FEARLESS
Vampire Hunter

K.M. Taylor

DEDICATION

Fearless Vampire Hunter is inspired by Robert E Howard's Solomon Kane, Bram Stoker's Van Helsing, and Jay Kristoff's Gabriel DeLeon. I also must thank Anne Rice, the creators of Vampire Hunter D and Hellsing, Supernatural's Dean Winchester, and, as always, the master, Brian Lumley, for influencing this story.
As usual, I am eternally grateful to my supportive family and dear friends, who always encourage and inspire me.

DISCLAIMER

All themes, names, characters, and incidents portrayed in this work are fictitious. Any similarities to actual persons, whether living, dead, undead, immortal, eternal, or similarities to items, places, worlds, or dimensions are purely coincidental.

This book is a satellite in the Codex Sohrakia series. You do not need to read Codex Sohrakia to enjoy this work, but if you want to understand the Dark Mythos behind this story, you will find links to order the series and its other satellites here: CodexSohrakia.com.

TABLE OF CONTENTS

I

FEARLESS VAMPIRE HUNTER

I've never kept a journal. Why should I? There was nothing about my life to write about. Who would want to keep a record of being bullied and lonesome all through their childhood and into their teen years? Also, I have never found it easy to talk about myself. Sharing the struggles and tragedies of my life is difficult enough; rambling on about me and my problems, well, it's just irksome, but here I go.

My name is Spencer Vale. At the start of this writing, it's the mid-2000s, and I'm in my mid-thirties. Look, I won't be putting any specific dates here, only a general idea of when and where events happened. Since I'm only now recording all this stuff, I can't recall exact dates anyway.

The reason I'm doing this? Well, this manuscript exists at the behest of a dear friend you'll meet during its telling. And I suppose, since it turns out to be a rather fantastic tale worthy of keeping a record of, it should be recorded, so I reluctantly agreed.

Don't get me wrong about my childhood; I wasn't exactly miserable. At home, I was happy. My older brother was my rock, and my folks were loving, supportive, and dear to me. I did have a few true friends over the years, but social life, for the most part, was nonexistent.

Being shy didn't help, either. I was terrified of looking foolish, of rejection, didn't have a bold bone in my body, so I kept mostly to myself, and, honestly, I was fine with that. I was a loner...a rebel! Nah, not much of a rebel, really, just a kid with his head in the clouds. Oh, the countless times teachers complained to my folks about me spacing off in class. My mother, rather than berating me for having such a dreamy mind, scolded the teachers for not encouraging a healthy imagination in me. Sure, she told me that I needed to pay better attention because I was there to learn, but that I should always dream when I was free to do so, just to be more conscientious about when and where I spaced out.

For most of my early life, we lived in a small, mountainous town in the Midwest. Family life was good, nothing astounding or particularly interesting about it. My folks were solid parents, sober, kind, intelligent, practical—all those positive things that lend to compassion and understanding, especially when raising two rambunctious boys like myself and my brother.

Jaren was older than me by about three years, so our school time was separated just enough to keep him ahead and me out of his sphere. The two of us were not entirely opposites, but we were different in many fundamental aspects. While Jaren was outgoing, proud, even brash at times, I was quiet, awkward, and, more often than not, locked up in my own head, lost in those wild fantasies. My brother always tried to yank my timid little ass out of the shell of my mind, but he had a devil of a time doing it. Not that I tried to fight him on that front. Heck! I adored him…looked up to him…practically worshipped the guy. But I simply could not be like him.

Tall, muscular, and ruggedly charming, Jaren strutted like a don and drew others to him like a tzar! He owned every room he walked into, and let me just say, not once did I ever feel a speck of jealousy of my big brother. Hey, I'll admit he *could* do wrong and did at times, but he always owned it, and now, looking back, he often used those slip-ups to teach me valuable life lessons so that I wouldn't make the same mistakes he did. He was as much a teacher to me as our folks were, perhaps more.

But me? I was a rail of a kid with a face like my Mama, pretty for a boy, skinny, awkward, and dreadfully clumsy. Thankfully, as I entered adulthood, those soft looks turned more rugged, and I sprouted up like a weed.

Always the loner, with my less than a handful of true friends, still, I was satisfied with life in general. My school friends and I enjoyed all the geeky stuff together: movies and comics, and I devoured books like they were "going out of style," as Dad used to say. Never was I begrudged any book I wanted to read, and my fancies were wide and varied. I loved fiction of all varieties: martial arts films, horror, fantasy, and science fiction books and movies. What young boy didn't love those? But I also ate up history, metaphysics, science, and mysteries, fearlessly letting my interests go wherever they wanted to. I certainly trod my own path, and doggedly so. About the only typical male interest I didn't have was sports, which should be pretty obvious by my bookish ways.

By the way, this isn't the first time I've endeavored to write a story, even though it is the first time I've written in first-person prose. Since I was a pre-teen, I'd piddled around with writing here and there. Whenever I read something that inspired me, gave me ideas, and awakened my writing voice, I would jot down bits here and there: at recess, in between classes, during boring lessons, or at home. Nothing that I'd ever share with anyone else! Oh, no! Anything I wrote was for *my eyes only*. My friends had no clue I'd written anything and never would!

But that's a lie.

One person knew that I wrote stories because she spotted me scribbling in my notebook and, unbeknownst to me, read over my shoulder. *She* was the very *last* person in the world that I would have wanted to read my trash!

Her name? Romayne Pierson...

It was sixth grade when I first laid eyes on Romayne and man! My heart was solid gone! Love at first sight? I can't deny it, and I was utterly helpless to it! No other girl...no other *woman*, as it turns out, could hope to trump her in my pitiful, besotted heart.

Oh, she was pretty, sure, but it was more than that. Something... moved me every time I laid eyes on her. No other human being affected me like Romayne did. There was no explaining it. All I could do was succumb to it, which typically meant me looking or acting like a damned fool in her presence. She was simply the most wonderful thing I'd ever laid my clueless little eyes on. A truly kind heart, she was always warm and considerate to me, no matter how rejected I felt by others. Unabashedly, she stood by me and made me feel like no one else could: important, like I mattered, like I meant something to *her*, which was the core of it, though I probably read into her kindness out of my feelings for her. It's hard to put those feelings into words, but I feel them even now; after so many years, it's always the same with her in my heart.

Rayn, as her friends called her, was not a part of the "popular" crowd, yet she was, in her own way, popular. She was "artsy," as she always referred to herself—an artist and actress who devoted her curricular and extracurricular hours to all aspects of the drama club: sewing costumes, building sets, makeup, and, of course, performing. And, man, I never missed her plays. She was good! Really good! And I admit each and every one of her characters made an appearance in my boyhood daydreams. I'm not shy to admit it. I still daydream about her to this day.

Her sneaky reading over my shoulder happened in algebra class, the only class we shared that year; it was eighth grade. We students were left to our own devices because the teacher was running late. I was so far away in my writing—a rather gory scene scribbled in pencil—that the entire room had vanished around me. Shit, I was concentrating so hard on that stupid little story, it was like I'd left the planet!

Then, out of nowhere, I heard, "What's that you're writing?"

Rayn's voice—she was standing right behind me! Her sweet voice was brimming with unbridled excitement, making me jump as my pencil flew out of my hand, and I hastily shoved the paper under my stack of books.

How much had she read? I thought in a panic, heart hammering and my face heating up as embarrassment surged through me.

But she only laughed at my reaction as she bent down, picked up my pencil, and held it out to me, grinning as I stared aghast back at her. "Sorry, didn't mean to startle you."

I took the pencil from her, still ogling and oozing shame.

"It's good," she tilted her head toward where my paper had been. "And scary!" Her big hazel eyes widened, and she made claws with her fingers, imitating a creepy monster. With her bright eyes and sweet face, all crumpled up like that; she was so fucking adorable my heart clogged my throat and, being the goofy kid I was, I could only mumble, "It's nothing," or some senseless thing like that.

Rayn rubbed her hands together like some mad villain, then leaned in close to me. She smelled of vanilla and lavender. My heart shuddered madly as she whispered in a conspiratorial voice, "I want to read it when you're done."

I think I nodded mutely just as the teacher entered, saving me from any real commitment and sending Rayn scurrying to her desk.

Of course, I never finished that story, and I never gave any part of it to her to read, even though she asked me about it several times after that encounter. I always made up some lame excuse and changed the subject, usually without being able to form coherent sentences, which was typical for me in her presence. I'm sure that's why she finally quit asking. How could someone who couldn't even speak properly ever write anything worth reading? God, I was pitiful around her!

Anyway, let's get back to what happened to turn my rather dull life, the Rayn-less portion of it anyway, upside-fucking-down.

Yes, horror was one of my favorite subjects. But never in my wildest dreams or nightmares would I have thought that real life could perfectly mirror my favorite old horror tales. Trust me, you aren't going to believe a word I say here if you're a practical person who "knows" there's no such thing as the supernatural or literal monsters. But hear me out because this is a wild, weird, and often tragic tale. That said, I hope to include some levity to balance out the awfulness. I'm not much of a funny guy, but I'll try, though there's not much to laugh about, either, so I'll just tell it as it happened.

About nineteen years ago…

I was halfway through my final year of high school when my family and I moved house. Thankfully, I didn't have to change schools. Oh, I wouldn't have cared one iota about that, except for leaving Rayn. *No way* would I have moved away from her! I'd have thrown the biggest tantrum. Heck, I'd have moved out and lived on my own before leaving her behind! Thankfully, I didn't have to, and my pitiful little heart was saved.

Not long after the move, everything changed. Every facet of my existence would be put through the wringer, and my perception of life, of reality, of literally everything I thought I understood would be turned completely upside down.

The first sign things were amiss was when Jaren started acting strange. My brother had always been an open book, a tough but warm guy. Funny, snarky, even a bit of a cad sometimes, at least to others, but never to me. But it was all tongue in cheek with him, that cool-guy attitude of his, all part of the show. He always knew himself well and utilized his natural talents openly, without pretense or fakery.

I thought Jaren was the bomb, to be honest. I'd do anything for him, and often I did. We were a bit like the brains and the brawn, although he was in no way dumb. It was his concentration that suffered, and I often came to his rescue, getting him through tests and tough, bookish things he never devoted enough time to. Jaren simply didn't have the patience to study. Studying was *my* thing.

I never did cheat for him. Never went that far. Not that he asked me to, at least not directly. He might hint at it with his humor…his ever-present sarcasm, but never did he push me or make me feel bad for not offering that level of "services." Basically, I tutored him, and he loved it. Or at least he acted like he did.

Nah, he loved it.

There was no animosity between us, not until things began to change.

God, I *hate* this part. I hate what happened to him, to us as brothers, to my entire family. Damn it, I know I should get these events down "on paper," but I don't *want* to revisit any part of it. Not like this, in all its horrid details. Oh, it haunts me every single fucking day, believe me! There's not a day, not a moment of any day, that I don't think of what happened and how life used to be before our nightmare…how it might have been had none of it ever happened…

Whenever those events surged into my thoughts, I pushed them out of my head for my own good…for my sanity! I never allowed myself to dwell on or entertain those memories because they might have driven me mad or made me give up, and I *could not* give up.

At the time this stuff was going on, Rayn didn't know, had not a fucking clue how I felt about her. If she did, well, I don't know how she'd have reacted to it. As sweet as she was, still, she looked at me like I was her brother. Shit, being around her made me feel like I was her *little* brother. I was, and still am, a complete, fucking idiot when it comes to her. Hopeless!

No amount of training or self-discipline can fix that part of me. Just the thought of her takes me right back to those gangly, stumbling, awkward days. But god, do I love her! If I could, I'd spend every waking hour with her, fool that I am.

I'd thought about telling her…how I felt…but I hadn't reached out to her since graduation, though I always kept quiet tabs on her, just to know she was okay.

Shit, I'm rambling like an idiot about my squishy feelings and procrastinating the awful stuff like a wimp.

Sigh…

Jaren began to pull away from me. That was the first sign something strange was happening. It hurt like hell, too. Truly, at that stage in my life, when I needed him the most, he wasn't there. I felt like a freak, my body changing, urges growing, all so intense. Well, all the normal adolescent stuff, obviously, but when it's happening to you at that age, it's the most dramatic thing ever.

Puberty was a bitch; I suffered alone. I never went to Dad with things. Not that I couldn't have, I suppose, but Jaren was my rock, or once was my rock. Dad was just there, in the background, working constantly and a bit "switched off." At least, that's how it felt to me. Hey, I never took for granted that I didn't have an angry, mean father. Never were we abused by him—never poorly treated. But I always wondered if something happened in his past to make him check out when it came to closeness. I loved my father, just didn't know him that well.

I'd sure love to talk to him now and ask him all those questions I never had the chance to before…

Mom? She was about the sweetest thing on the planet! That said, she was delicate. I don't know why she seemed so fragile to me like I couldn't go to her with anything that might upset or concern her. I felt fiercely protective of Mom. She was tender-loving and treated us boys like the universe revolved around us. She was the same with Dad, that sweet little lady surrounded by all these big males.

I was growing up fast, still not quite as tall as Jaren…yet, or even Dad, who stood just over six feet. Big guys ran in our family. My grandpa, Dad's dad, was a huge guy.

Sure, I was skinny, but I hated being taller than all the other kids when I was young, though it might have protected me from too severe pummeling at school. I always blamed my awkwardness on what I considered an unnatural height. I was constantly self-conscious about it, but as I matured and faced the things I've faced, I became grateful for it. Towering over others was now an asset.

As you can imagine, Jaren ruled the roost. He was such a massive personality; he overshadowed all of us in the best way.

But then, our rock began to crumble, and I cannot tell you the pain it caused my mother and me. I'm sure Dad worried internally, though he usually brushed Jaren's new ways off as some kind of phase.

The folks began to lean more heavily on me since Jaren was almost always gone. I didn't mind. It was good for me, so I ate it up. That was when I began to pay a little more attention to my body—just working out a few times a week, liking the changes in my physique, mostly due to puberty, since I really didn't work out that hard. It was easy putting on muscle, though. Glancing in the mirror, I began to see Jaren-like details emerging, which thrilled and kind of scared me, if I'm honest.

But things were only getting worse with Jaren. He would disappear for days on end, and his countenance was changing, too. He went from strong and vibrant to haggard and sick so quickly that I wondered if he was doing drugs. As impossible as that seemed to me, knowing him like I did…like I *thought* I did. Jaren was not the kind of guy to start doing drugs at his age. He was fiercely against things like that, always saying he hated being out of control.

I soon found out he'd quit going to the gym and lost his job, which utterly shocked me. The gym was a second home for him, and he loved that job: salvaging and restoring old houses. I had planned to start working with him but never got the chance.

But the real fear, the real horror, so unexpected, so inexplicable, happened one night when he came home in the wee hours and appeared in my room. It had happened a few times, always unnerving me, and so brief and strange I thought, at first, I'd dreamed it.

God, I hate it. Knowing what it meant now when I had no idea what it was all about in those moments.

Over the previous nights, from the moment he had gone missing, I'd been having freaky dreams. I don't recall now what they were about, but on the final night that Jaren came into my room, I woke from one of those nightmares with a jolt and nearly leaped out of my skin when I saw him standing again, for the third time, at the foot of my bed, staring down at me.

He mainly appeared in silhouette. My room was dark—a faint moon-glow emanating through my windows. I never used a nightlight, but I wished I had right then because what I was looking at didn't seem quite right. There was no doubt it was my brother, but the sheer wrongness of him had locked my throat into a tight column and sent my heart battering my chest as if it would escape from me, escape from *him*.

My room was dead silent, too silent, and I was holding my breath, trying not to make any sound; for some reason, I felt the urge to make myself as unnoticeable as I could, even though his face was turned toward me as if he was looking right at me. Yet his eyes were closed. And he made no sound himself, no movement, not even any natural shifting on his feet. His stance was too straight, rigid, awkward, more like a statue than a living human. I even wondered if he might be playing some practical joke on me. Had he placed some flat, cardboard standee of himself at the foot of my bed to frighten and make a fool of me? Would he burst into the room from the doorway any second and laugh his ass off at my helpless moment of horror?

Why do something like that? I wondered. Why keep coming into my room for several nights just to mess with me?

But, no.

That was no standee, and he was not playing around.

I then noticed his eyes again, which I could only barely make out in the darkness. There was a faint glow...a red glow...shining from *behind* his eyelids.

I blinked at him, not trusting what I was seeing, what I was feeling, not trusting any of my senses.

Finally, after what seemed like several minutes of unparalleled tension, when it appeared he would not move or speak to me at all...it struck me...was he sleepwalking?

Oh my god, I thought, *that has to be it!* He must be asleep! That was why he stood so oddly and so stilly and why his presence freaked me out so much!

Somehow, I'd omitted that most unnatural red glow behind his eyes in my misguided assessment.

Steeling myself with this new, if incorrect, realization, I finally found my voice.

"Jaren?" it squeaked out of me like the voice of some pitiful little kid. I fruitlessly attempted to remember how one was supposed to handle a sleepwalking person. This idea was new to me. Jaren had never sleepwalked in his life. None of us had. This was worrying on so many levels and not something I had the faintest idea of how to deal with.

Slowly, I crawled out of bed and made my way to his side. Whispering his name, unsure whether I should address him or not, I reached my hand out as his head, eyes still shut, slowly followed me. My eyes suddenly locked on his glowing eyelids, and my heart seized just as my hand touched his arm, and I suddenly remembered the red glow! That oh-so-*unnerving* detail!

The glow was brighter; I could swear it. And his skin was cold!

So cold…

Then he moved his body to face me with that agonizing slowness as his eyelids began to lift.

Terror!

I could not move. Not a fraction of an inch.

Then those eyes…those *searing* red eyes met mine as I finally forced my hand off his freezing arm. Deep within the blacks of his pupils, sharp, bright pinpricks of crimson light shone like burning candles, pinking his cheeks and making the soft, natural gray of his eyes appear lavender. He looked strong again, not sunken and drawn, though his pallor was ghastly pale.

I don't know if he stood still like that for minutes or if my mind froze as I took in this most preternatural thing that was once Jaren.

Lips trembling, after what felt like an age, I whimpered, "A..are… you…okay?" Such a stupid question; he was clearly *not* okay.

Now, this may seem passé to any horror fan, but I cannot express too strongly the genuineness of all I witnessed. As much as my mind wanted to believe I was dreaming, locked in some soul-crushing night terror that I could not wake from, I *knew* this was no dream. This was reality! *Real* reality, and I was suddenly living in true horror and true danger!

Jaren's lips parted. They peeled apart slowly, agonizingly, like tearing flesh, opening wide in a grimace that would put Cheshire Cat to shame, revealing pink-stained, too-long teeth like jagged bone scythes.

He was positively grinning at me, and as God is my witness, it felt like my entire world had been ripped right out from under me. Like a black hole had opened up and sucked me in soul-first.

That expression on his once handsome face was like some blasphemous pantomime of joy, some sick, twisted impression of glee. And his eyes, the look in his once warm and jovial eyes, was that of a beast wracked with hunger…fierce as a rabid wolf, a lion, some *monster* ravenous for…for…

I knew what it was…what he hungered for. That hot, viscous substance soared through my veins in a rush as my heart rammed like a mad thing against my chest.

I stumbled backward, heedless of my room…of where I was, or even who I was. Normal life was a distant memory. The shock, the *reality*—agonizing fear had utterly overwhelmed me.

The knob to my bedroom door poked painfully into my hip, bringing me back from a tunnel of terror, and I grabbed it as the world reappeared around me in a sudden rush of fight or flight. My mind grasped onto some semblance of focus, and I turned and yanked the door open, barreling and stumbling out of my room and down the stairs in a chaos of jumbled, straining, and shuddering limbs, not daring to look back.

If I'd realized what was about to happen, I might have remained in my room and tried to fight Jaren to save *them*…which would surely have ended things for me, and I wouldn't be here now, recording all this…

II
HEARTBREAK

I had to step away from this telling…get a drink. Needed something to…make this easier. Well, not easier, more like duller. Whiskey would do the trick. It always does the trick.

…

When I reached the bottom of the stairs, only then did I turn back, having heard no sounds of pursuit and seeing no one there as I peered up into the gloom. My heart was hammering, body vibrating, breaths coming in frantic gasps.

I was on the verge of running back up. The folks were up there, and I wanted to warn them, but just as I thought it…as if in answer to my concern, I heard a loud crash…and my mother's scream.

…

Fear fled from me in lieu of fresh panic, panic for someone other than myself, someone I loved with all my heart. I shot back up those stairs faster than I ever had. My parent's bedroom door was open; darkness beyond, but movement as well. Shuffling, which sounded wrong, and breathing that just wasn't right. "Mom!" I screamed, "Dad!"

…I…

God, I hate this. I said I would share all the gory details, but shit… shitshitshit, I don't want to!

…

She was already dead by the time I got there.

Mom was in Jaren's arms—those once loving arms and loving hugs, now the sick embrace of death. Of murder, so cruel.

11

I don't know why I switched the overhead light on. Why did I do that? Why did I want that glaring, blaring illumination of such heart-destroying madness?

My sweet mother hung limp and lifeless in my changed brother's strong grip; her skin was grayish white, her open eyes glazed, hollow, lifeless…her raw, red neck smeared in gore. Blood…her precious blood, running down into the trim of her soft, pastel nightdress. It dripped down Jaren's chin, too, smeared across his face, a face I no longer knew—the face of a monster I couldn't comprehend.

Oh, I knew *what* he was, as impossible and astonishing as it was. He was a creature I always adored. A fanged hunter of the night, a thing of fiction made real.

Blubbering and trembling so fiercely that I could barely stand, words failed me. All that escaped my quivering lips were whimpers and sobs so pitiful I never would have imagined they could be a result of my life.

Jaren dropped our mother to the floor like—like one of those garbage bags he always took out to the curb for her. And he was grinning again, that sickening, horrible, nasty grin—a bloody grin that made my gorge rise. The nausea hadn't hit me at seeing my mother's body; it was her blood on his lips, in his teeth, and his false and hateful joy that turned my stomach!

Suddenly, rage struck me like a blow just as I spotted Dad crumpled against the wall behind Jaren. He was not bloody or unnaturally pale and gray like Mom. But he was unconscious, and the wall was dented where his head likely struck the sheetrock; a hint of blood caked his hair.

Words seemed locked away in a shattered, unreasoning mind that I could not access, so I growled instead of yelling words, like a beast myself…a broken, unbelieving beast made only of pain. I flew at Jaren with my hands out, to…to what?…choke him? I don't know what I was thinking; I was seized with blind rage, grief, shock.

Jaren opened his arms to me and laughed, wet and guttural, as he absorbed my lesser weight. He was a wall, immovable, but I was scrambling then, punching, kicking, hitting him with all the power of my pain, but with a body so very weak compared to his. A flood of tears wetted my face as I screamed and roared at him, finally discovering words tossed in with the giant salad of curses, hollers, and wails. But he only laughed at me and my fruitless fight.

Next thing I knew, Dad appeared and threw his arms around Jaren's shoulders in an attempt to thwart him. He was yelling at me to do something, but I was so lost in my anger I couldn't reason out what

12

he was saying. Something about running. Something about saving myself.

Then, Jaren reached back with his left hand and snagged Dad by the nape of the neck. The old man could barely move as his head was pressed hard into the knot of Jaren's strong shoulder. And as I began to come back to myself, exhausted and screaming at Jaren to let Dad go, my brother turned his awful head, opened his horrible, shark-teeth-filled mouth, and sank his fangs into Dad's neck.

Our father hollered and vainly tried to fight Jaren off, as did I, but there was no hope for him. I knew he would join Mom soon, and then...then it would be me.

Only me...

The speed of it! Oh, God! How quickly Dad was drained...

I barely made it, stumblingly, to their open door—struck again by such profound disbelief and such bone-chilling terror, hopelessness, pain, regret...that I was on the verge of losing my legs right out from under me.

Jaren dropped Dad's body beside Mom's with absolutely no ceremony...no respect or caring. He then turned to me, his face inscrutable, his eyes burning so brightly I wondered how he could see for their fiery shine. Red, flickering, flaming fire locked onto my silvery metallic blue. Then, the oddest thing happened, which was the most disturbing yet...for me.

With a sigh, an almost natural Jaren-that-I-once-knew smile, his face relaxed, and his shoulders dropped. He was staring at me, and I was locked in place, ogling back at him, heart pounding and legs both wobbly and ready to run.

"Spence..." he said, his voice too low, too strange. But I could swear I saw warmth in his awful eyes as he shrugged, then barely chuckled, "I was...so hungry," Like he'd just stolen my piece of leftover pizza from the fridge.

...

If you're wondering what those empty ellipses are (...) that keep popping up after certain paragraphs, that's when I stop to take a stiff drink. And just so you're aware, no, I do not drink all the time, only when...well, sometimes it's all just too much. Writing this, reliving this, is bringing back details I haven't thought about in many years.

I miss them...with all my heart...I miss them, especially my brother.

...

So, Jaren was hungry, was he? *That* was painfully obvious, but it wasn't his apparent statement of the appallingly evident that broke me at that moment; it was the jest behind it. It was the false compassion I saw in his face, the lie of the warmth in his burning eyes.

"Just do it!" I screamed, the words bursting out of me like an explosion, shocking me even more than it apparently did not shock him.

But he shook his head and wiped his mouth with the back of his hand, smearing the blood of his father, his mother, licking his lips in, to me, what appeared to be a grotesque show of dominance or preening like some hellish demon showing me how awful and evil it could be.

"You, Spence?" He shook his once-handsome head. "No. Not you. Besides," he cocked an eyebrow and sighed like the cat that ate the canary, "I'm full. Satisfied…for now." Then he smirked wickedly, meanly, his voice a low rumble, "So, run! My sweet, innocent little brother. Go! Before I decide, I want thirds…"

And I did…I bolted because Mom and Dad were gone; there was nothing I could do for them, and I needed to get help before Jaren attacked others.

That's when it hit me…Rayn! I had to protect Rayn!

I ran for the car, snagging the keys that were sitting on the kitchen counter…where he always threw them. *Dad's* keys.

Jaren did not appear again as I stumbled into the garage and threw myself behind the driver's seat. I was shaking so badly that I had trouble getting the key into the ignition, and my eyes were flooded; I could hardly see anything for the helpless tears that wouldn't stop flowing. Finally, I got the engine going, but as I left our house— watched my home shrinking in the rearview.

I wasn't sure where to go at first or what to do with myself, so, I drove to Rayn's house, finding everything quiet and so normal it freaked me out almost more than the "unreality" I'd just witnessed. But it also flooded me with relief, and I passed her house by without stopping. I couldn't go there. I might lead Jaren to her, and what on earth could I say to Rayn anyway? How could I explain this hell to her?

Of course, there was no going to the police, either, and I had no family who lived close by.

Suddenly, a thought crashed my brain and nearly incapacitated me…what would happen when Mom and Dad's bodies were found? God, would I get blamed for their deaths?

A new kind of fear struck me then, the reality that I might live the rest of my life in prison for a crime I didn't commit—such an awful, brutal, cruel crime—that I would be ruined forever as a human being…

But as it turned out, I was not blamed for their deaths. For some reason, something I couldn't understand, Jaren had left a note confessing to everything and completely exonerating me. His fingerprints were everywhere…bloody prints on their bedcovers, clothing, and bodies, so there was never any doubt about his guilt and my innocence. In his note, he gave no explanation as to why he'd done it, and he stated that he planned to kill himself and that no one would ever find his body.

No one ever did, but I *knew* he was still alive…somewhere…

To the world, he was just another nutcase who killed his parents, then himself. And he'd have killed his little brother, too, had the boy been home at the time.

I was free, but I was never the same.

The first stop I made that night, when I finally did stop, was at a friend's house. Karl was one of my few real friends, my best friend. He typically had the run of his house since both his parents worked nights. I called in the murders from there. Not knowing about the note at that point; I did it anonymously.

The police soon tracked me down and questioned me, but they didn't drill down too hard when I said I wasn't home when it happened; Karl backed me up. I told them that I had been so distraught after finding my dead parents, and with nowhere else to go, I had stayed with Karl, which the cops seemed to understand perfectly well. I learned about the note during that time, and my innocence was established.

Once things settled down, I sold the house and got rid of everything in it. I gave away a ton of stuff and kept next to nothing myself. No way I wanted reminders of my past life and *no way* I could live there anymore.

My folks left me a small inheritance, so I sunk that money into high-interest accounts, gold, silver, and things like that. I was only sixteen, so Karl's family took me in for a few months until I turned seventeen, and I moved into a tiny efficiency apartment where I lived sparingly, saving every penny I could.

After some time, when my head and heart quieted a bit, I finally "got it together." I sought out my brother's physical trainer, and that's how I began my journey to really getting strong. I worked out regularly, improved my balance and coordination, and honed a few other basic skills. I landed various hard labor jobs. They were easy to get and helped me build muscle while keeping me out of my troubled head. It was mindless work that left me exhausted each day and drowning in perspiration as if I could bust my body and sweat out all the pain and loneliness rather than face those traumatic memories head-on. Time off from work saw me in Martial Arts, sword, and weapons training.

By the time I'd finished growing, those who knew me might be struck by my more-than-six-foot height (6'6"), strong arms, powerful legs, and, I suppose, handsome looks...

The ladies do seem to like me.

I let my straight black hair grow past my shoulders. But there was one time, when I cut it short again, that I sorely regretted that decision! I *hated* it so much that I never chopped it off again.

Rarely do I fully shave. Just like keeping my hair long, I prefer a bit of a shadow so I don't see the old me when I glance in a mirror. I refrain from growing out a full beard, preferring to keep myself a bit scruffy-lookin', more like Indiana Jones than Han Solo.

Despite my slightly unkept appearance (don't get me wrong, I'm a clean, fastidious guy otherwise), I have no problem garnering lingering looks from the ladies. Although, as much as they seem drawn to me, it also seems something in my demeanor tends to ward them off. I can be...quite intense, I admit it. How could I relax with what I know, what I've seen...what I've been through? There ain't nothin' normal about this bloke, ladies.

They sure would have loved Jaren!

Jaren...

God, I missed him!

I do favor my brother quite a bit, in coloring, mostly, and familial features, and while I might put off an air of strangeness, he never did; he took full advantage of the interest he received from what, to me, was endless female attention. Before losing him, he had tried to encourage me in that regard, but I was barely at the threshold of manhood when it all went wrong. So, he never got the chance to be a real "ladies' man" mentor during the time when romance and attempting to understand the female persuasion might have really mattered to me. It didn't matter anyway because it was all about Rayn once she entered my life.

Regardless of the trauma of those events, I never sought therapy, not with what I knew that I could never share with anyone. But I did seek knowledge, as I always had. Mine was, and ever is, an insatiably curious mind! Only, I found myself perusing books I'd never considered reading before, many of which I'd never have thought actually existed. Providence seemed to smile at me the deeper I dug. Vacations took me all over the country, seeking those mysterious and often forbidden books, journals, and artifacts, all in an attempt to understand what Jaren had become and to aid in the protection of myself and those I cared about.

I learned a lot, but only enough to be dangerous to myself and potentially others. I know that now, but then, I felt powerful, tougher than I'd felt in all my short life.

Oh, and don't think that Jaren was the only vampire I encountered. I discovered quite a few bloodsuckers over the years, and I destroyed my fair share of those bastards and bitches, before I reached the age of thirty.

At about eighteen years old, I started officially hunting—hunting for vampires in general, but also hunting for my lost brother.

I purchased a small, remote house for myself. It was a classic! Looked like something straight out of Evil Dead—located way up in the mountains, at the end of a long, winding dirt road. Small as it was, it was a pretty nice place. Not a wreck on the inside, although the exterior needed lots of work. I did very little to correct the derelict appearance of the outside, concentrating only on structural, functional repairs, employing clever ways of shoring it all up while keeping the cabin's broken, crooked facade. I wanted the structure to be unwelcoming to anyone who might approach it. I enjoyed driving up to the deceptively creepy-looking old place and then crossing the threshold into its nice, cozy interior.

My favorite feature was the library. The place had five rooms total: a living area, tiny kitchen, bath, bedroom, and the library—a mid-sized room lined with shelves floor to ceiling.

I bought the place furnished. Most of what had been left there was old but useful. I kept most of the things but got rid of the majority of old books, which were mostly novels, keeping only a few that interested me.

I also rented a P.O. Box to receive mail and keep my physical address use limited, and, as I planned to be traveling extensively, I needed a place for mail to go while I was away—not simply a hold, but a safe place to receive packages… I planned on sending important research home when I came across anything that might assist me in my hunts if it became too much to carry.

Oh, and cell phone, computer? Nope. Not me. I did utilize modern tech occasionally, when necessary, mostly via libraries. But I preferred to remain off-grid, keeping things simple and clandestine.

I don't think it's any stretch of the imagination to glean what my next step would be after how I lost my family. I had only two choices: to run away and spend my life hiding in fear…or to fight.

I chose to fight, to hunt down my brother and any others like him, and to rid the world of as many vamps as I could before my dying day.

Sounds epic.

It wasn't.

Well, mostly, it wasn't.

I spent nearly ten years working, training, and saving money before attempting my first hunt and achieving my first kill. During that time, I found no sign of Jaren. It was like he'd vanished from the face of the earth. Being a vamp, he would, logically, be outside of the typical human workings of the world. Still, I did begin to wonder if he really was dead. Could he have actually killed himself? Perhaps realizing what he'd done, could his guilt have driven him to take his own life? Somehow, I doubted it.

For the most part, I was alone through all this, but not entirely. Bringing others into my dangerous plans was not something I wanted to do, but I did have a few allies over the years. The first of which was Karl.

There was no way I couldn't, eventually, tell Karl everything that happened. Heck, he wouldn't let me continue to clam up about it. Jerk pushed me until I finally spilled all the beans.

At first, he was dubious. Who could blame him? I certainly couldn't.

But finally, after allowing it all to sink in, Karl replied, "Maybe Jaren started taking drugs, you know, that crazy, zombie shit, lost his mind, then pulled the whole vampire thing just to scare the shit out of you." But I knew better than that, and I told him so. I wasn't sure at first whether he'd ever really believe me, but eventually…he did.

He had to.

Karl stayed with me after I got the cabin. He didn't fully move in since the place was so remote that he didn't want to be stuck driving hours to get into the city each day. He usually stayed over on weekends; whenever I traveled, he'd look out for the place, pick up my mail, and such. Whenever I was home, and after begging me over and over and over again to let him come with me on my hunts, I finally relented.

I wish I hadn't…

But before telling you that tale and its ultimate outcome, I really should tell you about my first kill…

III
FIRST KILL

Whether it was the stench of blood or the rotten reek of decay, killing bloodsuckers always stank.

The new ones bled, just like us, and once dead, they descended into rot to coincide with how long they'd been a vampire—the old ones rotted away into dust, dust that smelled like a musty, putrid, open grave.

I never bother to clean up after killing the old ones. No need. All that's left is dust that won't make a lick of sense to anyone who finds it. But I always have to clear away the horrid mess of the fresh young vamps; the more recent, the yuckier.

But I'm getting ahead of myself.

That first time, the first time I killed—and don't think for one minute it didn't feel like full-blown murder. Dispatching new vamps always feels like murder. I did a piss-poor job of cleaning up...and dealing with it both practically and emotionally? I was so goddamn clueless. Since then, I've gotten—what?—accustomed to it? Hardened? Callous? Well, yeah. A bit of all those things. But mostly, I've learned a lot about what I was dealing with, and it's made all the difference.

Thank God, in those early days, with all my mishaps and mistakes, sometimes complete stupidity, I wasn't caught or implicated in any of the killings. Damn, but it's a miracle I'm still a free man, much less living.

Especially after that first kill...

I was covered in gore. The stink permeated me, and I trembled violently.

But let's back up. Can't leave you wanting for all those oh-so-gory details, now can I?

19

Five a.m., and I was up before the sun finished rising. Knew where I was going, had all my stuff laid out on a chair, ready to head out on my maiden slay: hunting knife, one of those big ones that made me think of Crocodile Dundee, a torch lighter, easy for a quick flame to burn the sucker, and a pistol with a silencer, to slow down the vamp, even if it wouldn't kill them. I had none of my current esoteric tools then. Shit, the danger I put myself in is astounding to me now, but for some reason, I dove in without fear. Well, at least without crippling fear. I was angry, with nothing else to give me purpose; I felt little need to preserve my miserable life.

Vamps rarely sleep alone, so I was prepared with one more weapon, a tranquilizer dart gun for the vamp's mortal guards. Occasionally, they only had a few, rarely only one, and most of the time, a small group of between six and ten. But at this stage, I had no idea about any of that.

Rising at the crack of dawn and heading out to slay early in the day came exclusively from my knowledge of the popular vampire lore. I was simply lucky that it was accurate. Later, I'd learn that vamps are literally dead to the world during daylight hours. The Sleep of Death, they called it, which made slaying the vampire without having to fight them "easy." *If* you could get to them, that is.

The one I was after had been snatching kids and lone walkers or runners off the nighttime street until the townsfolk had started avoiding ever being alone and never allowed their kids outside after dark, staying inside themselves in fear of attack. As you probably guessed, I kept a close eye on the news for such happenings; then, I'd stake out the areas until I caught the bastards, quite literally, red-handed.

It was imperative that I not blow my cover, so I had to find clever ways to distract the vamp from the kill if I could manage it, which was not always the case. Well, this being the first one, I had simply picked up a rock and threw it at a nearby tree, startling the monster and making them abandon the kid they were stalking. I was amazed it worked! Beginner's luck, no doubt.

Then, I was off, chasing the guy back to his lair.

Lair, that's a laugh.

The guy lived in a simple, small bungalow in an older part of town. From what I could tell as I staked out the place, the vamp lived with three mortals…people who were complicit or thralled (a term in fiction I'm sure you're familiar with). They never left the house, which would have been odd had I not known the little I did at the time.

I watched the place for about a week, unable to always tail the vampire himself because I wanted to know the ins and outs of the place, the mortals' comings and goings, and find a way to get in when the time was right. Truly, I hated not sticking by the monster...allowing him to go about his nasty business when I might have been able to stop him. Still, I worked alone, and I had to stick to my plan. I did notice that the disappearances lessened after I'd distracted the creature that one time. More law enforcement was out as well, which I also had to dodge. I didn't need my stalker's ways to implicate *me* in *his* wrongdoing.

Finally, I solidified my plan. It was...simple—some might even say stupid—but it worked, and here we are.

Eight A.M. and I stood at the door, dressed in a black denim jacket, jeans, and a white tee, hair pulled back in a band. I'd left my over-the-top Al Jourgensen-style cowboy/tricorn-folded hat behind. Felt it might have looked a bit too menacing. I was about as average looking as you could get, save the fact that I was loaded down with weapons, cleverly hidden in jacket and pants pockets.

When the mortals opened the door, two guys and one girl, all clustered in a triangle inside that narrow opening, I flashed them, especially the girl, my most genuine smile, and asked if I could use their phone: my car was broken down, simple as that.

They were about my age, without the slightest suspicion of what I was really there for. It was also three-on-one; should I be a baddie and try anything. So, after a few cautious glances between them, they agreed to let me in. I'm still amazed they didn't patently turn me away. Soon, it would be apparent that they were as green as I was.

Once inside, I stealthily drew my tranquilizer gun from my jeans pocket, keeping it mostly hidden inside my jacket as the girl led me to the telephone. The tranq dose was about right for an animal between 120 and 300 pounds, so without hesitation, I pulled the trigger, and a tiny dart lodged itself in the girl's thigh.

She yipped, probably thinking an insect bit her, and I caught her as her body went limp, and she dropped.

Stuff was fast-acting.

I sat her in a nearby chair and quickly slipped another dart into the gun just as one of the guys walked in. Didn't give him any chance to react before I squeezed the trigger, and he tumbled to the floor with a mild thud. That left me with only one to deal with.

Now, I had been training for months and doing hard work, so I was all muscle, like a coiled spring. Taller than all three of them, I felt more than ready to take on that final guy. Pocketing my dart gun, I strode into the room where last I'd seen him. I didn't mince words.

"Where is he?"

Catching sight of me and my apparent determination, the guy flew at me.

"Shit! Where are the others?! What did you do?!" He bellowed as fists flew.

The kid was untrained, so I promptly got him into a headlock. "They're fine," I husked in his ear, "just sleeping. Where's the vampire?"

His eyes met mine; then he glanced over my shoulder…he knew why I was there.

"No! You can't!" His eyes were wide with fear…panic.

"I can, and I will," I growled just as I released him, then used a haymaker on him. He was out just like his friends.

Thankfully, I hadn't encountered any super-strength. Those kids weren't any stronger than typical people, which was yet another hint concerning the nature of their vampire master. Green thralls, green vamp. At least, that was my uneducated guess at the time.

I stalked in the direction the guy had looked but found no sign of the vamp. Meandering through the house, I hunted for a basement door, the most logical place for a creature of the night to hide during the day.

At first, I found nothing, but then I noticed a bookshelf oddly placed against a wall that jutted out and left a space unaccounted for. Sliding the shelf aside, it hid a doorway. To the casual observer, it would not seem that odd. The hallway was wide, and a couch and chair were placed against the wall opposite the bookshelf, appearing like a makeshift reading spot. No one would have thought twice about whether there was a door there, nor would they have cared.

It took some work with my big Dundee knife to pry the door open. I listened for any movement beyond, but all was utterly quiet. The stillness of the dead, I thought to myself with a rye smirk. Then, I was down the dark staircase in a flash, hesitating for only a moment before switching a light on, a lamp perched on a chest of drawers at the bottom of the stairs.

Relief washed over me when the room was illuminated. It's a pet peeve of mine to flick on a light switch and get no illumination. I used to dream about it: constant, recurring dreams, where every single time I tried to switch on any kind of light, nothing would happen, leaving me in an oppressive dark. God, I hated those damned dreams! Oddly, after Jaren killed our folks, those dreams suddenly stopped. I still wonder if those dreams meant something.

The windowless room was nice...cozy—nothing like the basement hovel I'd expected. In most horror tales, if vampires weren't in a big, decrepit castle, they'd be in dingy old basements, sleeping in boxes or under floorboards or something. But this was a proper little apartment with comfy seating, a massive, large-screen TV, and a big bed at the far end of the room.

I approached that bed, which was not empty, of course. The thing lying there didn't stir. It just lay in its covers as if taking a nap, but looking quite dead: lips pale and eyes sunken...but its face was plump and fresh...freshly sated with some poor sod's blood.

Well, I thought to myself as I gazed down at that creature that looked like a man—a peaceful young man who appeared just a bit older than my eighteen years—*this is it.*

Slowly, I drew out my knife and, not knowing whether he would wake up or not, I held my breath and slashed down with all my strength right into his exposed neck.

Blood shot up and out, splashing the ceiling, my chest, and my face, and pooling crimson across his pillows and the mattress. But that cut, while deep, had not severed his head. I was shaking then, unable to stop myself from violent tremors that threatened to hinder my control. But I wasn't sure if it would be enough, just slitting his throat, so, in utter disgust, I pulled in a deep breath, hollered to cover the jangling of my nerves, and thrust that knife back down again, cutting deeper, then sawing through his sinew and spine as the gore spread out in all directions, its heavy, copper stink making it difficult to breathe.

The blood...it got all over me, all over him...*everywhere!*

Shock was setting in, and I nearly dropped the knife as I tried to get control of my frantic breathing. Last thing I needed was to pass out from hyperventilating!

This was a fresh vampire. Not so different from hacking into a living person. I was devastated and on the verge of utter panic at the thought that somehow I might be wrong, maybe even crazy, and I'd actually murdered someone!

But I knew better.

I had been right about a vamp's particular daytime weakness, which was the only reason why I'd accomplished this initial kill so easily.

But no, it was *not* easy. It was ghastly!

Relatively easy to get to him, perhaps, but the horrid job of killing him...it...was...

Finally, the head fell free, squelching as I snagged the hair and tossed it away from the body, following the dictate of vampire lore so that the monster could not rise again. Oh, and I forgot to mention that

I had pulled on work gloves as I descended the stairs, which were now soaked in gore. I could feel the sticky blood seeping through the heavy fabric and coating the flesh of my hands inside.

Suddenly, the room spun, and I leaned on the wall beside the bed to keep from collapsing.

As I said, this felt just like vicious, bloody murder, and I am not a man who would ever do this sort of thing to another human being. Yet, here I was, the *fearless* vampire slayer, and I had to remind myself that this was no human being. This was a creature that fed on and murdered innocents. This creature needed to die!

Peering at the remnants of my awful work, I felt gorge rise and emptied my stomach right where I stood, a quivering mess. Despite constantly telling myself this was right, my soul screamed at me, and my mind did not want to look at the gory destruction I had wrought.

I thought of Rayn; what would she think of me now? If she knew the truth of what happened, would she agree with what I was doing? Would knowing I'd done this violent act sicken her? What would my parents think? My brother…before, even after, he became a beast like the thing I just…killed.

Nausea only intensified, though there was nothing else for me to throw up. Guilt, like an old habit, kept niggling at me, trying to overwhelm my purpose, but I refused to let it.

Still, I felt stymied.

Before I could move to do anything, I sank to the floor, landing hard on my ass. Surrounded by blood and that severed head, which thankfully faced away from me, I tried to steady my nerves as I choked on rancid air.

But I had to move! Get the place cleaned up before me and my destruction were discovered by anyone. The kids upstairs should be out for a bit, at least the ones I'd plugged with tranquilizer. The one I'd sucker-punched might wake at any time.

Pushing myself up onto shaky legs, I set to work wrapping the head up in the blanket the vamp had been sleeping under, collecting it and the body into the large bedroom rug then dragging the bundle out to my car and stuffing it into my trunk.

Thankfully, the neighborhood was silent. Most people were at work, weekdays were good for hunting, too.

I returned and finished stripping the bed. The mattress was covered by a waterproof protector that zipped on. Made sense if the leech brought victims here, and it certainly worked in my favor.

Still, I flipped the bare mattress over since I knew no other way, at the time, to dispose of it, just in case any evidence might have slipped

24

my notice. I was working like a zombie, my head reeling, senses clogged with the horror of it all, and that foul odor, now beginning to be tinged with the putrid stink of death!

The kid I'd hit was beginning to stir as I left the place, so I caught his eyes as they landed on me and widened in apparent fear.

"You're free now. Be careful." I said flatly.

It seemed, by the way he looked at me, that he got my meaning, but I didn't stick around to find out. I brought the body to my cabin in the woods, burned it, all of it, the rug, the bed things, out behind my cabin, burned even my clothing. Then, I buried the ashes and bone remnants as deep as I could manage.

My energy was sapped as I stood watching that newly filled grave. I was only in my skivvies. It was chilly, but the ambient cold couldn't compete with the chill in my soul. Finally, I dragged myself to the house, to my bathroom, stepped out of my underwear, and into a scalding shower. I washed from head to toe, staying under the raining water until it went cold.

As I dressed in jeans and a tee, my mind ran through the day over and over again, like a curse upon me; it colored every aspect of my life, making all those familiar details around me seem monstrous, new, and forever changed...

And the stink hadn't left me, either.

Even after the stripping, burning, and washing, I could still smell the blood and the rot. The stench was in my skin, my sinuses, my freshly washed, wet hair. Would it ever leave? Was this Lady MacBeth's damned spot that would haunt and torment me forever?

Shaking again, my whole body giving way to tremors, I returned to my car, pausing only for a moment before starting the engine and pulling onto the long dirt drive.

Desperately, I needed something to cover the stink and dull my head. I had never drank alcohol before. Well, that's not entirely true. I'd tasted a beer with my brother not long before losing him, and I'd hated it. Tasted nasty to me, but the mild, giddy feeling it gave me, after only a few cringing gulps, seemed like the most welcome thing at the moment. That said, I felt like I needed something with more kick after what I'd just been through, so at the liquor store, I snagged a bottle of Scotch whiskey.

As much as I wanted to crack the thing open right there in the store, being the responsible guy I am, I waited until I got home, perched myself in my favorite chair, unscrewed the lid, then drank a big gulp straight from the neck.

I nearly choked to death from that initial burn. This was *nothing* like that mild beer my brother had given me.

Gaining control over my breathing again, I wiped leaky eyes with the back of my hand, laughing at myself until those tears turned to weeping. I took another, more careful sip, feeling the burn going down and the wave of heady numbness settling over me.

I thanked God for that blissful feeling…

The sting of pungent alcohol mingled with the hints of coconut and clove seemed to be doing the trick at deadening the lingering "scent" of blood. Carelessly, I tilted back some more, growing increasingly comfortable with the sharpness and the taste of the stuff the more I drank.

It wasn't long before my vision doubled; the room wavered. Oh, I was feeling better than I'd felt in an age! Heedless of any caution, I continued to suck the stuff down, fascinated as the room warped around me, my head felt light as a feather, and my body felt like a lead weight glued to my chair.

My thoughts then turned to Rayn. I wondered where she was, and like the besotted teen I was, I let my mind daydream just like I used to in my school days, if a bit less innocent. Thinking of her seemed to lessen the insistent memories of that first kill, so I let my imagination run wild, ravishing her again and again in a myriad of joyous couplings.

Vision cloudy, I gazed at my bed, imagining us together there, feeling a stirring in my dick; then it hit me: the intense need to urinate. Damn, that meant I'd have to move. The last thing I wanted to do was get up from that chair, which now felt like an extension of my big, heavy body. Sighing, I turned my head as I lifted the bottle to place it on the table beside me, and everything spun.

"Whoa!" I exclaimed, pausing to allow the entire room to right itself again, at least enough for me to put the bottle down. It hit the table harder than necessary since, with my vision so wonky, I couldn't tell precisely where the tabletop was.

With a grunt, I heaved myself up, gripping the arms of my chair as the room went topsy-turvy, and I tried to overcompensate, only just preventing myself from ending up on the floor. I then weaved my way to the bathroom and relieved myself. I could barely keep myself upright, leaning against the wall above the commode that swayed this way and that like a ship on rough seas.

Finished, I pushed myself up, then stupidly turned a bit too quickly, took about two faltering steps, then fell flat on my stupid face.

Glaring sunlight greeted me when I cracked my sticky eyes open. My mouth tasted like a cesspit, and my head felt ten tons heavier than it should. At first, I didn't know where the hell I was, but then I realized I was on the floor in my hallway, feet in the doorway to my bathroom.

It all came flooding back.

Groaning, weak, and trembling slightly, I pushed myself up onto my hands and knees and was hit with a freight train of nausea! I scrambled clumsily for the toilet and emptied my stomach into the bowl. It wasn't much since I had already tossed up yesterday's food after the kill, and I only had remnants of liquor in my system.

Dragging myself onto unsteady feet, I swallowed some pain meds, stripped naked, then repeated the previous afternoon's shower routine. Afterward, I fell into bed and slept the whole day away, waking just after dark, feeling a million times better and ravenously hungry! It was time for a steak!

Thinking over my first kill in a more reasonable manner as I ate, I decided on a few things. First, I needed to wear black from head to toe to hide the filth and gore. Also, I needed to be better prepared for clean-up afterward. But most importantly, I needed education! Movie and book vampires were not like the ones I would be facing, at least not entirely. I needed to understand the *factual* details of these things in order to deal with them more efficiently and to protect myself and anyone else involved.

While I had successfully accomplished my first kill, I knew that was a fluke. There would be situations much more complex and infinitely more dangerous than this one, and I needed all the help I could get... help to do it *alone* because I refused to drag anyone else into this nightmare!

Research began in the local library. This was before the World Wide Web, during the days of flip phones and microfiche. It was painstaking, time-consuming, and dreadfully tedious. And about the only thing I learned was that I'd need to go much older and much deeper into the lore, and I'd need to head to the old world to do it.

If I were going to find what I really needed, I'd need to go to Europe!

I had put that big, medium-rare steak away fast; then I returned to my living room, where that infamous, nearly half-full whisky bottle sat precariously on the edge of the table. In my drunken state, I'd tottered away, leaving it uncapped and heedless of its placement. Shaking my head, remembering both the bliss and the subsequent pain and sickness of the stuff, I snagged it, capped it, and stuck it away in my pantry. I had no plans to drink again, but who knew if I'd need the stuff at some point, so I kept it, just in case.

A knock on my door soon followed, but I wasn't surprised by it. I'd been expecting Karl. He would be spending the weekend with me, insisting I shouldn't be alone for too long, as I tended to be. It was a ritual. A couple of times a month, he'd come over, and we'd shoot the shit. Sure, we talked nonsense, but we also talked vampires.

Karl was now a believer after what I'd shared with him. He'd stuck by me after all that happened, the first and only friend I could go to after losing my family. I don't know what I'd have done without Karl! He was my rock. My only confidant. When I lost him, I nearly lost what little was left of my shit...

IV
THE DYNAMIC DUO

"No, and that's final!" I growled.

"Shit, Spence, you *need* me!" Karl growled back. He was bound and determined to join me on my next hunt. Bastard wouldn't shut up about it!

I'd had two kills since that first one, and it hadn't gotten any easier on me. I was well into what remained of that bottle of whisky, determined to deaden my senses without getting entirely shit-faced like last time. Seeing me drunk was something Karl had a difficult time getting used to. He'd known me all my life, or most of it anyway, and this new vampire hunter version of Spencer Vale was not at all familiar to him.

I couldn't blame him for his concern, but I was determined that nothing he said would change my mind about allowing him to come slaying with me.

"Spence, listen to me. It's destroying you," Karl sighed, making an effort not to let anger take over. "Are you listening to me?"

Staring at the light playing on the swirling liquid, I swung the whisky bottle around in a circle, allowing it to mesmerize me.

I was getting too drunk again.

"I'm already destroyed," my voice sounded dreamy in my own head, like talking in my sleep, "I've been destroyed since the day Jaren —" But I choked up and tilted more whisky down.

"No, Spence, you're not."

With raised eyebrows, I turned to him, surprised by the conviction in his voice.

"You're not destroyed, man. Not at all. Not *yet*, anyway." He shook his head and gave me a stern look. "You are amazing!"

That got me laughing.

"No," Karl exclaimed. He wasn't angry, but his voice was forceful, serious, and warm, "Shut your fucking mouth and stop laughing! You lost your family to this curse, this awful reality that no one is even aware of but me, and what do you do? You don't cave. You don't go into hiding or let paranoia overwhelm you. You don't sink into…well, you don't become a drug addict or a lousy drunk." He shot a warning look at my nearly empty bottle. "Alright, fine, you have a drink sometimes when it gets especially rough. That's not a sin; it's a coping mechanism. Seriously, how you *don't* drink yourself into a stupor every single day is beyond me. But Spence, you didn't give up and fall to pieces! What you did was train, you got strong, and you went out hunting for those dangerous creatures! You. Are. A. Badass!"

I could feel the heat rising to my cheeks, the liquor or the embarrassment; it was both. "Shut your fucking mouth," I mumbled, echoing him as I sat the bottle on the table and turned tired eyes to him. "You've got some unrealistic fucking romanticized idea of me, man." I chuckled ruefully, shook my head, feeling foolish.

"I'm not wrong." He insisted. "You are so strong. Man, I've never known anyone as goddamn strong as you are!"

"I'm dead serious about you shutting the fuck up, Karl," I demanded.

But he only laughed, and I love him for it. "Fine, but you can't deny you need help with this stuff. I'm fully capable, smart, strong—"

"You're a shrimp!" I teased. We both knew Karl was a tough guy. He was nearly a foot shorter than me, but that took nothing away from his strength. He was a stocky, muscular guy. Where I was unnaturally tall, lean, long-limbed, and T-shaped, he was a sturdy, stocky, perfect square.

"Shut up, shithead." He grumbled, but it was all play. We had the utmost respect for each other, and we'd always played these stupid games.

"Fine, but only once." I blurted out. It was the liquor. I'd never have said it, never have allowed it, if I was sober.

It took Karl a moment to register what I'd said; then, the moron was beaming at me like I'd invited him over for Christmas dinner.

30

"Great! Seriously, Spence, this will be the best. A vampire killing team. The dynamic duo!"

"I'm Batman." I hastily insisted.

"Well, of course," he huffed, "but I'm *not* Robin."

"Maybe Batman and Bat-Mite team up?" I joked.

Karl shook his head and glared daggers at me, "You're such a prick!"

"I thought I was amazing."

"Shut the fuck up."

Karl was right…initially.

Hunting was *so* much easier with his help! Heck, sometimes it could even be "fun!" From the day he joined me that first time, I hadn't picked up a bottle of whisky; it hadn't even crossed my mind.

I'm not saying there weren't difficulties. It wasn't like I didn't *feel* what we were doing. We both felt it, and it was rough. But we had each other for support, another mind to work off of, to find levity with, to unload on—someone else there who understood and looked at things with a different perspective. And we were *feeling* invincible!

But let's not get ahead of ourselves.

Our first hunt…

Not a week had passed since I agreed to let my best friend join me hunting, and I got my next vampire lead. The feeling was surreal as I shared the details with Karl, a friend, a person outside of myself, a partner, or a sidekick, as I continued to tease him.

"So," Karl was seated across from me in my favorite chair, fingers tapping the arm, ankle perched on his knee.

I sat on my bed, elbows on my knees, fingers steepled.

"This one's a woman?"

"Yeah," I hadn't hunted a female vampire before. Honestly, I was feeling more nervous than usual about it, not really sure if it was due to hunting with Karl or hunting a woman!

31

Could we do it? Slice a woman's head off?

He rubbed the stubble on his chin. "Doesn't matter, male… female…all the same, right?"

I shrugged, "Yeah, but it still makes me uneasy, I think."

"You think?"

Sighing, I sat back and ran my fingers through my hair. "This whole plan has me out of sorts."

"Hunting with me, you mean." His voice carried a hint of accusation.

"Look, I can't help it, okay? This is new to me. I've been alone, only having to worry about lil' ol' me since I started this. But now?"

"Now you feel like you're babysitting."

With a humph, I pointed a finger at him, conceding his point.

"Well," he continued, "I ain't no baby, Spence. I can handle myself as well as you can. The only difference between us is you've gone up against these things before and—"

"And that makes *all* the difference, believe me!" I cut him off.

Karl shook his head, scowling, "You're not backing out on me!"

There was no mistaking the warning in his voice. No, I wasn't backing out, but I wasn't happy, either. Not by a long shot. "Of course not. So let me have my concerns, alright?" I sighed deeply, "Let's go over the plan."

"Now you're talking!"

We were up the following morning just before the crack of dawn. Needed all the hours of light we could get to pull this one off.

"Why do they never do this in movies?" Karl said as he stretched and yawned. He'd slept on my small couch, which opens into a bed.

"Because it's not spooky enough for cinema. Got to have the full-on nighttime creep factor for movies. Bright, happy sunlight ruins the mood."

"Not if you're a clever and talented director!" He shot back, "I tell ya, done right, bright sunlight and horror could be particularly terrifying!"

I smiled, "It's been done with zombies, but not vampires, I don't think." Couldn't think of any right off hand.

"No *good* movies, anyway," he scoffed.

After breakfast, we suited up. I wore my typical all-black "uniform:" tricorn-folded cowboy hat, tee and leather pants, and a long leather coat. Karl also wore all black, at my suggestion and the detailed, gory reasoning I'd shared with him. I could tell the whole blood and gore thing made him squeamish. Movie gore is one thing. Real-life blood and bodily fluids were a whole other ballgame!

He wore jeans, tee-shirt, and a short denim jacket loaded down with weapons like the ones I carried, topped off with a plain black baseball cap. I ran over the details of the slaying with him again, going through the motions of decapitation, outlining the angle and way to take the head off in one cut. It wasn't foolproof, but it worked more often than not.

Karl couldn't hide his involuntary shudder, but I didn't tease him over it. Instead, I said, "Gird 'em up, boy. This ain't no larpin.'"

"I know," he replied thoughtfully.

I let it drop. "Thing we need to be prepared for is dealing with the thralls. From what I gathered, she's got at least five bodyguards, so you can bet they'll be big and strong. This could get ugly…and painful."

"I have a high tolerance for pain." He assured me, puffing his chest out.

"I hope so." I smiled gravely.

One thing I could say for Karl with regard to physicality is that he really was a tough guy in more ways than one! He could lay me out if he really wanted to, at least before my martial arts training. We hadn't sparred in years and hadn't gotten the chance before taking on this hunt. But he knew how to use an opponent's weight against him—how to feint and mislead them—how to read others and anticipate them. I wasn't too concerned about Karl coming up against the human guards unless they carried guns.

God, I really hoped they wouldn't have guns!

It was a ridiculous hope. *Of course*, there's no way they wouldn't have guns!

They had guns.

But I had my tranquilizers, and I was a good shot.

Still, it took us a better part of the day to finally subdue the bastards. Five big, burly guys, none as tall as me, but that doesn't matter a hill of beans if they have a gun and you don't.

This rich vampire bitch lived in a gated mansion on the outskirts of a neighboring city. Vamps usually like to live a bit apart, yet not too far away from bustling cities, where the hunting was easiest.

Not being too close to neighboring houses also made my job a bit easier. Staking places out, infiltrating, and the like was much harder in the center of a busy town or neighborhood with people everywhere: walking their dogs, jogging, kids running around. Remember, this is during the day, not at the dead of night.

Karl and I snuck over the wall at the back corner of the property after tranquilizing the first guard. Dart gun worked a treat. Four more to go...

"I'll distract them while you get inside." Karl offered in a harsh whisper. He was stating the obvious because that was our plan anyway.

I simply nodded, and he slinked off as I rounded a corner to try the glass doors off the rear patio. I struggled with the doors for a moment, hearing a commotion coming from where Karl went, confident he could handle himself.

Only a second later, Karl's voice rang out, "Spence, look out!"

I whirled around to find a big black cat slinking out from the opposite side of the house. What the hell? I hadn't spotted this thing during my stakeouts! And this was no house cat, mind you, but a big cat —a panther or something!

Richies have been known to keep exotic pets.

Everything moved in slow motion. Felt like The Matrix, but I was no Neo! As the feline sprang at me, I tried to grab my dart gun but fumbled it like the big idiot I was. Next thing I knew, the cat was on me, huge paws landing against my chest and sharp claws digging into me, right through the fabric of my shirt, sending the both of us tumbling into the patio furniture with a loud crash.

Thank heavens I didn't hit my head or fatally skewer myself on that metal furniture. I was going to be covered in cuts and bruises, or worse, by the time this was all over.

God, the sounds coming out of that thing, like a scene right out of Wild Kingdom! That thing was the hunter now, and *I* was the prey!

The feline was so soft I wanted to cuddle it, not fight with it, as I tried desperately to hold it back with my hands around its neck. I didn't want to hurt the gorgeous thing; it was just a cat...a big, deadly cat! Stronger than me, but not a preternatural monster!

Then, I smelled copper and realized there was blood all over me, but in my shock and frantic fight, I didn't yet register where the blood was coming from. On my back, fighting for my life, I wondered if this was how I was going to go out.

Suddenly, I felt the cat jerk sideways and away from me, realizing Karl had kicked the thing hard in its side, sending it sliding across the granite floor. I scrambled for my dart gun, only a few feet away, aimed, and pulled the trigger before the animal regained its bearings. Luckily, despite my trembling, jelly hands, it was a good shot, laying the cat out just as two more guards came barreling down on us.

Rushing to my feet, jamming another dart into the gun, I felt a wave of dizziness wash over me. A split second before the men were on us, hollering their threats and ready to end our sorry lives, I glanced down to find my shirt was torn to shreds and soaked red where the cat had scratched me—there were big gashes in my flesh from its huge claws.

So *that* was where the blood came from.

I felt no pain.

I was going into shock.

Fight or flight kicked in, and I whirled on the men, pulling the dart gun trigger as one of them lifted a pistol at me.

His shot went wild, thank god, while mine got him in the stomach.

A second later, he joined the cat in dreamland.

Just as Karl rushed at the other guy, and I was hoping he was the last one, another thug appeared.

"Great," I rolled my tired eyes.

Before I had to deal with the newest guy, I tried to dart Karl's opponent. But I couldn't get a good shot as they tousled, and I couldn't avoid the thrall that stalked swiftly toward me.

The two of us exchanged blows. He was big, almost my height, and a good bit thicker in build, but he didn't have martial arts training, so I had a leg up on him. But then *he* wasn't bleeding profusely, which gave *him* a leg up on *me*.

During our scuffle, he knocked the tranq gun out of my hand, sending it skidding too far from me to retrieve it. Then, just as I landed a good punch to the guy's jaw, sending him reeling, I heard a gun go off and spun to witness Karl and his opponent go down at the same time.

My heart stopped, and I froze for a second, praying Karl hadn't been the one to take that bullet.

Again, the world seemed to be moving in slow motion. My body was vibrating like a jackhammer as I saw my opponent reach into his shirt and drag out another pistol.

Before I could react, there was a shot, and my opponent collapsed. I turned and breathed a massive sigh of relief to find Karl up, holding my dart gun in both hands, smirking triumphantly at me. Then, seeing my condition, he rushed over.

"Shit, Spence! You're a bloody mess!"

Karl's strong arms grabbed me as I swayed, but I didn't go down. I was tougher than that.

"I'm fine, let's move and find the bitch," I ground out.

He nodded, but he regarded me dubiously. I'm sure I looked as pale, sick, and frightful as I felt—all gore-stained and barely upright, but the gashes weren't deep enough that my guts hung out, so I'd push through. Get the damned job done.

Placing a shaky hand on my sticky chest, I whispered an incantation, and a milky white mist sprung up out of my fingers, then danced over my wounds like Micky Mouse's brooms in Fantasia. Soon, the bleeding was staunched. It wouldn't last long, but it should hold me together long enough to finish the job and see to stitching myself up.

The *damned* damage was now beginning to hurt, but I pushed away the pain and got down to business.

"What did you just do?" Karl asked, eyes wide as he gawped at my no longer bleeding chest.

"Healing spell, not permanent, but sufficient. C'mon."

I shouldered past him and into the vampire's lair.

We searched the house, not finding any obvious place for the vampire to hide herself until we entered the master bedroom. The entire space had been converted into a dressing room, with endless, stuffed-to-brimming clothing racks, shelves loaded with high-end shoes and bags, and a dressing table like something out of backstage Broadway. It had a big, square mirror encircled with lights and a plethora of makeup and beauty products organized atop its surface.

Yes, vampires *do* have a reflection. Sorry to disappoint you.

Nodding my understanding, I turned to Karl and inclined my head toward the big, shiny, black, and gold-trimmed double closet doors at the back of the room.

Clever girl, sleep in the windowless closet and make the bedroom your dressing room.

Sure enough, opening the doors, which were not locked, we found a dark and cozy little sleeping chamber. Apparently, the vamp hadn't seen any need to lock herself in, never guessing that her gang of guards and big cat could be subdued so easily—well, it hadn't been easy. I was in a world of pain, but you get the point.

"No windows and no doors," Karl mused in the spooky voice of the Ghost Host.

Of course, other than the doors we'd just come through, he was right.

36

All the shelves, seaters, and such had been removed, and a huge California king filled nearly the entire width at the back of the closet. The furniture was modern but with that ornate Victorian influence: all cream and gold filigree, pillows, and bedding in Spode style, though red instead of the more common blue. Two narrow nightstands were the only other pieces of furniture present.

"There it is," I whispered, though I knew the creature would not hear me.

Lying on her back, arms flung over her head, was the vampire. She was naked, silk sheets clinging to her waist, breasts exposed. And she lay utterly still, no breaths making her chest rise and fall, no small twitches of her eyelids. Just as still as the dead man lying beside her.

A hearty-looking male, the same type as her guards, lay beside her on his stomach. She certainly had a type. His sun-kissed skin looked sallow, eyes and mouth agape, bite marks in several places, but very little blood otherwise.

This lady vamp was obviously fastidious, not wasting a drop—keeping her expensive linens nice and clean.

"Holy shit, Spence."

I looked up to find Karl leaning against the wall, gaping at the scene before us, looking almost as washed out as the corpse...almost.

"Told ya," It wasn't meant to be crass, but I had told him he'd see things he'd wish he hadn't.

This made him stand up straighter and give me a stern look as I pulled the hand scythe from my coat and advanced to the woman's side of the bed. "You have yours; get it out."

Awkwardly, Karl fumbled for his scythe, brought it out, and held it like it would scald him. I laughed, but not cruelly, "You take care of him, I'll get her."

Nodding at me, I watched as Karl swallowed hard and forced himself to grip the handle of that sharp, curved blade more tightly. We both moved to either side of the bed, and I nodded after we'd poised the blade tips beside those two necks.

"There's gonna be blood, lots of it, so...prepare yourself." I didn't tell him my kill would be far bloodier than his. All that guy's blood was in her, so I was the one in for a red shower.

Without any countdown, it seemed the two of us were subconsciously in sync when we lifted our blades and swung them down hard, slicing across those two exposed necks. Both of us achieved clean and thorough cuts; Karl's cut sent the man's severed head rolling off his pillow and toward the vampire. I had grasped her long, blonde hair in my gloved fist first, and my cut released a gush of red gore that soaked the pillows, bed, covers and drowned her victim's entire head.

Karl stumbled backward into the wall before regaining his footing and backing unsteadily toward the door.

As he struggled to get ahold of himself, I wrapped everything up in the bedding and handed him the woman, draping her mummy-like form over his shoulder as I shouldered the male.

Wordless, we swiftly escaped out the back, the way we'd come in, and hearing an inhuman groan, a feline groan, we hastened to my car, where we deposited the ghastly bundles into the trunk, and off we went.

The cat would eat well. And don't worry yourselves over it. Yes, I anonymously phoned Animal Control about seeing a huge black cat in the area. They got it. It was in the news.

The long drive back to my cabin was silent. Karl insisted on driving since I was in no condition. He seemed unwilling to ask or comment on the events of the day, and I was not in the mood to question him about how he was feeling.

Like a robot, Karl helped me unload the trunk, prep the funeral pyre, and bury the remains. Dragging ourselves into the house after all that, I let him shower first.

Later, once we were both cleaned up, we talked.

I'd gathered up my first aid kit, big ol' thing, loaded with all the self-help tinctures, gauze, and tools to right any wrongs, and parked myself in my favorite chair with a thud just as Karl sat on the couch. Eyeing my prep, he finally uttered his first post-kill words, asking me about that healing spell I'd used on myself.

"It's old magic I found in a rotting book in a dark corner of the occult section at The Book Chamber, that used bookstore that's been around our entire lives," I winced as I began to clean and stitch up those gashes in my chest.

He nodded his recognition of the place.

The bleeding had finally stopped naturally, but those wounds were raw and ached something fierce! "It was a tiny brown book of spells and incantations," I continued, "none of them worked except for this wound-stitch spell, which wasn't even a part of the book itself but handwritten in gorgeous cursive on the otherwise blank back page. I'd been flipping through several books before that one, looking for anything useful in prep for hunting, but coming up empty, as usual, and I'd given myself a pretty deep paper cut in the process of my search. So, I figured I'd test the spell on that since it was bleeding and hurt like the dickens! The spell actually worked, so I bought the book for a handful of bucks. Best purchase I ever made. Effects are temporary; worse the wound, shorter the duration. I still needed Neosporin and a bandaid to treat that cut later."

Karl shook his head, watching me work in morbid fascination, grimacing more than I was. "I can't believe you can do that to yourself! Stick that needle in and stitch your skin up like a granny mending socks!"

I shrugged, downed a nice gulp of whisky, more for the pain than to deal with the kill, and continued my work, "Had to learn to do and endure this kind of thing. Couldn't be dragging myself constantly to the emergency room, making lame excuses for how I hurt myself."

"Man, you're a beast!"

I laughed, feeling more like a tipsy piece of raw, shredded meat than a tough guy.

"You okay…after today?" Now that he'd broken the ice, I really did need to know how he was doing.

He shrugged, but I could see its weight in the stiffness of his shoulders.

"Yeah, I'll be okay." He looked hard into my eyes as I stared at him, needle poised between stitches, "Finish your work; it's unnerving me worse than dealing with those two vamps!"

I chuckled and went back to my stitching, but I knew it would take time for Karl to adjust. I knew it firsthand.

Karl and I hunted for two straight years together. The one stipulation was, now that we were a team, neither of us was ever to hunt alone, especially Karl! Although I hadn't been hunting that long myself, still, I considered him to be green and unpracticed by comparison.

Heck, for the most part, we were winging it because I hadn't yet set off for Europe to take that deep dive into the old, and hopefully rich, vampire lore we both so desperately needed.

Our slaying adventures were inconsistent. We fumbled one nearly disastrous kill, then utterly failed at another; that one nearly ended us both. That particular experience, or more properly, our inexperience, got me to book my first flight to Britain sooner than I anticipated. I'd planned to spend a few months over there and see what I could dig up.

Due to other commitments, Karl could not join me. But, initially, that worked out to my advantage because he could hold down the fort while I was away as long as he promised me *not* to hunt alone. He could gather intel, and we could resume our work once I returned.

In all my U.S. studies, everything had always led back to Europe. Nothing of vampire lore in the States was older than maybe the 1500s, and very little referenced history even that old. To go back to the roots, or at least to a better understanding of the origin and method of dealing with vampires, I *had* to visit Europe! I'd chosen the UK first, simply because I wouldn't have to deal with the language barrier, and I hoped, from there, I could find the threads I was looking for. Also, instinct guided me, which had been nagging me ever since I'd decided to become a hunter.

My plan was to return to the States occasionally to catch up on our to-do list, end a few bloodsuckers with Karl, and take care of important life stuff; then, I'd head back overseas as many times as necessary. Each time, I'd bring home more information, share what I learned with Karl, and, having gained essential connections, I'd set off again with a whole slew of plans.

Karl's pending marriage was one of the reasons he wasn't joining me on these trips, and once he tied the knot, I'd never let him hunt with me again. It was a good plan, but plans don't always go to plan.

V

LONDON

I flew first class. I could afford it, and I wasn't going to stuff these ridiculous long legs into those tiny, cramped coach seats for hours on end.

Once we were in the air, I relaxed to such a degree I could hardly keep my eyes open. Knowing that no bloodsucker was on board, I could let down my defenses since the flight would be in the air most of the day. I hadn't realized how tensed up I always was, never one hundred percent sure of my safety…expecting any moment to be discovered and attacked by some bloodsucker or their thralls.

But here, for these few hours, high in the sky in relative comfort, I felt as if I'd taken a liberal dose of tranquilizer as my ever-present alarm bells quieted.

A pretty stewardess asked if I wanted a drink, but I declined. I already felt a little drunk despite not having any alcohol in my system, and I was surprised when my response came out a little slurred. She smiled and gave me a knowing look; I didn't correct her.

Next thing I recall was the announcement we'd be landing in a few minutes. I'd slept the entire flight away and was grateful no one had woken me. Sure, I'd missed the in-flight services and felt mighty famished, but I also felt more rested than I had since I was a kid! It was euphoric!

I sat up, stretched, and took in the area around me. That attractive attendant was making the rounds, ensuring everyone had stowed their bags and no one was ill-prepared for a landing. Her gaze lingered on me with apparent interest. I did have that effect on the ladies, which I never quite got used to. Heck, I've been mostly a hermit all my life, especially since my hunting began. A hermit and an eccentric.

Once we'd landed in London, I made my way through the impossibly massive and insanely bustling Heathrow airport. It was simple hailing a cab, one of those classic and ubiquitous black Brit cars with the kindly cockney chap perched behind the wheel.

He drove me to a little Travelodge in Canning Town, just outside the city. It was cheaper than staying in the hub and not too far from the train station. I did like to save money, when I could.

The cabby, Kevin, gave me his card and told me he'd happily be my wheels while I was in town, and I took him up on that. What a godsend he was! It made my time there go much more smoothly than if I'd had to muck about on my own.

The first few days were spent getting myself acclimated. I caught up on some rest at the lodge, sleeping in, then hailing Kevin for a jaunt around the city.

Then, I spent a few weeks going back and forth to the immense London Library. That place was a dream for the likes of me! A bibliophile's Heaven. I practically lived amongst its vast and sprawling shelves, arriving early in the a.m. and departing just as it started to get dark. I struggled not to get distracted from my goal by so many things that drew my interest. No, I was not there to play! I was there to seek out relevant information about vampires, so I couldn't go around wasting time reading about history and science and random mystery stuff.

About a week into my studies, having planted myself in the oldest area of occult and mystical subjects, I began to notice I was being observed. It was the same man I spotted there each day, lurking casually nearby. He clearly had an interest in me but kept a respectable distance. Perhaps this should have concerned me, but it didn't. Nothing about him alarmed me, which, I admit, flies in the face of my typical borderline paranoia. What he did inspire in me was a growing curiosity of my own about who he was and what he wanted. But I refrained from confronting him about it, preferring to wait and see what he decided to do. Yeah, I'm still a bashful guy at heart, I guess.

Finally, one afternoon, I hadn't noticed him and wondered if he'd given up on me. I didn't dwell on it because I was riveted to an old book that a librarian brought to me from the back. It was a delicate manuscript, so I had to wear cloth gloves and handle it with the utmost care. I got the impression that the book was not typically allowed to be viewed by just any patron, but the kindly older woman seemed taken with me and couldn't refuse me when I asked for it.

I was so enthralled and deeply caught up in my reading and note-taking that I barely glanced away from my work for what was probably two or three hours.

"Excuse me," came a polite whisper from over my shoulder.

Turning to peer up at its owner, I realized it was that very same stately gentleman. I can't say I was surprised to see him.

Instantly, I was struck by the depth of his voice and his powerful demeanor. Tall and lean, he was dressed in a tweed suit that matched the tone of his hair. His eyes, also brown in that same russet tone, were perfectly paired with his attire, making him a picture of the British gent. I guessed he must be in his mid-sixties, and I was impressed by his full head of thick, dark brown hair peppered in the temples by streaks of white and cut short at the nape of his neck. He reminded me quite a lot of Christopher Lee in his manner and even a little in his rugged features.

His hand was extended toward me as I stood. I was, perhaps, only an inch or two taller than he was, which seemed to surprise him a little as he tilted his head slightly up to me.

With a smile, I took his hand and shook it.

Glancing briefly at what I'd been working on, he said, "I couldn't help but notice that book there. However, did you know of it? It is rather an obscure piece of literature."

I shrugged, "Perusing as I've been doing over the past couple of weeks, I was led to it."

"I see," he bowed his gentlemanly head and introduced himself, "Clannon Colfeld."

I couldn't help but grin and do the same. "Spencer Vale."

"A pleasure, I'm sure." He then inclined his head toward the table again. "May I join you, Spencer?"

"Yeah, yes…of course." We sat, and he tapped my notebook of messy scribbles with his finger. It seemed he wanted to say something as he studied it with a cursory yet intense glance. Scrawled there alongside my chicken scratch were symbols, graphs, and doodles from my memory that may or may not indicate connections to other things I'd studied. I could see his mind working as his eyes roved over the page, so I pushed it to him, inviting him to take a closer look.

As I mentioned, nothing put me off or sent warning bells ringing about Clannon. I liked and trusted him instantly, which was truly a rare occurrence for me.

He looked over my scrawling closely but did not comment. Then his gaze locked onto the back of my hand where I had tattooed the Wiccan Sofia to ward off bad energy. Didn't help with vampires, probably not. I wasn't sure why, but I felt a twinge of embarrassment. It didn't come from any reaction of his; he made no comment, nor did his expression change. But I still felt like a toddler that had doodled some nonsense on my skin. Somehow, I knew that this man knew things I could only dream of!

He spoke after a moment, where I had remained silent, allowing him to process.

"I think I can help you, Spencer." His dark eyes were quite serious as they locked with mine.

"You know what I'm looking for, I take it?" It felt as if we were playing a kind of word game, both of us knowing and yet dancing around the obvious.

"Vampires."

That was a short dance!

I nodded.

"And not the Hammer horror variety," his reply and expression proved to me that he knew all too well his resemblance to the inimitable Mr. Lee.

"Has providence smiled upon me this day?" I returned his knowing smile, unable to refrain from momentarily adopting his classic manner of speech, sans the accent, of course. I wasn't going to insult him by trying.

"Indeed, it has." He was smiling, yet the serious lilt to his voice and the powerful way he held my gaze moved me with giddy excitement. I might have had a sense about this man, but I could not have known then that I was making the most vital connection with regard to my mission I could possibly have made.

What he relayed to me next proved to me that I need not continue with that old library book and that he was far ahead of where I was in knowledge and experience. So, I returned the book, followed him out of the library, and hailed my cabby.

The pair of us set off for his home, a small apartment in the Mayfair district near the old stomping grounds of Beau Brummell. It was the very same Chesterfield Street where the Dandy himself had lived. A smart, clean, bright area where men's shops and everything from handmade shoes, suits, and the like could be purchased just like they had been back in those early days.

Stepping into Mr. Colfeld's place felt much like entering the residence of Sherlock Holmes rather than a modern apartment. This was a man of exceptional taste, education, and a flare for the macabre.

The walls, tables, and shelves were adorned with the most astounding things: unusual works of art, relics from all corners of the world, weapons, masks, and sculptures...all stunning and, no doubt, authentic. There was opulence here. But despite not coming from such a high place myself, I felt right at home amongst all that archaic class.

Actually, I was feeling a bit star-struck. Even though this was not *the* actor I had grown up watching. Still, being in the UK, in this iconic place, with this epitome of the English gentleman, and finding such a like mind felt a bit like a dream.

"Please, Spencer, browse to your heart's content," he moved to a small bar, an impressive antique, upholstered in black leather, with rich, shining ebony wood and silver trimmings. Three tall shelves of the same glossy wood overflowed with the most intriguing library. Those books had drawn me to them like a bee to nectar.

"Brandy?" He asked as he poured a glass.

"Sure." I'd never tasted brandy before, but how the hell could I say no? It was just so iconic.

He brought a glass to me, and we stood side by side, looking over his eclectic collection of books and knickknacks.

"This, my boy, is not the library you'll be interested in. I'll show that to you later, but first," he put a hand on my shoulder. "Let's sit. I want to hear your story."

As we moved to his tall, red leather, wingback chairs, he continued, "No one gets into this level of study without a story to kick them in this direction."

I sat, took a sip as he seated himself, and winced at the burn of the liquor. "I want to hear yours, too, Clannon. There's no doubt your story will be far more interesting than mine, and I hope not so horrible."

We exchanged knowing looks, his dark eyes filled with compassion before he sighed, "It is to be expected—tragedy in the wake of such fiends." There was no need to confirm that I'd experienced a vampire attack. I was to learn that we hunters always seem to recognize each other. "Let me say before hearing your sad tale, how sorry I am you had to endure it."

"Thank you," I sipped again, taking courage from the brandy and sharing my story with this man who so greatly impressed me. You already know what happened, and when I was done, Clannon apologized with such eloquence and feeling it was as if he'd committed the atrocities himself, but I waved him off. "As you said, it's to be expected, and it has become my drive, my singular purpose, to hunt and destroy all vampires." I then relayed to him the events of my first kill and the few hunts that followed prior to my coming into his country.

"Your friend assisted you, and yet, he, himself, had no prior experience with blood drinkers."

I nodded, "That's right. I really didn't want to drag him into it, but he refused to take no for an answer."

Clannon seemed on the verge of commenting, then hesitated before saying, "It's impressive what you've done, Spencer, and without any knowledge."

I could sense that that was not what he initially intended to say, but I didn't pry.

"Foolish." I laughed ruefully.

"Most certainly!" He chuckled with feeling.

"All I had was fiction to guide me, and it did the job, but I really do need the facts."

"And you shall have them," he assured me. "I didn't kill my first… *vamp*…" He used the shortened slang term in reference to *my* use of it during the telling of my story, "until I was in my thirties."

"Kindred spirits in vampire slaying!" I exclaimed a little too loudly.

"Quite so. But I was pretty well versed in their natures, abilities, and the like prior to my initial hunt. Unlike you, I didn't jump right into a mission of destroying all vamps. I spent many years learning to protect myself, traveling far and wide, as you can see by my unusual collections.

"Prior to my first life-changing encounter, when I was still a kid, I already knew vampires existed. But I didn't truly understand it or them. Oh, I believed the way a kid believes in Santa Claus, but I couldn't truly know until after…

"You see, my grandfather was a hunter and, despite my father, his son's, insistence that he not discuss such things with me, he persisted in secret, which I quite enjoyed, to be honest. Of course, learning such terrifying things from my grandfather, as exciting as it was for a boy so young and eager for the fantastic, did not prepare me for the awful truths that awaited me. No matter how dramatic and forceful my grandfather shared those stories, it was all just hearsay. The stuff of nightmares, unproven, yet held in my heart and mind like a kind of religious faith."

Clannon rubbed his chin, sipped from his glass, and stared across the room in deep thought.

I sat forward in my seat, my brandy glass empty, but heedless of this, I eagerly awaited his tale, which was sure to be enthralling—and terrible. He rose, took my glass, refilled us, and brought the bottle to the table between our chairs; then, as we settled back in, he began to tell his story…

VI

CLANNON'S TRAGEDY

Clannon took a deep breath, swallowed a healthy dose of brandy, then began his tale.

"I was in my early twenties when it started; my grandfather, who lived with us, had disappeared. Instantly, I blamed vampires since that was the one factor that, for me, made any sense. My father berated me to no end over my insistence that they had come for Grandfather after all he'd told me of hunting them and slaying so many of their kind over the years. I'd never seen my father so furious, so distraught and raging. His reactions seemed unhinged, even at my age. One minute, he railed at me for mentioning vampires and wild superstitions, then I'd find him digging through Grandfather's things, his secret hunter things, as if trying to find something specific.

"When he realized I was standing there watching him from Grandad's doorway, he rounded on me and stalked toward me as if to grab and shake me, or worse. Please understand that my father was in no way a violent man. He had only ever raised a hand to us, well, to me. My sister and only other sibling never did a thing to warrant any kind of punishment. He only struck my derriere when I'd patently deserved it, as all young boys do from time to time. I never begrudged him for it…not even when it occurred. I knew I deserved it, and it helped shape me into a disciplined man, for which I am ever grateful.

"But I digress. My father did take firm hold of my shoulders and stared hard into my startled eyes. Then, to my utter astonishment, he wept, and I was at a loss for words as he finally unloaded on me all his true worries, struggles, and frustrations.

"'Son,' he said finally, after regaining some composure, 'your grandfather never lied to you.'

"'I know,' I replied with calm assurance.

"He stared hard at me then, my father, always so strong in my eyes. He looked old to me for the first time, not as old as my grandfather, but old, tired, and frazzled.

"'I fear your assumption is correct," he continued, "that your grandfather *was* taken, or worse, God forbid, by...blood-drinkers.' It was as if he could not utter the word 'vampire.' The stigma associated with that term, from films and novels, made it as taboo a thing to consider as Bigfoot and the Loch Ness Monster.

"He then told me that, despite his pleading with my grandfather not to hunt at his age, he had refused to listen. And even though it had been many years since any vampire situation presented itself to him, something recent had occurred. Shocked yet again, Father told me he used to hunt with Granddad and that my grandfather had asked him to come along to assist with this current and necessary slaying. Still, my father had refused and made my grandfather promise not to pursue it.

"Now you must understand my grandfather, how stubborn he always was. Even more so in his doddering years. As he always told me, with regard to vampires, that nothing would keep him from his duty to deal with them. And I could imagine making a promise to my father would be one of those things he might renege on. Not that Grandad wasn't a man to be trusted to keep his promises. But when backed into a corner, if taking back a promise was, in his eyes, done for the greater good, then he would do it, I had not a doubt.

"At that moment, I decided that should the opportunity present itself, I would seek out Granddad and deal with the vampire myself. You understand we had no lead to go on, no idea where he went or what he might have gone after. We couldn't even be one hundred percent sure Grandfather *had* gone hunting a vampire. But it was unlike him to vanish for so long, and all intuition pointed to this being the case.

"Now, Spencer, my tale will mirror yours because new vampires often return to their homes, to what they know, to their loved ones. The last place, the last people that filled their thoughts before their mortality was drained out of them. Why? Well, there could be many reasons. Personally, I think it's familiarity—some residue of sentimentality or perhaps curiosity. Maybe some vain attempt to regain what they lost. Who knows.

"It was early evening, just after sunset. We were together watching telly, we three, not including my sister, who was traveling at the time. A loud sound came from the foyer, a cracking sound, like wood creaking and then splintering.

"Moments before this startling noise, I had noticed my father growing agitated and rising from his chair. Something had alerted him just before those noises sounded. Turning, we witnessed a sight that I..."

"Your grandfather," I whispered gloomily.

"My grandfather, yes, but no longer my grandfather. He appeared younger, taller, straighter. His skin was wan, ghastly pale, and he moved in an odd, frenetic manner as if he struggled to control his actions. But it was his eyes, his now glowing, crimson eyes, unblinking as he stared hungrily at us. I saw no recognition there. No love, compassion, nothing of the man I so adored. So imagine my shock, my pain, when he spoke and confirmed he knew precisely who we were.

"'Family,' he groaned, his face filled with an unnerving kind of barely controlled madness, 'my family. *Blood...*of my...*blood.*'

"Then, *he*...the *other* one, came—the one who had done this to my dearest friend. An old one that looked young. Slight of build, perhaps only in his mid-teen years when he was turned, with thick, golden brown hair and large, hooded eyes, shining fire in their cores. He...*it*... drifted into our small and humble place like some specter out of heaven, yet with the fire of hell in his bright blue eyes. Yes, he drifted, floated, levitated more than two feet off the floor and right through the *closed* front window."

Wide-eyed, I sat forward at Clannon's revelations. My mouth was agape as I shook my head. I'd never heard such a thing before! This was my first time hearing about the levitation and the passing through solid objects. I never imagined such things could be possible!

"That's right," Clan continued calmly, his eyes far away. "It floated and passed right through. These are skills a vampire can learn and hone over time...over long spans of time. That is how I knew this one was quite old, talented, and extremely dangerous! Those abilities, as well as the purely angelic presence the thing put off—a terrible kind of glory —a beauty on the edge of indescribable.

"The creature was across the room in an instant, that monstrously beautiful thing...hands grasping my father when he attempted to leap in between it and the rest of us, even to protect my grandfather, I assumed out of force of habit. And I was shocked, yet again, when the creature drew away suddenly, releasing its hold on Father, apparently losing its concentration as it fell from where it had been levitating,

49

landing hard on our wood floor. It was the wards, you see, the tattoos my father wore. His tattoos that I'd never seen before that night."

Clannon unfastened his shirt buttons, pulling it away just enough to expose a ring of runes around his neck.

"These tattoos were the reason my father had reacted just before the arrival. The ink burns when blood drinkers are near; it repels when vampires get too close, especially when they try to touch you. Grandfather had wanted me to get the tattoos when I was old enough to endure the pain, but Father would not allow it. I know, at that moment, he regretted that refusal. He screamed at me to keep back and protect my mother as he began chanting strange words like a mantra and advanced on the ancient vampire with bravery that made me both proud and frightened for him.

"My grandfather was also tattooed, so you might wonder how the vampire would have been able to turn him if he had been warded. I have a theory about that. I believe it was not an easy thing for the vampire to do, but it was possible, and here's why: the wards act most powerfully when coupled with the use of magic and the power of focused will. Granddad's mind had been slipping for some time: forgetting things, finding it difficult to keep track of time or even what day it was. Those failings, coupled with the powers of this very old vampire, would have made bypassing the wards a possibility.

"I turned to look for Mother and was aghast to discover my grandfather there, his face buried in her neck, his once loving arms locked around her in a most cruel embrace. Her gaze was filled with such pain, such anguish…for me! I knew it. Not for herself. Weak and weakening every second…her fair, peachy skin was swiftly turning gray, lips bluing, eyelids falling. It is…" his voice faltered, "difficult, even after so many long years, to share the details of such a—"

I lifted a hand, my face brimming with emotion…understanding, as I downed the last of my second glass of brandy. "You don't have to—"

He took my glass and filled both again, "Yes, I do. It is important we know and understand each other and our traumas."

When he paused, the powerful compassion we exchanged in that moment of charged silence solidified a friendship that would last the rest of our lives. I knew it all too well, the pain he had experienced… the anguish he suffered at that moment, reliving those heartrending events in the telling of it all. And I loved Clannon Colfeld then, like a father, like a brother, a most dear and cherished friend.

"To face them," he continued, "our traumas—it is our greatest strength and the foundation of our conviction."

Nodding, I sat back and took a sip, my head feeling light but my heart heavy as he continued.

"I screamed at my grandfather as he released his hold on my mother, and then I lunged, catching her up in my arms before she could hit the floor.

"'Hungry...' The old man mumbled through the gob of my mother's blood that coated his mouth. He was lost in a state of obvious bliss and twisted satisfaction. It was...the most terrible, most disturbing thing...

"'Hungry, so, so hungry...' his voice bubbled, like wet, sickening..."

Clannon shuddered.

"The room warped as I drowned in tears, anger, and desperation. Mother was gone, cold, limp in my arms. When I turned my swimming gaze from her pained, lifeless face, I saw my grandfather ambling toward my father and that deadly, radiant creature, the thing that has ruined our lives forever, held at bay by Father's strange utterances. I hollered at my father, who screamed back at me between snatches of his odd incantations to get my grandfather's scythe.

"Forcing myself onto fragile, wavering legs, I stumbled frantically for the study and the scythe hanging with other antique weapons above my father's desk. Hands were on me before I could even turn away from the wall, the shining, curved weapon held tightly in my hand.

"Grandfather was pulling me to him, sharp, awful fangs angling for my neck or whatever bit of flesh he could get them into. But I fought with youthful strength and panicked determination, somehow shoving my father's desk chair between us and causing the old man to lose his balance and stumble backward.

"I dashed for the living room again, scythe in hand, kicking a chair behind me in front of the old man, making him tumble over it as I shoved the door shut between us. I knew it was only a temporary hindrance, but it bought me enough time to throw the small scythe to my father.

"Tossing a scythe...not a safe thing to do, obviously, but in that kind of panic, I had to, and luckily, no damage was done to my father as a result. It landed close to him, and as he retrieved it, my grandfather seized me again from behind. This distracted my father, who halted his chant and lunged to my defense.

"But the ancient vampire was on his feet instantly, turning my father's attention away from me just long enough for Father to swing that scythe in an arc right into the neck of that young-looking, old creature.

"I gasped in astonishment as the thing's head flew free, unbelieving that my father had just slayed a vampire in so dramatic a way right there in our living room. Strangely, there wasn't much blood. The thing must have been famished to be so depleted, but I had not considered such details at that moment because I was struggling for my life against my grandfather.

"The events that followed happened quickly, yet felt as if they played out in slow motion.

"The thing that was once my grandfather moved so unnaturally fast that before I knew what had occurred, my father had crumpled to the floor, lifeless! Blood, my dear father's blood, stained my grandfather's face, his hands, and the front of his clothing. More blood had soaked his clothing than had been left after his attack on Mother. The attack had been more brutal. I do not know why the thing stopped then and stared at me so oddly, intensely, wordlessly, as his shining eyes, brighter in their fire than before taking my father's life, burned with such inscrutable emotion. But Grandfather's inaction galvanized me, and I lunged at him, like a complete buffoon, with no weapon but my bare hands.

"My life was unimportant to me. Only anger, red, heart-shattered anger, guided my hands.

"I heard my monstrous grandfather laugh at me. His laugh mingled with my desperate hollering as fresh, burning tears of pain and rage flooded out of me. I pounded the old man with harsh fists, and it took me several minutes, finding myself atop him, pummeling him in mad fury, to realize he was not fighting back.

"My mad attack came to a stop. Confused, I scrambled to my feet, gazing down at the old man who I had adored above all others. My best friend and teacher, so, so very dear to me, all bloodied and hideous, grimacing up at me, such an awful smile with those jagged teeth, sharp, deadly, bloody. He was not as damaged by my angry work as by the hideous work he had committed, but I struggled with seeing that face I knew so well. Love and hate mingled like oil and water within my heart as if the warring sides would tear that fragile organ asunder, and I would crumble into death along with my dear parents.

"But then he spoke, his once warm, endearing voice a clotted, guttural parody, and his words…I shall never forget his words, 'Clannon,' he rumbled, the sound of my name on those sickening, bloody lips wiping all thought from my addled brain. 'I…am sorry,' he said.

"I saw it then, the scythe in my grandfather's grasp. He had taken hold of it when my father dropped it. He lifted it as if to show me that sharp, sinister, curved blade. The thought that he might lunge forward and take my head and my life with it only fleetingly entered my mind. But no, that was not his plan.

"He moved swiftly, in that unnatural way vampires have, so quick that I could barely see the slash. Then his head rolled away as the blood he had just consumed gushed out of his open neck; the rolling of his head stopped not a foot away, and his old body went limp."

Clannon halted his tale, staring into the darkening room, his eyes distant and hand shaking as he lifted his glass to tip the last of its brandy down his throat. I remained silent, allowing him the time he needed, feeling the keen stab of pain as I imagined every sickening detail of his experience. He refilled our glasses, sank back into his tall leather chair, and sighed heavily.

"I knew what came next," his voice was low, quiet, filled with a dreamy kind of distance, "my grandfather had taught me well, so I did what I had to do. Just like you did, Spencer. I took it all, everything with even a droplet of blood on it, and burned them to ash. Well, all but that ancient vampire, which left nothing in the wake of its death but a pile of ash that I hoovered up and dumped into the bin. What a way to go, eh? For a body as ancient as that one to be treated. And yet, something about sucking that accursed dust up in a vacuum cleaner felt poetic." Clannon chucked but mirthlessly.

Overcome with the emotion of Clan's history, I took a sip from my glass. I was feeling quite drunk yet sobered by his harrowing tale. "Your grandfather, even after becoming what he was and doing what he did, had the wherewithal to end his own life." I was astonished, to say the least.

"Yes," Clannon replied in barely a whisper, "as if answering to a brief moment of clarity."

"I didn't know that was possible…for them to have any kind of conscience."

He turned to me then, his eyes dark and a little frightening in their intensity, "One of the most awful things I've learned about vampires is they are not mindless monsters, Spencer. While they are tragic and terrible things, they do feel, and they do, in ways I cannot understand, care."

"Care?" I exclaimed incredulously, "How the hell could they *care*? My brother, taking the lives of our parents with such cruelty!"

"But he left you alive, did he not?"

"He did, but I never saw that as anything but another act of cruelty. The most cruel thing of all—leaving me alone after witnessing what he'd done, as if to punish me, to torture me. Knowing I'd have to live with this pain—"

"And yet, he could have done much worse. You said he exonerated you in their murders as well."

"He did."

"He loved you."

"Don't," I downed my glass and slammed it down harder than I intended to on the table, then I sighed and sat forward, elbows on my knees, shoulders dropped, head in my hands. "I'm sorry, Clannon. I didn't mean—"

But he only laughed, a little laugh to cover the tears, "Please, I am not offended. How could I be?"

We sat in silence for a time; I'm sure his mind was running through everything we each had shared, as much as mine was.

"Where are you staying?" He asked finally as he took our glasses and returned the half-empty brandy bottle to his bar.

"Travelodge, out in Canning Town."

He laughed, "Canning Town! You're staying in Canning Town?! Oh no, we can't have that. Call your cabby and fetch your things. You'll stay here for the duration of your visit."

"I don't want to inconvenience you."

"Nonsense!"

The idea of staying with Clannon was thrilling for me, so I proffered no further argument.

Together, the two of us would embark on a journey of discovery, where I would gain the education and tools needed to most effectively hunt down blood drinkers and hopefully—if he did still live—find and destroy my brother, releasing him from his terrible curse.

VII
APPRENTICE

"I have dinner waiting for us," Clannon announced when I returned.

"You didn't have to—"

"Nonsense," he waved off my concern, "this first meal is on me; we can share the responsibility while you're here."

"Thank you," I had sobered up some and was starving!

We ate and talked a bit.

Clannon shared more about his life. His sister died a few years prior after a long-time illness. He never married, and his long-time girlfriend also passed away several years back of natural causes. As a hunter, he felt disinclined to attach himself more fully than he had during his time with her, and she never knew the true nature of his work.

With a fairly good inheritance from his father and good pay from his "day job" as a private investigator, and later a consultant to the British government in matters of arcane histories—yes, England's government was interested in certain less conventional subjects—he lived rather affluently, if simply. And his connections were mighty impressive!

After dinner, we retired to a small back bedroom that had been converted into a study. The books in this space were fewer than in his main sitting room library and of a different variety altogether.

"Ahhh, now *this* is a library with a difference!" I exclaimed as we stepped in. A large, stunning desk was placed central to the wall-to-wall bookshelf on the right side of the room. A plethora of far stranger, intensely curious trinkets and books with their arcane look, ancient bindings, and esoteric subjects…all made me feel like I'd set foot in a miniature version of Titus Crow's study.

This room was quite small, and I was amazed at how Clan had filled it so well and made it both comfortable and useful in that classical, British way.

"I hide these items from the average visitor. Might frighten away my…normal friends with such taboo things."

"No doubt." I ran my fingers over the bindings and gently flipped open a book or two that were lying on his desk, eager to delve into their most curious pages. "These are exceptional! Like new. Where did you find them?" Several books on his desk were pristine and immaculately bound, with covers so unique they were pure art. I'd only ever seen books that could be compared with these in very poor condition due to age and use. The oddest thing about them was that no titles were displayed, either on their front covers or on their spines. They were blank but beautiful mysteries!

"I bound those books myself," Clannon approached me and lifted one of them into his hands, proudly running his hand over the cover, "this is my creation, the design and execution." He turned it over to display the back and spine, then flipped it open, showing me the title page and indicating the way he had meticulously bound and tooled intricate designs into the leather. "See, this is the trick, making it even and securing it so that it's ready to endure many readings and endless perusals."

I was gobsmacked, as the Brits say! "Clannon…" I gasped.

He smiled broadly, "Take these," indicating a small stack of books on his desk, "they're yours."

"No, no, I don't expect…"

"Yes," he insisted. "Spencer, these are the most vital of the books you'll need, and I have the originals and can bind more copies at my leisure. See here," he opened his laptop, which sat in the middle of his desk, and showed me the files. "There they are, digitized and ready for print. I have an old friend at a print shop not far from here. He supplies the interiors, and I do the binding. My bound copies are owned by a handful of us hunters across the world. The only place no one owns these is America. You will fulfill that vacancy."

Shaking my head, I took the book from him. It was titled *Kor Borholden's Dark Whispers*. The cover was black leather, heavily textured with runes and shapes all woven together in a kind of Celtic fashion, yet not Celt at all. In the center was what appeared to be the head of a beast with a pointed chin, wide, angular eyes set with red rubies, and horns that poked out in a nearly straight vertical line from the sides of its head.

"What vacancy exactly am I filling here?" I could tell there was more to his statement than simply owning a stack of amazing, handmade, arcane literature.

"Let's discuss that tomorrow. I promise you'll know everything."

"Alright," I shrugged, curious but admittedly a bit tired for what promised to be a pretty involved discussion.

Clannon seated himself on a large couch, and I, book in hand, joined him.

The couch was one of those medieval pieces of furniture that looked too large in scale. It had a tall back and was as deep as a single bed. The thing was even long enough to accommodate my overly tall body. The piece was like new, immaculately upholstered, and very comfortable.

"You fall asleep here reading a lot, don't you?" I surmised.

"Often," he smiled. "You'll sleep here; it's the only place I can offer you."

"I'm not complaining; it's a lovely piece!" I ran my hand over the soft, thick fabric.

"It's a hobby of mine," he replied, "restoring old things."

Again, I was gobsmacked by his talent! "I noticed. It's ironic."

"Perhaps it is." He rose, waving for me to remain seated. "I know you're tired, so I'll leave you to your rest. The bath is just outside the door, in the hall to your left. Make use of anything you like. I have my things tucked away in the cabinet over the sink; otherwise, the space is yours. Tomorrow, we can begin your education."

I *was* feeling beat, my eyelids growing heavy as if his mention of rest had summoned my tiredness. "Thank you again, sir, for your kind hospitality." I got to my feet and shook his hand fiercely.

"You are most welcome, Spencer. I am looking forward to tomorrow and our burgeoning friendship."

"Me too," I replied.

He retired, and I grabbed a quick shower. Blankets and a pillow were laid out for me on that ancient sofa, so I crawled in, drew them over me with a sigh, and fell right into a restful sleep.

The following morning, we ate a traditional English breakfast: sausage, eggs, tomatoes, and beans, which I declined. I wasn't used to eating starchy stuff, and I didn't care for how it affected my digestion, so I explained that, and Clannon gracefully understood.

We then returned to that little library where I'd slept. I folded up my bedding as Clan placed himself behind the desk in his leather chair.

"That book you were perusing in the London library yesterday, I have an extra copy I can give to you." Without rising, he turned his swivel chair and pulled a book, the very same book, from his shelf. Only his was in far better condition than the library copy. Still, he advised me to use gloves to protect its ancient pages.

"I haven't gotten around to printing and binding that one yet, but I have it digitized."

I thanked him as he pulled cloth gloves from a desk drawer, handed them to me, then he drew forth yet another book. This one was altogether more creepy-looking than the first.

"This, my new friend, is *Encke's Grand Liber of Forbidden Truths*, it is a good start, more general, but still a vital resource, which will lead us on to other sources of greater detail and depth. This collection is a library unto itself, a sort of card index, if you will."

I moved to his side, peering over his shoulder as he cracked that sinister-looking book open and turned to the first page of its actual content. It was laid out like a dictionary or encyclopedia, and the handwritten text was tiny!

"How on earth do you read it without a magnifying glass?" I exclaimed, and he answered by displaying a large, ornate magnifying glass as he smiled up at me. He then reached around me and slid another large block of a book off his shelves. It was bound in deep, blood-red leather, with tooled figures on the front and tarnished silver corners. "The *Tome of Sohrakian Source*." He announced with no small measure of excitement. "This one is probably the oddest book in my collection and perhaps the oddest book in existence! It's an attempt at organizing a jumbled mess of insensate notes, scribbles, mindless mental meanderings, and bizarre sketches. It all, apparently, sprang from a nameless youth's dreams long ago—a kid who connected with some entity from another realm going by the name Whimm. And whim is certainly what the scholars thought of that weird, mostly incomprehensible journal. But I think it is the source, or at least one of the sources, for both Enke and Kor's writings, as well as others in my collection. Kor's book is a kind of glossary in poetic form, while Enke attempts to organize and make sense out of what mostly appears senseless. He does a pretty commendable job of it, too. These three books could be endlessly cross-referenced, and you'd never discover all the correlations!"

Standing, Clannon scooped up those books and inclined his head toward the sofa. "Come, let's do some digging!"

I seated myself beside him, and we spent hours perusing those pages, me asking questions, him imparting all the knowledge he had. As he'd said, we even discovered a few details he had not previously noticed.

"You see? Studying with another opens up new truths." He exclaimed, "I've been through this thing countless times, and with you at my side, suddenly treasures I had no idea were there are revealed!"

My head was spinning! The sheer breadth of knowledge this man had and the bizarre and astounding realities I thought only existed in the imagination…were all true! True and real and…

I needed a drink!

"Let's retire to the parlor for a drink," he said as he gently closed those reality-altering books and stood up.

"You read my mind," I replied with enthusiasm.

He checked his watch, "We should eat as well; it's been a while since breakfast." As we exited the room, he continued, "I often forget to eat in here when I'm reading."

"I can imagine."

He paused at the kitchen but waved me on, "Go make yourself comfortable. I'll bring us a snack. Make yourself a drink if you like."

I shrugged, "I'll wait for you on that. I…am not typically a drinker, or rather, I don't know how to make any mixed drinks."

"The brandy is refilled; make yourself a glass," he patted my shoulder, "you seemed to enjoy it yesterday."

"I did, thanks."

After pouring a brandy at the bar, I resumed the same seat I'd occupied the previous day and sipped the burning liquid. It was good, and I looked forward to the heady sensations it promised. Still, I needed to be careful not to make this drinking thing a daily habit— couldn't afford to become a lush or start relying on it, expecting it, and craving that drunken sensation.

Clannon entered a few minutes later with a snack of meat and cheese he called a ploughman's lunch. It was perfect, and despite my attempts to keep an eye on my drinking, as we talked and ate, I kept sipping until, between us, we had, again, polished off almost an entire bottle.

"If there is a blood exchange, then the change is more surely guaranteed." He was saying as he poured yet another serving in both of our glasses.

"Last one for me," I waved at my glass, smirked at him. "So," I sipped gladly, second-guessing my "last glass" declaration, "let me get this straight. A vampire drinks from a victim, essentially killing them, leaves them (no blood exchange), and the victim may, or may not, turn into a vampire."

"Correct."

"Or," I continued, "a vampire drinks someone dry, then gives them some of their own tainted blood, and there's still a chance the victim will die, but it's more likely they'll turn."

"That's right."

"Any 'likelihood percentage' involved with this, or is it just random?"

"It seems," Clannon rubbed his chin, thinking, "to be random… utterly random, in fact. But that said, you're right in assuming there should be a percentage because, according to the lore, blood exchange has a better guarantee. So, an educated guess, perhaps over sixty percent? I'm drawing that number, taking into account my studies from various sources and also a bit of experience. I believe my grandfather was turned via blood exchange. I have no way of knowing this for certain, of course, but it's a hunch. Maybe it's because his sire, what I assume was his sire, arrived with him at our home and relatively bloodless at that. Perhaps it was the blood on my grandfather's lips before he attacked my mother. Certainly, he could have fed on some other person or animal before coming to us, but I believe it was that vampire's blood. A blood exchange."

"Makes sense," I replied, sinking into my chair, boneless and euphoric.

"It's the arrogance and the vengeful way of blood drinkers to do something like convert a hunter. And it's not easy if a hunter is fully inked, charmed, defended. It takes old vampires to accomplish it. Strong enough to break through the wards. Grandfather had two things against him, faltering at his advanced age and running into an old vampire."

It was all so fascinating, but I had crossed a threshold and listened in a bit of a fog, watching with heavy lids and a silly smirk on my face.

Clannon laughed at me as he leaned forward and patted my leg, "You're right, my friend. I am more accustomed to these spirits than you are."

"Spiritss?" I slurred, then I understood. "Ah, yeah. Liquor." Then I grinned and tipped the last of my glass into my mouth. "I've never been a drinker." I shrugged.

"You're right to quit while you're ahead."

"I'm passsed ahead." I rolled my eyes, swayed a little where I sat.

"Have a nap, my friend. We've covered a lot today. That alone can addle the brain, liquor or not!"

I agreed, dragged myself onto unsteady feet, and, thanking him awkwardly for his wonderful hospitality, weaved my way to that oversized couch and crashed for a few hours.

Dreaming was a wild adventure colored by everything I'd learned, my own and Clan's traumas, and all we had discussed. I'm sure the alcohol played a part.

In those dreams, I was drunk the entire time, swooning, stumbling, and weaving around as I was beset by a menagerie of...*things*. It was a Lovecraftian heaven in my head...or more like hell, I guess, but I actually enjoyed it. Those eerie terrors bombarding me tried their damndest but could not seem to frighten me, not really, because I was too drunk to feel much of anything.

I'd never dreamed like that before—of being inebriated and chased by some sinister force—or forces. Sure, I'd dreamed of slaying vampires and other threats, both natural and supernatural. But this was like swimming in some netherworld that only I could see and feel. Again, HP would have loved it! Maybe he dreamed like that because if I'd had these kinds of dreams as a kid, I'd have written some kick-ass stories, too!

Well, I'd have *thought* my stories were kick-ass. Honestly, they probably would have stank. I was never a great writer. Yeah, I had some interesting ideas rattling around my head, but translating them onto paper...making them into a story was always a challenge for me. Still, Rayn had seemed, genuinely, to like that little snippet of a story she read over my shoulder. I always told myself because of that, maybe my writing wasn't as bad as I thought it was.

The headache wasn't too bad when I woke up, either—a slight hangover, which would likely clear up with some food and a shower, so that's just what I did.

Clannon had gone to run some errands but left me a note and some chicken for dinner. I put that away fast, showered, then retired to the small study and browsed through more of those hand-bound books laid out on his desk. Whew! They contained some wild stuff, but shit, I loved it all!

Did I believe it all was factual? No, honestly, I did not. Let me tell you, it's hard to swallow the stuff in those books! If I hadn't experienced vampires, I'd have thought the entirety of their contents to be utter hogwash! But, having been through yesterday's studies with Clan helped me to recognize and understand the things I read. I could see why Clan had wanted to start there, to prepare me for this whirlwind of sheer insanity!

He joined me a little while later, and we dove in again. His input, unwavering beliefs, and vast knowledge brought me around, at least to the possibility that some of the things in those books were based in fact. But there were things we discussed that even he doubted their validity. One could not help hanging onto at least some vestige of reason when faced with such fantastical, incomprehensible information.

I remained with Clan for the full six months of my UK stay; then, I returned home for a brief time to take care of business. Before leaving, Clannon assisted me in applying for dual citizenship. It was imperative that I be able to remain in Europe and not be forced to leave every six months. He had connections that he was sure could assist my application in getting approved sooner rather than later, so I went through all the rigamarole; then it was off to the U.S.

I wasn't long in my home country before flying back to England and, again, staying with Clannon at his insistence. There's nothing of note to share about that brief trip home. Mostly, it was boring, life shit. Action on the vampire front was nonexistent.

"My boy!" Clannon exclaimed as I stepped into his foyer again after some weeks, "I'm thrilled you're back. But I have plans for us since you were not away too long, and we don't want you deported if your citizenship takes longer than I hope it will."

He led me to my little guest room/his office with that massive couch and big old desk. Then, he outlined our first trip.

"We'll be in the UK during the first leg of our travels, 'seeing the sights,' to make the government happy but also to continue your apprenticeship. First stop, Glasgow, to get you inked."

Alright!

I was going to get those tattoos, the ones Clan wore, to protect and lend me other benefits during my hunts! "I'm past ready for this! Need those wards to hunt."

"Indeed, you do! Oh, and I made a discovery while you were away that I think you'll find most interesting."

My eyebrows shot up, "Really?" Whatever could this be about, I wondered.

"Your name, Vale, seemed familiar to me, so I did some digging. It seems you're not the first Hunter in your family."

My heart rate picked up, eyes grew wide, "What?"

"That's right. We keep an ongoing record of hunters going as far back as the first century." Clan pulled a carefully rolled sheet of yellowed paper from his breast pocket and handed it to me. As I unrolled it, he said, "The lists are not yet bound, though I have digitized the information and will bind them eventually. That is from a stack of very old, boxed papers."

Written in lovely cursive, clearly in an antique hand that looked like the late eighteenth, or early nineteenth century, was a list with dates, places, and other brief information. Running down the list, I spotted "Vale," then "Kilkenny, Ireland," and the dates "1731 to 1789."

"Hyroshian Vale," I gasped, then turned my astonished eyes up to meet Clan's smiling face. "My fifth great-grandfather was a hunter!"

"That's right."

"Is there any more information than this? Family, other life stuff, how he died?"

Clannon shook his head, looked apologetic. "Unfortunately, no. When things settle down, perhaps after your training, you can visit The Emerald Isle and do some digging."

I nodded. Someday, I'd have to look deeper, but just knowing I had a hunter ahead of me, that hunting vampires was in my blood, that I "got it honest," as Dad used to say, thrilled me more than I can tell you!

We set off for Scotland the following day, taking a small plane into Glasgow Airport.

VIII
GLASGOW

Glasgow, Scotland.

This was where I would get those strange and fucking awesome hunter tattoos. The artist was an old Nintach priestess, a rare and arcane teacher, magic wielder, and close friend of Clannon's.

Immediately upon our arrival, before heading out to the priestess' countryside home, Clan and I stopped at a little fish and chip shop. It was a tiny, narrow little establishment tucked inside a "close" between two old buildings. God, but that was the *best* fish I ever ate! I gave Clannon most of my "chips," aka french fries; wacky Brits don't know the difference between potato chips and fries! I ate three servings of fish, and those lightly-breaded pieces weren't small, either. But, as you can imagine, at my size, I can eat *a lot*!

Once we were satisfied, it was off to meet that mysterious lady, and that was an experience I'll never forget! She was a wee old thing, not even five feet tall, round and jolly, and filled with an air of mystique that drew me helplessly to her. I could imagine that unusual vibe of hers—a sense of great and ancient knowledge…forbidden knowledge —might put some people off, but not me. I was utterly fascinated!

Her name was Fedelma, or at least that's the name she went by. I never learned her last name and didn't ask. Clannon later told me Fedelma is an old Druidic name, which I was pretty sure must be rare these days. But I could be wrong about that.

"So," the old gal began as we three sat amongst her clutter of most interesting things in a space that was both comfortable and filled with intrigue. I was finding it difficult not to glance around constantly at this or that oddity, all so attractive to an ever-curious mind like mine. Yet again, being in this place felt like I was living in some horror movie, something by Hammer or perhaps one of those creepy Italian films.

"You're here to get inked," she grinned at me, and I was impressed by her straight white teeth. They seemed quite nice for a gal her age and didn't appear fake, like dentures. She had to be over seventy but there was a youthfulness about her that made her ageless.

Returning her smile, I shrugged, "Always wanted more tats but never knew what to get." I held up my hand to show her my only tattoo. She ignored it or did not care.

"He'll have what I have," Clannon stated as if he were ordering dinner for me.

Fedelma's face grew serious, "The kid's sure 'bout what he's takin' on? What he's gettin' 'is handsome self int'a? He surely looks like he can handle himself! Never seen one that looked more capable!" Her eyes sparkled at me from across the room, and I think I actually blushed.

"He's already been at it." Clannon reclined into his overstuffed cushion, hands behind his head. We weren't seated in chairs, but large round poofs, a bit like beanbags, but with soft, yet surprisingly supportive stuffing inside, rather than beans, and not so casual. They looked Indian, like something a Maharaja might have scattered about his harem. The whole room was adorned in the colors of the Far East: deep burgundy, peacock blue, gold, rust orange, and midnight purple.

"Hunting?! Without protection?!" She gasped dramatically but not at all jestfully. There was genuine and intense worry in her reaction, and her eyes bore into mine with accusation, reminding me of my mother whenever I stepped out of line.

I loved her then and felt a twinge of sadness as I thought about how much I missed Mom.

"Killed multiple vamps before flying over here." I smiled disarmingly. "Went as well as it could. I'm here, aren't I?"

"Nothin' to make light of, young man." She scolded. "But I'm glad yer here, prettin' up my place."

"Flirt," I smirked, feeling my cheeks heat up again. There was just something moving about being teased that way by a mature woman of obvious power. Oh yes, I could sense power radiating off her. I never knew us mere mortals could be powerful like that in the real world. Magically powerful, I mean.

A giddy rush coursed through me over knowing her, what we were about to do, and what I was involved in.

Shit, my life was strange!

"So, Fedelma, tell me more about you, what you are, this whole Nintach priestess thing," I asked.

She smiled sweetly, and I could almost imagine how she might have looked when she was young. She seemed a little surprised and quite pleased that I'd shown such interest.

"Alright, handsome. I'm sure Clannon told you the Nintach are old as time, or nearly so. I'll not be sharin' much since it's better if you don't know it all. Nintach priestesses and our secrets are well guarded, even among hunter-kind. We implement a plethora of means to keep ourselves concealed from vampires and other dark things."

She scoffed, then laughed at herself, "Just look at me sayin' 'we!' There is no 'we,' it's only me. I'm the last one, and I keep myself well out of confrontations with blood drinkers, just as my kind always have. We are, *I* am, far too important, and my secrets too vital to take any chances.

"I'm sure ya also know that a vampire can make a psychic connection with mortals when they drink yer blood," she continued, "They can learn things from ya, vital things that could be the difference between life and death when hunters go up against 'em, which we can't allow. So, you'll be warded in more ways than one. Locked within your runic protections will be obfuscatin' powers that prevent vampires from discoverin' the likes of me. They even hide the lion's share of a hunter's own secrets from the fiend by temporarily blurrin' or even completely blankin' out the hunter's memories as the creature drinks, makin' it impossible for the vampire to learn anything.

"Also, while the runes will prevent young vampires from piercin' a hunter's skin—only the bite, mind ya; other weapons can still get ya—it may not hinder an *ancient* blood drinker from chompin' into ya."

It was a lot to take in after my oh-so-simple slaying strategies. Magic? Wards? Sure, I understood all that in a fictional sense. But the whole "this is the real deal" thing was madness! Awesome, fucking, madness! I was eating it up!

"Well," she huffed a little, "before I go marrin' that nice skin o' yers, let me teach ya precisely what I'll be doin' to ya and why. Not a centimeter of ink will I stain ya with until ya hear me out and state yer approval. Otherwise, it'll all be meanin'less. It's all vital stuff, and it *will* change ya. Fundamentally, yer life'll be altered, and ye'll have to agree to it all before I can e'en begin."

That was cryptic, but no going back now.

"Of course, I accept."

"Not so fast, young'n!" she jumped on me again, disciplinarian that she was.

"Like I said, I'll accept nay promises from ya until ya hear me out. Impatient thing!"

I laughed, "Patience has never been my strong suit."

"Well, make it one!" she demanded, "nothin's more important than patience in this awful work!"

Her point was well taken, "Yes, ma'am."

This garnered another grin before she sighed and turned serious again, if not so severe. Then she began her first lesson. Pulling the neckline of her moo-moo down, I saw that she had the same runes around her neck as Clannon, but she also had other tattoos he didn't have.

"These here," she indicated those particular shared symbols in a wide circle, about three inches from the curve of her neck, they dipped below her collar bones, then all the way around in a circle, "are runes of Sohrakia, taken from a book, the true origins o' which no one knows, but its strange teachin's are effective, so that's all that matters."

"*Tome of Sohrakian Source*," Clan interjected.

"Quite right. This here serves as repellent, warnin', and protection, and I'll be drawin' this all over ya, which I mighty look forward t' doin'!"

The old gal sure was relentless with her come-ons. That naughty look on her cute little old lady face nearly made me laugh aloud, but I held it in and winked at her instead.

She smiled back at me, then gave Clan a pointed look and a nod of her head. He promptly stood up and disrobed, keeping only his boxers and socks on.

She then proceeded to run through all the tattoos I'd be receiving, using Clannon's bare chest, back, arms, and legs to illustrate. Those Sohrakian runes encircled all of his limbs, coiling around them like skinny snakes, and there were many other strange markings there, too.

"If we were alone, my boy, I'd show ye mine," she giggled at me.

"Why so shy?" I cocked an eyebrow at her.

"You Hush!"

I had finally gotten *her* to blush, made me feel accomplished.

With a finger pressed to Clannon's heart, she explained the rune there: a triangle, point up, with a spiral at its center and what looked like some embedded stone. I wondered how that was accomplished, getting that rock to stay in Clan's flesh like that, so I asked.

"Magic," was all she said. I didn't push it.

There were angled strokes of ink spiking off the triangle. They poked out in pairs from each of the triangle's three sides. Runes, different from the Sohrakian digits and unfamiliar to me, graced each space between those spikes, three to each side of the triangle.

"This here's a heart seal," the old priestess explained, "powerful blood magic, makin' it difficult for vampires to take yer vital life juices. It can also hide what ya are, the hunter ya are, from their senses. The older the bloodsucker, the more powerful they can sense ya, an' they can sense a slayer real easy if you're not careful. It's like they can smell the slaughter off ya or pick up on yer revulsion to them. There's more to this seal, much more, but that's not important right now."

"Not important…. Not important *good*, or not important *bad?*" I quipped.

She waved a dismissing hand, "Never you mind! It's not going to hurt ya, so let it go."

Fine then, I let it go.

"Now…" Running her finger slowly down, she halted at a tattoo that circled Clannon's belly button. "You heard of chakras, yes?"

I nodded.

"Then you'll notice markin's on each one," she continued, "each unique, another form of protectin' ya. No special details to outline 'bout them, but any little bit helps, eh?" She stalked over to me and grabbed my right hand, then ran her fingers over the Wiccan mark I had there. "Not bad for wingin' it. Won't do squat against vampires, but it's a nice thought." She patted my hand, cutting her soft brown eyes at me. More flirting, so I wiggled my eyebrows back at her, and she blushed again before dropping my hand and returning to Clan.

Uttering an odd string of strange noises that barely sounded like language or words at all, she dragged the forefinger of both hands in unison over areas of Clannon's skin, on his chest, shoulders, and back, that were not tattooed; suddenly, those blank spaces filled in with more of what appeared to be Sohrakian runes. But these runes glowed red; they were larger than the black-inked versions, and they wavered and pulsed in a regular rhythm.

"These'll warn ya, *and* ward ya, and, in a fight, they'll enhance yer thinkin' and reflexes. I made 'em glow just now, but vampires don't make 'em glow. Yet other dark beings…certain Darklings, do set 'em off, and if they're very, very old, they'll light up like a flickerin' brush fire. See 'em pulsin'? That's Clannon's heartbeat. These're intimately tied to yer life force and work in tandem with that heart shield."

Mesmerized, I couldn't take my eyes off them. They seemed to trace the path of the largest arteries, right where a vampire might decide to drink from, even circling that triangular heart symbol, making me think of Ironman's Arc Reactor.

69

"Darklings…" I mused. "You mean the creatures outlined in some of the books I've been studying with Clan?"

"Aye! That's the ones."

Honestly, I had a really difficult time believing any such creatures existed. Maybe because I had grown used to the idea of vampires, simply due to my first-hand experiences with them, but these other things?

"Have no doubt about Darklings, boy." She was watching me like a hawk, reading my mind simply by the expression on my face or my body language.

"I wasn't—"

But she only snickered, "I can read ya like an open book, handsome! That's more trainin' you'll need! Gotta learn to school yer thoughts, but especially manage and utterly control yer expressions, emotions, yer whole body! You think *I* can read ya? Nah, even I ain't got nothin' on them vamps! If yer not in utter control of yerself, you'll give the game away. They'll use the expressions of yer exposed thoughts and feelin's against ya without a lick of hesitation!"

What she said took me back to Jaren, how he'd acted with me, seemed to see right through me, but he *did* know me so well, better than anyone, at least back then, so I had chalked it up to that. It was probably a bit of both.

"Thing is," I shook my head, "I've never had to face a vamp while they were awake. I only ever hunted during the day to avoid that."

"Handsome *and* smart! Good thing, too! Ye'd probably be dead by now if ya had. Would'a been such a loss!" Her eyes twinkled, and I felt my cheeks heat up again despite myself.

Again, she grew serious, "Ye'll deal with walkin' talkin' deadly-awake vampires soon enough, no doubt. The young'uns pose little threat to a learned hunter, but the old ones…?" Her face went grave, and she exhaled dramatically. "The older they are, the more vicious and deadly! Effortlessly deadly, boy! Even seasoned, warded, magic-wielding hunters better watch out 'round them!"

"I understand," This made me all the more anxious to learn everything I needed to know and get on with the tattooing so that I could jump back into the fight!

Fedelma proceeded to expound on the other smaller inkings on Clannon's body and a few unique symbols on her own flesh for the next few minutes: symbols for healing, to subvert attention, to illicit dreams of portent and precognition, all sorts of wild and esoteric things! I listened, enraptured. The tattoos were many and varied, hence

70

our plan to be in Scotland for a few months time, to study and get it all, or at least the ink like Clannon wore, drawn onto me, all over me!

I was going to be in a world of hurt and wasn't looking forward to *that* part of this new reality.

When she finished and looked hard at me, wordless and expectant, I grinned and bobbed my head once with an, "I accept this calling and will devote my entire life and my whole self to its cause." I wondered if my great-grandfather had done this very thing and what his priestess was like.

A broad smile broke out on Fedelma and Clannon's faces.

"Good boy," she exclaimed, "and a thorough acceptance at that!"

We finished the day with food and drink, retired early, and got plenty of rest before many days of burning flesh, long lectures, and a whole lot of pain.

Each day began in earnest! I did not simply lay there and take it during my intense tattoo sessions. Fedelma and Clan taught me in much more depth all about the various symbols, related effects, and magics. I say "magics" in plural because the magic skills they imparted came from many different sources; some even mish-mashed together to create new and unique spells. There weren't a thousand spells to learn. Instead, there were only a handful of key bits with precise uses against vampires.

Not having to memorize a gazillion things was a massive relief to me. That said, I am fairly adept at memorization and tend to quickly pick things up that stick in my head forever. My trick, if I have one, might be that everything has a rhythm to it, whether smooth and catchy or dissident and out of sync.

I might struggle with something that doesn't have a clear, natural flow or pleasing "beat" to it. For the most part, spells do tend to be pretty easy to put a rhythm to that I can essentially rap to myself or even sing if that helps me to recall them. No, I do not sing spells out loud. No one wants to hear that out of me! But I do sing them in my head as I draw each syllable forward in my mind, like recalling the words to a favorite song. I do not have a photographic memory, but I have my techniques.

During the times I was in healing mode, in between the inkings, that's also when I studied a little chemistry. Well, not so much scientific stuff, although it felt a lot like science class back in school, with the beakers, blending, and chemical reactions—it was the physical or alchemical side of magic. I loved this part because I loved science, big geek that I am. Heck, I love every bit of this stuff—magic and molarity, spell casting and synthesis, "fantasy" and horror. All my favorite things!

Without the *real*-life horrors of pain and death, that is.

I even began to love the tattooing. That unique kind of pain, or discomfort, of getting inked became almost addictive, although, once my tats were done, I had no desire to add more. My body, everywhere beneath my neck, was inked nearly from top to bottom. Not every inch of my skin, but I was sufficiently covered with those runes running all around my torso, arms, and legs.

Oh, and don't think Clan and I didn't go out regularly to hunt vampires! We kept ourselves busy hunting almost every day once my tats were mostly finished. Arguably, this might have been the most useful part of my education. In the field, first-hand training was indispensable, honing my knowledge and skills to sharp edges and fine points. I've said before that vampire slaying could be "fun," and I can say now that this time, cleaning up Glasgow with Clan at my side was a total blast!

But my fun time in Glasgow was interrupted when I got an unexpected call...

Karl's fiancee had reached out to the phone number I'd given to Karl before I left. It was a line provided for me by Clannon, and the message was delivered through his answering service. The call was forwarded to Fedelma, and she handed me the line instead of Clan, which was the first sign something wasn't right.

An intense, sick feeling settled over me as I took the phone, and my heart began to thunder in my chest. "This is Spencer Vale."

"Mister Vale," a woman's voice greeted me. She was all business, though not particularly cold about it. "It's nice to make your acquaintance, sir. My name is Sarah. I...suggest you seat yourself for the following message from a Miss. Markam."

"I'm sitting," I lied. Then, suddenly feeling a little weak in the knees, I moved to obey her, returning to the cushion I'd first sat on weeks before.

"Alright. I regret to inform you of this news, sir; please forgive me. Miss. Markam sends word that her fiancee, Karl, has been killed… Murdered, she says, but they don't know by who or why. According to the police, it seems the young man was attacked in one place, then moved to another and left for dead because very little blood was present at the scene, but Karl had been stabbed repeatedly."

The woman paused, obviously feeling a bit overwhelmed by the news she had to deliver. After a moment, not receiving any response from me because I could not speak, she continued, "Miss. Markam then added that Karl had insisted if anything were to happen to him, she was to relay any and all details to you as soon as possible. That was the end of the message. Needless to say, the young woman was quite distraught over her loss, but she still wanted me to apologize to you for interrupting your travels with such terrible news."

I was frozen. My mind locked up. My body was a cold, hollow statue of ice.

"I am…so sorry, Mister Vale." The kind lady broke into my whirling thoughts.

"Th-thank you," I replied absently. Then, like a zombie, I handed the phone to Clannon, who was standing closest to me.

He thanked the service, then hung up the line as I collapsed inside. My head dropped into my hands because I could not hold it up. I struggled to think clearly, to form coherent thoughts, but I couldn't accept it! It would not form in my head as any kind of reality! The rending of my heart and the loss of someone else, yet another being so vitally important to me, it could not be true! And yet, I knew it was true. Could feel it was true in my bones.

Karl was no longer in the world.

My best friend and brother from another mother was gone.

It was time for me to leave. My time in Glasgow was coming to a close anyway. I was still healing, but all the tattoo work was now complete.

"I have to go," I mumbled through my hands.

"What's happened?" Clan asked, his hand on my shoulder and his voice heavy with concern.

"Friend died…it's…bad." I wasn't crying, not yet; it was too fresh, too impossible, and I was in shock.

"I'm sorry, Spencer."

Fedelma wrapped her arms around me, pulling my head into her soft stomach, "Yer all done here, my dear boy. Go and do what needs doin'."

"I'll return as soon as possible," I replied airily. My head was floating; I was having a devil of a time getting a hold of myself as I stood on wobbly legs and tried to remember which way was up.

That gentle hand on my shoulder and another on my arm from Clan and Fedelma assured me of their caring and friendship. I smiled at each of them, but it was a hollow expression, detached. They understood, of course. They had lost loved ones, both naturally and due to this most unnatural line of work. There was no pain like it, and it further cemented our deep and growing connection.

Clannon booked my flight for me as I packed up my meager belongings and left within the hour. A short flight into London, then back across the ocean.

Hours to think and to grieve, yet I was so numb and in shock that my feelings remained locked somewhere inside, waiting for some catalyst, some proof that what I'd been told was actually real. Nothing about the flights out of Scotland and then on to the States roused my addled head. None of the interactions or the time in those cab and airline seats seemed tangible. Every bit of the trip felt like an alternate reality, some mad dream I'd wake up from any second.

I kept going over that phone call, the message from Karl's fiancee, again and again in my head. I'd given him Clannon's answering service number only for an emergency and told him not to give it to anyone else. Apparently, he'd had good reason to share it with his fiancee, whom I'd never met. He must have known something bad could happen to him…

Then it hit me!

The bastard had gone hunting *alone!* Why hadn't that been my first thought? There was no other explanation!

Found dead, barely any blood!

Fresh shock overwhelmed me. I had allowed this! Allowed him to hunt with me, and the dumb ass had gone against my wishes—against our vow, and gotten himself killed! The rage and pain worked me up so badly that I had a difficult time controlling it. But I was on a flight with two hundred people. I couldn't let myself lose it, so I caged those emotions inside, which must have finished zapping my strength because I finally fell away into troubled dreams.

When I woke, as we approached our final descent, I cannot tell you how disappointed I was that the awful truth was not actually a dream.

Took a taxi home. They let me out at the end of my long drive, and I walked the rest of the way, finding my little cabin perched there in the dark, looking a bit eerie and inviting, its familiar, creepy, yet welcoming arms waiting to enfold me.

A sudden, profound loneliness descended on me like a heavy black cloud as I dragged my feet to the door.

IX

BROKEN

Entering my little shack of a house felt surreal. I'd only been gone a few months, but now everything had changed. Rather than feeling familiar to me, as the outside had a moment ago, the interior felt like an utterly foreign space, and *I* felt like an entirely different person. My tattoos were still healing, uncomfortable, and my head was filled with an overload of information, all crashing and careening through its squishy bends and curves: magic, mystery, and mayhem, all the stuff of wild and incomprehensible nightmares that I'd learned and experienced during my time away.

But now, suddenly, here I was back home.

And Karl was dead.

I'd *never* see him again…

Never sit and laugh with him, drink and shoot the shit with him, hunt with him…

The house looked almost exactly as I'd left it despite feeling so alien to me. There were small signs that Karl had been staying there since I left; things shifted slightly, the TV remote on the couch, not on the table where I always left it…

My throat tightened, my chest constricting as I dropped my pack to the floor with a thud. My feet seemed planted in that spot, just inside the front door, unable, for the moment, to proceed any further into the house. I let the memories, pain, and loss wash through me like a tidal wave, washing away my most recent past, struggling to accept this new reality, struggling to make anything around me feel real!

Shitshitshit!

"Goddamit, Karl!" I yelled into the void, "Why'd you go hunting alone, fucking dumbass bastard! You *promised* me!"

Then, like a bull, I was moving…

Into the kitchen to the pantry. Thank god it was there! Whisky now in hand, I returned to the living room and fell into my chair, making its legs grind, scratching short, deep grooves into that old, wooden floor.

Down went the first big gulp, straight from the bottle. I exhaled deeply, head laid against the chair back, my throat burning and tears leaking down the sides of my face and into my hair. But I couldn't rest; I was too worked up to just lay there, so I sat up straight, took another long swig, and let my eyes wander the room. It was then I noticed the spiral binder lying on the table beside me. I didn't recognize it. It was a big one, more than an inch thick.

I plopped the thing onto my lap, opened it to the first page, and recognized Karl's handwriting immediately.

He had been keeping a journal!

The next couple of hours were spent reading and drinking. The binder was by no means full, but Karl had filled it to nearly half with all manner of thoughts, details, and info from his observations and scoutings. He threw in musings only he and I would understand: jokes, comparisons to our favorite fiction, even personal feelings about the whole vampire thing, and the effects his hunter work was having on his relationships, especially with his fiancee.

At first, reading Karl's words made me feel a warm yet sad sentimentality, somehow drawing all the realness back into my shattered reality. But as I reached the end of his entries, I grew increasingly furious and distraught. God, the level of frustration surging inside me was barely containable!

Finally, I reached the part where he described his decision to go *alone* against the vampires. Despite our understanding, his promise to me, and any sense of smarts that I *thought* he had!

I can't wait for Spence this time. Man, he's going to fucking kill me for this, but these beasts are attacking innocents every single night! Got to handle it despite the dangers. I told Sarah to call that UK number Spence gave me should anything happen to me. Told her not to hold any details back.

Whoa, that sure did set her off!

She demanded to know what the hell I was talking about, what I'd gotten myself into, and why I thought anything was going to happen to me. So, of course, I lied to her. I'd been lying to her all along, and I was too good at it for my own comfort. Never would I lie to her about anything else, and the dishonesty with

78

the one I loved the most was really getting to me. But how could I possibly tell her the truth?

'Hon,' I'd say, 'I'm a vampire hunter, see? And I've got to rid the world of a handful of nasty, bloodthirsty creatures that are out there killing innocent people. You understand, don't ya? Now let me go and be a hero, okay, and quit badgering me!'

Yeah, right!

Creep that I am, I laughed her concerns off. I told her it was nothing at all serious, just that I loved Spence like he was family, my brother of choice, if not of my blood, and I wanted him always to be kept in the loop about my life.

She screwed her pretty eyes up at me. I knew she didn't buy my excuse, that something was going on and had been going on for some time. But she quickly realized she wouldn't get any more out of me, so instead, she grilled me about Spence, wanting to understand him, suspicious he'd been involved in some international espionage or some such thing that I was now dragged into. It was much easier to dissuade her in that regard since it wasn't true, at least not the way she had formulated it in her vivid imagination.

Still, it was incredibly hard leaving her today, knowing where I planned to go, what I planned to do, all by myself, and her…completely in the dark about it.

So, I've been keeping this little record of my life, my secret *life, ever since Spence left for Europe the first time. Maybe it was a way of satisfying the need to confess all that I now know and continue to learn since I couldn't tell anyone else outside of Spence, and he was gone; I was alone, left with all this fantastical and freaky knowledge, and the awful things I've seen, burning a fucking hole in my head!*

Tonight, I hunt…

Alone for the first time…

If the vamps don't kill me, Spence certainly will when he discovers what I've done!

I'm going to leave this journal right here beside his chair so he finds it when he gets back if I'm not around anymore.

The address where these vamps live is downtown, 8989 Vanburen Street, in an old warehouse with gray paint and three faded red stripes on both front corners. You can't miss the place; it used to be a big car factory.

And Spence, if you're reading this, it means I'm a goner. Thanks for being the best-damned friend, the best damned chosen brother a guy could have. You're a fucking rock, a beast, an inspiration! I wish I had half your courage and conviction.

Now, Spence, if anything happens to me, don't you—

"Fucking *idiot!*"

Roaring in fury and frustration, I threw the journal to the floor, lunged to my feet, and stalked around my living room, drinking like a fish and raving like a madman!

79

Soon, I'd drained the bottle dry. I was smashed—hadn't been that drunk since my first kill, staggering about, cursing everything and everyone, especially Karl...especially *myself.* With a growl, I threw the empty bottle at the wall, shattering it. Dumbass fool, it was the wall right over my bed. Shards were everywhere.

I sank to the floor, tears streaming, heart straining, head swimming. Like a baby without his Mama, which, of course, I was, I curled up into a ball and cried my sorry self to sleep.

Some hours later, I woke up furious and sick as a dog! But the pain in my head only served to increase my rage—it was now a controlled rage, motivational, demanding action. I showered, cleaned up the broken glass, ate, took a long walk in the hills behind my house, which restored me like a miracle, turning my fury and hangover into sharp determination and a mercifully clear head.

It was evening when I returned home, but I didn't care; I suited up and headed out on the hunt. The vamps that took Karl's life would not live to take another!

Never had I felt so sure of myself, so powerful, so *fearless,* and brimming over with red, deadly revenge!

It was a slaughter!

I found the vamp's lair easily, right in the oldest part of downtown, exactly as Karl had described it. I felt the effects of the creature's proximity via my tattoos. The sensation was interesting, a burning, yet not quite like heat, almost electric. And the closer I got, the stronger it was. It didn't hurt, per se—not so much pain as mild discomfort.

I could sense three vampires holed up there, all male—youngins! Interesting that the wards seemed to lend me a psychic understanding of those kinds of details. According to Karl's notes, there had been four of them before he paid them a visit.

So...he had taken one of the shitheads out before they got him! Good boy!

Made my job that much easier.

And in a way, it made me feel a smidgen better that his death was not entirely in vain. He'd killed a vamp and gotten himself killed. It was in no stretch of the imagination an even trade, but he hadn't left this

Earth empty-handed. He'd delivered that demon right into Hell's burning hands. A fucking fantastic way to go out, if you ask me!

God, I'd love to know what actually happened, all the details, or maybe I wouldn't. Didn't matter now anyway. I was there to finish the job and wreak my revenge.

Accessing the place was a breeze, magical lock picking. Nice! The knowledge, skills, and protection I'd gained in Europe made hunting here at home an entirely different experience. Despite the horrid purpose behind this particular hunt, I loved the confidence and the drive I felt.

Outside, day was giving way to night, and all the creatures were stirring, along with all the mice! Or the rats, more like. Yeah, sure, I was being reckless, but how was I supposed to feel the accomplishment of my revenge if I ended those bastard vamps while they slept? No, I wanted the assholes to see me and to know, beyond any shadow of doubt, why I was there.

I pulled on my leather gloves. In my right hand, I grasped the scythe, and in my left, the tranquilizer gun, locked and loaded. The once-warehouse was now converted into a large, open living space, furnished with several mismatched couches, tables, many chairs, and a plethora of things likely lifted from this or that property, stolen from kills, as was the bloodsucker way. Dead center was an enclosure, a big box constructed with no windows and a single door in the middle of the front-facing wall.

Sleeping quarters, formerly warehouse staff and management offices, I guessed!

Just as I took in the sparsely furnished surroundings, the door to that box opened, and out came those three surviving vampires.

My prey.

The tallest vamp had short ash-blonde hair spiked straight up—his pale eyes wide, furious, lit with those ubiquitous red cores just like all vampires. He had a long, angular face, a pointy nose, and a slightly receding chin that he tried to hide with a thick soul patch. It didn't work.

The next one, emerging on his right, was about the same height. He had dark, shaggy hair and rounder features and was a tad more heartily built than the other. Last but not least, the final vamp burst out from behind the other two, moving with preternatural speed as he darted to my left. Dark-haired, shorter, stocky, and apelike, he crouched as he moved, ready to pounce.

I uttered a quick barrier spell, flicking a hand nonchalantly at the apelike vamp to keep him back, sending a wave of energy out of me that rushed at him, bringing him to a halt, then it curved to the right and fully encircled me.

Suddenly, there was movement elsewhere just before a flurry of voices came from my right, left, and behind me.

"Hey, who the fuck're you?!"

"What the hell?!"

"How'd you fucking get in here?!"

All the usual exclamations, plus a mixture of colorful expletives to follow.

I ignored them, headed straight for the first two vampires as the others, three non-vamp guys, the human thralls, surged forward. I'd have to deal with those non-vamps first since my wards did little against other humans.

One...

Darted and down. He'd had a gun, useless now as it skidded across the floor and disappeared underneath a huge cabinet against the wall.

Two...

Didn't want to cause any fatal or permanent damage to the normies, so I muttered another incantation as I thrust my hand toward the second, sending him flying into the far wall. I heard the air escape him as his back slammed into the wood, and he crumpled to the floor, out cold and out of breath but alive.

Three...

My hand met the last one's jaw, sending him sprawling before he could bring his pistol to bear. He didn't get up, but I hadn't killed him.

The vampires were on the move!

In one swift movement, I stuffed the dart gun away and dragged my "Dundee" knife from its holster. Two vamps came at me head-on while the third, the stocky one, skirted around behind me. Those tattoos I wore were stinging like mad, burning my skin, but the discomfort only urged me forward with higher confidence. I felt mad rushes of power and a strong sense of invincibility. I let all of those feelings take me over, knowing these young vampires couldn't get their teeth into me due to the mysterious runes that protected my flesh and my blood from their feeding.

They had no fucking idea what I was, what those wards were, what I knew, or what I could do! Poor fucking sods!

And sure enough, they were hanging back, hesitating, looking at one another in astonishment and fear. Yeah, fear! Of me! God, I loved it!

"You can feel it, can't ya?" I goaded them on, gobbling up the miasma in the room that filled me with courage, pride, and righteous indignation, "Fucking bloodsuckers!"

"Who the hell *are* you?" The tallest one, still shorter than me, growled incredulously.

"Death," I replied in a low, guttural voice. Its ominous resonance surprised even me.

I had no desire to waste another second talking to those freaks. But I did want them to know I was there for Karl and that they were about to meet the reaper, so I added, "You fucking blood addicts took my best friend from me, and I'm here to take your sick, cursed lives from you."

I could see the recognition and realization on their faces as the truth dawned. They added it up quickly because I was a hunter, and so was Karl. Sure, he didn't *feel* like I did with my magical wards, but he'd come for the same purpose—a not common thing for these creatures. And now, they had offed one of my own, and I was here for payback.

"Fuck you! He tried to kill us, took one of *our* own; of course, we ended his miserable life!"

What the fuck? I could hardly believe my ears! The smart-ass vamp was daring to defend *their* actions. Furious, I snarled at them, but I was also in full control and feeling mighty bold, so I stalked toward the two in front of me and felt the tingle of the runes as the one behind followed close on my heels. Still, the ward continued to hold them back.

I wondered what the vamps felt when they came up against my wards.

"What's it feel like, eh?" I smirked wickedly.

They glanced at each other, backing away, step by step, as I advanced. I couldn't help the sinister, knowing grin I gave them, brandishing my scythe and wiggling my knife in the air as if I were offering candy to a bunch of kids.

"Does it *burn*?" I guessed it might feel a bit like the burn I was feeling as the tattoos reacted to their presence.

They didn't answer me. I hadn't expected them to.

And, anyway, words…normal words, were unnecessary. Strange syllables began to tumble from my lips, spells that rippled out of my body, out of the very core of who and what I was. Their magic surrounded all four corners of that structure, hemming in the three creatures and trapping them within a circle only feet from me.

Would they have attempted to run had I not blocked them in with magic?

Perhaps.

But I wasn't going to give them any chances. I wasn't interested in playing with them anymore. I wanted them dead, plain and simple.

So, I went to it.

One...

The vamp behind me crumbled to the floor after I spun quickly and sliced right through its thick neck in a perfectly aimed arc. The vamp's head flew free, spinning and rolling away. Blood twirled in the air like a sprinkler, leaving a trail of red gore in its wake.

Two...

The tallest one lunged at me once my back was turned, unheeding the effects of my warding, whatever those effects were in him... hollering in a strange mixture of anger and pain as he resisted those repelling forces. The vampire met my big knife right in the gut! Then, a swing of that dripping, red-stained scythe right across the skinny column of his neck, and just like the first, his head tumbled and rolled. I pushed his body off the knife with my booted foot, letting it crumple in a heap to the floor.

Three...

Flinging blood from my weapons, I whirled on that final vampire. He stood like a statue of tension, burning hatred, and terror, glaring daggers at me—loathing and abject fear for his miserable life radiating off him in a miasma that competed with the magic in the air.

I might have schpieled at him then, given him a nice, classic, wordy monologue, lectured him about the death of Karl and the pain he'd caused me and so many others. But I didn't have the stomach for any more talk. Instead, I barreled down on him.

He spun away and attempted to run from me, coming up short against my magical barrier. That last vamp struggled to push through those mystical forces...hollering in panic and pain, filling the air like some terrible soundtrack of hopelessness as he tried fruitlessly to get away.

Without hesitation, I stuck the knife in his back, right at his heart, and held him there, dangling a few inches off the floor as if the knife was a handle to control him by. Then I propped my knee in the small of his back, released the knife, and grabbed his lank, dark hair. Scythe fisted in my other; I slid it right across his sorry neck.

In a swift move, I tossed the head away, yanked my knife free, and surged away from the corpse as blood sprayed. Then I turned my back on the lot of them as those magical walls fell away.

Groaning as they came to, those now free mortals provided background noise for my brief clean-up. I used the sink—a big industrial contraption located in the back corner of the huge space—to clean the blood from my face, neck, and clothing as best I could.

Then, I headed for the door and threw a quick incantation at the human guards, two of which were slowly dragging themselves to their feet, further befuddling their confused minds so that they couldn't describe me to anyone else. The tranqed guard was still out cold, but the spell would work on him, too.

Back home, I got fully cleaned up, then booked a flight back to England for that very morning. I snagged my bag, which I hadn't even bothered to unpack, and I was off—traveling far away and leaving no trace of my "crime," despite doing not a damned thing to clean up after myself.

I *had* left something behind, though, an anonymous call, a lead, stating that the "fuckers" who murdered Karl lived at a particular downtown address. What law enforcement would make of that, and what they might find in that warehouse, I had no clue and didn't care, but it felt good since there had been no suspect and no leads for Karl's murder.

And there was no way they could tie any of it back to me, not knowing who I was or having any clue about what I'd done.

I took Karl's journal with me, not only because I didn't want it landing in anyone else's hands but because it was the last of him I'd have, and I cherished it. I was gutted for his family, friends, and fiancee. God, I wished I could tell them what happened, that his death was noble (if stupid), and that he had been avenged. The best I could do for them was to continue killing vampires. Save others from dying or being turned. Thank goodness Karl had stayed dead. No word of any untoward resurrection, family or fiancee suddenly taking ill. A normal death and funeral. That was a godsend!

On the way out, I drove by Rayn's house. The neighborhood was so quiet and peaceful that I felt as if I'd entered an entirely different world. And essentially, I had, which was such a massive relief it nearly brought tears to my eyes. Her car was parked in the drive, lights on in her windows, and a petite shadow moved casually through her living room in the direction of the kitchen. I sighed happily. She was alright! With all my heart, I hated leaving her again and not being able to talk to her, to warn her, but so far, all was well, and I had more work to do. I put a spell of protection on her property. It wouldn't last too long, just a few days, but it would ease my mind enough to get me on that plane and back to my studies and training.

85

Returning to the UK was blissful. Again, I slept most of the way on the flight. And shit! What dreams I had! Not nightmares, per se, but dreams weird and so vivid I was shocked when I woke up and the plane was beginning its descent.

Romayne played a big part in purging my subconscious mind as I slept. Her presence was ubiquitous throughout my dream wanderings across Europe and various vampire interactions that made not a lick of sense to me. In those dreams, she and I were best buddies with blood drinkers, as nutty as that sounds. We hung out with a plethora of vampires and other…things, like some oddball family reunion. Clannon was there, and the other hunters made appearances as well. It was all so chummy and kumbaya, the complete antithesis to everything I'd experienced; upon waking, the nature of those dreams made me wonder what the hell my bloody brain was up to!

After landing at Heathrow, my faithful cabby, Kevin, drove me to the station, where I jumped on a train and traveled the countryside to Scotland. I took the extra time to reread Karl's journal, slept a little, stared out the window a lot, and let my mind think and process everything that had occurred. It was an ideal time to calm my brain and come to terms with Karl's death and my future.

Part of me felt oddly relieved not to have to worry about Karl anymore. Of course, the fact he was gone hurt me to my core. It was the same pain as losing my family, and I knew I'd never truly get over it. He *was* my chosen brother, not blood, which some might say is stronger still because that kind of connection was made by choice.

Now, back in the States, I only had to worry about Rayn, which served to drive me that much harder in my vampire hunter education.

Clannon met me at the train station in Edinburgh, and seeing him again thrilled me more than I can say. We'd only been apart a couple of days, yet oddly, it felt like weeks had passed!

We clasped arms, and he gave me a powerful hug, "How are you?" He asked as I slid into the taxi beside him.

"Good, fine; I'll tell you all about it later." Didn't need the cabby overhearing those gory details!

We rode in peaceful silence until we reached the Old Town…

X

EDINBURGH

The Ancient City!

Unlike London, with its mixture of old and new world buildings—gothic cathedrals perched next to soaring silver skyscrapers, castle walls glowing with scattered reflections of modern lights—this city was more fully antique and brimming with unbridled character. I adored the cobbled streets, superannuated structures, and the big castle on the hill. The whole vibe spoke to me more profoundly than either London or Glasgow.

Clannon took us to a little pub run by a couple whose family had owned the place for six generations! That was mad to me! Blew my simple little mind. They were adorable, both of them stout, bubbly, and full of energy despite being quite old. I was ready to adopt them, having lost my grandparents on both sides when I was only a boy.

They served us a haggis dish, with potatoes and whisky sauce. So good I sucked it all down, doubling up on the protein since portion sizes were small compared to the States.

We stayed with local hunters and close friends of Clannon, Byron Craig and his wife, Kenna, in a humble flat just off the Royal Mile.

Byron was yet another large man, though not as towering as I or as svelte as Clannon. Broad of body, yet not overweight, with long, thin legs and wide shoulders. His dark brown hair was a bit scraggly and hung just to the nape of his neck. He was a jovial fellow, and his amiable smile warmed me to him instantly. It took me a bit of time to adjust to his heavy Edinburgh brogue, spoken so quickly that it was difficult for me to understand. However, I soon adjusted. I seem to have a knack for picking up on difficult accents.

His wife, Kenna, was a tiny thing, an adorable waif of a girl with chestnut hair, delicate features, a sweet demeanor, and a sharp mind. I had a hard time imagining her hunting vampires, but apparently, she was a swift and efficient vamp killer. I'd never have guessed such a thing by looking at her. I really wanted to see her prowess for myself, but she had quit hunting some time ago when the couple decided to try and have kids, which hadn't happened yet. So it seemed I wouldn't get the chance to see Kenna in action.

It was from Byron that I acquired the next addition to my arcane book collection, *Pashan's Forbidden Treasures*.

"Whenever I run across these extremely rare works," Byron exclaimed as he laid the book in my hands, "even if I already own a copy, I simply must buy them. I just cannot leave them out in the wild! But it is good to send this one off with you to the States. The new world has never seen the like, I assure you! That book has been lost for centuries! Well, not *that* particular copy, but the manuscript it's translated from. A treasure far greater than all the treasures described within its pages! You know, old pirate legends mention Pashan and his giant cache of priceless booty. It's the source of all of those deep sea riches that the old-world buccaneers went on and on about. There are some curious stories in pirate history tied to Pashan."

I cocked an eyebrow at him, "Are they in here? Those pirate stories?"

Byron shook his head, "Nope, but I do have a few sources in journal collections if you'd like to borrow them while you're here."

"Hell, yeah!" I exclaimed, "I'm a sucker for classic pirate lore!" *What big kid isn't?* I thought.

Over the following days, the four of us traveled to a few places around Scotland, doing a bit of hunting and exploring. We drove out to the countryside, to the ruins of a castle—a bonafide medieval structure of chunky gray stones, tiny windows, and towering turrets, just like every fantasy story I ever read! I was beside myself with joy, though I held it together, put on a calm face and an easy demeanor. No sense spazzing out around those new, easy-going, classy friends of mine.

A fairly large portion of the structure was still intact and possibly, though barely, livable. The rest was a pile of crumbling bones open to the heavens, its floors carpeted in bright green grass.

The castle's neighbor was a tiny, deserted church, also constructed of stone, with an ancient graveyard filled with medieval, tottering markers all carved with wonky skulls, spooky cherubs, and quirky designs. I wanted to see every single one, all different, all fascinating, but it was the castle we spent most of our time with.

There was a small farm in walking distance, ringed in by a rickety wooden fence and rolling hills of green and heather that surrounded us in all directions.

We walked the area for a bit, then returned to the castle and stood in silence, just taking it all in.

"Former residence of an ancient fiend, this place," Clannon finally said, gazing up at its jagged walls. "Byron and I might have died attempting to put that one down!"

"Might have died? Attempting?" I cocked an eyebrow at him. "You didn't succeed?"

He shrugged, "We didn't. The whole encounter was..."

"Baffling." Byron finished it for him.

"Haven't seen hide nor hair of the creature since."

"We spent years trying to track that one down again." Byron elaborated as we stepped into a massive "room," which was now a big roofless area, "That first encounter happened during our earliest days. The way it played out, how we survived it, I'll never understand. We walked in with no magical tattoos or spells to protect us. Yet here we are! Dumb luck, I guess."

"You're going to have to tell me all about that one, you know," I replied.

"By all means!" Clan exclaimed, "Coming face-to-face with an ancient creature like that!" He shuddered, "From what you've told me, you haven't faced any old vampires before."

"Just youngins," I shrugged.

"That's normal for the Americas." Byron added, "I'd be surprised if there were many truly ancient undead over the pond."

But Clannon shook his head, "Oh, I don't know about that. The American *continent* isn't young. I'm sure some old ones made their way over there at some point." Then his dark eyes wandered those blank rock walls, reminiscing, "This one, the thing that was here..." He looked genuinely terrified. It was a look I never thought I'd see on Clan's face. Honestly, I was taken aback by it, made my chest vibrate.

He seemed to notice and gave me a grim look. "It's smart to feel fear when coming up against such a creature as the one we faced here."

I nodded, "I can only imagine." But when I thought of facing a vampire like that, some dangerous, archaic thing of immense power, rather than feeling fear, I was filled with a rush of morbid excitement. It just showed how far I'd come since the beginning. Run toward danger rather than away from it—a true hunter.

We spent the rest of that afternoon roaming the balance of the castle, then strolling through the graveyard and the church before heading back prior to sunset. Even though the old creature was long gone, as the day waned, I could feel Clan and Byron's uneasiness and eagerness to leave.

That night, after dinner, we gathered in Byron's small living room with drinks while he and Clannon proceeded to tell me all about their failed hunt at the castle.

"You want to tell it, Clan?" Byron gestured nobly to his friend, offering him the floor.

"Alright," Clan lowered his voice, sounding exactly like Lee's Dracula, "It was a dark and stormy night…"

We all chuckled.

"Actually, it was a dark and stormy *day*." He corrected with a smirk before diving into the tale. "I'll not go into the details of how we discovered the fiend. Suffice it to say, we had done our due diligence and followed the breadcrumbs, or the blood, as it were.

"Byron and I pulled out of the drive before the crack of dawn. We wanted to arrive at the castle just as the sun was coming up. The sky was dark over the horizon in the direction we were headed. Seeing the horrendous weather, we nearly changed plans, but we also knew the job could not be put off any longer. Too much was happening, and we needed to put a stop to it. So, we forged on."

Byron jumped in before Clan could continue, "The castle was in better condition back then, not *much* better, but the vampire lived in it, so it wasn't as derelict as it is now. That intact portion, surrounded by the ruined bits, could even be called inviting if you didn't know what lurked within. Anyway, go on…"

"Thank you, Byron. Are you quite sure you want *me* to tell the tale? You're perfectly capable and obviously eager—"

"No, no! Go ahead."

Clannon shook his head and smiled patiently before continuing, "Byron and I were pretty well 'book-educated' before striking out, but neither of us had actually killed a vampire before. As I previously mentioned, I was in my thirties when I started, and this was my first hunt. It frightened me so badly that it nearly put me off hunting from the start. Byron had encountered his first vampire on the streets about five years prior, but I'll let him tell you that story another time."

Raising his hand to halt Clan, like some kid in class getting a teacher's attention, Byron looked eager when he said, "No need to wait; here it is. It's short and sweet, so let's get it done with. I was out one night and stumbled on a vampire feeding in a dark corner mere steps from Edinburgh Castle. It was off the main street, away from shops, and the streets were quiet anyway. I was on my way home after working late.

"The guy, the vampire, spotted me and vanished. The woman he'd attacked…killed…lay, leaking blood from her neck in several places. I couldn't do a damned thing about it except try to find help. Freaked out, I bolted, unsure where to go or where the creep had disappeared. He seemed to disappear instantly, right before my eyes, but it was very dark, and I figured he must have slipped into the shadows.

"Of course, I never knew vampires existed. They were just movie monsters to me, and even having seen what I had, I told myself that some maniac was playing the part of a bloodsucker, not believing for a second that the guy was an actual vampire. Heck, a nutter acting like a vampire was unnerving enough for me!"

Clan jumped in, "I caught sight of Byron as I was leaving the pub where I'd just had dinner. I was in Scotland for business, and it was kismet that I happened to be there at that time. I saw this man gesturing wildly, telling two constables about a 'stabbing.' But there was something in Byron's delivery, something that grabbed my attention and set my scalp tingling. So I kept back, waited, and watched."

"After I led the policemen to the woman," Byron continued, "and after the bobbies left me, Clan walked up, introduced himself, and asked what was going on. For some reason, perhaps because I couldn't tell the cops that I *thought* I'd seen a vampire, and it was really bugging me that I had to obfuscate certain details to them, I said, 'I think I just caught a vampire killing a woman.' Clan gave me a look, *that* look, the one he gives when he's dead serious about something, and said, 'Did you tell them that?' I laughed nervously and shook my head, 'You're kidding, right? I'd never tell a constable I saw a vampire!'"

"We stared at each other," Clan added, "because it hit us—somehow, we both knew that our lives would never be the same. Well, mine had been irreversibly altered years ago, and now, due to happenstance, us being in this particular place at this particular time, this man was joining me in my dark reality."

Byron nodded, "The look Clan gave me told me that what I'd seen *was* real. My head was whirling. It was madness! But I couldn't doubt it.

"The cops called an ambulance, and I was questioned in more detail at the station. I gave them the best description I could, feigning ignorance when they mentioned she had several bite marks on her. Told them I'd seen the blood and thought she must have been stabbed in the neck. They bought it, thankfully, and let me go. After that, Clan and I were inseparable! I studied with him, and so did Kenna. She and I were already together then, about to get married. I was so relieved when she believed me! Of course, it probably helped that Clan was there to share his own experience."

"I didn't know what to think," Kenna interjected, laughing, "I've got a pretty open mind, and, of course, I believed that Byron believed what he'd seen. Then there was this friendly, if imposing, gentleman backing it all up. Honestly, there was a moment I wondered if you two were taking the piss. Playing Hammer Horror on me or something."

We all laughed. "I can totally see why!" I exclaimed.

Byron sighed, "So, that's it. Before the castle debacle, that was my one and only vampire experience."

"Neither of us was properly prepared for what we were about to face." Byron and Clan shared a long, intense stare, exchanging silent and apparently intense memories between them.

"Alright, fellas, c'mon, let's get back to the meat of it!" I rolled my eyes dramatically.

Clan picked up the tale with a playful huff, "The castle was silent when we arrived and made our way onto its grounds. We figured human guards would be watching, fully awake and ready for us. There was no doubt in our minds they would know we were there.

"Our first gaff was not being properly warded. I'd studied a lot over the years but had yet to meet Fedelma, and most of what I'd learned seemed outside of any real-life experience. A sane mind can't help but compartmentalize such things. And you know how time can be, how it steals away the reality of unusual or amazing things. Dulls the burn of tragedy. Well, from late teenage years to thirty-one, that's a long time and a lot of life lived in between. It wasn't that I'd forgotten all I'd lost, but the information was stored in my mind as a kind of dream…a nightmare that, while it drove me to my research, hadn't, until this first hunt, solidified as a thing of reality. And having no wards meant we stood out like a dog with two tails! Enthusiastic as we were, we were dumb as rocks."

"Hey!" Byron exclaimed in mock offense.

Clannon ignored him, "Oh, we *were* dumb! Be assured. We should never have gone to that place! The creature, a truly ancient vampire, was wily, of course; he most assuredly knew we were there, yet let us waltz right into his castle, the livable portion of it, and meander about for quite some time before finally making himself known.

"The place was…well, there appeared to be no thralls, not one human protector. But the castle veritably crawled with ubiquitous shadows that moved in perpetual agitation, always just out of sight. I cannot tell you how unnerved we were after crossing his threshold and being surrounded everywhere by those inky black things!"

"Shadows? What do you think they were?" I'd never encountered anything like what Clan was describing during my hunts.

"At the time, we assumed they were a part of the vampire's powers. An illusion or manipulation of the existing, natural shadows. And perhaps some of them were. But now, after our extensive studies, we believe they were Nethers."

I nodded, recalling those human- and sometimes inhuman-shaped blacker-than-black shades whose true origin was only speculated upon in the texts I'd read.

"Entities from some other dimension, apparently, that like to attach themselves to vampires." Clannon shrugged, "Why they choose to cling to a vampire, I'm not sure. Perhaps they are drawn to the darkness because, while different creatures, still, vampires may be considered one of their own. Or, perhaps they're connected in some other way."

"Demons?" I asked, though I had my doubts about that, at least from the biblical perspective. I wasn't particularly a religious person. Even after learning vampires were real, the idea of angels and demons in the traditional Christian sense just didn't fly with me, not when taken literally. Yet, from Clan's description, those shadows seemed to fit the bill pretty well.

But Clannon shook his head, "No, not biblical demons; at least, I don't believe so. Don't ask me why I categorize them differently, but I do. The more you read, the more I think you'll understand why I feel this way."

"I tend to agree with your assessment already." I was more comfortable believing in trans-dimensional shadow people than demons from a literal Hell, perhaps because there could be a scientific aspect to it.

"Another anomaly," he continued, "we were not molested by those shadow creatures in any way, simply unnerved by them. I assumed, and still do, that it was because the vampire wanted us all to himself. He held them off, as it were. Of course, that's only a guess.

"It was midday before the creature made his appearance," Byron said.

I gasped, "Broad daylight?"

Clannon nodded, "Broad daylight, but a day darkened by heavy clouds and rain. The fact that he was up and about during the day at all was a sure sign of his great age.

"The vampire didn't actually show himself initially." Clan continued, "The first thing we experienced was his voice. *That alone* was enough to send any large, mature male scampering away like a terrified child.

"'Impostors,' it rumbled in a growl like rolling thunder, shaking the rafters, making my chest tighten and the very air vibrate. A voice made of menace as if menace was a physical substance, yet it was playful in a sickening way, brimming with wicked, vicious intent...

"Nothing, no amount of bravery, no justice-fueled determination, could prevent the overpowering desire to flee. Simply hearing that voice triggered a fight or flight response like I hadn't experienced since my grandfather's attack. But we were also stymied by that very same terror. I could hardly make my legs move as Byron and I backed up slowly, trembling so badly I thought I might trip over myself!

"But before we could even think to bolt out of there, the *creature* appeared! It strode across the landing high above us, halting near the wide, curved staircase. His big, powerful hands, with their strong fingers tipped in sharply pointed, jet-black fingernails, rested on the railing, tapping the old wood in a steady rhythm.

"This monster was a thing out of time—a massive, rugged fellow; surely he had been a large, rough man during his mortal life, which had only been intensified, and to an astounding degree, by his vampirism. The embodiment of ancient Scotland, he was. The way he pronounced 'imposters' was the first sign of his age, using an old Scottish-Gaelic form of the word in a brogue heavier even than Byron. But it was also in his manner, the gate of his walk, the tilt of his head, not only monstrous but antique!

"Let me give you a bit more physical description outside of how utterly *un*modern he was so that you can picture him as we saw him.

"His ash-brown hair was cropped short to his head, which seemed a bit unusual since, in those hoary days, men typically wore their hair long, like Byron or yourself. He had an oval face with powerful features, a high forehead, and a short beard trimmed neatly. Wide-set, scrutinizing eyes regarded us with unnerving intensity, burning bright crimson, brighter than any vampire I've seen since. His broad shoulders and thick chest gave him the look of a mob boss or, more likely, the leader of some long-dead Scottish clan. His legs were long, and he was quite tall, probably as tall or taller than you, Spencer. His intelligence, knowledge, and countless years of experience radiated out of him like a physical aura that filled the room. From floor to ceiling and wall to wall, his energy ruled the very air of that place. I guessed he'd lived there for centuries. Perhaps he'd been the one to have the castle built; that's how completely it felt like an extension of that vampire.

"We didn't want to breathe it in, to draw that tainted air into ourselves. Byron had ahold of me now and dragged me toward the door as the thing's voice again reached out to us from above.

"'Ahhh,' the ancient creature sighed, 'What brings ye here to invade *my* hallowed halls? To enter the walls of Kaedon Erskine's domain? Was it yer plan, mortal scum, to rob me?' the thing chuckled, and it sounded like the cracking of great stones, 'Petty thieves, ye mortals. To think ye would have the foolish audacity to steal from the likes of *me!*'

"Apparently, our host did not know who we were or why we were actually there. That gave me a small surge of hope. We were only simple thieves in the beast's eyes. *Good!* I thought. It was better he saw us that way rather than as hunters who were there to kill him. I found myself nodding, even smiling back at him…awkwardly, to be sure. We both knew there was no hope of killing a thing such as that, so we simply needed to get away from it with our lives! *Not so simple*, I thought to myself shudderingly.

"'No, no,' I exclaimed, addressing the vampire with a quavering voice, 'we were simply c-curious, that's all. We don't w-want any of your th-things… W-we thought this p-place was abandoned!'

"It was a very dumb excuse; clearly, he knew it was balderdash. Then his eyes raked over us, and he spotted the thing I held grasped in my hand. When first we arrived, upon entering the place, I had pulled a large machete from my coat, and I now held it behind me, unable to put it away again without him spotting it. Yet he'd seen it anyway.

"Suddenly, like mobile clots of ink, those shadows began to move with purpose, spreading up and out, revealing walls, ceiling, and floor, all previously pitch-black. Yet, still, they hung back, even as they ringed threateningly around us.

"Thinking the shadows were likely an illusion, I mumbled a short incantation, suddenly remembering a protective spell I'd memorized that would protect me from mental manipulation. I heard Byron pick it up just after I did, and our low voices, uttering that magical prayer, met in unison as we finished it. But the shadows remained. Which meant they were real, tangible, not figments born of imagination or formed of psychic conjuring. A reality that set fresh panic bells ringing in my head!

"Then, to our astonishment, the creature took swift steps forward despite having nowhere to go without running into the balustrade. Yet he did not run into it; he passed right through the heavy wooden railing, descending to our level with a sickeningly monstrous smile that froze our veins like ice. His large hands were spread at his sides like some twisted imitation of a religious icon. Of course, I'd seen it before, a vampire passing through solid objects, but that did nothing to diminish the shock of it. The mind simply does not handle witnessing such things well. It breaks reality, distracts the thought processes, and sends one into a jumbled mess of panic and confusion.

"I was frozen, utterly useless, as the beast approached, drifting forward like some specter from Hell. 'Sealgair!' it grinned with beastly glee, 'Hunters...Aye, it has been an age since I have encountered hunters! But you? You mere...wee...*boys*? You...would hunt *me*?' It laughed menacingly as, with cold, immensely powerful fingers, it took hold of my chin." Clannon visibly trembled, drew in a deep, steadying breath, then continued, "The moment that creature touched me, I was a child again, a helpless young boy whose father grasped my face and forced me to look up at him. But this thing was not my father; it was... death, and the unnatural gleam in its burning-coal eyes, the beastly spread of its dagger-filled mouth, promised an end most painful.

"To be honest, peering into the nightmare of that thing, I had given up. I knew, without any shadow of a doubt, that I would be with my dear family soon. That I would go out of this world the same way they had, which felt right and proper somehow. And it was the strangest sensation to face death so assuredly that I felt instantly, and inexplicably, calm, even serene. Slowly, my senses returned, and the whole of my body relaxed as the fear fell away from me and was replaced by surrender. I could feel Byron's hand grasping my arm tightly, and the vampire had released my chin. Yet still, I held my head high, tilted up to meet his red gaze almost defiantly. Everything was silent and stagnant for a long moment as the three of us stood opposed.

"Then, to our complete shock and consternation, the beast threw back his terrible head and laughed uproariously! We did not know what to make of that as he stepped back, threw his hands out, locked eyes with Byron first, then with me, and spoke words I'll never understand.

"'Go!' he exclaimed, 'go from here and better yourselves. Make your bodies strong. Make yourself uamhasach…formidable, then return to me when ye think ye can destroy me.' It paused, tilted its awful head to the side, then in a low, grating, sinister voice, it said, 'Tell me yer names, leanabhs, so that I may know who my foes shall be.'

"Leanabhs, it means infants. I didn't hesitate and told the creature my name, then waited for Byron to follow, but he kept silent. Oddly, the vampire did not seem to care. 'Make for me an airidh nàmhaid, Clannon Colfeld, become a *worthy* foe that I may find utmost joy in ripping you apart and a' cromadh sìos your hot, red blood, that most precious fuil…' he chuckled, 'yes *fuel* for such as I, as my reward, only after much turmoil in our battle and oh, so much pain!'"

I was shocked, mystified, shaking my head in disbelief, even before Clan finished the tale, "He let you go?!"

Clan nodded, "He let us go."

"Two big men," Byron shrugged, threw up his hands, fell back in his seat, where he'd been sitting on its edge throughout the telling as if he'd only just heard the story for the first time and hadn't lived it himself, "There we were, two big men filled with rich, red blood. He could have drained us dry in mere moments, sated himself like the leech he was, but he let us escape, vanished before our very eyes after promising us pain and torture upon our eventual 'return.' We wasted not one measly second getting the hell out of there!"

"A few years later, once we were warded and well-trained by Fedelma, we did return, Byron and I, only to find the castle truly abandoned. Much, but not all of Erskine's things were still there, but he was nowhere to be found and not seen again."

"Are there other hunters who could have offed him?"

Clan shook his head, "No. Not any that I know of working in our 'official' capacity."

I stretched and yawned hugely as Clannon rose from his seat. "It's been a long day, lads."

We remained in Scotland, mainly in Edinburgh, for about six months. Clannon returned often to London. Sometimes, I went with him; others, I remained with Byron and Kenna. We hunted regularly, honing skills, protecting others. It was a very fulfilling time for me.

XI
PARIS

A lead brought us to France, just Clannon and I. We met up with another of those rare long-time hunters, Gerard Landry, a lone wolf like me, only more well-seasoned. Gerard had studied separately from Clannon and Byron, yet he'd found his way to Fedelma, as all European hunters had since she was the only one of her kind, which caused no small level of concern.

Repeatedly, the hunters had begged the old witch to teach one of them, or at least someone else, her special skills, only to be rebuffed by her. Always, she insisted that she knew no one with the proper qualifications to do what she did, promising that if ever she did meet that unique someone, then she would pass her craft and full knowledge on to them.

What exactly those mysterious "qualifications" were, no one had any clue, and there was no swaying Fedelma on the subject. She would do what she would do, come hell or high water!

It was late afternoon before we reached Paris. Gerard picked us up at the Eurostar train station. We had just stowed our meager luggage into his trunk and were about to crawl into our seats.

"I asked you here because I need help with this one," Gerard informed us as he yanked his mane of rust-brown hair back into a messy bun at the nape of his neck, tying it off while giving me a curious look.

Gerard was probably in his forties but looked about ten years younger; wiry, almost a waif of a man, but according to Clan, he was swift and deceptively strong. To me, next to the two of us big guys, he looked like a shrimp, but I kept that opinion to myself until I could judge his rumored effectiveness.

The French hunter stood just under six feet tall with slender limbs, honey-fair skin, attractive, well-refined Scandinavian features, and that long mass of tight, natural curls. His manner of dress could be described as retro-fashionable, another detail that reminded me of myself, although his outfit was not all black, as mine always was. Instead, he wore dark, fitted trousers tucked into calf-high leather boots of the same brown tone, a black fitted shirt with a high turtle-neck collar, and a mid-thigh length burgundy leather jacket cut similar to an eighteenth-century frock coat with weapons of the trade installed in this or that hidden pocket or tucked into his boots.

That jacket was badass; I was jealous.

Of course, Gerard was tattooed, as all hunters were. He wore a positively gaudy charm, which he told us he had stitched tightly into that snazzy leather jacket's lapel using heavy nylon thread to ensure he wouldn't lose it.

"Sohrakian rune, 'tis the best protection, mon amies."

I showed him my much simpler charm hanging on a chain around my neck, "Fedelma made sure I'm well warded."

"Ha, I've no doubt she did." Gerard laughed.

"That thing looks like a granny clasp; where'd you get it?"

My little tease didn't phase him one bit; he positively grinned, tapped it with his fingers, squared his shoulders, "Designed by moi, fashioned by a jeweler in Paris, then christened with la magie! C'est one of a kind!"

I liked Gerard. Couldn't help myself. Grinning back, I said, "Must've cost you a pretty penny."

"Nah," he replied, "argot pour dire qu'on doit une faveur: owed me a favor." He translated with a wink, "Perks of this nasty entreprise."

He drove us into the heart of Paris, where his flat was located. It was a gorgeous night, so we took to the streets. The City of Light was crammed with tourists and positively crawling with vampires! The runes in our skin remained in constant flux, stinging and burning so much that the three of us were positively itchy. We finally employed a little magic to ease the discomfort.

I was also itching to do some slaying, but Gerard insisted he'd have it all under control; it was "the old one," the maker of all these young ones, that must be dispatched first before dealing with the rest.

Honestly, I didn't like leaving vamps stalking the streets, drinking up innocents, and having their way, but this was the Frenchman's domain, so Clan and I were forced to acquiesce.

Enamored by those bustling old city streets, streets that I'd seen countless times in film and read about in fiction, I couldn't help but fancy Lestat and his brood of undead, haunting the old cemeteries, lurking in the shadows or frolicking in the modern lights.

That is, until we faced an archaic beast so wholly unlike Anne Rice's creations as to wipe such fantasies right out of my head!

But I'm getting ahead of myself. Before embarking on that insane part of that French adventure, we ate.

Clan and I hadn't had a proper meal prior to leaving Scotland, and the small snacks on the train just weren't cutting it. We were famished! Gerard treated us, and as we snarfed down a late lunch, he informed us that we would be going to the French Alps. It would take us nearly six hours to get there, and we would be lodging in a small hotel until morning…hunting time!

Clan and I spent a restless night of broken sleep on the floor of the Frenchman's tiny apartment before setting off the following morning.

Behind the wheel of his little gray Peugeot, Gerard began to fill us in on the details of our quarry. "The Chateau de Laque sits high in the Alps, a veritable castle of stone built right into le side de le mountain, like an extension of its natural face. For ages, de Laque has been thought derelict, but no, the place *has* been occupied by an old and très terrible thing. More than one terrible thing. An ancient blood drinker, and possibly…other things, from what I have surmised. But the nature of these others, I cannot know."

"Others," I mused, mostly to myself, yet I did want to understand what he was referring to.

"Oui, amies, other things. I am sure that you have read of Darklings?"

"We have, but other than shadow entities, are any of the things the books mention actually real?"

"Truly, I do not know," the Frenchman shrugged, "Shadows, oui, and perhaps more. The energies surrounding de Laque are, well, not like things I have previously experienced. Accablant, unnerving, you will see."

"You say old; I assume the vampire is an ancient." The uneasiness in Clannon's voice was mild, but you couldn't miss it.

"My guess? Oui. The beast that rules his roost is quite old. It is difficult catching him out. Trying to spy upon or to follow le ruse monstre has been a chore."

As you've noticed, the Frenchman often liked tossing words from his native tongue into his speech, but it was done in such a way that I was able to understand him or at least get the gist of what he was saying. I'm writing the things he said the way I recall them, with the help of a French-to-English dictionary for spelling, so if you happen to know French, please forgive my ignorant mistakes. I simply want this narrative to feel authentic. Wouldn't be the same without that quirk of his. Anyway, back to it…

"So, there are shadow entities there." Clan commented.
"Oui. Certainly, more than one being lives beneath that roof, for I have witnessed much mouvement during my reconnaissance. We will hunt in la lumière du jour; bright daylight should assist us, but le chateau's windows are never still, ever active, even when the sun burns high."
"Sounds to me like it could simply be a shit load of mortal thralls living there." I shrugged.
"Perhaps…perhaps. Or, les shadows, les ombres. We must prepare for the worst, par des amis."

The chateau on the mountain! What a sight!
Chateau de Laque sat cradled in the vast, jagged arms of the sprawling French Alps. Their craggy peaks tipped in snow. Those gargantuan mounds, an awe-inspiring sight, marched from horizon to horizon, propping up a vast, azure sky bearing not a single cloud.
It was a warm day, but a chill wind blew down off the peaks, wafting over us like some portent to our "nefarious" plans, causing the three of us to shiver and pull our coats more tightly around ourselves.
"We have a climb ahead of us, les gars." Gerard had parked his car well off the main road in a cluster of trees. The concrete roadway veered off sharply to the right and away from the overgrown path that led to the old Chateau. There was no way to drive up there, so we had to hoof it.

"How far is it?" I asked as I ensured I had all my trusty companions stowed securely in my coat: scythe, dart gun, butane lighter, big knife. My tattoos were already tingling, and I unconsciously grasped the Sohrakian rune hung on the silver chain around my neck.

But before the French hunter could reply to my question, the three of us jolted and turned wide eyes to each other.

"You two feel it, yes?" Clan asked cryptically.

"And see...*them*," Gerard replied.

I glanced around us between the tall, skinny trees that shot up into the sky like sentinels in all directions, and there they were, a plethora of shadows lurking where no shadows should be, interrupting the glare of morning sunlight that lanced through the trees' tangled branches.

"He knows we come," the Frenchman's voice was casual, even nonchalant, as he shrugged and gave us both a look of resolve. "They are always here, these ombres, watching, but they do not molest, so we go."

Gerard locked the car and trudged up what once was a dirt drive, now clotted with overgrown flora, winding the entire way up the slope to the grand edifice.

The forest crawled with shadows, and that's not some figure of speech or some colorful description to give the scene more oomph; shadows were *literally* everywhere! But only on the periphery. Like those annoying eye floaters, you couldn't focus on one if you tried. My eyes were darting, my head jerking this way and that. Clan grasped my shoulder as if to say something.

But Gerard beat him to the punch, "Shadows are alive here, Nethers, watchers."

"Yes, Nethers," I repeated.

We went silently, keeping to our thoughts. With every step we took, those shadows followed. It seemed to me they urged us on, pushing us from behind and gathering barely in sight at the threshold of the forest. Were they doing this stalking on their own, or were they being guided by the vampire?

I shivered internally with...

Delight!

Anticipation!

I felt not a shred of fear—only a giddy need to return to battle.

The "taste" of my previous confrontation, wiping those vampire brats off the planet in that warehouse of death, returned to my mind like a delectable enticement, and the bloodlust I felt shocked me!

What was I becoming? Well, that was easy; I was fully embracing the hunter within. Having lost my sensitivity to blood, to the killing...

the killing of these preternatural beasts, you understand. A killer? A man-killer? I was not. I had no desire to commit murder, and it sickened me to think of killing a mortal person. But there was no hesitation or revulsion within me now over killing a vampire!

The journey was quick along that path, yet it took us close to an hour to reach our destination. Shivering inside, but not from the temperature, I studied the place up close. Built of stone quarried out of the mountain it rested on, it really did appear to grow right out of its face, and it did look abandoned as we approached. No lights gleamed within its windows, and there was no movement anywhere in the surrounding area.

Those ubiquitous shadows no longer followed us. It seemed they had returned to the castle. Could that be why every window in the place appeared black as night? Were those things of darkness watching us with their burning matchstick eyes?

Oh yes, Nethers also have red in the cores of their eyes, not just like vampires. Apparently, it's a trait all Darklings share, and it is the only thing of color about those shadows. Writings describe how the Nethers will hide their eye-shine by closing or perhaps covering their "eyes." That's when they appear as pure blackness. And they can see just as well with their eyes covered as without!

Those damned, freaky things greatly disturb me, more than I like to admit. But we were there for the vampire, and I would not be put off by a bunch of shadows!

Chateau De Laque was an awe-inspiring sight! Unlike the crumbling castle ruin in Edinburgh, this ancient chateau was whole and amazingly preserved, which I found odd, simply because this place was clearly much older. A hoary structure built in the earliest of medieval times perched there like some melodramatic scene straight out of dark fantasy, this was a structure plucked right out of the wildest imagination with its jutting spires and thick stone walls of slate gray, black, and thin, white veins.

The whole area reeked of stygian miasma, a horrible taint that was not wholly unfamiliar but so powerful as to be far beyond what I had sensed from the baby vamps I'd faced so far.

I was...astounded! I shook my head, gaping, utterly fascinated, for a place such as this to exist in the modern world was incredible to me. I felt transported in time. Like I was thrust into the middle of some ageless horror, a page ripped straight from the world of Lumley's Necroscope!

"Holy shit, we're actually going in there!" I gasped. And yet, despite the foreboding, like Death's shroud waiting to drape itself over us and rip us from the living world forever, I remained buoyed by my lifelong love of all things dark and creepy. The horror, monsters, and mystery that had always spoken to me. I was a boy again at that moment, filled with the reckless burning need to see and to know! Real danger be damned, I *wanted* to get inside that wicked-looking place—that nightmare stone monument crouching like some hungry, wild beast between the towering cliffs of those massive peaks.

Since it seemed clear the vampire knew we were there via his shadow watchers, we entered, unmolested through the massive front gate. The courtyard was wide and narrow, unkept and barren, without a speck of greenery, and decorated only with remnants of what might have been a fountain and a few low, stone-lined areas.

Inside the castle proper, we found our "friends," those Nethers, lurking all about us yet still avoiding any attempt at direct observation.

On my left, Gerard crossed his arms and glanced about as if waiting for an old friend to emerge any minute from one of several arched openings. While on my right, Clannon was visibly tense, his dark brows screwed down, brown eyes scanning the area warily.

A crumbling flagstone floor spread before us, and narrow stairs hugged the left wall. They were rock walls with failing, powdering lime mortar adorned here and there with sculpted figures and friezes, all falling into ruin. Yet, still, the place felt lived in, if not maintained. There was a massive arched fireplace to the back of the room and three doors: one directly across from the entrance, now behind us, and two to the left, one in front of, and one beneath the stairway.

It was a large room, sparsely furnished, yet the furnishings and other items bore a mishmash of patterns and seemed to come from varying eras. It appeared, upon cursory inspection, that no two pieces belonged together. Simply a gathering of seating, tables, and other items that may have originally been there or were acquired out of necessity for basic comforts.

The space was much darker within than it might have been had those shadows not huddled everywhere so thickly. And it was utterly still and silent, like the ambiance of a gigantic tomb.

Suddenly, the air around us shifted, becoming active, vibrating, and rushing through our bodies like an electric charge or a magical one. It felt as if the edifice had suddenly awoken due to our unwanted presence; the castle stirred like a great lion and seemed to draw in a long, ragged breath.

Hastily, the three of us drew on our magical protections, uttering spells with habits we'd all developed during studies and practice.

Of course, before leaving to come on this hunt, we had pre-prepared ourselves, utilizing the typical anointings and cloaking magic to their fullest. But at a time like this, when those dark powers raged against us, the first instinct was to shore up the spellwork we'd already cast.

If nothing else, we would keep our heads clear and unaffected and not be manipulated by whoever...or whatever we were about to come up against.

As if summoned by our mumbling words, a voice encrusted with archaic knowledge, struggle, and the bitterness of centuries buffeted our senses and turned the air of the room ice cold—a psychic cold that only intensified the natural cold of those old, stone walls and floors.

It was the accent that gave me the first hint of who the creature might be. Well, his accent and the aghast look of recognition that erupted on Clannon's startled face.

Turning to Clan, I knew.

And the vampire's words confirmed it. "Clannon Colfeld..."

Holy shit! This was that ancient Scott that Clan and Byron had failed to kill all those years ago!

"Erskine!" Clan gasped in reply.

The monster's voice was like the rumbling of a massive stone sliding against jagged rock or a giant boulder rolling away from a moldering tomb, and Clan's description had been spot on; its heavy Scottish brogue put Byron's to shame!

"Aye!" By the sound of the beast's voice, it was elated to see Clannon again. Emerging from the shadows, the thing grinned its monstrous grin, its mouth so large it almost literally went from ear to ear.

As the vampire approached, those Nethers formed a tight, inky crowd all around it, which parted like a curtain of jet to reveal their master in all his horrible "glory."

"Ye've come back to me, wee hunter, just like I told ye to, found me all the way oot here, ev'n." it chuckled, "And ye've brought chairdean wit' ye, yer friends. How...delightful."

Just like Gerard, the vampire's archaic tongue slipped into his speech here and there. But I was able to glean his meaning, even without knowing what some of those words or phrases meant.

"Ye'll try to kill' me, I ken, with yer weak, mortal hands," he sneered, his pale lips quirking up on one side, pasty skin looking like animated death.

106

I couldn't help sneering back in disgust.

The creature was massive. I'd never seen such a big vampire and rarely seen such a large man. Was sheer size a sign of an ancient? Clan had mentioned that Erskine might have been taller than me. No fucking kidding! The beast towered over my six-foot-six frame by at least half a head!

From Clannon's description, I recognized the vampire's looks instantly, surprised at how closely my mental image came to the real deal. And yet, my fervent imagination could not match the monstrousness of the beast that loomed before us, even as the general features came remarkably close.

The ancient Scotsman wore heavy trousers, a coarse brown tunic, and furs flung over his thick shoulders. He regarded us, puny mortals, through pale, pewter-gray eyes, shot in their cores with radiant carnelian flames that surged and waned.

And, oh, was this one dripping with arrogance! All vampires were arrogant. At least those I'd encountered. But in this thing, there was pride with a difference. I could see hints of what the man might have looked like, even been like, before his change. It seemed clear he'd always been a man of power and high standing. Still, long centuries of vampirism had truly altered him, making what might have been once attractive features into something utterly unnerving, molding those natural details into a bona fide monstrosity.

The strength in his broad shoulders, powerful muscles, and those large, jutting bones gave the monster an even more inhuman aspect—a physical structure disturbingly...*wrong*. And his hands, like the massive talons of a great bird of prey with their long, yet thick, powerful fingers and knifelike onyx nails, big enough to lay that huge palm atop my head, and each digit could grasp me beneath my jawline.

I recalled Clan telling me that each vamp changes uniquely over time. Some take on inhuman traits and features, revealing the horrors they are, while others grow more beautiful as time goes by, eventually becoming so stunning, their visage so ethereal, that they could be mistaken for angels, and often were. These beautiful creatures might so easily entice and seduce that they likely found hunting to be the simplest of things.

At the same time, the ugly, twisted vampires would have to hide away using metamorphosis, which was rare and not well understood by hunters, or develop powerful charm abilities to obscure or alter the perceptions of those who saw them. I had yet to see a vampire that was in any way angelic, though I had seen a few attractive ones. But attractive or not, they were always just beasts to me.

The three of us were stuck in place by some unseen force. No, not by any mesmerization or magical power on the vampire's part, simply the pause before the battle…calm before the storm.

Erskine's glowing, crimson-slitted eyes studied us minutely. He was taking his time, weighing us as boxers size up their competition in the ring before the big fight. But no, not that. Because boxers are typically, at least for the most part, evenly matched, and there was nothing fair about *this* confrontation. This single, most formidable beast would have the upper hand even with the three of us up against him. And should he be assisted by his shadow pals, or if we were set upon by some other unseen helper…? Either way, it wasn't looking good for us.

Angry suddenly at my gloomy thoughts, I shook myself inwardly. What the hell was I doing? We were hunters, warded, trained, and deadly! No way I would let myself wilt before this thing like some dying flower—like the bullied boy I once was. I was hungry for this!

As if my change in perspective awakened something within him, the old vampire turned his brutal head slowly my way; his too-wide mouth split open, and his formidable jaw seemed to dislocate in an impossible grin that morphed into a maw of mad proportion. Long, serrated, razor-sharp fangs glinted as his furnace eyes widened, and the light behind them surged like the stoking of coals.

Excitement, that's what it was: joy, the anticipation of some keen and long-awaited enjoyment. It swelled within him, within *me*, as muscles bunched and attention became riveted between us. I saw—felt —Clannon and Gerard step slightly away as I, alone, the first of us, stood to face off with this beast of a thing.

No, they were not running from the fight, simply allowing the process to take its course. They knew I was strong, and I'm sure they sensed in me the desire for this, as well as my lack of fear. They would let me "take first watch," as it were, and join in as the fight progressed. I appreciated this more than I can say: their trust in me, in my strength and determination, buoyed me up even further.

"Strong," Erskine's clotted voice rumbled.

God, the sound of it, so very inhuman, so ghastly, it sent a fresh surge of thrill coursing through me.

Was I a masochist?

Was I even still sane?

Who knows? I only knew I wanted that experience, that looming battle, just like a druggy needs a hit.

"Hungry," I replied to him with my own rumble, widening my eyes ravenously, brimming with rage, fierce anticipation, and eagerness to draw this thing's blood.

108

The demon cackled; the cracking whip of his voice, coupled with our pent-up energies, charged the place like a Tesla coil!

"A worthy foe, aye, at least judgin' by yer enthusiasm. Let us hope so. But we'll see... We'll see. Give me yer name, laddie, so that I may speak it back to ye, the moment I tear yer sweet throat out."

I spun the scythe in my hand, round and round, an action I'd gotten so good at over the years I hadn't even thought about doing it. "It's nice to finally meet you, Kaedon Erskine. Name's Vale, and mark my words, monster: *you* will squeak *my* name from your dying throat when I take your fucking head!" It was a threat to match his own, which made him laugh that much harder, rocking the place with fresh thunder. But it wasn't a laugh of derision, though perhaps that was a part of it; it felt to me as if it contained a level of respect for my boldness, infused with the promise of a battle worth fighting.

Keeping to my typical style, which was not to make the first move, I let the creature dictate the start of our confrontation. And I didn't have to wait long...

XII

A WORTHY FOE

The air between the four of us—hunters versus beast—hung heavy with expectation, yet no sign of fear.

I say no fear, but you must understand, there is fear and there is fear; being frightened into inaction or running away, or knowing and accepting the magnitude of the dangers you're facing while embracing the healthy fear that motivates, drives, and pushes one to perform acts of bravery and strength, perhaps beyond normal human abilities.

The latter was the "fear" I was experiencing. That furious, driving force! Karl used to call me The Fearless Vampire Hunter, which I always scoffed at. But he did it because I never showed an ounce of hesitation, and I never let him see if I was scared. Honestly, by the time he joined me in my hunts, I truly wasn't scared anymore. The only time I felt anything one might consider "fear" was over *his* well-being, never my own.

So, at that moment, facing my first ancient, monstrous vampire, I trembled from limb to limb. But with anticipation and eagerness, not terror! Those emotions rocked my body with the burning need to move, to cut, to draw the fucking thing's blood.

I'm sure old Erskine was feeling much the same as I was, though his form of bloodletting would be quite different from mine. Not that I would give him any chance to get at my vital fluids!

We hunters were powerfully warded, as you know, so sinking his teeth into us would be—I might have said impossible if we were dealing with a youngin', but we weren't—so let's say difficult. At least not as easy as biting into an unprotected mortal.

111

My eyes moved to his talon-like hands with their long, curved, ebony fingernails and big, hearty fingers. Suddenly, a thought struck me. With an ancient vampire's ability to pass right through solid objects, he could probably reach right into my chest, without even breaking the skin, grasp ahold of my heart, and squeeze it like a ripe melon! I certainly hoped our wards would prevent *that*!

"Aye," Erskine rumbled low in his throat. "Ye're nay mere lambs come to the slaughter, eh? Well warded, ye are! I sense it as it buffets me where I stand."

Knowing vamps can't literally read minds unless they're feeding, it still felt like he'd read my thoughts.

"T'will nay be enough, lads," he continued, smirking cruelly, hideously with that creature's mouth of his. "'Tis nay the buffeting of a mighty wind I feel from yer meager magic, merely a gentle breeze. Ye think yer the only ones with magic, eh? I've had centuries to master the draoidheachd."

That's the word for magic in old Scott-Gaelic, by the way.

"Good for you." I snarked.

Then Clan replied through clenched teeth, "We'll see about that."

He and Gerard stood right behind me like the stalwart friends they were. I felt warmth well up in my heart for them, which nearly evolved into worry for their safety. I hoped they'd make it out of this confrontation alive—hoped we all would! But I shoved those concerns down hard, deep in my gut, then drew in a sudden breath just as the vampire moved!

I was coiled tight, ready to spring, but the expression on the creature's face halted me. His attention was diverted, his eyes locked on the Frenchman's lapel as he took a short series of quick steps forward. I realized suddenly that his focus was riveted to that brooch Gerard wore so proudly.

"Ye would use The Dark Lord, *my* Lord's mark, against me?!"

Erskine was clearly furious, and his words sent my mind whirling back to the many things I'd read about that symbol of Sohrakia, and I wondered what he meant by a Dark Lord. Had I seen a Dark Lord mentioned in connection to that symbol? Could Pashan be the Dark Lord he was referring to?

But I didn't have the luxury of distraction.

Erskine's hand reached out so quickly that none of us could have stopped it. He grasped Gerard's lapel, snagged that gaudy brooch in his massive claw of a hand, and yanked it, tearing it and that brown leather it was pinned to easily away, leaving a gaping hole in the Frenchman's stylish jacket.

A lot of good that thick, nylon thread did! I thought to myself. And it seemed, at first, that the Sohrakian rune had no protective effect, either.

Gerard had flinched in utter shock at first, but then he threw up his arms and clawed with his hands, attempting to thwart the vampire and get his precious brooch back. But his efforts were in vain. It was like watching a small child struggle against a huge grown man.

The vampire swung his arm up, the same hand that held the jewelry, and whacked Gerard under the chin, sending him flying across the room.

Reacting immediately, I swung my scythe up and sliced into the creature's pale, gray arm as Erskine brought it back down again. The hand holding the brooch jerked away as my blade cleaved his flesh, and blood spurted up and out of that deep wound. Then, I caught a glimpse of the vampire's palm just as he yanked it back, and that Sohrakian symbol—the Dark Lord's symbol?—had been burned into Erskine's flesh, just like the headpiece of the staff of Ra was imprinted into Toht's palm in Raiders of The Lost Ark. I had to assume that the symbol of the "Dark Lord" had burned Erskine due to some anointing of the piece by Fedelma, which she performed on all of our special charms and jewelry, but that was only a guess since I couldn't stop and ask Clannon about it.

The brooch was flung to the floor, tumbling away in the same direction Gerard had fallen.

I thought the Frenchman might avail himself of the chance to grab it, but it appeared he was out cold.

One down.

Hopefully, not for long, and hopefully, Gerard wasn't too badly hurt!

Clan had immediately rushed to Gerard, and now spun to face Erskine while shooting a fierce glance my way as we both advanced on the creature.

The vampire grunted, ignoring his sliced arm, which was probably already stitching itself up. The old ones healed extremely fast, apparently. He stalked toward me because I was closer to him. Blood had sprayed from that deep cut, coating his furs and even splashing into his awful face, only making his visage that much more disturbing.

Clan had a big stride with those long legs of his and came up behind the vampire just as I met the thing's advancing claws with my weapons and a hastily worded spell's repelling force.

Since magic is only so powerful against such an old monster as this, it did not work on Erskine as effectively as it had on those baby vamps back home. His black taloned fingers came to within an inch of my tender flesh as I leaned away from his advance, barely in time.

Clan was on him now, big, shining blade arcing down and into the monster's back just before the beast could turn and block it.

The creature howled, more out of anger than pain. Oh, it felt the pain, to be sure. Vampirism did not prevent the agonies of physical damage. But this thing had experienced eons of it, from my guess, even before he became a vampire, and his tolerance must have been incredible!

"Insect!" He roared, then laughed like a madman because he *wanted* this…wanted *us* "worthy foes" to give him a real challenge, and so far, we were, but the fight was only getting started.

I dodged his attack as he lunged at me again with that knife sticking out of his back, just behind his right shoulder.

I knew that Clan had been aiming for Erskine's neck, missing the mark when the creature moved.

Ducking low, I swung my "Dundee" knife up and sunk it deep into the vampire's gut. It made a faint squishy noise as it pierced him just above his waistline, and I felt it scrape against bone. He barely made a sound this time.

Then, utilizing a bit of my martial arts training and his own weight against him, I pushed into his big body with all my strength and swung my leg out, attempting to kick his legs out from under him. But those fucking things were like tree trunks, so firmly planted it was as if they grew right out of the floor!

My shin smarted as if I'd kicked concrete, but I swallowed the pain as Erskine grasped ahold of my body, constricting my ribcage with both of his monster hands, and lifted me right off my feet as if I were a wee lass. He swung me around, tossing me and sending me crashing into Clannon. We were both pushed off balance, landing in a heap several paces away. I scrambled to my feet, and Clan moved with me; I was relieved he was okay, though he was a bit slower, and I could tell he was in pain.

Then, I felt strange energy pounding the air around me, attempting to dig itself into my mind, but Fedelma's wards were doing their job well. I was not influenced one iota by the old creature's attempts to muddle my thoughts.

"Might as well give it up, Ersk." I exclaimed.

He chuckled at me, then, in the next second, he vanished before my eyes. Yet his voice remained close but non-localized as if coming from the very air itself. "A nickname, eh? Are we pals now, Hunter?" he teased.

This was another ability to control the very atoms of his body. To vanish in much the same way as he passed through solid objects.

"Aye!" I imitated his old-world expression, my head turning this way and that, muscles bunched, and weapons held firmly in my hands as I concentrated on the tattoos on my body to help locate the fiend. "Why not?" I shrugged. "Just two pals sparring."

His chuckle made the air shiver. The tats tingled on my right side, and a little behind me, and the feeling was slowly intensifying. I could tell the beast was moving ever so slowly closer.

Controlling my immense urge to turn and throw myself at him, I waited. Not allowing my body or any small movement to indicate I knew he was there.

As the burn of those particular runes suddenly surged, I knew he was practically on top of me.

Calling upon the powers of those mysterious Sohrakian runes, the invisible ones, and concentrating the brunt of magical energy on that side of my body, I thrust out a surge of power. Then, I heard Erskine grunt as the force hit him, and I swung myself around, scythe angled for his neck.

I knew the magic would only startle him temporarily and hoped to seize that brief opportunity to take his head. But damn it, the beast was quicker than me.

He reappeared for only an instant as he leaned out of my blade's path, then promptly vanished again.

To me, it seemed he had moved to my left, but it was too quick to be sure, and the burning in my tattoos had evened out again. He was not near enough for me to sense his position.

A movement to my left made me turn that way with a jerk. It was Gerard, up again with weapons out and his ruined leather jacket discarded. He looked royally pissed, mostly about the jacket, I assumed. A cursory glance at his pants pocket, with scraps of his jacket fabric poking out, told me he had hastily shoved the brooch in there.

The three of us stood in a triangle, eyes scanning the area around us.

"Damn it, where is he?" Clan exclaimed, just as I saw a ripple of movement in his direction.

"Duck!" I yelled, and Clan dropped immediately. I threw my big knife at the beast.

Erskine warped into view, the blade sticking out of his thigh. He had shed his furs, dressed in brown and black leathers. I had to admit, the tooling of the tunic, belt, and boots was stunning! Fit the creature like a glove. Obviously, custom-made for his unusually massive frame.

115

Who's your tailor? I thought to myself, feeling kind of rotten for putting a hole in his leather pants.

Erskine yanked the blade out and weighed it in his hand before sending it flying back at me with magic. Again, he was too quick for me; I wasn't prepared. No time to duck, and it was headed right for my heart!

This all happened in a split second and felt like slow motion.

But thank god Gerard was prepared, sending a thrust of magical energy between me and the vampire, knocking the knife off course by about two feet and sending it sailing past me. Shit, at that velocity, if the thing had got me, I would have been skewered all the way through and possibly pinned to a beam several feet behind me. The knife hung there now, stuck deep in the very edge of that huge, thick chunk of wood.

Before I could get my bearings after such a close call, the vampire began to utter a string of words I could not make out.

Shit! It was another spell, and he was hurling it at Gerard, who had engaged him in a fierce, if brief, attack!

Even in such a short observation, I could see that the Frenchman was, indeed, a superb fighter!

Clan screamed a protective spell as he rushed to block the magic and keep it from striking Gerard, but Erskine's massive, clawed hand flew out just as the beast's presence wavered again and shifted instantly right into Clan's path.

Those long, deadly nails raked Clan's face, digging into his cheek and jaw.

"Shit!" I cried out in shock and concern for my friends, just as Clan hollered in pain and the vampire's mysterious spell hit Gerard.

The Frenchman dropped like a rock, utterly still in an instant.

My heart sank!

Clannon was bleeding badly from his face as he stumbled away, mumbling a quick healing spell to staunch the bleeding, and Gerard just might be dead!

Fury!

In an instant, my entire body erupted with fresh, fierce adrenaline!

I surged forward, descending on the vampire like a freight train! My wards were pulsing like crazy, energized by my surging emotions, my determination, and deadly intent!

Erskine turned slowly, his every move a show of dominance, of self-indulgent pleasure and superiority.

Every move he made seriously pissed me off!

We came together in a fierce clash of claws versus blades, teeth versus wards, magic versus magic.

I fought him with all I had as Clan hurled spells to assist me and to hold the demon back.

I knew two things.

One, Erskine was toying with me, and two, I would need to employ the strongest magic and every ounce of my strength to have any chance of beating this thing…all while mostly doing it alone.

But I was used to working alone, and I really wasn't entirely by myself. Clan might have been out of the physical fight for the moment, but with some magical sutures and that unyielding determination of his, he'd be back in the thick of it soon.

My strength was buoyed by those special tattoos, the invisible ones. Those secret markings could be utilized via psychic conjuring, meaning one would not need to speak a spell out loud to draw from their energy. Giving the vampire no idea that any magic was being employed against him.

Meditation training taught me how to activate them and pull their magic up from the core of my being, even in situations where I could not properly meditate.

During practice, once I'd made that initial connection to my core, I'd learned what unique powers were available to me and in what form. It's different for everyone, dependent on one's singular personality, their gifts, and even their sentimentality. All are unique.

For me, my magic was based on physical strength, an almost precognitive instinct during battle, and the protection of others. Namely, based on those attributes, I could imbue my weapons with added magical strength.

Those powers, *my* powers, flowed to me now from deep within, and they came without causing my body any diminished energy, which was a boon I cannot praise enough!

So, as Erskine and I exchanged blows, the blades of his long nails leaving me and my clothing covered in tears and scratches, and my metal blades doing much the same to him, I had drawn from myself that magical boost to imbue my blades with a much stronger cutting force, sharpening my ability to anticipate his moves and increasing the power of my blows.

My ultimate goal, obviously, was to take the fiend's head! But to slice through *that* formidable column of a neck, I would need every ounce of strength I could muster and more!

The vampire's many wounds healed constantly, right before my eyes—all those cuts and any damage I inflicted fading away in mere seconds.

While I? Well, I was a real mess!

Clan had joined in again, but he was finding it difficult to insert himself into such a fierce one-on-one battle. Instead, he hung back, doing what he could to help by hurling a constant stream of healing and protective spells my way. He was a godsend, I'll tell ya that! Helping me keep up with Erskine's constant, preternatural healing, although mine would only be temporary...

Fine, as long as the magic kept me going long enough to finish the job!

Clan moved behind the vampire and finally yanked his other blade from Erskine's back. He proceeded to stab the monster again and again, slicing into his shoulders and arms as he tried skewering his neck, all while dodging the creature's attempts to throw him off.

Finally, he got the knife into the back of the ancient creature's neck. I could see the tip of the blade emerge in the front just as the beast swung a massive fisted hand into Clan's chest, knocking the air out of him and sending him soaring across the room again.

Taking that oh-so-brief opportunity while Erskine's attention was divided, I grasped the handle of Clan's knife, which stuck out at a forty-five-degree angle from the left. At the same time, I hooked my scythe on the opposite side of Erskine's neck, and just as the vamp turned back to me, I yanked both blades with all my strength.

With a gurgling growl and talons like battering rams, Erskine shoved me away. I went flying, luckily landing on a couch where he had tossed his huge, thick furs. They provided me with a soft landing as the wooden furniture below them crumbled away, and I hit the floor with a dull thud.

Clearly, I had not succeeded in removing the monster's head yet, but how far had I gotten?

As I leaped to my feet to take stock of the situation and pulled another knife from my jacket, not quite as big as my Dundee, which was still stuck in that column and too far for me to reach, I saw Erskine's neck gushed blood. Both blades seemed to be lodged there, wedged together, possibly in his spine.

He warbled, bubbled, and spewed blood and froth from his mouth and nose as he fought to pull them out.

Grinning with a kind of mad glee, I rushed at him, throwing my full weight onto him.

With all of his staggering and struggling, he was already off-kilter, so we both went down, a mass of weight smashing into a heavy table, reducing it to splinters.

Atop the monster, my fresh blade in hand, I stuck it deep in his neck, dead center, right along with the others. I could feel the resistance as it pierced his spine, the grinding of metal-against-metal and bone.

"Vaaale…" The monster squeaked, rasped, spewed.

I smirked wickedly down into that hideous face, whispering harshly through clenched teeth, "And what did I say you'd do with your dying breath?"

The beast's eyes were blazing fire, burning me with their hatred and disbelief as if made of true flame. I locked my ice-blue eyes with his searing orbs, willfully extinguishing his sinister heat.

A flicker of powerful emotion suddenly passed between us: unreadable, unfathomable—a span of eons in a single instant—it nearly threw me for a loop, but I held my ground, leaning all my weight into that final blade while grasping the handle of my scythe again and yanking with everything I had.

Blood gushed like a geyser, pooled beneath him, coated my arms, stained my front and my face. His horrid, ghastly mouth hung wide open, inhumanly wide, with its jagged, razor-sharp teeth, like an angler fish from the depths, gaping his shock.

There was a grinding scrape. Then wet, squelching as I pushed, straining my muscles to their max.

Then, a snap…and a crackling pop.

Snap. Crackle. Pop.

And the head rolled free.

But I didn't move fast enough to escape what happened next.

That huge body of his suddenly began to vibrate, jerk, and twist madly beneath me. Caught in the things flailing arms just as I attempted to scramble away. They suddenly locked around me, and I was yanked down into that mass of arcane muscle and bone.

I was pressed hard into his ruined leathers and coarse fabrics, all soaked in blood, mere inches from his red, raw, squirting neck.

Those massive arms were like vises holding me there, talons digging into me through my own leather coat, growling, pushing, and wriggling frantically to free myself.

Then, I felt one of those large limbs go limp, and other arms encircle my middle, pulling me back and away from the dying thing.

Coming to my feet, I stood unsteadily in front of Clannon as he kicked Erskine's severed head like a soccer ball toward the fireplace.

My legs were shaking as I turned to watch the unending thrashing of that headless body. One arm, cut almost completely through just above the elbow, lay limp, but the rest of the thing seemed to rage on and on in an endless fight for—what? Life?

"We need to start a fire! Now!" Clan's voice rang out, pulling me out of a kind of morbid fascination. Using my lighter, we scooped up all that broken wood, threw it into the fireplace, and got the flames started.

"Grab the shoulders!" he moved around the thing, trying to get at its thrashing legs, which was simply impossible.

I did as he asked, dragging the body close to the fireplace. But then, something odd caught my attention. A sight I'll never forget. A thing that will forever live in my darkest nightmares. It sent my sensible, reasoning mind to a place I hope never to go again.

I dropped Erskine like a hot potato and stumbled back, shaking my head, eyes wide, unblinking, and my entire body shuddering uncontrollably.

"Wh…what the h-hell?!" I stammered, unable to tear my eyes away from it.

It was Erskine's neck, that red, raw, bloodied neck that no longer bled. But it wasn't the lack of bleeding that stymied me, made me feel faint, broke my brain; it was the expansion of something from within its center—that utterly wrong, utterly inexplicable shape emerging from inside!

A dome…

A tuft of ash brown hair…

What looked like, but could not possibly be, the top of a *new head*!

"Quick, Spence! We must get him into the fire!" Clan hollered at me in all earnestness, practically growling at me to get my shit together.

My hunter training kicked in. That, and something more, deep within me that I can't explain!

I lunged forward, grabbed the thing, and practically all by myself, dragged that abomination's body into the slowly emerging flames, then I snatched up his severed head and tossed it in after.

The fireplace was massive, large enough to hold a single bed and more. Clan, using a large poker, hastily spread the wood out, and I scrambled to gather more wood, covering the entire width of the body and lighting small fires along the way. The flames caught in Erskine's clothing and soon the vampire was roasting from shoulders to toes.

The—corpse?—continued to move spastically, so we had to stand clear as its thrashing threw sparks and wood splinters in every direction. Soon, the flames covered the entire firebox and swelled into a raging inferno. It was so hot that our exposed skin was beginning to singe.

Finally, and quite suddenly, the body fell completely away to ash—dust…the dust of ages.

"He's gone." Clan said almost reverently.

There was reverence to it, an instant peace, so astounding, so utterly opposite to only a second before, that both of us swooned.

Recovering quickly, as that oppressive energy had fled so completely, Clan scooped up Gerard. Thank goodness the Frenchman was alive, but we could not rouse him.

"He's under some spell, and it's not lifting, even now that our vampire is dead and gone. It must be powerful magic." Clannon had laid Gerard on a small couch as we watched the fire fully die away, and there was nothing left but those ruined leathers for the flames to consume.

"Too bad, that was some gorgeous leather work," I commented, mostly to myself and in a most delirious way. Body and soul, I was beat! The battle was catching up with me, and each limb felt ten times heavier than it should.

A warm hand on my shoulder made me turn to find Clannon smiling tiredly at me. He was a mess, too, his face gouged by three long cuts, held together by magical threads. "Let's get going. There's nothing more to do here." He said.

It was then I realized that the shadows, those mysterious Nethers, were gone. It also hit me that they had done nothing to assist Erskine in his fight. I had expected them to play some part in our battle, but once we got rolling, there had been no sign of them. Well, perhaps they lurked in the corners watching us, but I was too caught up in the fight to notice them. Now? They were nowhere to be found. Every dark corner was lit by the natural light of the midday sun, or was it late afternoon? I'd completely lost all track of time.

"They're gone," I commented, "the shadows."

Clannon simply shrugged, and we carried Gerard to the car. We cleaned up as best we could right there in the woods, refreshed our magical healing, and Clan drove us back to the hotel. I tried to get him to let me drive, but even with his wounds, he wasn't as spent as I was.

I went in alone to check out since the damage to Clan's face was more dramatic than mine. All of our things were already in the car, so there was no need to return to our room.

While I was settling our affairs, Clan had made a call and found us a chambres d'hôtes, or what we call in English a bed and breakfast. It was a private house, with no one living there, so we could stay the night, rest up, and figure out what to do next, primarily concerning our friend—Gerard had still not regained consciousness.

Once we put the Frenchman to bed, cleaned ourselves up, and as we shared a bottle of scotch, Clan commented, "There is only one place I know we can take Gerard for help."

XIII
ROMANIA

They came to me in the night with their wild black hair, big dark eyes, and berry-stained lips. Not vampires. Gypsies, or Roma, as they preferred to be called. I had wondered why Clannon and I were separated into different tents and why my presence had gandered such enrapt attention upon our arrival.

They knew Clan pretty well from previous visits, but apparently, I was a new and fascinating novelty. I couldn't help but think they saw in me a steed worthy of breeding.

There were three of them, all mocha skin and long limbs, slinking like cats into my tent. Beautiful and timeless, as if I'd been thrust into the past, nothing modern about them…nothing touched by technology or any century beyond the Middle Ages.

The tallest and oldest of the three, probably in her early forties and just as gorgeous as the girls in their early twenties, led the charge. She crawled atop me as I sat up groggily, utterly confused at their sudden appearance, questions in my eyes but mute to forming any words, as astounded as I was.

All three of them wore long, layered skirts but otherwise were naked.

Honestly, at first, I truly thought I was dreaming as I gaped at them —mouth dry and heart racing. I quickly grew hard just as I realized I was actually awake, and this was indeed reality. The pain from my arousal increased as the other two joined the first, hands tugging at my clothes, chocolate brown eyes glistening hungrily in that dark tent, barely lit by early morning light.

"Wha—?" I barely whispered before the woman on top of me placed her fingers over my lips to shush me. Her other hand had unfastened my pants and found my twitching cock, grasped it with a force that made me gasp, and worked it vigorously, knocking my mind off kilter and taking full control over my body.

I collapsed onto that cot with a raspy exhale, moaning helplessly, losing myself to her insistent touch. I didn't bother to fight the undressing. Didn't resist their eager and well-practiced hands all over me. And how they each took their turns, pulling me along with well-practiced skill and relentless ardor in this—my rather late—sexual awakening. By the time the sun was fully up, I'd had them all more than once. Utterly exhausted, I fell into a dead sleep, not waking until late afternoon.

Coming to in a lingering cloud of utter bliss, aching in nearly every muscle, especially that one most used, I lay there as the lurid details of that orgy slowly emerged in my memory.

Despite such a night, I couldn't help but feel used. But was I complaining? Nope. As much as I hesitated to admit it, I realized I'd needed that release for a long time. Their soft bodies, searing touches, and me…spilling myself into their wanton heat again and again both thrilled and cleansed me. But the strangest part? None of them, not at any point during the act, pressed their mouths to mine. Oh, they tasted the instrument of their need with their plump, soft lips and swallowed my seed without hesitation, but to kiss my mouth seemed… I don't know, too…personal? I could only guess.

It didn't bother me. The only lips I wanted someday pressed to my own belonged to Rayn.

Thinking of her, covered in the sweat and sex of those gypsy ladies, I felt arousal surge again. But my stomach growled loudly, and I needed to relieve and wash myself, so I dressed and went to take care of those other basic needs.

"No warning." I gave Clannon a smirk as I approached, having bathed and now feeling more ravenous than before.

He laughed knowingly, "Like thieves in the night," then he held out a bowl to me, "Breakfast, or more like dinner."

Clannon knew my tastes, so my bowl was heavy on meat, light on vegetables. I washed it down with water collected from mountain streams, sifted, boiled, allowed to cool. Filled with rich minerals, it was the best water I'd ever tasted, and I guzzled it like a desert rat. Then, I shoveled the soft-cooked beef and vegetables into my mouth with fervor.

"Quite a welcome, eh?" He mused.

I just smirked, kept eating.

"I knew they'd come for you," he continued. "My three are over there," he tilted his head to a large tent at the opposite end of the camp. "It's the same welcome every time I pay a visit. Those two young men," Clan gestured with his spoon to a pair of handsome lads only a few feet away, talking to one of their elders, "they're mine."

I nearly spit out my mouthful of stew but then realized that to be shocked by such a revelation was ridiculous. At that moment, the real purpose of those visitations actually hit me. "What? They're breeding with us?!" Sure, I'd considered it jokingly at first, but now, I knew it was fact.

Clan shrugged, smiled, sat his empty bowl down: "At first, I also found it strange after being presented with my sons as infants the second time I visited. My reaction was quite dramatic, as you can imagine. I felt obligated to provide for the boys, send money, or do something. But their mothers and the clan chief, or Rom baro, insisted there was no need.

"Two of 'my' three ladies became pregnant, but I was assured they would not expect me to be a father to the boys nor a husband to them. The clan would be their family." He shrugged. "By the time I left, I'd somewhat gotten used to the whole thing. Although I do send what I can to help them, and I visit yearly, sometimes more often. The boys are happy, healthy, thriving, so what more could I ask for? I've offered to bring them to London with me, just for a visit unless they might want to stay. But so far, they have politely declined."

This was something I wasn't sure I could get my head around. "Kids," a strange, uneasy feeling washed over me, "Those women want to have *my* kids."

"I know what you're feeling."

"Yeah," I replied with a frown. "I'm not sure how I feel about this, honestly."

But what was I going to do about it? I changed the subject, "How's Gerard?"

"Better; I checked on him after I woke. These people work miracles."

We had rushed to Romania to this particular gypsy band because they had the know-how to help Gerard after what Erskine had done to him. For ages, the Roma had worked with the hunters, even before Clannon joined up. He'd discovered their existence in a collection of letters he'd stumbled upon during his studies and developed a quick rapport with them.

"I have no doubt you'll have children by at least one of those vixens." Clan commented, studying me and my unease closely. "There's no need to feel concerned, Spencer. I was told by the eldest of their group that in times past, this band of Roma suffered maladies and illness due to inbreeding. They learned from this, and every other generation or so, they bring in new blood…new DNA, to strengthen their stock. You and I, big, strapping males, well, it goes without saying."

Chuckling wryly, I felt heat rise to my cheeks. But my head was bowed over my bowl, long hair hiding my dumb embarrassment behind a black curtain as I ate. Between mouthfuls, I mumbled, "If they want to breed giants, more power to 'em!"

Clannon laughed, then grew silent as we finished our meals.

Basking in the unique energy and stunning views of the Carpathian Mountains of eastern Romania was absolutely breathtaking! Their power poured out of them and straight into my soul. It felt like healing, which I'm sure it was. I needed this reprieve, we all did—this stunning natural beauty after what we'd witnessed!

We spent a few weeks there, in the foothills, with the Roma Lovarti. Their sprawling camp was located beside a large lake of indigo water, so clear you could see right to the bottom. The colorful tents and wagons dotted the landscape, adding to the beauty of the scene.

Our wounds were tended to and we were healing up nicely. Gerard continued his treatments to overcome the spell he'd been hit with. They had roused him on the first day, but he still had a long way to go.

There was also a lot I could learn from these people. Different skills, not recorded in books, only passed down by word of mouth, in tales old as time, which Clan and I went over together, with the help of several of the villagers.

I also got to know Clannon's sons, Ion and Iza, quite well. The boys might have turned Clan down when it came to visiting his home country, but they stuck close to him nearly the entire time we were there.

Both of the boys greatly resembled their father, tall, lithe, but strong, with his dark coloring only intensified by their Romani blood. And Clannon was fiercely proud of them. It warmed my heart to share in their family time together. I felt a bit like an uncle and sometimes another son. Clan was like family to me now, and these young men, less than ten years my juniors, were the closest thing to brothers I'd had since Karl's death.

"You hunt the vidmă, the striggoi; how did such a mission start for you?" Ion, the older one, asked me as we visited one evening. They already knew Clan's story, of course. So, I told them mine. I also shared what happened to Karl, which seemed to touch them deeply.

To be honest, our time there was uneventful on the blood-drinker front. I thought that coming to Romania would provide the most vampire-slaying action yet, being in the very heart, the very birth land of vampire legends. But it turned out this place was the most peaceful yet. These Romani tribes have been hunters since time immemorial. They, and their grandfathers, and those long before them, kept the lands clear of vamps.

Yet, their magic was different from what we used, and their wards and weapons, while similar—because the method of utterly destroying a vampire is always the same—were uniquely forged and constructed by the tribe rather than purchased at the nearest sporting goods store.

The quality time spent with them had been highly informative, if often redundant to what we already knew. Obviously, having come here often, Clan was fully aware of what I was only just learning, but it thrilled me all the same.

I was given many gifts by the gypsies: trinkets, sheets of parchment scribbled with this or that incantation or tidbit of vital knowledge, and several unique weapons. There was a long needle, sunken in a gun-like contraption, that, when pressed to a vampire's heart or to the base of its spine, would immobilize them temporarily. It was only the size of a small pistol, though with a slightly longer muzzle, and could easily be carried in a pocket of my coat. There were also blades, beautifully fashioned in warm, gorgeous wood and gleaming, etched metal.

One of those special items left me astounded and speechless. Something so archaic they couldn't tell me how old it actually was or where precisely it came from.

127

"It is not ours, not created by us, not even of this world," Iza said as he handed it to me. "You will sense its strange energy if you hold it in the palm of your hand."

I took it from him gingerly and held it up to the firelight to check it out. There seemed to be nothing too special about it upon first inspection. It was simply a silver locket hanging from a thick chain with no clasp, composed of what appeared to be the same metal. There were no markings on the charm, nothing to distinguish it.

"The item of import is inside," Iza instructed me, taking hold of the locket and pressing it between his thumb and forefinger, which seemed to unlock it. The thing popped open and embedded into the metal within, carved of what appeared to be bone, was a symbol I knew all too well. "The Symbol of Sohrakia, or of Pashan," I commented. It was the same symbol of the tiny charm I wore around my neck and of that gaudy brooch Gerard adored so much.

"It was originally the Sohrakian symbol, adopted later by Pashan," Clan added, "at least that's how we understand it."

Ion spoke up as Iza released the locket, and I cradled it in my palm.

"That symbol is made of bone," Ion continued, confirming my suspicions. "It is rumored to be carved from The Dark Lord himself and, perhaps, gifted to Pashan."

The Dark Lord! That's what Erskine had said. But who, or what, was this Dark Lord?

"We know from old stories that, eons ago, it was given to someone, though no one knows for sure who." Ion shrugged, "Perhaps it was Pashan, or another, before Pashan. Per the histories and old pirate tales, The Dark Lord and Pashan were both creatures of metamorphosis or maybe they were one and the same being. No one knows. There are no tales, no records to explain it. The legend goes that The Dark Lord has many names and many forms. He can give of his physical essence without losing anything of himself and would often create things or gift his Darkness to others. That is the rumor, anyway.

"Whether these tales are facts or simply stories and parables, we do not know. The bone may, instead, come from a Darkling or even a disciple, or it may simply be a human bone imbued with something no one understands. But it does have power. Inexplicable power that often defies logic. If a vampire, or even a victim who's been bitten, touches the charm, it will react. You will know. They will not like it."

Yes, just as I had sensed Fedelma's power, I sensed this thing was imbued with something inexplicable. And they weren't kidding about the power; I could feel it vibrating against the palm of my hand. It

128

tingled like a soft, electrical charge. "I…appreciate you giving this to me. But I feel strange taking it from you. It seems so…important!"

"No, it is as it should be," Iza waved his hands and shook his head.

"Iza dreamed last night that he gifted that to you. The dream was a sign, so you must take it." Ion insisted.

"Thank you," I bowed my head to them and gently deposited the necklace in my topmost inner coat pocket since I didn't know how to put it on without a clasp on the chain.

"Here," Iza reached out a hand, asking me to hand him the necklace, so I did. "Now watch and listen. Prin voinţa sohrakia, eliberează această închizătoare."

Suddenly, the chain separated, and Iza handed the two ends to me. "Go on, put it around your neck and touch those ends together. They will re-join. They desire to be united."

I did as he said, and they connected like he said they would. The charm now hung from my neck.

"Now," Iza smiled, "I will teach you that spell so that you may also unclasp the chain."

We spent a couple of hours on it, finally working it into phonetics so that I could put a rhythm to it and commit it to memorization.

We remained with the Roma for about two weeks. It took more than half that time for Gerard to finally be up and about again. The magic that Erskine had used on him was very old, powerful, and it took very old magical skills handed down for ages to reverse it. Unfortunately, the Frenchman would end up suffering ill effects from that curse for the rest of his life. Somnambulism, to be precise. He would now fall asleep at the drop of a hat, completely unexpected and at any given moment. Which meant he could no longer be a hunter.

But that was okay to Gerard. Didn't seem to faze him. He accepted it, shrugged it off, even seemed to be pleased by it. "I have fought many a battle. It is time for resting. I can still help to support other hunters and train, oui?"

Clan and I had agreed, hoping Gerard wasn't hiding any real disappointment. But what could he be disappointed about, really? Vampire hunting was a severe, dangerous, nasty business. And he was out of it, lucky sod. No, not by choice, but by necessity. And he had fought hard and earned his respect, so more power to him and his new, less harrowing life, I say!

As our time drew to a close, Clannon invited Gerard to return with us to England, which he readily accepted. But me? I had other plans.

"It pains me to release you, Spencer. I could not have imagined meeting a friend and brother such as I've found in you."

My eyes burned, "I feel the same. You are family to me, Clannon. That is how I love you." I hated to leave, but it had been months away, and with no one to look after my property, now that Karl was gone, I felt I needed to return to America. Also, there was this niggling thing hovering at the back of my mind. It was a constant distraction pushing me to get back. And whenever those kinds of intuitive, pestering emotions struck me, I always obeyed them.

We embraced tightly, then pulled apart, slapping backs and grasping arms.

"May this not be goodbye forever, my friend." his soft, deep voice choked.

"It won't," I replied with a sad but grateful smile.

I left the following day on a small flight to Amsterdam, then on to New York, then home. This time, my mind was so preoccupied I found it difficult to sleep, and the trip seemed to last for-ev-er! When I finally drifted through the front door of my little cabin, the musty smell, after being closed up for so long, hit me like a slap in the face. But I was too bone tired to do a damned thing about it. The jet lag was seriously settling in, and I felt as if I'd been drinking, which I hadn't, and I was even a little nauseous.

After a shower, I crashed into my bed and slept for nearly twenty-four hours straight. Waking, I felt a bit better, yet not quite one hundred percent. So after opening some windows to air the place out, I took to the hills, walking in the cool evening air. It was fall, and the days were warm, but the nights were chilly, making the evening air perfect for a long walk.

When I got back, I set about refreshing the place, cleaning, dusting, and laundering my bedding and travel clothes.

I was famished after the long walk, then nighttime housework, so I headed out to grab food.

The next morning, I picked up my mail and shopped for groceries and household needs. Upon my return, I ate until I was satisfied. I decided to spend a little time simply living in my solitude, getting reacquainted with the place and the quiet of being home again.

A small pile of mail awaited me, I never received much mail, so sorting those out didn't take long. There was also a package from Clannon, which baffled me. It had to have been sent before I left Romania, but when had Clan made time to mail a package off?

Opening it, I found a brand new laptop computer and a letter.

I laughed and shook my head. What the hell was I going to do with a computer?

The note read, "Spencer, my friend, I am sure this little gift will surprise you. But I felt it necessary to do this for you since you told me you didn't own a computer. You see, I am spoiled—spoiled to this whole new email, instant communication. Sure, the two of us could chat on the phone, but then you said you didn't have a mobile. So, I decided to send you a laptop. It is convenient in that I could store many things on there for you and preload manuscripts and information that you might find useful. I know you are concerned for your privacy, which I heartily agree with, of course. So, I took the liberty of signing you up with a PPTP (Point-to-Point Tunneling Protocol), an encrypted connection through my employer, that will make everything you do completely private. You'll find info on that in your computer files under 'Documents.'

"Now, since you have no internet connection where you are, as you described it to me, 'way out in the boonies,' you will find pre-installed info on satellite internet, also through my work. Signing in should be simple; no need for wires or techs to come to visit your place, either. It's all wireless.

"I do hope this gift of mine will be accepted. I hope this letter finds you safe and well, back in your cozy little cabin. I will greatly miss your company, my dear friend. Please drop me an email as soon as you can. You will find contact information for myself, Byron and Kenna, Gerard, and even Fedelma (yes, she's online, too) in your address book. I hope you won't find yourself too lost in the computer/internet age! Oh, and lest I forget, your password to get into your new computer is 'Fearless.'

"Cheers, Clannon Colfeld."

I couldn't help but laugh. Me? With a laptop! It was preposterous! Alright, I *was* curious, and this was quite the astounding gift; not cheap and completely over-the-top, in my humble opinion. I admit I felt a little giddy unpacking it, plugging it in, booting it up. I henpecked

"Fearless" into the login and was greeted with a scene of Erskine's Scottish castle ruins.

Again, I wondered when exactly Clannon had shipped this thing to me.

It had to be before we went up against the ancient vampire. There simply was no time for him to do it after that. I piddled around, figured out how to activate that satellite internet and security "PPTP" thing. I wasn't quite as clueless about computers as Clan thought I was. I *had* utilized the library computers before, many times, so I basically knew my way around. My first order of business after entering the World Wide Web was to drop an email to my most excellent British friend.

"Clannon, you dog! A computer? Seriously? Well, you got your wish, my man. Here I am, dropping you an email just like all those normal modern humans. I got home, finally, after what seemed like forever, and now I'm all rested up. The place was stale from disuse, as you can imagine, but unmolested, thank goodness. It's all aired out now and fresh again. I'd missed it, but now I miss you and the gang. Any new developments over there? How's Gerard, adjusting to normal life, alright? Let me know what's up when you can.

"Cheers, and thank you, Spence."

We exchanged emails regularly, keeping tabs on both personal and hunter work. The best exchanges came from Fedelma. My god, that woman! I've never known anyone so quick and so ready on the mark with innuendos! She always left me either red from laughter or embarrassment. Wicked, wicked woman!

XIV
CLUB NETHERWORLD

I was enjoying being home again after my long stint in Europe. The extra luggage I'd taken with me empty; I'd filled with all the books and few other items gifted to me by Clannon, Byron, Fedelma, and the "Gypsies."

I spent quiet time looking through my little arcane library more closely. A few titles I hadn't studied as much as others, and I was eager to crack them open.

Let me summarize for you since I haven't yet included them all here.

You're familiar with *Kor Borholden's Dark Whispers,* that index of darkly imbued creatures and things. Custom bound by Clan, just like the other books he'd given to me.

Then there's *Och The Alchemist: Formuli,* which I don't think I've mentioned before. A massive collection of "recipes" for concoctions, tinctures, and other magical, medicinal, and alchemical creations, some for dealing with vampires, others for basic things like healing, and yet others, forbidden and potentially dangerous.

Pashan's Forbidden Treasures, a list of fantastical treasures and their descriptions, collected by a mysterious man—or creature?—named Pashan.

Charms of Ftorthin, a tome of unique, and frankly confusing, magical spells. Only Fedelma could make any sense of them.

Tome of Sohrakian Source, which has been mentioned, though I feel I should elaborate a bit more about it. It's definitely the wildest book in the collection, containing a jumbled mess of bizarre descriptions, explanations, and origins of all things dark. When I read some of it with Clan for the first time, I thought most, if not all of it, was utter hogwash. It was the largest book in my collection and, according to Clannon, the most difficult for him to bind.

Finally, there's *Iter et Journals de Andronicus*. A fascinating collection of ancient diaries, writings, and other snippets from an apparently exceptional man of mysterious origin: an explorer, a rumored immortal, possibly a vampire.

Along with the books, I acquired several artifacts, various talismans, an amulet of protection, and useful charms to enhance the magic spells I'd learned.

Europe was a massive help in my understanding and growth, but the best part? I was now a part of something bigger than myself, and I'd gained dear friends that I'd cherish for the rest of my life!

I missed them, although I did love being back in my ramshackle little cabin. But otherwise, being home again was strange. Everything about my hometown looked and felt so vastly different. All the progress and growth of the surrounding towns and cities made them nearly unrecognizable to me! Had I really been away long enough to warrant that many transformations?

It wasn't only the new construction everywhere, the alterations to roads, and most of those trusted businesses now long gone…it was the feeling in the air. Something had shifted—something familiar, and not in a good way!

Europe has a certain air about it. There's this antique kind of energy, especially in cities like Edinburgh, Sibiu, and the French Countryside. There are dark areas, too. Places that seem to reek—in an energy sense, rather than olfactory—of death. And now, certain parts of my hometown, especially downtown, felt unnervingly and worryingly familiar to my hunter senses.

Soon, I discovered why.

Restless, one night, I decided to walk the downtown streets and do a little scouting around. Yes, that's right. It was nighttime, and I was out hunting. Since getting inked, acquiring all that magical knowledge, and battling old Erskine, I had truly become fearless. I was far less concerned about running out of daylight now, especially when offing those weak little "baby" vamps.

I was not out on a whim, I was actually following a lead that I'd spotted in the local news. It was flimsy at best, yet just odd enough to attract my attention: rumors of kids acting out as "genuine" vampires, gathering at nightclubs downtown. This would not concern me, on the face of it, but there were also reports of blood loss and potential killings. I hadn't hunted for weeks, and I was most definitely jonesing for a slay.

If I should find a vamp this night, I'd be more than ready to scratch that proverbial hunter itch.

A small string of nightclubs, all owned by the same person, appeared to be attached to those reports. They had all sprung up in the heart of downtown just when the rumors began to circulate. So I followed my instincts and took a stroll by one of them, Club Netherworld.

Then, I sensed it: the heavy black taint of the undead!

Damn, I loved it when a hunch paid off!

Lined up at the door, waiting to enter, were a menagerie of goth kids and a few adults barely hanging on to their youth. All decked out in their black clothes, leather, and lace, faces paled out, some as white as the full moon that hung like a ghost in the velvety night sky.

Dressed as I was, my typical getup, tight black tee, tapered, fitted black pants, boots to my knee, and, since it was cold out, my long black coat and signature black cowboy hat, wide brim curled into the shape of a tricorn, Al Jourgensen style… Well, I certainly fit right in with that overdressed bunch.

Several of the ladies ogled me, which didn't surprise me, seeing as I looked so much a part of their dark little gang.

I never left home without some kind of weapon on me. Dressed as I was, it was easy to hide them, and as the crowd slowly entered the thumping building, I noticed that no one seemed interested in checking bags and coats at the door for any nefarious belongings.

So, the best way to scope out that vampy vibe was to pop in and have a look around.

I slipped in line behind a group of barely-covered females. They wore what looked like bondage gear, the tallest one topless, with only tape over her nipples. She wore a leather jacket to cover herself until crossing the threshold, throwing it off behind the counter immediately and thanking the employees for holding it for her. They were friendly enough, these goth kids, as they smiled and greeted me, the new guy, with great interest.

I simply nodded at them with just enough cordiality not to appear too rude. Luckily, they weren't pushy with me—typical goths.

Stepping in, a tall, striking woman cut her dark eyes up at me. Her skin was a milky brown, obviously once a rich chocolate. The faint burn of my tattoos told me this girl was a recent vampire. I'd been hunting long enough now that I was unfazed by that fact, and I let on nothing as I smirked at her.

135

"No cover, right?" I asked knowingly.

"No, sir."

Her eyes were just beginning to show that pinprick of red that I also knew to look for. They couldn't hide it without wearing something to cover their eyes.

"We make our money on our drinks." She added.

"I'm sure you do." I knew the "no cover" thing was used to lure as many humans as possible into the establishment. This was a feeding place, perfectly disguised behind the goth lifestyle. Vamps could take a little here, a little there, without anyone thinking a thing of it. But they were slipping up, kids landing in the emergency room with low blood counts, some dying, just enough to alert a hunter like me.

To go barging into a place like this, "guns a-blazing," was not smart, obviously. Hunts like this were tricky. Dealing with vamps deeply integrated within society, mixing intimately into mortal social circles, about all I could do was stake them out, track them to where they sleep, and take them out the same way I always did. At least it would be easy compared to battling the old Scott!

But did I really want "easy?" No, I didn't.

I was missing Europe, something fierce!

The music soared around me as I made my way to the bar, causing the floor and every cell in my body to vibrate—god, they played it loud in that place. Music wasn't bad; sounded okay. I'd heard goth music before, couldn't criticize it, but I'd have preferred to listen to it down a few decibels.

Ordering a drink, nothing too strong—had to keep my wits about me—I turned and let my eyes scan the growing crowd of dancers and minglers. A few attractive girls, lots of dolled-up boys, a…

My heart stopped!

Eyes bugged.

I nearly dropped my glass!

There she was! Romayne Pierson!

I hadn't seen her, not properly…not this close…in what? Nearly two decades? Sixteen damned years, and she looked exactly the same like she stepped right out of my dreams!

My heart went from calm to frantic fluttering, and I felt perspiration bloom on my neck and forehead. How could she look so good after so long?

I say she looked the same, but honestly, she looked even better than the last time I saw her—those chestnut curls piled atop her head as if she stepped right out of the nineteenth century. She wore a corset of deep purple with black lace that seemed to tickle the mounds of her milky-white breasts. Her tiny waist was cinched in, making the curve of her swaying hips utterly mesmerizing. A cameo choker of violet and black lace hugged her smooth, pale neck.

I was mesmerized!

But her face…God, that wonderful face that stole my heart so many years ago, it trapped that very same straining muscle all over again: big, wide, hazel eyes, lightly outlined in smoky gray, unlike the heavy makeup most of the girls there, porcelain cheeks with their gentle curve, so soft, so enticing, I wanted to kiss them, both of them, in that European fashion. And her lips, delicate and perfectly bowed, made my mouth water.

I was on my feet and striding toward her before I knew what the hell I was doing.

She wasn't looking my way at first, but as I drew nearer as if summoned by my fevered approach, she turned to me, and instantly, I was back in that young, blundering boy's body. I tripped over my own damned feet and was only saved by a man that had stepped right into my path in passing. I ran right into the guy, which halted my fall. Then, I apologized, growling at myself internally for being the bungling idiot I was. Gathering myself, looking up, I started.

She was right there, standing directly in front of me.

"Spencer?!" she gasped, her eyes wide, bright, so beautiful I wanted to cry. I forgot to breathe. "Oh. My. God!" Her sweet face beamed, "I barely recognized you! You're…you're huge!" Her laugh was like music as her arms flew around my waist.

I held her firmly to me, feeling like a moron as my eyes burned. Shit! Was I on the verge of fucking tears? I swallowed hard and pushed them back before making an even bigger idiot of myself.

"I have grown a few inches," I chuckled, refraining from nuzzling her hair. She was so tiny next to me, I'd have had to bend down quite a bit to do so.

She stepped back and took me in with those luminous eyes. I had to look away. She was just too lovely. My heart couldn't take it.

"Damn, boy! You're handsome, too!" She grinned, nudging me teasingly, like a sister ribbing her little brother.

I shrugged, found my eyes rested on her bosom, then quickly looked at the floor. "You don't look any different, Rayn. Gorgeous as always."

Suddenly, I was jolted from our joyful reunion by a presence that struck me like a freight train.

It made my tats burn like sparking tinder.

Glancing around in alarm, I spotted him almost immediately—a full-fledged and potentially quite old vampire. I could pick them out in any crowd now, after what I'd experienced overseas, not only due to my wards but because they reeked of particularly dark essence, and this one wore it like Dracula wore his cape. He threw that force around like magic, like a lure, the Pied Piper tempting his flock, and the adoration from the crowd surrounding him as he slowly traversed the space was just as palpable.

My "necklace" of strange runes, tattooed in a wide arc around the base of my neck, had flared up like a brand—a physical sensation, nothing anyone could see—and I lifted a hand to touch my burning skin. Several of my other tattoos were reacting as well, protections warning me of this unexpectedly powerful vampire's proximity.

Then I recalled my single, completely sentimental tattoo. The letters "R-A-Y-N" tattooed on the inside of my wrist, just below the palm of my right hand. Romayne's signature, taken from a note she'd given me during our school days. Thank god that one was hidden beneath the fingerless leather gloves I wore. It wouldn't have been good for her to spot *that* one!

"Hey, you okay?" Rayn's voice yanked me out of my shock. I turned to look back at her, my heart skipping a beat again as our eyes met.

"Y-yeah, fine."

Good god! My precious Rayn was right here in the lair of the vampire! I'd utterly forgotten where the hell I was, distracted by seeing her again, by the sudden reaction of my wards. Shit! I had to get her out of there! Warn her! Protect her!

My inked skin burned harder, making me look up again to search for the vamp.

I nearly leaped out of my skin to find him striding right up to us. Then, as if going from dream to dreaded nightmare, Rayn greeted the vamp warmly, like a close friend, and they embraced!

No! I screamed inwardly. *Nonononono!!!*

But what happened next sent my head and my heart into a tailspin. They *kissed!*

Mouth to mouth, the filthy beast pressed his filthy lips to hers. It was short, due to my presence, or perhaps being in public in general, but it was intimate, and my heart plummeted right into my fucking boots! What the bloody hell had my Rayn gotten herself into while I was away?!

Oh yes, I was *burning* with mad jealousy as fiercely as those wards burned my flesh!

138

My mind shot back to high school, to those times when Rayn had a boyfriend, and I caught them walking the halls together between classes or happened upon them (only twice) kissing.

But *this*! This was so much worse! So drastically different and so utterly horrifying that I lost all capacity to think clearly. All those years of honing my mind...schooling my self-control, it all fell away like so much ash. Fedelma would have been so disappointed in me!

Growling, my fingers curled into fists, clenched so tightly that I felt nails digging into my palms; I stared at the vamp with pure, unfiltered malice. It took all of my strength not to rush him right then and there, scythe in hand, ready to part his head from his scrawny neck!

The fucking blood sucker's eyes, black as night, turned up to meet mine and locked onto me like a fish on a hook. His irises were utterly black. I saw no red in his pupils, but I was unmoved by this because I could tell the thing was wearing contact lenses that hid that sure sign of his true nature.

Don't doubt for a second that this thing knew precisely how I felt. I attempted to rein myself in, to blank out my mind and control my body, but I was having a devil of a time doing it. My rage and distress were written all over me, not only on my face but every curve, every angle of my body language spoke to my soaring emotions.

"Spence, what's wrong?" Rayn's sweet voice struggled to reach me through that sea of desperation. The most important person in that crowded room had essentially vanished for me until I heard her speak again, rising into my perception like a distant birdcall. I blinked and turned my gaze down to her, but I had no idea what to say. My thoughts were in turmoil!

"Aurel," she turned back to the beast, that handsome, horrid beast with his long, blonde hair, unnaturally fair skin, and eyes black as night. She hesitated slightly, seeing my obvious disdain, her hand resting on his heartless chest, "This is an old friend of mine. I need to speak to him for a moment alone, okay?"

"Of course, love," fucking Aurel replied with sickening cordiality. He was a foreigner, which was clear from his accent. And the name, Aurel, sounded Eastern European to me. But his features and that nearly white, blonde hair appeared distinctly Scandinavian. He nodded at me stiffly before bending down to her again, his ebony gaze locked onto mine in clear challenge as he pressed his awful lips to hers, then he turned and sauntered away.

Rayn rounded on me then, her expression brimming with confusion and teetering on anger. "What's wrong with you, Spencer? We haven't seen each other in forever, and you're acting—"

"Jealous?" I blurted out, feeling my own mix of anger, hurt, desperation...

She shook her lovely head, and all I wanted to do was take her into my arms and hold her! No, not *all* I wanted to do; I wanted to grab her and drag her pretty little ass right out of that place, away from that damned, fucking shithead, Aurel!

With a huff, Rayn snagged me by the bend in my elbow and dragged me toward the exit, "C'mon. Let's get caught up and have a little talk." Her tone was scolding, and I felt like a child about to get a whippin'.

YES! I thought gleefully, warily...let's get the H-E-double-toothpicks out of this fucking place and away from *him*!

Outside, to the left of the entrance, was a seating area where people gathered to talk and smoke. No seats were available, so she led me to a spot further down the sidewalk.

But that wasn't good enough for me.

"Come with me, Rayn," I took her hand in mine...realizing it was the first time I'd held hands with her, my heart accelerating, emotions colliding between being with her again and the circumstances we were in. "We need to leave here...*now*. There's a lot I need to tell you, Rayn, and I...I'd prefer to do it as far from this place *(from your fucking vampire boyfriend)* as possible."

But she planted her feet right there on the concrete and refused to move, shaking her precious head at me, "I'm not leaving. I'm here with friends and look, Spence, we've known each other a long time, you and me, but it's been years since we've interacted. I knew you once, but this...the way you're acting, I'm not so sure I know you at all anymore."

My heart shattered, "You *do* know me, Rayn. *Me!*" I pressed my palm to my heart in earnest, "The *real* me is in here, always the same, even if life has changed me on the outside, even if I've been altered due to..."

Her eyes regarded me intensely as if she were trying her damndest to figure me out.

But there was no way she could understand me...without my telling her...telling her *everything*...

"Can you tell me something, Spence?" She echoed my thoughts, folded her arms across her chest, and sharpened her gaze, "Tell me why you're jealous of Aurel, a man you've never met after not seeing or speaking to me in *years*! I didn't even get the chance to introduce you two before you turned into Bruce Banner on the verge of hulking out."

I laughed, momentarily disarmed by her reference, "Nice one," but my voice was flat, serious: "Rayn, he's *dangerous*."

140

"Dangerous?! What?"

I nodded, determined to say something to convince her, but what could I say without seeming like a complete madman?

"Spencer Vale, you…" Then she paused, studying me, perhaps seeing the intensity in my eyes, the utter conviction in my stare. "Alright, I want you to tell me why you think Aurel is dangerous. I can see this is important to you, and I'm not going to discount what you say without a full understanding."

Smiling, relieved, yet trembling over the importance of this opportunity, I attempted to gather my thoughts. How much could I tell her, and how could I tell her such incredible things, even if I kept it to the barest of basics, without losing her confidence forever?

"Okay…" I took a deep breath and, well, I tried…

"Rayn, after my family, well, you know…" Instantly, her face softened as if remembering my tragedy. But I held up a hand and gave her a wan smile to tell her I wasn't upset with her for being upset with me, then I continued, "My life took a path that I have no doubt would shock you. No, I'm not going to go into all that right now. But what you must understand, what you *must* believe, is that I *know* what I'm talking about. Look, I am not going to stand here and ask you to simply trust me. But please, *please* trust me.

"No," I shook my head; I'd never found organizing my thoughts to be this difficult before. "Actually, I *do* beg you to simply trust me because I am not being flippant or manipulative or…or jealous when I say to you that Aurel is an extremely… dangerous…man!"

Even before I ended my tirade, Rayn was shaking her head in vehement denial, "I can't believe that. Aurel has been wonderful to me —"

"Oh, I'm suuure he's been sublime!" I harrumphed. Not controlling my disgust at all. How could I, after all I'd seen and done? "Manipulators are not unkind to the manipulated."

I regretted that adjunct the moment it passed my lips.

Rayn gasped, which, I admit, from her limited understanding, should have been totally expected. "Manipulated!" She exclaimed, "What the hell is that supposed to mean? I'm not being manipulated by Aurel!"

"I'm sorry," I tried to salvage the exchange, though I was not sorry for speaking facts, only for upsetting her. "Look, I…" My eyes burned. I was beginning to panic. How could I convince her? How could I make her trust *me* over *him*? And how far had he gotten with her? I didn't see any bite marks on her neck, but there were other places he might have drunk from.

141

That thought made me feel even sicker.

"Will you tell me why you feel this way?" She urged.

I could tell she was trying to hear me out, and my heart took courage from that.

"Do you know something about Aurel's past?" She continued, "Do you two *know* each other?"

"In a way, yes—" but that was a lie, literally, not figuratively.

"In a way? Speak plainly, man!" She half-joked in a fake British accent.

Her humor was like that: a little unusual, always quirky, with a flare for the dramatic in the most unlikely of circumstances. I gave her a wilting smile. "I know his *kind*, Rayn."

"What *kind?* Goth?" She shrugged in annoyance.

"Vampire." It burst out of my mouth before I could stop it.

"Yeah?" She shrugged again with a 'so what?' attitude.

"Yeah!" I shot back determinedly. "I'm not kidding, Rayn! He is a vampire."

We stared at one another for a long, tense, silent moment. Then she tilted her perfect head at me and cocked an eyebrow. I wanted to smash my lips to hers and confess my soul.

"You're serious." She gasped.

"I am. Dead. Fucking. Serious. *Un*dead! Fucking! serious!" I demanded. Sure, vamps aren't actually undead, but the reference strengthened my argument.

It seemed, for a moment, that the wheels in her mind were turning, fervently attempting to make sense of this bizarre revelation. Perhaps, I fancied, she recalled odd things about Aurel that she'd witnessed. Instances that struck her now, suddenly, as being vampire-like. Well, I could not read her mind, of course, so it was only a guess. But any hope I had of convincing her was shattered when she laughed at me. It wasn't a cruel laugh, just a laugh of incredulity and complete dismissal.

"Aurel may love playing the part of a vampire. Heck, don't all Goths? It's Goth pinnacle, after all. But Spence, Aurel is just a very pretty guy that owns a club and enjoys spooky crap and great music. He's kind and clever and talented. You should see his art; it's incredible!"

"I don't give a fucking shit about his art! He probably stole it and claims it as his own—" Typical vampire. They lived on theft: money, homes, valuables, and, of course, life.

"Spence!" She slapped my arm, "It's *his* art! I've watched him paint for hours at a time!"

"Fine, he's a fucking talented vampire that paints. But he's a *real* vampire, and he *will* kill you, Rayn!"

A distracted glance over my shoulder made me turn and follow her line of sight, unsurprised to find the devil himself striding up to us.

"You've been gone for a while; I thought I'd check on you." He smiled at her as he shot a harsh glance at me.

That little exchange between the two of us males was not lost on her, and she rolled her eyes dramatically.

"Boys, boys, you're both pretty!" She teased, "I won't put up with these testosterone-filled challenging looks between you two."

The blasphemous couple was arm-in-arm now, the vampire placing a slow and determined kiss on Rayn's forehead, making the pain and rage in my heart surge like a hurricane, but I did my best to tamp it down, at least outwardly. Still, the beast saw it and looked infuriatingly pleased with himself for riling me up.

He couldn't know what I was, but if he did feed on her, then he'd learn what I'd said from her blood. I felt my heart clench at the thought that if he hadn't already drunk from her, he might be more curious now. Had I hastened her demise?

Shit and damnation!

God, did I relish the day I'd slice that "pretty" head right off his "pretty" shoulders and send his sorry, sickening ass right to hell!

"Look!" Rayn sighed, halting my raging thoughts, her arm around his waist, her other hand reaching to take hold of my arm. She looked at me, into my eyes, as she addressed him, "Aurel, this is Spencer Vale. He's a very old friend from school that I haven't seen in a long time. Despite his attitude tonight, he is kind, funny, and a bit out of his mind, but he *is* a good man."

She then turned her eyes to the vamp bastard, and his hungry gaze locked onto her, making me crazy with fury and anxiety as she addressed me.

"Spencer, this is Aurel Lonescu, my boyfriend, an amazing artist, savvy club owner, loving, friendly, and the most powerful vampire in the city!" She *joked*.

Lonescu was an old Romanian name. Where'd he get that blond hair from?

I saw him start, ever so slightly, at her vampire declaration. The tongue-in-cheek way she turned to me when speaking those words made him scrutinize me more closely. I did not hold back when my eyes snagged his in a clear, threatening challenge.

Don't you doubt it, you bastard, blood-sucking menace! I'll end you!

That's what my eyes relayed, and I could tell he got the message loud and clear because the look I got in response was pure, unfiltered hatred. It was then I regretted letting him see those thoughts because she was locked firmly in his accursed arm as I stood there like a complete moron, feeling helpless and hopeless.

"Come, my dear," he gently coaxed Rayn away, shooting one last burning glare at me, "I'd like to go back inside now."

"Okay," she readily agreed. And just as distant thunder rolled and drops of rain began to fall from the sky, she turned to look back at me with a forced smile. "It was nice seeing you again, Spencer." But the look in her eyes said differently. I had scared her, and not in the way I'd wanted to—I had made her scared...of *me*!

XV

ONCE BITTEN

There was no way I was going to leave this alone. My mission now was to save and protect Romayne Pierson from goddamn Aurel Lonescu! So, I hung out in the shadows outside that club until Rayn and the bastard left, then I followed them. But that damned vamp was clever. I knew that *he* knew I was there. He had caught my scent, so to speak. Sneaking up on him, at night anyway, would be impossible now.

He might not know, yet, the truths of precisely *who* I was, or what I do, or how many of his kind I'd sent to Hell, but he would find that out soon enough because I'd show him the hunter firsthand, and take his head while I was at it!

For now, he knew I was tailing them, and damn it to all hell; I lost him only a few blocks from his stinking club. The sudden thunderstorm hadn't helped, either. It had lasted into the night and hindered my ability to keep them in sight. I searched the area for a bit, driving the streets, checking nearby neighborhoods for his car or any sign of them, hoping my wards might alert me, but found nothing.

Would he have taken Rayn back to his lair? Would he be with her at her place if he took her home? Goddamnit, the thought of them together tore a hole in me I could barely fathom. It felt like myriad knives slicing my heart and soul into carpaccio.

But I had to get ahold of myself, so that's what I did. I drew in a deep breath and let it out slowly, calling up my hunter training, which had fled me this very evening after what I'd seen and discovered.

Shit, for me to lose it so badly and so easily after years of training and practice! Get it fucking together, Spence!

145

Alright, I centered my thoughts. Should I go to Rayn's house, in case that's where they went?

Rayn lived not too far from my parent's old place, in the same house she grew up in and apparently inherited from her parents, who had passed away during the years I'd been gone. Being an only child, there were no other contenders for the property.

Like I said, I always kept tabs on Romayne; that's how I know this stuff. No, I didn't know everything about her. Just things I'd heard here and there when I was in town.

Before running into her at the club, every time I was home, I'd wanted so badly to approach her, but I refrained. Fought with myself constantly over how to do it and what to say to her, always talking myself out of it for an endless list of reasons, the greatest of which was protecting her from me and my lifestyle. Protecting her and not making an utter fool out of myself in front of her. What she thinks of me is now...?

At least now, hiding my vampire-centric life was a non-issue—cat was out of the bag, for better or worse.

Going to her place was all I had left to do since I'd lost them, so I staked the place out for the remainder of that night, through the next day, and into the following evening. I was feeling a bit bleary but so caught up in my purpose that I hardly noticed it.

No one arrived as I watched. Her car was there the entire time since he'd driven them, and apparently, she hadn't needed to go anywhere.

But I could tell she was home because I saw the lights in her windows go on and off. It seemed the vampire had brought her straight home after the club and dropped her off while I was searching for them. I'd lost precious time, damn it!

Was he in there with her?

I felt sick.

But no, he wouldn't stay with her unless...shit, I hoped he wasn't in there! If he were, that would mean...

More deep breaths to steady myself.

At about six p.m., I was on the verge of rising from the curb, where I sat across the street, to knock on her door. But just then, Rayn emerged. My heart leaped into my throat, and all of the tiredness fled me in an instant.

She wore casual clothing: a teal, fitted tank top with a scarf around her neck—warning bells—and gray sweatpants. She carried her purse and wore black cat's eye sunglasses, odd for the evening with the sun sinking away. This prompted a louder jangling of my already heightened nerves.

Judging by her body language, she appeared tired as she turned to face me and jolted upon seeing me rise to my feet.

The weather fluctuated constantly like it didn't know what to do with itself. While the nights were chilly, the days were warm. It was dropping again as the sun began its descent, so I had slipped on my long leather jacket and plopped my hat on my head. My Dundee knife was tucked in the back of my pants, under my shirt, always prepared!

On my person, I wore sparse jewelry: one of my protective talisman necklaces, Charm of Ftorthin, bracelets containing Irouquat Stones, particularly good for warding off negative energies. I also had a gift for Rayn, which I prayed she'd accept from me.

It was the necklace, given to me by Clan's son Iza, with the strange Sohrakia symbol carved out of bone and embedded inside a plain locket. That runic shape looked a bit like the letter "T" with an "S" lying horizontally across the T's vertical stalk.

The thing repelled vampires; that was all I cared about.

The two of us came together on the sidewalk in front of her house just as it began to sprinkle. She grumbled as she eyed me warily through those dark shades. Made my heart sink to receive such a reception.

"Spencer, what the hell are you doing here? *Please* don't tell me you're stalking me!" She was exasperated, and I was distraught.

"I'm *not* stalking you, Rayn. I'm looking out for you." God, I didn't want her to see me as some crazy stalker! But that's precisely what her eyes held for me.

Shit!

Her face seemed worried, tired. "Are you okay?" I asked softly, feeling my concerns grow the more I looked at her sallow complexion. I knew that look all too well: that drawn-out, fatigued countenance.

"I'm just fine, Spencer." Her tone was clipped, yet not mean, just a bit annoyed. At least, that was how she sounded to me, like she was trying to be civil and not hurt my feelings. She turned away then and stalked back up the drive toward her car.

Tenaciously, I strode along right beside her, glad the rain was so light it was barely noticeable.

"Where are you going?" I couldn't keep the suspicious tone out of my voice.

"To the corner store," she ground out, "I need a few things."

"It's almost dark—"

"Yeah," she cut me off with a huff. "I realize that."

147

Ignoring her terseness and the lump in my throat, I took hold of her arm just as she arrived at her car door, and she reluctantly turned to face me.

Knowingly, I asked, "Did you sleep all day?" For some reason, in my state of concern and frustration, I suddenly felt the urge to challenge and push her. I was annoyed by her abruptness with me when all I wanted was her wellbeing.

She shrugged and gently pulled her arm out of my grasp. "I sat around and watched TV all day, happy?"

I was not happy. Far from it. "Why didn't you go to the store *earlier* today?"

"I was tired and didn't want to go. It doesn't matter when I decide to go to the store, Spencer."

"It's not safe after dark, Rayn!" I reached over and yanked the scarf away from her neck.

"Hey!" She exclaimed, grabbing for it as I held it too high for her to reach. Easy, being freakishly tall as I am. I peered at her neck.

My skin prickled, and heart plummeted to find bite marks just below the curve of her jawline. Right in her jugular!

"Aha!" I exclaimed as my heart raced, and I felt a little nauseous, "He bit you!" My voice was a growl filled with anger at fucking Aurel and brimming with distress.

"Yeah, so what if he did," she growled right back at me, and I felt my heart quiver. It was all I could do not to crush my lips to hers!

But her reaction floored me! So what if he bit her? I gaped at her in disbelief. "He *drank your blood*, Romayne!"

But she only laughed. *Laughed!* What the hell?

"No, Spencer, he did not drink my blood!" She was incredulous.
I was flabbergasted.

"Have you never heard of a love bite?" She almost laughed.
Love bite?

"That's no love bite!" I gritted my teeth as I thrust my hand into my pocket and pulled out the gift I had for her. Her eyes widened as if expecting I'd draw out some kind of weapon. Oh, if she only knew, I'd never hurt a hair on her head.

I opened my palm to reveal that mysterious necklace. To her, it was just a plain, silver locket on a chain.

"What's that?" She crossed her arms, her expression a mixture of trepidation and curiosity.

"It's a gift…for you." I reached forward and placed the palm of my hand, cradling that magically imbued charm right up against those bite marks.

148

Immediately, Rayn flinched back, away from the touch of the locket, with a yelp, "Ouch! What the hell?"

"Shit!" I exclaimed, pulling my hand back and placing my other hand on her shoulder to steady her and keep her from leaving me, "I'm sorry I hurt you, Rayn, but I told you so. That is no fucking love bite," I was sneering, barely able to contain my fury, but it wasn't at her, of course; it was the nasty taste of the word 'love' in relation to her bloodsucker boyfriend. I held the necklace out to her then and demanded, "Touch it!" Staring hard into her big, beautiful hazel eyes, my heart strained in my chest.

But she hesitated to do as I asked, and honestly, I couldn't blame her.

Oh, how insane I must have seemed to her. My heart was breaking.

"Touch it!" I insisted, swallowing my emotions and shoving the necklace toward her again. "Please, Rayn!"

Irritably, she complied, but when her fingers gingerly brushed the charm, she didn't react, and I breathed a deep sigh of relief. "That must have been the first time he drank from you."

"This is ridiculous!" She huffed, but I could see a twinge of fear in her eyes—the beginnings of conflict in her expression. Was she starting to believe me? To doubt bloody Aurel?

I took heart.

"It must be the first time he bit you because while touching this to his bite, it stung you, but touching it with your fingers did not. Right?"

She nodded.

"Do you understand?"

She shook her head, "No. Of course, I don't understand! I don't understand any of it. Look, Spencer, I'm trying to be patient and compassionate with you. You've been through a lot; I get it, and my heart goes out to you, it does. But suddenly, you show up out of nowhere and presume to order me around, ask me 'twenty questions,' and blame my gothic boyfriend of being a *real* vampire? Do you know how insane that sounds?"

"Yes," I replied flatly, then I sighed and took her shoulders, the necklace hanging off my right wrist. "But I've seen things—"

"you people wouldn't believe..." She cut me off and smiled warily.

Rayn could never help quoting from movies or songs, especially when she wanted to lighten the mood.

I sighed, "...Attack ships on fire off the shoulder of Orion..." Then, I gave her a sad, pleading smile, wanting so badly to take her into my arms and confess my undying love for her.

"I'm sorry." Releasing my hold on her, I dropped my arms, gathered the necklace into my hand, and stared at my closed fist. I had to get her to accept it from me, somehow.

Gently, she took hold of both of my fisted hands, brought them together, cradled them in her own, and gazed up at me with feeling, "I know you believe this vampire stuff, but—"

I cut *her* off, "I believe it because I *live* it." Then I thought better of elaborating, not yet. She was not ready to hear my truth, to really believe it, but I had to at least get her to take and wear that necklace if I had any chance of protecting her. As much as I wanted to, I couldn't be with her 24/7, so this was my best chance until I could end Aurel.

"Will you take it? Wear it? Even if you don't believe me? I mean, it's just a necklace, right?"

She regarded me then with a look of defeat and a warmth that, again, gave me a spark of hope.

"Alright," she sighed heavily.

I let her take the charm from my hand and examine it. Her brow creased as she ran a finger over the deceptively simple locket and unusual chain, "It's odd."

"It's very old."

"There's no clasp." Mystified, she pulled the chain through her fingers, searching for some way to open it.

"There's a trick to it." The chain was magical and could only be unclasped via a particular spell, but I didn't tell her that. "Here, let me," I held my hand out to take it from her, and she placed it in my palm again.

I mumbled the words to that spell under my breath, and the chain came apart. Then, I draped it around her neck and allowed the closure to fasten on its own.

There was no way she didn't hear my weird mumbling, but I played it off like nothing happened.

"There." I smiled at her, so pleased that she wore it and that she would be unable to remove it without me.

Warily, she gave me an intense glare, her fingers gingerly touching the charm, eyes narrowed, brow furrowed.

I laughed as disarmingly as I could, "It's okay. It's just a spell of protection. I'd *never* curse you, Rayn. I…"

Love you…

We stared at one another for a long moment, my nerves calming, her uncertainty plain.

"Can I come with you to the store?" I asked as if nothing odd had just occurred.

"Wow," she shook her head, her voice a faint, astonished gasp. The audacity of me, assuming she'd want me to remain in her presence any longer after all the strangeness.

I simply shrugged.

On the way to the store, I kept my head on a swivel, checking the streets around us, which were mostly clear. I kept catching Rayn serendipitously glancing at me, but I pretended not to notice. Probably scrutinizing the wackjob idiot beside her. Worth it to get her protected, even if it meant she'd hate me forever. I sighed inwardly. We didn't speak a word. I'm sure she was profoundly confused, and I had no idea what I could say to her now. A weight was off my shoulders, at least. But her negative opinion of me was now solidified, and it was killing me.

We stopped at a small convenience store, and since there was only one way in and out of the place, I let her go in and shop on her own. I didn't want to annoy her any more than I already had.

During our short trip back, I finally tried to ease her mind about me, voice trembling as I struggled for words, "Rayn, I...I really am sorry. I can't stand that you think I'm a nut. Honestly, there are real and valid reasons why I gave you that necklace, and please understand, I have first-hand experience with this stuff...as crazy as it sounds."

Her eyes were locked on the road, a good excuse not to have to look at me, I figured.

"I believe that *you* believe it, Spence." She exhaled, her expression filled with pity for her certifiably crazy old schoolmate, "You have suffered an incredible trauma. No one can go through something like that without being affected by it. There's no—"

But I laughed ruefully, "Fine, if that's what it takes for you to humor me. I'll take what I can get. Throw me and my outlandish ideas in a nuthouse and be done with it."

She turned then as we sat at a red light, and when her eyes met mine, and my heart surged, I could swear I saw a spark in her gaze as she stared back at me. Something moved inside me as if I had seen something move inside her. I forgot to breathe...

Then, a car horn jolted us out of that brief connection, and she proceeded through the now-green light.

"Can I take this thing off if I want to?" She asked.

We parked in front of her house; I exited the car, then turned to her over the car's roof as she closed her door. "Nope, and I don't want you removing it, either. You need it since I can't stay with you all the time."

151

The look in her eyes as she stared back at me was inscrutable. It was almost welcoming, considering my comment. Was she about to invite me to stay with her, or was she about to tell me to go the hell away and never come near her again?

"Fine," she barked, then stalked toward her door as I scurried around the car and met her on the sidewalk.

I could see the raging conflict of emotions on her face, the struggle in her eyes. I knew the necklace would protect her to a degree, but vampires are clever, and it was in no way foolproof. As much as it comforted me knowing she had it, still, I was mortified at the idea of leaving her alone.

She stood before me on that quiet evening, so stunning, so helpless to this thing she did not believe in, couldn't possibly understand. And how could I make her understand?

"Please, come home with me," I blurted suddenly. Ridiculous of me, I know, but there it was. My voice broke as I said it, and I hated the weakness of it, how pitiful I sounded when I needed to be strong for her.

In taking *her* blood, that damned thing had literally sucked the blood straight from *my* heart. And this sweet and innocent woman before me, who owned me, heart and soul, and didn't even know it.

"Just give me your mobile number, and I'll call you if anything untoward happens."

"I don't have a mobile phone, or any phone for that matter."

"You don't have a phone? What century are you living in, Spence? You, with your pseudo-pirate-slash-cowboy hat and long black coat? You look like a cross between Al Jourgensen and Neo!"

I laughed; that was pretty spot on. "Nailed it!" I snapped my fingers as if I'd accomplished something, then rolled my eyes. Honestly, I hoped she liked the look and didn't see it as some cheesy attempt to appear cool…which, of course, it was, although it was also practical. Well, the coat with its hidden weapon storage and concealment and the all-black attire was practical. The hat? All for show. I just liked it! I suppose it did obscure my face, though the overall look might attract some attention.

I took her hands into mine and dropped to my knees, my head bowed. God, she was so beautiful I couldn't even look at her. The mere sight of her stripped my brain and stole away my words. But I *needed* to look into her eyes for this, to prove to her my earnestness, to *make* her hear me. But I just couldn't lift my head to do it; I could only stare at the sidewalk as the words poured out of me.

"Rayn, I...you, you mean the world to me. I know I sound mad, a-
and maybe I am, a little. Mad for *you*, a lot! But I know what I'm talking
about, as bonkers as it seems. God, Rayn, if *anything*...if he turns you...
kills you, I-I couldn't go on! Not if you...not if... Because I...I..."
Why did I hesitate to say it?

Damn it all, just *say it*!

"Spence, please look at me."

Her tender voice flowed to me like a cool summer breeze, easing
the heat of my emotions. But could I lift my head and look at her?
God, I wanted to. I held tightly to her delicate hands, my fingers
moving constantly, rubbing, pressing, caressing her soft flesh.

Attempting to gather my wits, my weak heart rushed as I slowly
turned my head up, and my gaze locked with hers. Those bright hazel
eyes staring, the gentle arch of her brows etched with concern, even
warmth. I sank before her heedless power again, inside rather than out.
She wanted me to look at her as I spoke, so I was determined not to
shirk any longer. But to conjure words seemed impossible after locking
eyes with her. My tongue was snagged by the fierce anguish of my heat.

As we stared, I felt my eyes burn.

Shit, was I about to cry?

Maybe I should cry! Ladies loved tears, right? And mine would be
pure and genuine...maybe they would finally convince her.

"Rayn..."

My voice choked. I felt my lips quiver, so I pressed them together
tightly, setting my jaw, determined not to look any *more* the fool in front
of her. I thought I'd, maybe, regained some measure of control over
myself, but I was an idiot.

Then I felt it: a cool line of moisture cleaving a slow path down my
cheek.

Her arms were thrown around my neck in an instant, her heat, her
scent of vanilla and jasmine engulfing me, and I clung to her as my
heart raved and my mind lost its focus entirely. All I could think of was
the years of loving her and how I had longed to hold her against me,
just like this.

"Don't cry, Spence," she whispered in my ear, "I know you've been
through traumas I can't possibly understand; losing your family like
that, god, I can't even..."

I was too choked up to speak at first, and I couldn't bring myself to
release her, not that she made any attempt to pull away. I buried my
face in her hair and finally said, "My family was killed...by a vampire."

At this point, I don't think this surprised her. Surely, after all my raving and emotions, she must have figured that's what happened…or what I *believed* happened.

Her hold loosened, and I felt her pulling back, so I released the embrace and scrubbed my eyes with the back of my hand. Again, I couldn't look at her, embarrassed and overcome by her sweet, pretty face, I had to look away. It wasn't difficult to avoid her as I stood up, towering over her with my unnatural height.

Finally, she touched my hand, and I looked down at her upturned face. "Spence, I cannot come home with you, okay?" There was such pain in her expression…and that other emotion…pity.

I knew then that she wouldn't be swayed by my tears, as pure as they were.

"Have a good night, Spencer, and please take care of yourself." She then headed for her door.

I watched her as she entered her house, gave me a smile filled with forbearance, then closed the door behind her.

My shoulders dropped as I exhaled and shut my eyes. The rain finally began to come down heavier, as if in response to my troubled emotions. I accepted both my success and my defeat as I headed for my car. I needed a shower and some sleep. Before pulling away, I left a ward on her house as an extra measure. Whatever happened next, fucking Aurel would not find drinking from her to be so easy, at least not while that necklace graced her delicate neck.

The next move would be to find and end his miserable hide and continue to monitor and protect Rayn. I would have to keep out of her path, though. As sweet as she was, I didn't want her getting a restraining order against me for stalking.

All hope that maybe, someday, somehow, she'd learn to love me was dashed. But before I could allow myself to sink into despair, I had to hold it together to keep her safe!

XVI
REAL

I had a TV and a couple of players, VHS, DVD, but no cable. I also had no phone. Why have cable and a phone with what I do? Better to "not exist" in my line of work. If I needed to call someone, I could drive up to the little town, to a motel or corner store, and use theirs, which I rarely did. I pay for everything in cash, no credit cards or loans. Keep it simple and untraceable. Vamps are clever, but none have discovered me yet, and I plan to keep it that way.

After cleaning up and snatching a little nap, I spent the afternoon hunting for the bloodsucker, which was proving harder than I'd anticipated. Seemed he was as good as I was at keeping himself hidden from society. No luck with that, so as darkness approached, I was off again to watch over Rayn. Despite the wards I'd left with her, I just couldn't help myself.

Would Rayn be seeing Aurel so soon? Maybe…maybe not. I couldn't take any chances. I didn't want her to deal with him alone, even wearing that necklace.

When I pulled up, her car was there, right where we left it.

Good.

A gentle knock on her door, and I inhaled deeply, letting it out slowly, as I tried to get my pulse to chill out.

"Spence," she peered out at me through a narrow opening with a faint smile, which sent a surge of relief through me.

"Come on in," she sighed, exasperated, and moved aside as I stepped in.

It was a small, quaint little bungalow, probably built in the fifties. The place and Rayn's petite little body made my giantness stand out that much more. I felt like a bull in a china shop; had to be careful about my surroundings, or I'd knock this or that knickknack over. The ceilings were low, too, but plenty tall enough for me, yet still, I ducked my head a little as I followed her into the living room from the entryway.

"I should have expected you back so soon. But I figured after giving me this oh-so-special, *protective* necklace that I can't take off, you might not feel the need to watch over me anymore."

Rayn said all this as we moved into the center of the living room, then she turned to face me, fingering the charm around her neck.

I went straight to business, "Are you seeing Aurel tonight?"

"Maybe."

She'd expected me to ask that, obviously.

We stared at one another. Her hazel eyes were wide, their centers moving over my face with interest, as if she were truly looking at me for the first time since we were kids. I cut my eyes away, self-conscious at the intense scrutiny. I checked out the room instead, taking note of her eclectic taste in goth decor with smatterings of colorful antiques and strange items representing Egypt, Asia, and Greco-Roman cultures. When I looked back at her, she was smiling at me, and my heart lurched into my throat.

"Yes," she finally answered me, "I will be seeing Aurel tonight. We have a date at his place."

I felt a thrill to have a lead to his lair, but my heart sank; she said it so casually, just a date...with a damned vampire! Well, sure, they *were* dating, and he had bitten her...a fucking "love bite"... but had they...?

I felt suddenly ill at the thought she might have slept with that creature!

But I wasn't going to ask about *that*.

"Tell me, is it the first time he bit you?" I gestured to her neck, those bite marks she hadn't bothered to cover.

She nodded.

"First and only '*love* bite,' that's good!" I scowled.

"What's Aurel going to make of this, I wonder?" She lifted the charm, swung it like a pendulum, watching me with interest.

"He won't like it, that's for sure." My face remained locked in that show of disapproval. "I want to follow you tonight. Watch over you, just in case."

She frowned then but didn't immediately respond; just gazed at me with that burning look I couldn't quite decipher.

"Okay," she finally said a bit hesitantly, as if she wasn't too sure about that decision. Still, her acquiescence buoyed me up, and my frown turned into a smile of relief. I felt the need to ease her mind.

"Look, I've done this surveillance thing countless times. I'm very stealthy, and my wards..." I pulled down the neck of my shirt to show her a hint of my tats, "will make me all but invisible to your vamp boyfriend. He won't have a clue I'm there unless I want him to know."

Rayn's eyes lit up, and all hesitation seemed forgotten in an instant as she moved toward me.

"Can I see them? Your tattoos! I never thought of you as a tattoo-type guy!"

She was positively giddy over me being inked. I couldn't help but chuckle at that. I suppose the geeky boy vibes I used to put off wouldn't lead one to believe I'd get tattooed.

Gathering up the hem of my tee, I lifted it to reveal my bare abdomen and chest.

A gasp escaped Rayn's lips, and I watched her gaze roam over me as her cheeks turned soft pink. Suddenly, I felt embarrassed, and my face and neck got hot.

Was she checking me out?

My body *was* well formed now after years of hard work and endless training. There wasn't an ounce of fat on me—I was all muscle if a bit on the pale side.

Her fingers tickled me as she traced them over the runes that snaked around my collarbones like a wide necklace. She then slid them over the inked threads that ran down my lower chest. But she withdrew her hand before reaching my abdomen.

Didn't matter, I was still getting hard, and I dropped my shirt, pulling my long coat closed to hide the bulge in my pants. Hoping she hadn't noticed that!

"They're odd," her eyes cut up to mine, and I could swear she was flirting with me. Her pink cheeks made my heart flutter, "but they're beautiful," she continued. "So the runes make you undetectable?"

I nodded.

"Who did those for you?"

"An old Scottish woman and a real character." Was I imagining it? Surely, she was just toying with me. She always liked to tease me.

"You'll have to tell me all about it, that interesting tattoo artist, what they mean, how they protect you."

Her tone was tinged with a patronizing kind of skepticism—at least, that's how it sounded to me. It was clear that she still struggled to believe me…thought I was a kook…even after touching the necklace to those bite marks and getting that inexplicable reaction.

I didn't respond to her request.

"What time are you meeting him, and where does he live?"

"Nine p.m., and he lives downtown, high-rise apartment, tenth floor."

Well, that was brazen for a vampire, living up in the clouds.

"I assume he'll buzz you in. So you'll have to let me into the building with you."

She nodded, then gave me a stern look, "I'm doing this so you can either prove it all to me or so I can prove you wrong. I don't want you harassing or harming Aurel—"

I cut her off, "He's a vampire, Rayn. I'll do more than harass him; I'll destroy him."

Her hand went to those bite marks, and her frown deepened. She didn't know how to respond to that! I felt I needed to set her mind at ease.

"Not tonight, I promise, unless I have to, okay? If he threatens you —"

She cut me off this time by raising her hand, "He won't threaten me, Spence. He's only ever been good to me."

I felt my jaw tense, "Let me tell you a little story, Rayn. Years ago, my mother got taken in by a phone scammer, telling her she'd won lots of money in some sweepstakes, but the funds couldn't be released until certain fees were paid. Fees that seemed never to end. Dad caught on after she'd already sent three big payments to those crooks. You know what her defense was for those shithead scammers? 'They were so nice to me!' Yeah, like they're not going to drip with sweetness while they're draining your bank account…or your *blood*."

My point was taken as I saw Rayn's expression soften and her shoulders sag.

"You need to be careful," I insisted, "especially careful tonight."

"I will, but how will you be there when I'm shut up in his apartment with him?"

"Don't worry, I'll get in."

Her look was skeptical; she dropped her head and pinched the bridge of her nose.

"Trick of the trade." I winked, but she wasn't amused.

First, I was warded, so the vamp shouldn't sense me, and I was a sneaky bastard so that he wouldn't spot me either. Then, there was my magic. Locks were no barrier for me.

"Just get him away from the entrance in the first five minutes, and I'll slip right in."

"If he sees you, I'll be so embarrassed!"

"That would be the least of your worries."

She sighed, shrugged, and shook her head. Again, I saw the wheels of her mind turning. What was she contemplating? The sheer madness of it all, then how that locket had burned her? A contradiction she couldn't ignore. Then I noticed how she kept scratching her skin beneath the locket. She saw me watching and stopped.

"Yes, it itches. And I can't remove it." Her annoyance was clear.

"I'm sorry, but that just shows you're on a dangerous precipice with him."

Her face softened, seeing my profound concern.

"A real vampire. It's just too much."

"No kidding!" I replied with feeling. If anyone knew that fact, it was me!

I followed her to Aurel's apartment building just as more dark rain clouds gathered over our heads. We drove separately, of course, and I kept back until she reached the door to get buzzed in. It was a swanky place, which was no surprise. I wondered what rich person Aurel had manipulated and killed to steal it or how many he'd sucked dry to get the money to afford it. Certainly, his little nightclubs wouldn't make him enough money to land him there.

The door clicked, and Rayn stepped in; I followed.

After one last wary glance, she set off, completely ignoring me as I followed well behind. Her body language brooked no evidence that anything was different from a normal girl heading to her boyfriend's place for a date. She was relaxed, even peppy in her step. Clearly, she utilized her talents as an actress. I was impressed.

She had already told me his floor, 10, and apartment number, 101. It was a corner suite.

My heart sped up when he opened his door and let her in, not a sign of trepidation on her part, and nothing of suspicion in his…not yet. It wouldn't be long before he noticed that charm she wore, and only God knew how he'd react to it.

Outside, the storm now raged, but the building was so tight you could barely hear the rolling thunder. I put my ear to the door, heard them just inside, listened for silence. I couldn't make out all they said, but my heart was in my throat as I waited—vial in hand, cap removed, poised to move. Finally, quietly, I tipped the oil onto my finger, rubbed it onto the lock mechanism, and whispered the short incantation. There was a quick flash of light, the mild smell of metal and burning, then the lock clinked open. I recapped the vial and stowed it as I carefully slipped inside.

Immediately, I heard them in the adjoining room, so I drew closer, silent as a mouse, and tucked myself into a corner between a tall antique chifforobe and the entrance to the living room.

It was a modern gothic space: clean, crisp lines paired with old-world curves and filigree, lots of black and smatterings of silver, red, and purple. Opulent, yet goth-boy quirky. Two walls were windows, floor to ceiling. Hundreds of paintings filled the two windowless walls and were propped up on the floor. They were good, I had to admit: portraits, still-life images, landscapes, all spooky, quirky, eerie. Shit, I'd have been a fan of his work were he not what he was! Aurel…the "wonderful vampire artist," I scoffed internally.

"A gift from who?" Aurel was asking, his tone controlled and slightly accusatory.

The necklace!

Rayn laughed, "Just a friend. You don't like it?"

No immediate response from him.

My chest was vibrating with anticipation and concern for Rayn. I peered around the corner to watch them. I was deep in shadow where I stood, but if he happened to look my way, no amount of darkness would hide me from vampire eyes. I could have applied a veil of magic to hide myself more effectively, but I didn't bother. I knew how this night would end. Rayn would be safe, and that creature destroyed! But I had to prove what he was to her first so his destruction wouldn't throw a deeper wedge between us.

I hated putting Rayn in this position, but I was confident I could handle it, and there was *no way* I'd let anything happen to her!

"You don't *like* that thing, do you?" He motioned toward the offending piece of jewelry, "It doesn't seem to agree with you." He waved his long, pale fingers, tipped in dark purple nail polish, at her, indicating her pink, irritated skin just beneath the charm.

I watched her face, wondering how she'd respond to that. For an instant, a mere blink of a second, her eyes narrowed, then she relaxed and yanked gently on the chain, "I can't get it off. Can you help me?"

She turned her back to him, lifted her hair, and dropped her head, exposing the chain and the back of her neck to the *vampire*!

Tantalizing, for him and for me, but for wholly different reasons.

He stepped up to her—I readied myself—he gingerly reached for the chain, then paused, "I don't see a clasp."

"Really?" She feigned ignorance. "There has to be one! Can you help me look for it?"

The instant she felt his fingers against her as he touched the chain, she turned the necklace so the charm fell against his hand. It was purposeful but appeared natural, an accident.

Clever girl.

But my muscles were bunched, everything tensed and ready as the vampire hissed and stepped back.

I held my breath.

Rayn turned to him with an innocent, "What's wrong?"

The vampire looked stunned, confused.

"Tell me where you got it!" He barely controlled his…anger?…his panic? "Who gave you that…*thing*?" He hid the burn on the back of his hand beneath the other.

Rayn's mouth hung agape, and she shook her head. "Why, does it m—?"

"It matters." He ground out, "Tell me."

A second of mental deliberation crossed her face before she spoke with resolution, "Spencer gave it to me; the guy—"

"From the club." Aurel *did* growl that time without reservation.

"He told me what you are, Aurel." Her tone was bold, demanding. She stood facing him now, arms crossed, expression set and determined. She was not frightened of the vampire. She was far too comfortable with it for my liking!

"What I am?" Aurel smirked, snickered, did everything but roll his dark eyes.

"He believes you're a vampire… A *real* vampire."

The *vampire* laughed, but Rayn wasn't finished.

"That you're a vampire and that this charm would protect me from you."

Silence fell.

Dead silence.

Then Rayn took steps toward Aurel, and I had to muster every vestige of self-control not to jump out and put myself between them. I watched on, morbidly curious and wracked with worry.

"*Are* you a vampire, Aurel?" She asked, almost seductively.

Was she actually toying with him? Taunting me?

I felt a mad surge of jealousy, but I held back, staring, transfixed, at the unfolding scene.

161

She was no more than a foot from him now, and I was ready to spring.

"Funny," she continued, "if you are a *real* vampire, I can't really say I'm that surprised. I always fancied you a vampire, with your natural, *un*natural pallor, your fangs, which I thought were the work of a dentist, and your last name, Romanian, very rare here in the States. I thought initially you'd made it up to be cool, to sound like you stepped right out of Necroscope or something, but it's real, isn't it?"

Whoa! Rayn read Necroscope?

Quit geeking out, Spence! This is not *the time!* I chided myself.

Aurel stood utterly still before her, his tall, lean frame ramrod straight, head dipped to look down at her upturned face, his long, blonde hair hiding his features like a funeral shroud.

"Real…" his voice was low, musical, like a tragedy. "*Real* fangs. *Real* name."

Rayn's eyes were wide with wonder as his response confirmed everything I'd said.

"Real," she gasped, "and you drank my blood."

His chuckle was guttural, wanton, hungry, "*Real* blood."

The vampire moved so quickly with its preternatural speed that the eye could not follow. He grabbed her forearm, holding on like a vise as she attempted to pull away. But he remained as still as stone as her helpless body pulled fruitlessly, beating against him with her fist.

"Don't you dare!" She screamed.

This all happened in seconds, and I was out of my hiding spot at the very same time. Tattoos prickled, and muscles ached as I threw myself at the vampire.

I hadn't pulled out the scythe yet because they stood too close, and I didn't want to cut Rayn accidentally.

As my larger body slammed into Aurel, we both toppled into his coffee table. Thankfully, it wasn't glass but wood lacquered in gloss black; its legs were crushed by our combined weight.

I felt Rayn's slight body fall into mine as she cried out in surprise, then saw that the vamp still had a hold of her arm. The bastard wasn't letting her go.

The scythe was out in the next instant, and I lifted it high to slash down, intending to cut or sever the creature's arm and free her. But with his unnatural speed, in a flash, Aurel was on his feet with Rayn held firmly against his chest, facing me, where I crouched on one knee, weapons held to the ready.

Right hand held the scythe, left, my dart gun. Tranquilizers wouldn't do much to a vamp, but it might buy me time if needed. I didn't shoot, not yet…not with Rayn in the way.

His arm held Rayn firmly around her waist and against his body while he pulled her wrist to his mouth and paused there. Mostly for my benefit, he kissed it slowly, then licked it, running his nasty tongue slowly up her inner arm, from near her elbow to her wrist, staring me down with those hard, black eyes…their red cores hidden behind dark contact lenses…taunting me with everything he had.

Oh, I'd kill him slowly and enjoy every fucking second of it!

But how could he hold Rayn like that when the charm was supposed to ward her? Either the charm could not protect anything but her neck from his bite, or he was enduring its repelling force in a brazen show of defiance.

I guessed the latter.

His energy did feel old, though something about him also felt modern. The creep was a conundrum. If he *were* ancient, he might withstand the charm's power, but I wasn't sure.

I rose to my feet and held my hands up to stop him from biting into Rayn's wrist. I did not drop my weapons, though.

Rayn's other arm was free, and with a growl, it shot up. She reached her clawed fingers behind her as she attempted to scratch Aurel's neck and face with her nails. He seemed unaffected as she dug into his flesh, her teeth bared and animalistic, determined sounds escaping her throat.

I was floored by how fearless she was!

The vampire laughed at her valiant attempts, his attitude almost playful with her, like a lover's game, teasing, taunting, foreplay…?

God, I hated him!

Her scrapes barely affected his unearthly skin. The breaks in its pale surface mended themselves almost instantly, leaving little crimson traces behind on her fingers and under her nails, but any vestiges of blood left on his flesh were absorbed back into the creature through its pores. Waste not, want not, I guess.

And, that fast healing proved he was no youngin'.

Keeping his black eyes on me, he dipped his head down, his mouth beside her ear, and whispered just loud enough for me to hear everything, "I was good to you, wasn't I? Do you think me a monster, Rayn? A demon that would harm you?"

Calmly, so calmly it shocked me yet again, Rayn replied, "Would you have told me what you are? You drank my blood, Aurel. *Without* asking me. Without my permission? What was your plan? Would you change me into a vampire without my consent? I can't believe you'd have killed me. Are you going to kill me now?"

That seemed to affect him in a way I couldn't accept. His features softened, his black eyes wavered as they held mine. The emotion there made my heart sink.

The vampire actually *had feelings for* Rayn!

Beauty and the Beast.

I felt sick again!

But did she love him?

It certainly seemed that way, judging by her lack of fear, her comfort in his presence, her steady voice, and calm demeanor.

I was stumped, tongue-tied, devastated.

Finally, the vampire closed his eyes and pressed his face into Rayn's hair. I couldn't hear what he said that time. It was only for her, and I wanted to explode as I waited there, feeling awkward, like I was intruding on a tender moment between lovers!

Finally, she spoke.

"Go," Rayn said in a soft, kind, but firm voice. "Go away now, Aurel, and I'll be happy."

With a sigh, the vampire turned his eyes back to me, searing me with his disdain and a stern look of warning. He spoke not another word, not to me, not to her, and in the next instant, he was gone.

Rayn staggered, left unsupported when he seemed to vanish into thin air, but she righted herself just as I reached out to help support her.

"You let him go." It was simply a statement without accusation. Though I'd wanted to end him, I wouldn't have wanted to hurt her in the process. She really did seem to care for him, and I hated it so much I can't even tell you!

God, I hated it!

But I wouldn't let her see that.

What right did I have to her heart, anyway?

Still, *he* was a monstrous creature, and *she* had owned my poor, wretched heart for decades!

I sighed inwardly but kept my voice and demeanor strong on the outside like I always did, or at least tried to do.

"You okay?" I offered her a hand.

"I'm okay."

But her voice shook, and I saw her hands trembling. Without thinking, I grasped them in mine and caressed them to try to calm her.

"What did he say to you before he left?" Perhaps I shouldn't have asked. It was clearly personal, meant to be between them, or he'd have

164

said it so I could hear it. I thought she might refuse to tell me, but I was wrong.

"He said he would never kill me but that he wanted to turn me. That he was lonely and felt I'd be an ideal companion. He struggled with telling me what he was. That if I didn't want to be like him… If his leaving would make me happy, then he would go. My body tensed when he said it because I worried he might come after you. I said nothing, but he seemed to know my thoughts, or at least gleaned them, due to the fact I'd brought you here. He told me he would not menace you or seek your death as long as you let him be. So, I told him to go."

Before I realized what I was doing, I had pulled her to me. We embraced tightly for a long moment before parting. Her body melted into mine, and I felt a sense of relief that she relaxed so completely in my arms.

"We should go so that Aurel can have his apartment back." She said in a voice tinged with sadness as she pulled away.

"Okay." I felt strange abandoning a kill but also relieved that Rayn was safe so that I could easily put my concerns aside for the moment.

My concern? That Aurel would go back on his word and come after Rayn. Could he truly let her go? Could a vampire even be trusted? Eternity was a long time, and if he did love her and intended to make an eternal companion of her, could he just give that up because she told him to?

Time would tell, and I would protect her until the day I died!

What if he came after me? Well, I'd be ready for him! I wasn't concerned at all about that.

We returned to her house, where she asked me to stay with her that night. Of course, happily, I agreed.

Neither of us could sleep, so we sat up with her TV droning in the background and talked…

I confessed it all to her then, my immense crush on her and how important she was to me. As inexplicable as it might seem, having been apart for so long and never more to her than a casual friend at school. Still, she was my heart's world. I couldn't imagine anyone else coming along that could fill that space, and I told her so.

She took it well, calmly, sweetly, but I couldn't be entirely sure how she felt about me. I mean, she'd suddenly lost her boyfriend. How long had she been seeing him? How serious were they? I asked carefully, and she said they hadn't been together long but were pretty close. God, I was relieved *that* was over! I hoped it was finally and forever over.

She begged me to tell her all about my vampire experiences, and I promised to tell her everything when the time was right.

XVII
SPENCE & RAYN

The next morning, I woke on Rayn's couch, confused as to where I was before it all came back to me. Sitting up, I turned as she strode into the room, fresh and dressed for the day in jeans and a v-neck MST3K tee shirt that hugged her curves and made me feel fresh butterflies.

"What time is it?" I asked a bit groggily.

"Eleven-twenty," she beamed at me.

My heart fluttered, and I was sure my nervousness showed, so I occupied myself with a morning arm stretch to cover my giddiness.

The couch depressed, and I turned to where she'd plopped down beside me.

"You told me last night that you have a place out in the country. A safe place."

"Yeah," I searched her eyes. She looked worried.

"Can I...come there with you? It's not that I don't trust Aurel, but...he knows where I live, and when you leave, I'll be..."

I stifled a grin, giving her a calm smile...far calmer than I was feeling. "Of course, you can stay with me as long as you like, Rayn. I *did* beg you to come back with me already, remember? So you know I don't mind."

"You did, I know," she gave me a shy look, a look of apology.

"Get your stuff, and we'll head out. My place is not close. It'll take us a couple of hours to get there. I'd like to leave in time to be out of town before nightfall."

Standing up quickly from the sofa, she saluted me like Benny Hill: back straight, fingers pressed to her forehead, tongue out. "Yessir!"

I laughed and shook my head, nerves jumping, but I hid them best I could.

She then bounded off to the back of the house, and I watched her with a dreamy smile and a swirling chest filled with anticipation and anxiety.

"Spencer!" She gasped, taking in the rather derelict-looking cabin as we pulled up.

That two-hour drive flew by as we talked about everything under the sun, mostly her story, about her folks passing and her life I'd not been a part of.

I shut off the car and turned to her with a big dumb grin on my face. I was elated to have her there—overjoyed that she finally believed me about Aurel and vampires in general—that she agreed to stay with me and that she seemed to have warmed to me again after so many years. Honestly, it felt like I was living in a fever dream. Felt less real than vampires, to be honest!

Alright, I know it's annoying, and I'm sorry if I gush over her too much, but you must understand, even having not been in Rayn's presence, in an intimate way, for most of my life, this girl had some strange and wonderful power over me.

Staring at her seated beside me as she gawped at my spooky little abode, I could fully understand those love stories like Romeo and Juliet, Heathcliff and Catherine, Jack and Sally!

The air was heavy with moisture, and the skies were leaden as more rain threatened. Gave the whole place a true horror movie vibe!

"It's straight out of Evil Dead!" She exclaimed.

High praise since that's just what I was going for. "If you like the exterior, you're gonna love the inside!" I exited the car and snagged her luggage, which was simply a single large bag of clothes and other necessities. "After you," I beckoned with a gentlemanly wave of my hand.

Shooting a skeptical glance my way, she headed for the porch, hesitating before taking the first crooked, rickety-looking step.

"Go on, it's fine." I urged her, snickering internally.

Of course, it was far sturdier than she would have expected by looking at it, not actually decrepit at all as she stepped up onto that unsafe-looking board. Gaining trust, she proceeded with more confidence and seemed to marvel at how solid that derelict old porch indeed was. At the door, I reached around her and unlocked it, allowing her to step in first.

"Whoa! This is nice!" Her exclamation of shock made me feel a surge of pride.

The very air of my little cabin seemed to sizzle as I followed her over the threshold. It was her cherished presence, finally gracing my little home, a daydream I'd entertained countless times.

I laid her bag on a chair, then spread my arms wide as I turned to face her. "Home sweet home."

Her head bobbed up and down as she turned to me with a knowing look, "You make the outside look like a rundown, shabby ol' abandoned wreck on purpose."

"Yes, ma'am," I beamed, "Go on, have a look around. I put a ton of work into this place."

"And it shows!" she replied, leaning into the bathroom. Then she made her way to the library, "I'm going to spend lots of time in here," and finally, to my tiny kitchen. That was pretty much it.

"You like?" I asked when she joined me again in the living room, which was only composed of two chairs, a small sofa, two side tables, my bed, and a television.

"I do!" She moved in front of me, glancing here and there, "Where can I put my things?"

She was right; there was very little space for anything besides my stuff. I'd had no time to pre-prep for her stay since I hadn't expected her to take me up on my offer.

I jumped into action, clearing a small shelving unit between the living area and kitchen and shoving my things under my bed.

"Here you go!" I proudly presented the shelf to her. "It's yours—however you want to use it, and the bathroom, too. Set yourself up any way you like in there. Heck, you can have full run of the place as far as I'm concerned."

But my grand enthusiasm and generosity only made her laugh.

"Thank you, sir!" She bowed, then rising again, our eyes locked, and the spark that shot between us felt like lightning to my soul.

That could *not* have only been me!

She *had* to have felt that, too!

Suddenly, it was like I was back in high school. My stupid nerves jumped, and I felt stupid and giddy and nothing at all like the big, tough vampire hunter.

Turning toward my kitchen, I had intended to offer my cherished guest something to eat or drink, but my long legs got tangled up, sending me tumbling into my chair, dragging it down with me as my big, awkward body crashed to the floor with a loud thud.

"Spencer!" Rayn exclaimed, and I could tell in her voice she was trying hard not to laugh at me.

"Shit and damnation!" I cursed, but I was laughing at myself, seated down there with the chair on its side and the table beside it all askew. My shoulders sagged as I turned embarrassed eyes up to her.

Rayn really did laugh then; she just couldn't help herself, "You look like a lost puppy... Well, more like a giant lost wolf or something." She offered her hand, and I shook my head.

"You think you can pull *me* up, little girl?" I ribbed her, taking her hand anyway.

"Leverage, dumb ass," she teased.

I got to my feet, straightened myself up, cheeks burning as I righted the chair and table. She rested her hand on my forearm, and I looked down at her.

Lawd have mercy; she was so pretty and so petite, only five foot two, delicate, but no waif. All deep curves and supple flesh, lean but strong. My heart was performing acrobatics.

"Don't be embarrassed." She rubbed my arm lovingly, her face filled with compassion and even apology as if she'd made me fall on purpose. I think she still felt bad for having treated me like I was crazy. And I could swear she looked at me with more than just friendship... with...*desire!* Her sweet voice, her gaze moving up and down from my eyes to my mouth, and her words came out breathy, her hand growing hotter as it soothed me, comforted me, did *other* things to me.

I smiled, nerves jumpin', but feeling so very happy. "You have that effect on me, Rayn." I said, referring to my clumsiness, "I...I'm an idiot around you." I shrugged, "Can't seem to help it. Always been that way." Gently, I rested my hand on the side of her head. She didn't pull away, even leaning into my touch, so I dug my fingers into her thick, chestnut hair as she turned her cherubic face up to me, those bright hazel eyes locking with mine.

"Who'd have guessed you'd turn out so..." Words seemed to fail her, then she smirked wickedly, and I felt my knees go weak at the look she was giving me.

Her voice went full-on sultry when she said, "I could eat you up, head…to…toe."

My heart went utterly mad!

"Brazen hussy," I rumbled.

"Only for you," she gasped as I pulled her to me and crushed my lips to hers.

Fireworks!

Oh yes, it ain't no myth! It was the Fourth of July in my head; my heart—groin all fired up as our tongues danced and our mouths filled with moans and groans of utter delight.

We stumbled to my bed, our bodies a tangled mess of desperate bliss, just as the skies outside opened up and rain poured from the sky in great buckets.

I thought nothing during the process of removing our clothing. It was effortless, sudden, and magical, as if our shared, bare, unencumbered flesh were the most natural thing in the world.

The bed was narrow but long, firm, and welcoming as I guided her to lie below me, and we continued our lascivious exploration.

God, the taste of her, her scent, the feel of her hot, smooth, milky skin, I was utterly lost in her…my dearest Rayn. Finally, the object of my heart lay beneath me, and nothing in my life had ever felt so true, so natural.

*Super*natural, even.

Destiny was working its magic, and I had no doubt my feelings were shared as she breathed my name, her hot breath warming my ear.

I kissed her again, deep and slow, then moved down her body, hands and mouth tasting, teasing, discovering every hill and valley of her forbidden lands. Not an inch of her flesh did I leave untouched by my hands, my mouth. And god, but she tasted divine!

Her fingers raked my scalp, scraped my shoulder, my back, and I hoped she'd leave marks there, marks that would never heal, like the ones she'd left on my heart.

While I was no virgin, I had not *tasted* another. Those Gypsy lovers had come to me for one thing, and I wondered again if I had children growing within them. It was a distracting thought at that moment as I dipped my head between Rayn's legs and breathed in her sweet sex.

So I put those memories out of my mind and obeyed her pleas, running my tongue slowly over her wet folds as her back arched and writhed in response.

"S-Spence!" She exclaimed.

So I obeyed, with tongue and fingertips, digging into her, experimenting, finding her most tender places, and ministering to her until she shuddered, whimpered, and cried out with abandon—until I was hard to bursting, and she begged me to enter.

I rose to see her flushed, desperate face, the most frazzled and stunning vision I'd ever laid eyes on. All because of me and my ravenous work.

I must have also looked a slutty mess myself, drunk on her and desperate.

She glanced down to find me fully extended and ready to go, and I saw her eyes go wide.

"Whoa, that thing's supposed to fit inside me?" She joked breathlessly.

I gave her a crooked, sheepish little smirk, then a shrug of my shoulders as I positioned myself at her chasm, my anxious tip teasing her threshold, her glistening eyes begging despite her playful reservations. Gently, I pushed in; she tensed, and I felt the gentle resistance of her maidenhead.

She was a virgin!

Only for you. She'd said.

Only for *me*!

My beautiful Rayn. All mine!

All. Fucking. *Mine*!

"Are you okay?" I asked in a voice filled with gravel, choking on a surge of sudden emotion.

She nodded, wet eyes bore into mine, grasping my heart like a fist. "More…" she pleaded.

And I complied, watching her sweet face, plunging deeper the instant her expression showed no indication of discomfort, increasing my speed when she gasped for more.

Rising…rising…

I slammed my eyes shut as she clenched around me. So hot, so tight, her voice crying out as her body fell away into mad trembling, and I tumbled in after, utterly lost in fierce waves of orgasmic bliss! I tried to hold on, to last as long as I could, but soon, too soon, I crested and gave way to that blessed release.

Afterward, I sank down on top of her; there was nowhere else to go on my little twin bed. Nowhere else I wanted to go. My swimming head was nestled between her glorious breasts as I hummed with delight, then nuzzled my face up into the crook of her neck.

We were a sticky, hot mess, and I was in heaven.

Later, I woke to the feeling of her baby-soft cheek pressed against my forehead and her fingertips brushing hair from my face. I hummed happily, kissed those fingers, and mumbled, "Shower."

God, we needed it!

Although, part of me didn't want to wash her off.

As we meandered to my bathroom, she was a vision of tousled hair and tired eyes. I got the water going. I was getting hard as stone again, and she noticed. Her milky cheeks pinked, making me ache as we entered the steaming bath.

"Did a vampire give you those?" She asked about my scarred chest.

I shook my head, "Big cat."

"Really!" Her lips grazed one scar, pressed softly to another, "It's not the years, honey," she sighed between kisses.

"...it's the mileage." I finished it for her with my best Indiana Jones impression.

Then she noticed her name etched on my wrist.

"Spencer!" She gasped, snagging my arm and turning my wrist up to see her signature scrawled there in permanent ink. She gawped up at me, luminous eyes round and astonished.

"I had it done a long time ago, after losing my family, to keep me motivated."

She cocked her head, staring as she traced those letters on my wrist, "My name...to keep you motivated..."

I dug the fingers of my other hand into her hair, and she turned her face back up to me.

"To protect you, that was my motivation."

"But we hadn't seen each other for so long."

"That didn't matter." I chuckled.

Her arms encircled my waist, and we held each other for a long moment.

"I went to your house after it happened, you know." She nuzzled into me. "I wanted to comfort you, to...I don't know...be there for you. But you were gone, and I didn't know where you were."

This shocked me; how could I have missed her coming to see me and not known about it until so many years later? "I was staying with Karl's family." I explained, "Then I moved to an apartment and finally ended up here. If I'd known...I'd have come to see *you*. I did check on you pretty regularly, but I didn't know how to...to... After all that happened, and the longer time went on, there was just nothing I could have said to you to—"

"I know," Her arms tightened around me, and she tilted her head up, resting her chin on my chest. "We're making up for lost time." A sly little smirk curled her lips, and I returned my own.

"Little minx."

Her eyebrows bobbed. I laughed.

We lathered each other and ourselves in a dance of washing and exploring. Giggles and moans replaced words; it was sharing beyond discussion, and I took her again with ardent gusto. She ate it up...ate *me* up...as hungrily as I did her.

Before letting the shower go cold, we emerged, and after toweling off, Rayn pulled on my discarded tee to avoid getting a chill. I didn't bother dressing for the day, just skivvies. I was too preoccupied with my cherished guest, and I was too warm to be cold.

We made a beeline for food.

As you already know, I primarily eat meat. It's quick and simple to cook with just salt, fills me up, helps me put on muscle quick-and-easy, and I can go long spans without having to eat again.

I had nothing else to offer her, but she didn't seem to mind, inhaling her steak with fervor.

Her fair complexion positively glowed, eyes sparkling and clear, cheeks rosy, smiling, laughing and filling my little house with the heaven of her presence.

We parked ourselves on my sofa and popped on a movie, Logan's Run, but barely watched it. I couldn't leave the poor thing alone. Constantly slipping my hand under that tee, which swallowed up her darling little body...

I nuzzled into her sweet warmth and kissed her neck; the wounds from Aurel's bite had nearly healed. Feeling them beneath my lips galled me, but Rayn was mine now, safe from him, I vowed, and he would be gone by my hand soon; I sealed that vow with a sweep of my tongue across those accursed marks.

Rayn squealed lightly and shuddered deliciously, and her giggle was music to my ears. Our lips crushed together, and we kissed deep and long before parting, and still close, we locked eyes in a staring contest of pure adoration. My hand wandered down, finding her hot and wet for me; I dug my fingers in, making her cum again and again until, finally, after another copulation, she lay quivering and gasping, her legs draped at my sides as I slid out of her, then bent and softly pressed my lips to hers.

"I love you, Romayne Pierson." Words straight from my straining heart, yet not good enough to relay the true depth of my feelings for that precious creature.

174

Tears filled her luminous tired eyes, and she positively beamed up at me, making my heart go utterly mad and my damned dick stiffen up again.

"Spence…" She searched my eyes but seemed to check herself before expressing her feelings.

"Don't hesitate to say it to me." I whispered earnestly, "Whenever you're ready. You couldn't speak those words to anyone safer than me." I knew it was true concerning *my* feelings for *her*. But I also knew the nature of my work put me in constant danger every day—the ever-present threat of death…or worse! Still, is it so different from professions like law enforcement, firefighting, or other deadly, normal-life things that could tear loved ones apart in death? But I shoved those morbid concerns aside and kissed her again, slow and tender.

Pulling her to me as we readjusted ourselves and the movie ended, Rayn cupped my cheek in her palm, and I turned to face her.

Her look of resolve and determination halted the beat of my heart.

"I love you, too, Spencer Vale." Her lip quivered, and we shared a heartfelt smile as my eyes burned and hers spilled over. Then we laughed at our sappiness and fell into a fit of tickling and squealing before heading back into my shower.

Clean again and fully spent, we tumbled into bed. I slept like a rock until the following morning. Apparently, she did as well, but only after laying awake longer than I had.

Ravenous again, we sucked down a breakfast of bacon and eggs; then, it was time for our promised discussion.

I was kind of dreading it because I knew I'd have to relive things I didn't want to think about, but I'd wanted to tell her for so long that my eagerness far outweighed my reservations.

"So," she sat beside me on the sofa, one leg pulled up as she turned to face me, all decisive and ready to hit me with a million questions. But she only said, "Tell me everything!"

This garnered a pitiful look from me as I raked my hand through my damp hair. Rayn watched me with hungry eyes, but we both refrained from losing ourselves to sex yet again, at least for the moment.

"Everything…" I replied airily, then gave her a tired smile. "All right, well, barring the lurid details, I'll tell you exactly how my family was taken from me and what came after."

Patiently, she waited, her face filled with compassion, her hand on mine, so I grasped it, and we both squeezed. I proceeded to share it all with her, as I've already shared with you and my hunter friends.

It killed me to see her reactions, the changes in her face, the pain in her eyes, for me and my tragic family. She brightened when I got to my travels; sharing those thrilling details was like a healing endeavor, minus the "gypsy" orgy, of course. Oh, I'd tell her about that someday, but this was not the time!

"Spencer, your life…" Her voice was a breath of astonishment as my tale came to a close.

"Yeah," I shrugged, "it's about the only choice I had, becoming a hunter. Well, the only choice I would consider."

Running her finger over the tattoos on my arm, following that snake of strange symbols, she shook her head, "I'm so relieved you have these protections!"

"Me too!" I laughed ruefully.

"I want to help you."

"Help me?" My brow knit, then I smiled. "You *are* helping me," I wiggled my eyebrows at her; she rolled her eyes, and then I got serious again. "By being here, with me, so I don't have to worry about you as much."

But she shook her head, her shoulders squaring, face as determined as I'd ever seen it. "No, Spencer. I want to join you in your hunts. To hunt with you!"

"No!" My reaction was instant, nearly cutting her off. I sat up straight, my voice harsher than I intended. "No, Rayn! No way!"

That lovely face scowled at me, and she crossed her arms, "I held my own with Aurel—"

"No! Shit, there's *no* way I'd let you get involved in this!"

"But I *am* involved in it! Spencer, I—"

"Rayn." I groaned, squirming where I sat. I thought of Karl, how I'd lost my best friend to this mission of mine; there was no chance in hell I'd lose my precious Rayn, too!

"You're thinking of Karl, aren't you?"

She could read me like a book.

"I'm thinking of *everyone*, Rayn! But mostly, I'm thinking of *you*! Sure, it's predictable to say I'd never forgive myself if something happened to you, but it's the truth! The goddamned truth."

"I'll get the tats, like you! Karl didn't have the tats, right?"

I shook my head, "No, he didn't. But why the hell do you want to do this? Seriously, Rayn, why would you *choose* to participate in the violent and ugly work of vampire hunting?"

"Because I want to be *with* you."

My heart soared. I couldn't help it. She wanted to be with me, and I never wanted to be parted from her, either.

176

"Look, I feel the same about you. You have *no* idea how much that means to me. But this life is not some fantasy, Rayn. Not like your acting gigs—"

"I *know* that!" She exclaimed incredulously, "I'm not a simpleton—"

Gently, I placed a hand on her leg to calm her, "No, you're not; that's not what I meant. But hearing my tragedies and triumphs told like a story makes it sound romantic, epic, even fun. Heck, I can admit that some of the hunts were…'*fun*.'" I made air quotes. "But the fun and games only last until tragedy strikes. Then it's just pain. Awful, life-shattering, fucked up pain."

My voice choked, and I dropped my head. Her arms were around me in an instant, her lips on my cheek, my forehead.

"I'm sorry. I'm so sorry!" Her hand stroked my hair, and I hummed contentedly as I rested my cheek on her chest. "But…"

Was she still going to argue it? I lifted my head and gawked at her.

"But," she smiled mischievously, "if I'm warded like you and with you at all times, educated like you, then I'll be an asset to you. And I will *not* let *you* go, risking yourself, leaving me alone at home to dilly-dally around and wash your laundry for you!"

There was no way I couldn't laugh at that. Then it hit me: she expected us to share a home together…for good, not just for now!

Amazingly, I began to change my mind. To actually consider allowing her to hunt with me. What was I thinking? How could I ever accept such a thing?

"…and what if you leave me here, all by my lonesome, to go off hunting," she cleverly insisted, playing on my feelings, using my worries against me, "and a vampire comes looking for you, or me, or simply stumbles upon this place with little ol' unprepared me inside, just like a sitting duck, untrained and unprotected! Better that I'm with you, all trained up, protected, and ready to defend myself!"

She was good!

I gazed upon her flawless, creamy skin and hated the idea that it would be marred by the same tattoos I wore. My face must have shown that cringe, because she slapped my shoulder lightly with her hand.

"What's that look for? You think I couldn't do it? That I wouldn't be good at it?"

I laughed mirthlessly, looking hard into her eyes, knowing how smart she was, how creative, how brave. "You'd be a superb hunter. Maybe even better than me, at least when it comes to smarts."

"Aha!" She grinned, squaring her shoulders again. "See, now, that's it, right there! You be the brawn, and I'll be the brains!"

177

My thoughts turned to Jaren...*I* was supposed to be the brains, while *he* was always the brawn. I must have looked sad because she suddenly took hold of my hand, "I'm kidding—"

But I shook my head and smiled, cutting her off, "I know. Just reminded me of Jaren and I, that's all."

Tenderly, she kissed my fingers and rubbed my hands lovingly, "You're strong *and* smart, Spence!" She declared.

I laughed shyly, "If we do this, I'll have to get over my clumsiness in your presence."

"We'll work on that, but I can't make any promises." Her eyes teased me, wantonly tempting me.

But I was serious, *dead* serious. "Rayne, if you were to die, I would follow you. I could not live without you in this world—not now that my world utterly revolves around you."

"Spencer, no—"

But I shook my head vehemently and grasped her hand to hush her; she had to know the depths of my feelings, especially if this was happening, "If you should be turned, become a vampire, then I will follow you into an eternity of deadly thirst. I will seek out that tainted blood, drink its poison, and beg fate to make me like you."

She threw her arms around my neck and grasped onto me as if to prevent me from taking such drastic actions. But I only chuckled a sad and desperate chuckle and held her tightly, feeling how perfectly our bodies melded together...how whole I felt in her embrace. Never had I felt so complete. I nestled into her heat and the swoon of her scent, drowning in her. She was like a blanket to my shivering soul, sheltering me from the chill of my life, my losses, and my awful duties.

And I *would* do it! Not a word of my promise would I hesitate to perform for her, to be with her.

XVIII
INITIATION

As much as it went against my feelings for her, I now had a new partner, and I would ensure her complete protection in the entire process of initiating her.

Part of what made me accept this and allow it was Byron's wife, Kenna. And Rayn had been right that leaving her alone while galavanting about hunting and slaying didn't sit well with me, either.

So, after filling Clan and the others in on our plans, it was off to Europe with my girl!

After landing in London, we took the train to Glasgow. I gave Rayn the window seat, knowing how much she'd love watching the English countryside during our just-under-five-hour trip. Hand in hand, we traveled, and in contrast to my concerns, I was the happiest I'd ever been in my life!

This was the truest desire of my heart since the day I first laid eyes on her, to have her by my side. Still, if I allowed my mind to dwell on the dangers of a hunter's most treacherous world...

Anxiety!

It was a constant war within me: the inexplicable, even destiny-filled joy and the terrible guilt and resistance I felt at allowing it to happen!

"Quit worrying, Mister Vale."

I turned my gaze from the window down to her sweet face.

"This is destiny, can't you feel it?" she whispered, smiling tiredly up at me, her tender voice so serene it contradicted the turmoil I struggled with.

There was that word again... *Destiny*...

Yeah, I felt it, but was it real? "Is it, though?" I asked, feeling like I was betraying some inescapable truth.

She squeezed my hand, laid her head on my shoulder, sighed, "I can feel something more in all this than the love between us. I keep getting this rush of excitement like something is coming—something weird and wonderful."

My head raced hearing her describe my own feelings back at me, even better than I could contemplate them to myself.

Fear assailed me, coupled with morbid excitement.

Weird and wonderful…

Oh, yes. I felt it, too.

Something weird, wonderful, and *immense!*

But what on Earth could feel so profound now, after all of the Earth-shattering nightmare realities I'd already come to terms with?

Were we marching straight into the arms of Death?

Certainly, *death* would be more profound than the menagerie of profound stuff my life had already turned into.

Hugging my arm snuggly, Rayn squeezed my hand in both of hers, and I squeezed back.

"Just roll with it, baby," She singsonged those words, Steve Winwood-style, and I smiled, recalling how she'd sung that same tune to me years ago when I was struggling with those bullies at school. I pressed my lips to her head, and we rode along in silence. Lulled by the rhythm of the tracks, I drifted off to sleep.

I had brought Rayn to Scotland to meet everyone and, most importantly, to get her own protective warding: tattoos, spell instruction, etc.

Fedelma and Rayn got along instantly. God, but that old gal had the filthiest mind I ever encountered! The way she talked to Rayn, about me…about *us*, intimate jokes and innuendos all right *in front* of me, and Rayn joining in right along with her, it still makes me blush!

Not once did I leave Rayn's side as she got inked. I held her hand, talked to her, explained details, and provided constant education alongside Fedelma. I helped Rayn in every aspect of her initiation. It took a month, as it had for me, and I babied my woman the entire time.

Like a faithful servant to a queen, I waited on her every need, applied salve after each inking, and did all I could to keep her comfortable.

In between times, when her tattoos needed healing and she wasn't studying, the two of us loved walking the highlands together: the wild, rolling green hills, cool, inviting temperatures, and clean air of the Scottish countryside were something I'd grown to love deeply.

"God, I love it here!" Rayn exclaimed as if she'd just read my thoughts.

She did that a lot, and it only proved how often our minds followed along the same track.

I smiled and squeezed her hand. "It's magnificent. It makes all the strangeness of this life seem more real somehow, and the struggles seem to lessen."

We continued in silence, lost in our thoughts and in nature. But as much as I felt the calming effects of our stroll, the truth of why we were there and what I'd gotten Rayn into still haunted me. It would never *not* haunt me.

"I still can't believe I'm letting you do all this." I sighed.

Rayn smiled and squeezed my hand. "I love you too, Spencer."

Gently, I halted our stroll and cupped her pretty face in my hands. It was one of the only places I could touch her, for now, as the final tattoos had been inked and were still uncomfortable during the healing process. The invisible, magical ones were even more painful than the standard ink tats. But I knew just where they were located on her so that I could avoid accidentally touching them.

"As much as I hate the marring of your tender perfection," I complained, seeing her creamy cheeks turn cherry, "I do feel a sense of ease knowing you're properly warded. This is a protection I couldn't have provided to you alone, and now I know I'd have wished this for you even if you weren't joining me as a hunter."

Her delicate hands rested on mine. Her smiling face and shining eyes looked up at me with such love that I felt the strangest melting sensation—melting into her, forever, and not only my heart but everything that was me.

"I'd have wanted it, too, and since we're being so forthright, I *am* nervous about our first hunt. I know it's silly to say so. I mean, how could anyone *not* be nervous about that? But I... I can't help but have doubts."

"About joining me?" I cocked an eyebrow at her.

She sighed, cast her eyes away, frowned, "No...yes..." Then she shrugged and cut her gaze up to me again, meeting mine with

181

conviction, "Getting these tattoos drove it home. It was already real for me, after Aurel, but the killing. I'm nervous about the killing."

I caressed her baby soft cheeks with my thumbs and smiled wanly, warmly, helplessly back at her, "I can't give you a lick of comfort there, lovely. The killing is nasty. It's utterly disgusting, and it…changes you. There's no way it couldn't. In some aspects, killing old vampires is easier to stomach. Not easier to *do*! Aw, hell no!" My over-the-top impression made her smile, but it barely lightened the mood. I sighed and continued, "Ancients are not as messy unless they've just fed. They stink of the grave, and it's a nightmarish, surreal business. Unnatural in every way."

She shuddered, then wrapped her arms around my waist and embraced me tightly, heedless of the discomfort her tats might cause her. I gently returned the hug, burying my face in her hair, breathing in her sweet scent.

"Leave the kills to me unless completely necessary, okay?"

She squeezed me tighter, "Let me do it at least once, to…break the ice…harden me up to it."

"Once won't do it. It never gets easier, not really. But yes, you should learn to do it first hand, so you are best prepared."

"There's something else…" she signed into my chest.

I pulled back, held her close still, looking into her upturned face.

"Fedelma, she wants to pass down to me her knowledge, teach me how to ink and—"

Fedelma had chosen Rayn as her successor?!

The shock and understanding must have shown on my face because Rayn stopped and grinned at me. "I haven't even killed a vampire yet, and she chose me for this! When I expressed my doubt to her, she shook her head vehemently; you know how she is; it's her way or the highway. Not that I would have turned her down. I'm excited about it. She said it was my energy, my soul. A resonance she recognized and that she'd been waiting for. So I suppose I'm destined for this."

Shaking my head, I grinned back at her, then hugged her to me, gently, carefully. "It makes perfect sense. Perfect sense." Was this the big destiny thing we both had been feeling?

We remained wrapped together, warm in the cool breezes that rushed off the nearby ocean, surrounded by those lush, impossibly green Scotland hills—nature's magic tainted, or perhaps enhanced, by our unnatural duties.

Early morning, some weeks later, after Rayn's initial training and education were complete, we set out. We would return to Fedelma later to begin the more intense work, passing on those unique skills only known by the old priestess.

This was the first hunt for Rayn, and butterflies were raging in my stomach. Still, we, Clannon, Byron, and I, had picked what we thought should be an "easy" job. A young vampire Byron had been tracking for a while. The creature had caused a bit of chaos with the local youth, but otherwise, the vamp mostly kept to himself. This one had been abandoned or simply ignored by his sire. Left not knowing which way was up, he had no clue how to hide and protect himself.

This would be a mercy killing and a true trial by fire for Rayn.

It *would* feel like murder...murder of a youth, with all the blood and the gore and the painful, sickening guilt afterward.

God, I dreaded it!

Dreaded her doing it.

At my request, Clan and Byron hung back, letting Rayn and me deal with it on our own unless things happened to go south. As much practice as I had working alone or with the others, I felt that she—well, the both of us—would prefer the moral support *after* it was all done. And it was always good to have backup nearby—something I hadn't had back home before hunting with and after losing Karl.

Clan and Byron went on ahead as we remained at Byron's car and suited up.

Rayn wore all black, as we all did: fitted clothing, a short leather jacket stocked with weapons of the hunter that I'd given to her, gloved hands, short boots, and hair pulled up in a tight bun. She looked like some cat burglar ready to drop down from the ceiling and rob a museum or something—a gorgeous cat burglar who had already stolen my heart.

Ha! And what do you think I did as I stood there, daydreaming of her in her tight little outfit committing grand larceny?

That's right, I moved to take a single step toward her, stumbled over literally nothing, like the moron I am, and nearly fell on my face!

God, I'm such a freak!

Recovering quickly as she giggled at me, I pushed the worries out of my mind, placed my black cowboy hat atop my head, and turned to

Rayn with a rakish grin—perfect way to cover for my bungling idiot self.

Giggles were suddenly gone, and her eyes grew wide as they stared up at me; her lips parted, and I could swear she swooned a little. My face heated up, and I looked away, fiddling with the handle of the small scythe I had tucked in the inner pocket of my long black coat.

Without a word, she grabbed my collar and yanked me down to her, pressing her lips to mine. I lifted her off the ground with one arm, tilting my hat back and holding it in place with my other hand as her arms locked around my neck. We laughed into the kiss before getting lost in it.

She really was swooning as I sat her back down again, and so was I.

I wondered if Clannon and Byron were watching and what they made of our antics leading up to this awful job.

"God, you're hot in your hunter garb!" She exclaimed, shaking herself as if to clear her head and whip her body into shape. "Well, you're *always* hot, Spencer, but…you know what I mean." Then she frowned, "This might be a problem, you know. I'll get distracted by your overwhelming hotness, and you'll be tripping over yourself like you always do in my presence. *Great* approach to vampire hunting! We're doomed!"

I laughed, but she was right.

Then, I grew serious because I had to. "We'll be fine. I've learned to school my emotions and my mannerisms when going up against these things. So have you, like I taught you to do. You're good at it, Rayn, and you're brave…"

Her hands were on her hips as she playfully scolded me, "How do you know I'm brave? This is our first slay!"

I shrugged, "Aurel."

"That was brave?" She acted incredulous, but I could tell she was still playing with me.

I nodded resolutely, and she grinned with mock arrogance.

"Thank you."

"Don't mention it."

We made our way around the side of a derelict building where the kid slept during the day. Our friends were nearby, unseen, but watching —a testament to their talent for stealth.

Silently, Rayn and I crawled through a broken-out window into a large, dimly lit room littered with at least two feet of fallen ceiling tiles, broken desks, chairs, and other furniture, and mounds of trash. There was an odd stink in the air, moldy, dusty, with a faint hint of rot. Dead animals, probably. I didn't believe the vamp would kill where they slept, and the smell was so mild, not likely to come from a large body.

The place was probably built in the seventies, with all the bland square lines, eerie liminal spaces, and office layouts you might find anywhere in the modern world.

"The creature," I whispered, preferring not to humanize them by calling them 'he' or 'the guy,' "will want to place himself in a space that's well hidden and difficult to find. If he's clever, he'll not fall asleep in a bathroom stall or someplace where urban explorers might stumble upon him. Remember, vamps are like dead bodies during daylight hours, at least the younger ones are, so the last thing they want is to be found and carted off to some morgue."

Rayn nodded, and we moved further in.

"Careful where you step," I warned, "no telling what's under all this stuff."

Just as we passed deeper into the place, suddenly Rayn stopped and grasped my arm. I turned to look down at her and saw her eyes fixed on something across the room. She was staring at an open doorway, but when I followed her gaze, I could see nothing there to get excited about.

"What is it?" I asked.

After a brief pause, watching the expression on her face shift from alarm to a scrutinizing frown, she replied, "You don't see him, do you?"

My head shot up and I looked around again, back at that door, heart leaping into my throat, but still, nothing was there. "Who, him?" I asked, looking all around us, finding no one.

"Whoa."

Her whisper drew my attention back to her.

"Spence..."

I stared down into her face as her eyes tilted up to meet mine, filled with wonder, which only confused me further.

"What, Rayn?" I hissed out of confusion and concern, "What is it?"

"Come on, hurry." She rushed ahead without explaining herself.

"Hold it! Shit!" I exclaimed. It only took a couple of strides for my long legs to catch up with her, but I saw how in earnest she was and decided not to halt her to demand an explanation. It was clear she'd seen something, and I trusted her, so I let her lead the way.

After navigating a few smaller offices, passing through them, and down a narrow hall into a room with no windows, she paused and looked around as if expecting to see something.

"Rayn." I controlled the frustration in my voice.

She sighed and turned to me. "I lost him."

"Lost him? Our quarry? But I didn't see anything."

Smiling patiently, she took my hand and grasped it in hers, then looked up at me and held my confused gaze like a parent about to explain something to a child—not in a condescending manner, but in a way that alerted me to the importance of what she was about to tell me.

"Spencer, I saw a young man, blood on his face, his mouth and chin, and on the front of his shirt. I know he's our guy. He darted this way, and I caught glimpses of his movement which led me here, but he's vanished completely, although I can still hear him panicking, confused."

"Wh…wait!" I gaped at her.

"I think I saw his ghost, Spence." she breathed excitedly.

"Hold on…" I took hold of her shoulders. "You can see the spirit of the vampire?"

"Yes, sir." She nodded.

"Have you ever seen spirits before?"

"Nope."

We both stared at one another for a long moment; then it struck me.

"Aurel…"

And she finished it for me, "You mean when he drank from me, something remained? He left something with me?"

"Maybe," Now, this could be handy, even as I felt concerned. I'd need to tell the others about this. Get their take, especially Fedelma. "But wait, the vamp kid isn't dead…so…"

She shook her head again, "You said they sleep during the day as if they were dead. What if it's a kind of astral projection?"

Brilliant, I thought. "Right, that idea never occurred to me, that their souls might vacate their bodies during their death sleep. It does make sense. Okay, let's be quiet here for a minute and let you *feel*; maybe you can pick him up again."

We did that, and it didn't take long.

"I hear him still, but he's babbling now. Really confused, not sure if he wants…"

Her words ceased, eyes closed as she concentrated, shaking her head. Then she opened them and looked up at me with such tenderness, even sadness, that I felt a sinking feeling.

"He isn't sure if he wants us to kill him or not. He's fighting with his nature. His desire to feed because he's so hungry and out of control, but he still feels a sense of wrong in what he's done and what he will do. It's pure madness, Spence. His mind isn't reasoning properly.

186

It's like he can hardly think like a human anymore...like he's become only hunger and need. He just wanted blood, but he could feel the coming of the day encroaching, and he knew he needed to hide. He hadn't fed properly and went down unsatisfied. Ravenous! God, he's so ravenous! I can feel it as if I were hungry, too. But for me, it's a hamburger, while for him, it's..." she shook her head, the compassion for this creature radiating off her, "So his sense of humanity is wavering drastically, faltering and fading more with every second. He's miserable and driven! So driven! Fighting with himself now after witnessing us here and having an idea of what we are and our ultimate goal, to kill him."

"Is he speaking to you in words?" I asked.

"No, not speaking. He screams at me...at us, but no. It's not a discussion or a verbal kind of pleading. It's all inner thoughts and emotions manifest through his soul body." Her eyes were brimming as she held my astonished gaze. "We must free him."

It was my turn to nod, "That's why we're here."

We shared a sad smile, then I grew serious again, "Can you try to reach him, reason with him to let us know where he sleeps?"

"I'll try."

She shut her eyes again and drew in a deep breath. Then, after only a moment, her eyes popped open, and she looked at me with renewed conviction. "There's a basement under here, in this room, but it's hard to find because he set it up that way...to be well hidden."

Together, we searched the floor, carefully shifting all the junk with our feet and gingerly moving furniture with our hands until we found a spot where ceiling tiles had been piled haphazardly, but they wouldn't move. It appeared the kid had used some hardware adhesive to bond the haphazard-looking stack together, then affixed that pile to the trap door so that he could slip inside and pull the door closed, making it appear like a pile of junk no one would care about. He figured it unlikely kids would bother to move that stack. It might not have been completely foolproof, but it also might serve to protect him until he found a better hiding place.

I then spotted the caulk gun and discarded glue canisters scattered within the other trash. "This guy's more of a clever bastard than I would have given him credit for," I exclaimed. We couldn't remove the glued cluster, but I could lift them along with the trap door. So I yanked it open as its hinges screeched, then descended a wooden staircase that felt more like a ladder than stairs proper. I assisted Rayn as she followed me.

It was utter darkness down there. I searched for a light, but the overheads did not work. I growled inwardly. As always, flicking a light switch, or, in this case, pulling a chain on a light that didn't work, seriously annoyed me! I snagged the flashlight from my coat and switched it on, moving the beam over the whole area in a wide arc. It was a dank, musty, windowless place with a very low ceiling. I had to duck to avoid slamming my head into the beams. Curtain-like cobwebs adorned the crevices and corners, and not much of anything else could be found there.

Rayn had her hand over her mouth as she scrunched her nose up at me.

"Yeah, nasty." I agreed—the place stank of mold, moisture, and rot even worse than above.

Finally, I paused the beam, and there he was, our unfortunate young vampire, seated against the corner of the wall across the room, utterly still, legs crossed, head down, sleeping his death sleep.

I felt Rayn shudder beside me.

"He really does look dead, and God! He's positively screaming at us right now." She cringed back, hands up as if to ward off some unseen thing that was getting in her face. Which, apparently, he was.

"Calm down, calm down," she repeated, obviously unsure how to deal with her oppressor.

Me? I stalked across the room, drawing the scythe from my coat, ready to get it over with.

"C'mon, Rayn. You want to break the ice and set this guy free, then put the poor sod out of his misery!" Once I stopped to look over the vamp's prone body, I turned, scythe in hand, handle held out to her.

To my surprise, and yet not, because I knew how tough Rayn could be, she walked bravely toward me, but after taking the first few steps, she visibly shivered.

"Uhhhh!" She exclaimed, "I just walked right through his ghostly ass!" Then she took the blade from my hand, and I stepped aside to allow her access.

It hit me then that this was it! My love was about to kill her first vamp, and I felt the most intense wave of fear and anguished nerves I think I've ever felt. Actually, that moment felt a lot like the night my brother—

"Okay," her voice halted my morbid reverie, and I watched as she leaned over the vampire."

I moved to his other side and gently grasped his hair, pulling his head back, exposing his neck. Rayn started, and I could see recognition on her face—the bloody face of the spirit she'd seen.

Placing the scythe beside his neck, its pointed tip touching the wall beside him, her stunning face turned to me, almost pleading yet filled with such fierce resolve I felt instantly proud of her.

"You remember what I showed you," it wasn't a question; I knew she remembered.

Nodding, I saw her muscles bunch, and her body go rigid. Her jaw was set; then, with a growl and both hands grasping the handle of that deadly tool, she yanked it hard across the vampire's neck.

Blood gushed and sprayed like a sprinkler.

The body did not move or react in any way.

Yelping, Rayn stumbled back, dropping the scythe, which I instantly snatched up from the floor. Waving her arms before her, she squealed and hollered at something that I could not see. But I didn't let the odd display hold me back. She had cut the vamp's throat deep, but the head remained attached, so I lunged forward and hacked it clean off with a single swing.

The head rolled and settled right at Rayn's feet just as she stopped squealing. Her eyes fell on it; then she scampered in my direction and away from the gory mess we had both just made.

My lighter was out now, and I lit a piece of trash from the floor and threw it onto the body, which began to smolder immediately as the first small flame caught on the kid's clothing. Once I was sure the body would burn past any chance of reanimation, I threw the head onto it.

Then, I prepared to put out the fire once all that was left was ash so that it wouldn't take the whole place down—not that the ruined structure needed saving, but if we let the fire run wild, we could have a real disaster on our hands.

"He's gone," she said in a haunting voice. I knew what she meant. The ghost of the vamp was, I assumed, at peace now. I nodded, and we shared a brief exchange of understanding.

As I worked, Rayn stood close by, hands to her mouth, eyes big and brimming. Me? I was all business, knowing the process and familiar with enough scenarios to handle almost any circumstance. We ascended those ladder steps and closed up the cellar. I then made the place look "derelict untouched" again. When it was done, and I was satisfied no trace of us or what really happened could raise suspicion; we left and met Clan and Byron behind the building.

"How'd it go?" Clan asked as he handed us several implements to do a quick cleanup before heading back to the car.

Coming down and adrenaline fading, I simply nodded, then turned to Rayn, who seemed amazingly relaxed, if a bit subdued. It hit me again, knowing what she had just done and how she must be feeling. I

189

pulled her to me and held her in a snug embrace. Her small, soft body tensed at first before relaxing completely into me.

"We need to get you two properly cleaned up." Byron placed a hand on my shoulder and squeezed.

"I need a shower," Rayn's muffled voice rose from where she was pressed into my chest, "a thousand showers!"

Rubbing her back to ease her struggle, I couldn't agree more.

XIX
SUCCESSOR

In the car, on our way back to Byron's place, Rayn whispered in my ear that she needed time alone with me, so after hot, long showers, we immediately retired to bed. Clannon slept on Byron's couch while Rayn and I took the tiny spare bedroom. We shared a twin bed, and despite being awfully knackered, we couldn't help but mess around. I could tell she needed me in that particular way, and I was more than willing to be there for her in any capacity, especially that one.

My blood was up, hers was, too, and we both could use a release.

"Think we can do this quietly?" Rayn asked with a sparkle in her radiant eyes. It amazed me to see the level of ease she displayed after the day we'd had.

"I'll do my best," I watched her hungrily as we both disrobed. Then I stretched out on the bed, hands behind my head, smiling at her. "You're the noisy one," I teased, winking when she humphed back at me.

Naked and stunning, she joined me. I was taking up the entire bed, top of my head right at the wall—there was no headboard—and feet sticking out over the bottom edge. Beds were small in Britain.

"Oh, look! Little Spence sure is excited about something!" She smirked at me and gently flicked the tip of my penis as it stood at attention like a good little soldier. It twitched in response. I was just about to give her some clever retort when she grasped hold of it and began to rub.

Gasping, my back arched, my head fell back, and my hips bucked of their own accord. I forced myself to look at her again, finding her

191

watching my face intently as she moved that precious hand up, down, up, down with fervor.

I must have looked like a dazed and mazed fool, head swimming, mouth agape, groaning and moaning beneath her. Eyes rolling, I fell back again, unable to help myself relenting to her utter power over me.

Then I felt her other hand move slowly up my abdomen, my chest…then the velvety soft tips of her breasts, with those hard nipples, and her lips and tongue all sliding up my body as well. She continued to work me, deftly controlling me via my oh-so-eager joystick. Her lips and tongue explored, finding my nipples, twirling, tasting, sucking… I was falling apart fast, but I held on, my hands moving hungrily over her lean body, soft skin, and deep, luscious curves.

She was kissing my neck now, scraping her teeth over my jaw, then her mouth found mine, and we kissed deep and harsh, humming and grunting like mindless animals.

Her hand left me suddenly. I was so hard it ached! Her soft, wet opening found me there, rubbing against my straining tip in a tease I could barely endure.

Breaking the kiss, she abruptly sat up, hovering above me like the temptress she was: her succulent body writhed, hips swayed, her flushed, astoundingly beautiful face ogling down at me with the most adoring wickedness.

God, I wanted to scream. I was on the verge of exploding and mumbled something to her, probably some incoherent gibberish, as my hands left the heaven of her soft breasts and moved to grasp her hips, intending to push her down on top of me. But she robbed me of that action by dropping onto me with her full weight, taking my quivering rod deep into her, all the way to the hilt!

I cried out despite myself.

Now, everyone in the apartment would know just what we were up to.

I was utterly lost, ramming into her relentlessly; the soft ringing of her laugh and gentle moans of delight sounded distant and lost in my swimming head.

Making a valiant effort to keep any further noise down, I muffled myself with the pillow I'd yanked out from under my head just as the orgasm rocked me and sent me soaring away. Rayn had covered her mouth with her hand as she peaked and shuddered in her own mad bliss above me.

We took the bumps and curves of that euphoric ride until the climax waned, and we both began to come down.

With a long, satisfied exhale, she collapsed onto me, hot, tender, and humming contentedly.

Just about to drift off to sleep, I was roused by the feeling of dampness on my chest. I shot awake instantly when I realized she was crying.

"Hey," I hugged her tighter, rubbing her back slowly, kissing the top of her head as I pulled the blanket over the both of us and tucked it around her.

"I'm okay," she whispered shakily, nuzzling into me.

"I know you're not, but you're not alone, Rayn. I'm here. Not only for fuck healing." I joked.

Nodding, she dug her face into my neck, sending sweet shivers through me when her lips grazed my skin.

"I know. Don't worry, I'll adjust."

There was resolve in her voice, strength despite her tears.

"You're amazing," I whispered in her ear, then kissed the side of her head.

"Hush and go to sleep." She settled into me and sighed.

I was so exhausted I obeyed her almost instantly.

The following day, we stayed home, talked, and got to know Byron and Kenna better. Again, it was instant chemistry and effortless camaraderie. Knowing all these hunters was like satisfying destiny, which had my mind going off on all sorts of strange journeys: We would learn so much from Byron and Kenna, that husband and wife long-time vampire hunting team! It was a godsend having them there so that Rayn wasn't alone like I had been on my first kill. Kenna had done it for so long and had already worked through that most harrowing start, and she knew just what to say and how to help Rayn adjust, which filled me with immense gratitude.

"What a contrast to my first time," I said to Byron as we watched Rayn and Kenna talking across the room.

Clan topped off our drinks, hearing what I'd just said when he arrived. "First kill is the most difficult. Something snaps after that, and even when it's awful…even though it's always awful, somehow the second, third, and every subsequent time, those particular emotions seem more distant."

"Scared me shiteless when I felt less affected the second time," Byron added.

I shrugged, "Took me a handful of times before I really noticed a difference. I was a soft kid. Too soft."

But Clannon shook his head and grasped my shoulder, as he liked to do, "Soft, no, Spencer, you're about as tough as they come! What you did alone before coming over here still amazes me."

"She'll be okay," I assured myself. Watching Rayn, as happy as I was that we had these indispensable friends, still, I worried for her.

"She'll be fine, she has you…"

I turned to Byron.

"…and us," he finished.

With a grateful smile, I took a drink; it burned like a physical manifestation of contentment as it slid down my throat. Then Rayn turned and smiled at me, so calm, sweet, as if to ease my mind, and I returned it just as the liquor went to my head.

We'd be okay. I told myself.

We had to be okay.

If I'd known what that really meant at the time, maybe I'd have done things differently.

Then again, probably not…

Back to Glasgow we went, so that Rayn could start her new phase of training with Fedelma.

It was just Rayn and me this time. Since there was nothing for Clan to do, he returned to London for a time to take care of personal business.

I had no idea what to expect going in, not that I would be a part of it. This was secret stuff, one-on-one priestess stuff, and a whole new initiation into an extremely limited, exclusive order. So exclusive, there would only be two once Rayn's initiation was complete.

Fedelma had chosen Rayn, felt a kinship with her, felt a certain energy or spirit about her…perhaps the same thing that drew me to her myself. It certainly felt right, yet I was a bit nervous, I can't lie.

But Rayn was excited! It seemed, after her brief tears and then talking with Kenna, that she was fully invested in this new direction. And the best part? The Nintach priestesses did not hunt. They were protected from vampires more stringently than any other person on the planet!

That was a relief, hard to put into words. Funny how Rayn's insistence to join me, and my insane choice to let her, would lead to her potentially being safer from vamps even than I was!

I wasn't sure how I'd spend my time while Rayn was wrapped up in her studies. But I found enough in Fedelma's library, exploring the town and roaming the hills, to keep me busy.

Actually, I got good long naps in during most days because my evenings and nights were…busy! I'm not sure what it was about the training, but there was a power, an energy growing in Romayne that frankly floored me. It started after the third day. I'd just waltzed in from a long walk. The ladies trained in the cellar where Fedelma kept all the secret stuff. God, I really wanted to go down there, see it all, watch the process, but I was forbidden.

No one was around, so I slipped into the shower to get cleaned up. I wasn't there two minutes before Rayn joined me. It was…god, it was good! She was on fire, a little vixen all roaming hands, mouth, tongue, and I was her most willing and eager meal. This most intense fervor… this ardor, it seemed to be an after-effect of her training.

You know, I'd almost decided to go with Clannon, to let Rayn and Fedelma do their thing and not "get in the way," but after I realized how this trip was going to be for me, for us? I was so glad I decided to go with Rayn to Glasgow!

We shared a bedroom there in Fedelma's house, which was pretty damned comfortable compared to Byron's place. Sizable bed, essentially a huge cushion on the floor with endless pillows, blankets, and soft stuff. Very private, on the opposite end of the house from Fedelma's bedroom. After that amazing shower, I floated by Rayn's side to our shared room, her leading me by the hand, me her faithful pup.

"What do you two gals get up to down there?" I asked dreamily, a little skeptically, as I sank naked into our bed.

"Oh, it's nothing like that, Spencer. It's…I guess it must be the power that surges as I learn. Working and growing in this thing, it awakens all this love, this…joy, and I just want to…" She made a little growling noise, like the purr of a cat, then proceeded to nip me with her teeth: my nose, the soft lobe of my ear, my jaw, and finally, my bottom lip. She pulled back but stayed close, her gaze roaming my face adoringly. I wanted to melt. I *was* melting. "We work intimately with our core beings, spiritually," her soft breath tickled my ear, "with the powers of soul, in order to enhance the sacred feminine. Maybe that's what makes me so hungry for your sacred masculine." Her eyebrows moved up and down suggestively, "Makes me so—"

"Enthusiastic?" I smirked just before she crushed her lips to mine. I pulled her to me, and we lost ourselves in another ravenous kiss. Like a sap, I actually felt my eyes stinging over how much I loved her, but more how I knew she returned that love. Honestly, it frightened me a little. But I shoved that away, buried it with all those other worries interned deep in my gut.

Suddenly, it hit me how naughty and quick Fedelma always was with innuendos, and, putting two and two together, I figured it had something to do with this sacred feminine power the Nintach priestesses used.

Tired after our workout in the shower, I could feel my head wanting to sleep, but Rayn's closeness and her eager exploration of my body had my other brain standing at attention. Well, no rest for the weary, so I flipped us over and paid Rayn back with dividends. We proceeded to enjoy each other for a few heady hours, after which I fell into a heavy sleep, dead to the world.

The following morning, I woke late and alone. There was a cold coffee perched on the table beside the bed and an omelet, just as cold, cut into the shape of a heart. Silly, lovey-dovey stuff…I ate it up, both figuratively and literally, and it was the best coffee and eggs I'd ever eaten.

Spent the day on cloud nine, floating around with a big grin on my face and a spring in my step. I met a few nice folks, walked the local cemetery, and felt relieved not to have any alarms go off on my tattooed skin. There were no vamps nearby, which was good…

A little strange, but good.

Or was it good? Honestly, I would have enjoyed a slay-fest! Just like the slaying got my blood up and primed me for shenanigans after, shenanigans had my blood up and primed for vamp slaying! Ah, a good slay seemed as satisfying to me now as a good lay! I chuckled to myself as I made my way back to Fedelma's place.

Stepping in, I was surprised to find the ladies in the kitchen, not down in their secret dungeon.

"Well, what's this?" I announced myself as I entered.

They had a plethora of ingredients laid out, ready to make… something.

"It's time fer dinner and some special tidbits for our inductee here." Fedelma replied with a knowing wink, "They go down easier with a little food."

There were herbs, various preparation tools, dishes, a mortar and pestle, but there was also a huge slab of pork shoulder. "Nice!" I exclaimed.

"That's for you," Rayn bounded over to me, throwing her arms around my neck just as I leaned down to receive her, and planted an enthusiastic kiss on my lips.

"Go on and have a little fuck time before dinner!" Fedelma instructed so casually it almost sounded like something my mother would have said, though never would she have said such a thing.

I laughed as Rayn and I broke the kiss, and my girl, my beautiful, sweet girl, pulled me toward the kitchen door and said, "C'mon, let's get to fuckin'!"

What was that old lady doing to my Rayn?!

Look, it wasn't that Rayn couldn't be a bit crass, typically when she was being goofy, and she certainly was a spunky, enthusiastic little thing, but this was a new level. And hey, I'm not complaining! Noooo sir, not one iota! I was about the happiest camper you could ever see!

We scampered to our bedroom like two kids about to steal from the cookie jar. Before I even got myself undressed, Rayn and I were losing ourselves in another delicious tryst. It was playtime, laughter, tickling, tasting, and fucking. It was heaven!

"I asked Fedelma about seeing that vampire's ghost," Rayn said as we lay, utterly spent, staring at the ceiling.

"Oh, what did she say?"

"It wasn't Aurel's bite; it's this...part of my Nintach priestess energy. It was awakened when I got the tattoos."

I nodded, "Ah, well, that makes sense."

"And speaking of tattoos, mine are a little different than yours, you know."

I turned to my lovely lady, lying on her back beside me as she turned to meet my gaze. "They are?" I hadn't noticed, hadn't studied them that closely.

She nodded, "The female wards are different from the male. Since they are linked to our essences, they have to be. Here," she sat up, turned her luscious naked body to me, cross-legged and smiling. I moved to sit up as well, but she placed a hand on my chest, so I settled back into the cushions.

Playing instructor, peppered with a little flirting, Rayn pointed out various details, runes, and placements that were unique between us. Her finger touched the ink on her skin, then teasingly, ticklingly, traced those on my flesh that were different. "There are more on our backs

197

and in the ones that we can't see. Just small, yet fundamental differences."

I was fascinated and now aroused again after her tender touches and the low, slow, taunting way she delivered the information. We fell back into fondling and frolicking until we heard Fedelma call from the kitchen. "Get yer nasty selves cleaned up, then come eat!"

Hastily, we rushed to bathe ourselves, dressed quickly, then hurried to the kitchen. The house smelled divine! We ate like starving children, talking and laughing all through dinner.

Fedelma gave Rayn about five different herbal concoctions. One was a dry blend that actually vibrated in the little dish it was in; Rayn had to fold it into a thin slice of meat to control it so she could eat it. The second, third, and fourth were all liquids that Rayn took in shots between bites. Only one of those did she scrunch her face up at. Must not have tasted too good.

The final dose was a gas, some kind of smoky substance. It was green, and it swirled in a disk before Fedelma, who used her fingers and a spell to form it into a Gobstopper-sized ball. That sphere of smoke then drifted over to Rayn, who pressed her lips to it and sucked it into her lungs. I was amazed she didn't cough or choke on it.

Rayn turned her luminous eyes to me, and I mean luminous! They shone with that same green, bright and swirling in their irises, then it slowly faded. I must have been gaping dumbly at her because she asked, "What?"

"Your eyes were glowing green, just like that smokey stuff," I replied.

"See, I knew she was the one!"

We turned to Fedelma, her face filled with pride, smiling at us. "That's the final proof, right there. A spell to test the inheritor, the successor. It can't be done right away; I had to wait until certain practices were, well, practiced. That's why it's good to have instinct, and I've got an incredible instinct! Never doubted I'd found my girl!"

"Do you feel anything?" I asked Rayn, unable not to feel a little concerned about her.

"Nope, just a little tired."

Well, that was no wonder after all our messin' around!

"You two go get some rest." Fedelma waved at the kitchen door with her hand as she stood up and shooed us out. "Let yer lady sleep, mister; this initiation is catching up with her."

"Yes, ma'am." I scooped Rayn up and carried her to our room. Laid her down in our bed and crawled in beside her. Wrapped in a nice little bundle, we fell right to sleep.

Those blissful weeks soon came to an end, and Rayn's initiation was over. We were set to leave. We had packed our things and were planning on flying back home because Rayn needed to handle a few things back in the U.S. But before we could schedule our trip, which we planned to do from Clannon's place in London, Fedelma sat us down and stared hard at us for several long minutes before finally saying, "There's something here you need to do before you go."

"Something else?" I asked.

The old woman nodded, "It's, well, I can't explain it, but the both of you need to go exactly where I tell ya to go."

Confused, I narrowed my eyes at Fedelma. I did not like the strange, cryptic way she was acting. "Spill it. What is this all about?"

She locked her eyes on mine, her expression firm, "You remember how I told ya I have incredible instincts. Well, this is that. So trust me, and just do it. There's a house in the hills, an energy there, and I need the two of ya to go take care of it."

"Take care of it?" Rayn asked, "In what way?"

"However you see fit."

I was getting angry, "What's that supposed to mean? Is it a vampire that needs killing?"

"There is vampire energy there."

"Vampire energy…" I shook my head, "But I've sensed nothing. No burning, no alerts, and I thought Rayn was now out of it."

"She is. This is different. There's another energy; I don't know what it is."

The old woman was acting stranger than usual, and I was becoming increasingly unnerved. "Alright, fine, but *why* does Rayn have to come?"

"Spence!"

Of course, Rayn would be pissed with me for wanting to exclude her. "Look, Rayn, you're a Nintach priestess now. Doesn't that mean you're supposed to stay *out* of this stuff?"

"Well, yeah, but if Fedelma says I need to go, then I need to go. She wouldn't send me out on a fool's errand."

Rayn was right; why would the old gal do that after taking so much time and effort to train her as her successor? Maybe I was making a bigger deal out of this than I should. Maybe this was a part of Rayn's training, some trial for her or something. "Fine, we'll go. So, where are we going?"

Fedelma handed me a hand-drawn map. I recognized the terrain. The old lady was a pretty good artist, and the map was surprisingly detailed. I saw a mark where we were to go. It looked pretty average, a small remote cottage high up in the northern hills, hidden behind lots of trees.

"Well, let's get suited up." I turned to Fedelma, "We're suiting up, yes? Do I need to treat this like a hunt?"

She nodded, "I would, yes. But don't act rashly."

"I don't *act rashly*. I calculate. I never strike first." I replied a bit harshly.

But she didn't seem to take any offense. "Good, Spencer, that's good."

It was midday when we headed out, and the weather was a little overcast, a tad on the cool side. Rayn and I had changed into our hunter's gear, taking the rental car, since the distance was too far to walk.

When we were well away from Fedelma's house, where she could not watch us through her windows, I stopped the car and took hold of Rayn's shoulders. I looked into her eyes and ran my thumbs over her baby-soft cheeks.

"I don't know what this is, and I know the old bat wanted you to go with me, but—"

"Don't you say it, Spence!" She warned me with a harsh, determined look.

"Alright, fine. Off we go. But—"

"No buts!"

So, we were off, into the hills, up winding roads, barely speaking since neither of us was sure what to expect.

I felt like I was on autopilot, my head full of a plethora of thoughts: of the road I'd taken, of my past, our future. It had been some time since I allowed myself to do these mental exercises… exploring the many what-ifs of my life.

What if the vampires had never turned Jaren? What would have happened to me? Where would I be now? It wasn't really worth thinking about, and when I did mull it over, I never seemed to get anywhere with it. Would I trade all that I'd seen, done, and learned for a "normal," mundane life? A "safe" existence? Is there even such a thing as a safe life in this world? Not really, and yet, if I'd still ended up with Rayn, I'd happily live the most mundane life with her and with full contentment!

But would I give up all this, the reality-shattering things that both thrilled and terrified me? Would I turn in all the strength that I'd worked myself to the bone for, to possibly end up with my skinny ass behind a desk and a boss wagging his finger at me and peering over my shoulder, working my tail off in a completely different way only to fund *some other man's* extravagant lifestyle?

Damn it, no! I wouldn't!

Despite all the pain, the blood, the tears, and the terrors, I'd turn down any opportunity to alter my course. I'd keep doing this most frightening and violent thing until it killed me, or I got too damned old to keep up! I treasured my new friends, the forbidden knowledge I'd gained, and every muscle I'd built and scar I'd earned! Hell, I'd—

"You're looking mighty intense there, Mister Vale; what's on your mind?" Rayn cut into my thoughts. I turned to her briefly, seated there beside me with those inquisitive eyes as I navigated those mountain roads. I wanted to grab and kiss her, to thank her for being with me, for putting up with me, for making me so damned happy!

Shrugging, I laughed it off, "I was just thinking about life. Would I ever give all this vampire-hunting stuff up if things were different?"

"Really? Are you having doubts? That kind of surprises me."

I shook my head without any hesitation, "Nah, no doubts, just mental exercises. There is no way I'd go back to an average life, even if I could. Sure, if I could, I'd bring back those I've lost, save them from their fates. But I'm actually happy doing this stuff. Happier than I've ever been, with you here." I winked at her. "And more than that, I'm grateful to know Clannon, Byron, and all the others. How could I ever wish for a life where we'd never known them?"

My dear woman scooted close to me and hugged my arm, "Life is so strange..." she began, then in a sing-song voice, she continued, "When you don't know..."

"...how you can tell, where you're going to..." I finished the lyrics for her, and we both laughed.

But my mood, deep down, remained uncertain. I was feeling that strong sense again of something coming, something different, something...inexplicable...

XX

THE ANCIENTS

What was it I had only just said to Rayn on the road to this place? That I'd never give up this violent life of battle against dark forces?

Well, now, I was having second thoughts.

Who...or *what the hell*...was *that*?

Standing at the other end of a room, in that little, quaint cottage, way up a hill in the Scottish countryside, was a...a...man? No, not a man, not a human man, anyway. And yet, he was manlike. An alien? A creature of...*some* kind, but *what* kind?

Can a monster be beautiful? Well, sure. To myself and other horror enthusiasts, creatures like Giger's aliens or Lumley's Wamhyri *are* beautiful in a most hideous kind of way. But this creature was both marvelously unsettling and disturbingly stunning to look upon.

Positively towering, his head nearly touched the ceiling. I think he might even have been taller than Erskine but much narrower in build!

He had a well-sculpted, long face with pronounced aquiline features, a well-shaped, unobtrusive nose, a high arching forehead, and a deep widow's peak of long, stark-white hair that draped in a curtain over his straight shoulders and cascaded to midway down his back. His almond-shaped eyes were almost too large for his face: electric blue, bright and iridescent, clear as a mountain stream, mesmerizing! They had no whites at all, their liquid indigo filling the entire orb. That ever-present red prick of fire, exactly like a vampire's, glowed at their cores where his pupil should have been, making a lavender stain within the blue, in a perfect circle where his iris would normally be.

Full lips, even cherubic in their fullness and round shape, were perched above a slightly pointed chin, and his cheekbones protruded high on his face, the flesh of his cheeks concave as if he'd chewed them away inside, making him look gaunt, yet the effect was surprisingly beguiling. It lent him nothing of illness or anything of advanced age, at least not in the way a human might age, which seemed a contradiction considering his pallor and the hollows around his wide-set eyes. Oh, he was old, this being, so old it might be incalculable; at least, that's the effect he put off.

His unusual yet somehow attractive head sat atop a tall, thin neck and an exceedingly narrow body; he was long-limbed, moving with slow, determined, even ghostly grace. Tapered fingers and pale, sharply pointed nails gave the effect of spider legs, ever-moving, grasping, tapping, thinking…like some mad scientist or devious villain making his felonious little plans.

His skin was marble-like fair gray, not quite white, with a faint hint of slightly darker gray veins just under its surface. He wore light gray wrappings and white layers of draped fabrics that may or may not have been stitched together in unseen places. The effect appeared as if he'd stepped right out of an old movie or more like an ancient sepulcher—ghostly, monotone, but for those gleaming indigo, lavender, and scarlet eyes.

Again, there was no feeling of frailty or weakness about this being. Instead, there was *strength*! Its power…unmistakable as the vibration of its presence filled the entire space, radiating from him like a raging furnace fire. Yet there was no heat, nor was it a feeling like electricity; it was simply energy. Energy far greater than Erskine's, which, until that moment, had been the strongest I'd ever encountered. Well, that, and Fedelma, but her powers were not forceful, not…male, as were both the old Scottish vamp and this being's aura.

He was not the only unusual thing present there in that humble space. Standing with him was a female, clearly his companion. But she appeared to be a human or at least a former human. It was obvious she had been heightened by some preternatural gift. God, she *was* jaw-droppingly gorgeous! Nothing monstrous about her! And yet, she carried an air and manner that was similar to his, some inexplicable power, an ancient power…

Standing close beside her creature lover, the woman's creamy skin was milky, like natural pearl. Her light brown hair shimmered with a metallic sheen of honey brown, gold, and copper hues. Wavy, loose curls hung in a curious twist over her left shoulder, and her eyes were a striking lavender, probably actually gray or pale blue, which, like his, the color was altered by burning red cores. She was also lean and long-limbed, giving her an illusion of height, though she was not unusually tall as he was. She was certainly a vision of spectacular, angelic glory next to his eerie, yet also alluring, strangeness.

They both burned with dark forces—ageless, even youthful, especially the female. There was something modern about her, too. Something contradictory that I couldn't quite put my finger on: her mannerisms, the look in her eyes? A quality both ageless and twentieth-century, while he was entirely archaic and unfathomably ancient! Is that a word? Shit, I don't care. It's perfect.

One thing I was sure about, they were not vampires. But how did I know that? They certainly might look like vampires: both of them had that unnaturally light pallor, although different somehow from vamps. Both had the fiery red prick of light in their pupils, a trait of all Darklings. Both had sharp teeth. Why sharp teeth if not blood drinkers?

Maybe they *did* drink blood.

Maybe they were so damned ancient they no longer set off vampire wards, or at least the effect on those wards was different—or maybe they were something entirely different...

Either way, they were *not* vampires in the traditional sense. Oh, they did set off a portion of my runic tattoos. Still, it was a wholly different set from those the vampires affected, which also excited my skin in a wholly different way, creating an entirely new sensation.

While vamps made the black, inky runes burn with a warm heat, these—beings—made them tingle, which was not entirely unpleasant, although it further disturbed me; it was the activation of the invisible tattoos, the red glow, and the euphoric vibration of my skin that I'd not felt until now.

I recalled Fedelma's words, *"Vampires don't make 'em glow,"* she'd said of those hidden runes, *"but other dark beings...Darklings...certain ones will set 'em off, and ye'll light up like a flickerin' brush fire."*

Watching from across the room, I couldn't take my eyes off them. The way the pair gazed at one another, positively mooning, and their intimate closeness and warmth, yes *warmth*, even so much as heartwarming to witness... It certainly appeared to be adoration, perhaps even love. Pure, deep, genuine love! I couldn't help feeling its effects, like a tangible thing, and I even recognized myself and Rayn in their dynamic. I could feel its palpable truth, and I admit, I was deeply moved with a kind of empathy and even compassion for these nonhuman, or beyond human, beings.

But despite their show of love, their strange and moving beauty, and their ethereal aspect, something about *him* utterly disturbed me!

You may assume, by the nature of how my tattoos were reacting, that no actual vampires were in that place, but you'd be wrong. There *were* vampires somewhere there; I could feel them…feel the burn of those other runes on my skin, which I knew instinctively was not caused by these two. And the effect was mild. So, the vamps were keeping their distance, holding back, possibly waiting for something. For what, I couldn't guess.

Vampires weren't the only other dark creatures present; just as Erskine's place had crawled with shadows, those Nethers clung to every corner of this place, clustered more thickly around the creature and his lady. And, as it was with the ancient Scott, they simply watched us with their unblinking, shining, red eyes.

"You keep strange company; I can sense your vampire friends," I said to that tall male when he turned to me, breaking the silence that felt as if it might have lasted forever had I not said anything. The couple knew we were there, Rayn and I, but only just turned to acknowledge us.

The creature smiled and cocked his strange head, "I am a benevolent succorer to other Darklings; it is my calling."

If there was anything about this creature that completed the hair-raising experience of being in its awesome presence, it was its voice! Deep like thunder, yet smooth and soft, like gentle winds rustling leaves, droning…hypnotizing, with a strange accent I could not place. Were I not well-schooled and practiced at checking and controlling myself around unnatural monsters, I just might have lost myself to that voice's mesmerizing effects. How easy it would have been to succumb and let my head slip into complete serenity.

Rayn had a tight grasp on my arm, pulling me out of my haunted thoughts. I turned to her, finding her eyes locked on the creature. The features of her dear face were slack, eyes wide, wondering, utterly unchecked. She was feeling everything I was, no doubt, but her body language was far too open, too exposed. I didn't blame her. She was far less practiced than I was.

Hastily, I placed my palm on her cheek and turned her head to me.

"Sui temperantia," I said, which is Latin for self-control. I use that saying as a quick reminder, both for myself and anyone I might be with, to pull back from a vampire's hypnotic trance. I chose Latin mainly because the average person, or younger vampire, doesn't know the language. I prefer keeping my enemies unaware of what I say. Give nothing to inform them.

"A worthy practice," I heard the creature say in response to my comment. Of course, *he'd* know Latin, old as he apparently was.

Again, inexplicably, I knew he was old. So old, he made Erskine seem young!

But my attention was now on Rayn. She nodded, if a bit dreamily, and after a moment, her eyes came into focus on mine. I returned her nod emphatically, and when I felt sure she was back to herself, I turned again to our host as he began his first steps toward us.

The haunting way he moved was almost as enthralling as his voice. Every step seemed controlled, somewhat like a dance...a dance of death—walking, gliding, spider-fingers wiggling, making me cringe inwardly despite being just as drawn to him as I was repulsed.

"I'd appreciate it if you didn't work your mind tricks on us." I kept my voice level, hiding my uneasiness.

It smiled.

Unnerving!

I shuddered inwardly.

"I work nothing on you, mortal," he replied, "It is simply my natural effect."

"Involuntary," I stated flatly.

He nodded.

"But I'm sure you can willfully rein it in...control it."

His lip quirked up, and he nodded again, only once.

That pervasive sense of dreaming lifted like the clearing of morning fog, yet the threat and sense of morbid wonder remained.

God, but I could seriously have geeked out over this damned creature! He was, in my boyhood words, the coolest damned thing ever! I'd have been utterly obsessed if I'd been watching him in a film! But I checked my inner geek, cleared my mind, and relaxed just as the creature moved more swiftly, striding determinedly toward me.

His hand reached out slowly, gracefully, not at all in a threatening way... But that's not entirely accurate. It wasn't that I didn't feel threatened; I felt like there was no real threat in it. Or, perhaps he was *making* me feel that way, with some preternatural influence. Whatever the case, I did not move out of his path.

Both Rayn and I stood our ground, as still as statues. At the time, it didn't feel as if I was being controlled by an outside force, but later, I did wonder if we had been manipulated.

Normally, I was ready, even eager, to pounce on any threat. But I hadn't even drawn my weapons; it didn't even cross my mind.

Then, suddenly, he was right there, looming over me by more than a head! What would that make him? Over eight feet tall?

Before I could register what was happening, he touched my neck with his spidery fingers, and those typically invisible rune tattoos placed strategically all over my body flared so bright that I could see them glowing in my peripheral, shining beneath my clothing.

As shocked as I was at that, it was the fact that he was in no way repelled by any of my wards that really astonished me!

The new, tingling of my flesh increased, sending warning bells finally ringing and my thoughts into helpless panic.

Fearless?

Nope. Not me! Not at *that* moment when the very air in the room suddenly grew thinner, the vibe became stifling, and the thing's mood turned precarious. Not when I had the love of my life, the most important person in my life, my one and only reason to live, standing right beside me, right beside this monstrous thing, facing as much danger as I was.

"Ssslaayer," the creature suddenly hissed in my face, the red in its huge, gleaming eyes flaring wild crimson, the powers behind them holding onto me as firmly as the creature's hands that now stiffly cradled my head. And I knew that those spidery hands were strong enough to crush my fragile melon in an instant.

God! Please, not with Rayn right there, grasping my hand so tight it hurt.

I couldn't form words; thoughts and reactions were locked up in my mind, but my eyes pleaded desperately with the creature. All pride and bravado had fled, leaving only my fierce desire to protect *her*.

The being's strange eyes had grown wide and raging, and its fingers moved against my hair, itching to do me in with a single, deadly squeeze that would end my mortal life. There was no mistaking his intent. It radiated from him in palpable, barely checked fury.

But then, as suddenly as it manifested, his demeanor slowly shifted. While his hands remained where they were, cradling the sides of my head almost lovingly, their constant movement had slowed…stilled, and the flames in his eyes shrunk down and settled again into small pinpricks of light—just before his gaze broke from mine and moved down…

To *Rayn*!

I saw then that Romayne's other hand, the one that was not grasped in mine, was gently resting on *his* arm. She was touching that horrifying being, and her bravery astounded me as her pleading eyes captured his.

Please don't destroy my love; her powerfully emotional look implored him.

My own eyes burned as I watched their exchange. I glanced up to gauge the monster's reaction as I swallowed hard to keep from crying, and it seemed he was actually moved by her earnestness! Perhaps even by her sweet, pretty face. Certainly, he appreciated beauty, judging by his companion.

Words failed me. My throat was a column of hard tension. I could barely breathe as I stood utterly still, waiting to see if this would be our end!

From behind our aggressor, his mate approached. She placed one hand on his back, the other on his arm, just above where Rayn touched him.

Not a word was uttered by that unearthly woman, but a similar pleading showed in her eyes, imploring her lover not to kill me or *my* woman! But why? Why would *she* care to spare our lives?

The creature met his woman's imploring look, then turned to me just as a damned tear escaped my eye and slid unwanted down my cheek...

Weakness!

Damn it!

Revealing my emotions at a time like this!

I fucking hated it!

No, actually, as a new surge of emotion enveloped me, I realized that I loved it!

You see!? I thought scathingly at him! *How human I am! How deeply I can feel! You unearthly, unholy monster?!*

But just as I fell into my typical hateful thoughts, my fierce disdain toward vampires, I realized it made no sense to feel that way about him. Such indignation and pride over how *I* felt was silly. It was all too clear that these two beings bore their own depth of devotion to each other. They loved as deeply as I loved Rayn! They didn't deserve my ire, and they weren't even vampires.

Being in his presence was the oddest thing. I felt befuddled and scrambled, as if I couldn't think clearly, yet I felt like I was perfectly capable of ordered thoughts. The haze had lifted when I asked him to rein it in, but this must be some other effect, something he either could not control or used to control us on purpose.

Still, he held me physically, firmly, unwilling to release me...fingers so long that they nearly swallowed the whole of my head. Then he moved those awful hands until his cool palms caressed my cheeks, and we stared at one another with the passion for life versus the finality of death.

He *was* Death.

Figuratively...literally...

This thing could actually be *The* Grim Reaper! I imagined him donning a long, black, hooded cloak, snatching up a massive scythe, then going about his terrible work.

But I, too, was a reaper, a hunter with my Dundee knife, my butane lighter, and my little mini scythe, all of which would do me little good here.

"Please…" Rayn's sweet voice was like a salve on my soul, breaking the silent exchange between me and that thing. She was pleading with it for me, and it broke my heart to see and hear her terror and anguish.

His angelic lover turned her lips to his ear, coaxing his head down to her as she whispered just loud enough for Rayn and me to make out her words. "They are like us," her fingers stroked his arm up and down as she smiled sweetly, even reassuringly at me.

My heart raced with hope, but my mind struggled to understand why the woman was protecting me. Could she have recognized our shared love as I had recognized theirs?

"Like *us*…?" her lover scoffed, making my heart jump despite myself. He then removed his left hand from my head and cupped Rayn's cheek, holding the both of us like guilty children gazing up at their parents…wondering what our punishment might be.

My heart froze.

Rayn looked so tiny, so fragile, with his massive hand cupped around her head like that. I wanted to scream as his long, inhuman thumb stroked her flushed, fair cheek, the cheek I'd caressed and kissed now a thousand times.

Why the *hell* did I *ever* agree to let her come with me?! I'd have done anything at that moment for her to be back home, safe in her little house.

"…*are* they…like us, my love?" The male creature mused, eyeing Rayn so intently and so closely that it almost appeared he might kiss her.

"Yes, my Sweet Eternity," his woman replied.

This only made the creature laugh before he answered in his smooth, hypnotic, sepulchral voice, "Nay, dear Ulgania, how could these fresh, new things be anything like us, who have loved each other for the better part of an eternity?"

But she was undeterred. "You remember, dear Viarudian, in the beginning? Surely you do, with your incredible mind, so ancient yet capable of recalling details from a past so inconceivably distant? Remember how it was? How we loved long ago before you were so cruelly locked away from me?"

I could see his gleaming eyes glaze over as his thoughts traveled back in time. I tried to imagine what he must have been like so long ago…had he been mortal once, altered so much by the Dark Essence and by eons of time as to achieve this most unnatural state? Or had he always been this timeless, inexplicable thing?

"We were new then," his angelic lady continued, her luminous gaze moving from me to Rayn and back again. "So very young and fresh, were we not?" She was telling their tale to us as much as reliving it with him, "Young, devoted, desperate. And you, my love, taken from me far too soon… No, I do not want to see these two destroyed. I would not enjoy seeing them suffer a separation such as ours. How many long centuries did we wait to be reunited, dear Viar? Do not revisit our pain on these fragile mortal lovers."

Viarudian turned his eyes again to meet his love's, finally removing his hands from us in order to cradle her face as the pair stood close and shared their intimate exchange.

I wanted to separate us from them but couldn't find the will to move. Rayn also seemed to hesitate, leaving us helpless and frightened, as well as confused as we stood mutely, waiting on what might be our final demise.

"I could kill the both of them," the creature said in a voice more suited to a tender sentiment than a threat of death. "That way, they would be together in the Realm of Souls. Would that not please you or at least ease your mind?"

"No," Her response was quick, nearly stepping on his last word. "My precious, it would not."

Viarudian turned his burning stare back to me and locked on. I could not look away.

"This hunter…he and his woman have killed our kind. Mercilessly, they have acted without remorse."

Rayn spoke up, her voice stronger than I might have expected, yet still vibrating with emotion, "I have slayed one vampire, but it was not done mercilessly. It was done out of compassion. The hunters—"

But the male hissed to stop her, "That is your judgment on my kind, and it is not yours to make." He turned to me then, and the look he gave me was less of fury and more of testing, even teasing.

"My dear Ulgania," he continued, "allowing these two hunters to live would only show that we acquiesce to those continued killings."

"Perhaps not," she argued softly, then turned and addressed me, "You have brought your most precious love with you into this violence."

Her clear accusation stabbed my heart, and I flinched inside. Rayn grasped my hand tightly, but I did not turn to look down at her. I couldn't face her as my guilt surged, but I knew her expression regardless, that bull-headed determination of hers. She *wanted* to be there with me, come hell or high water.

Still, I should never have agreed to let her join me, and yet I was so grateful at that moment to have Rayn by my side. God, what would I have done without her there? Surely, I would already be dead with a head of bloody pulp had Rayn not been there to show those beings the depth of our feelings, to be a mirror of their own relationship.

But would it be enough to save our lives?

XXI
ANOTHER CHOICE

"Is there not a better way?" Ulgania's voice was filled with hope, even sweetness. There was no ire there, no blame towards us or what we'd done. "Could we not bargain for a different way?"

The woman's statement finally turned the tall male's ageless gaze back to her from where he now stood several paces away.

I frowned, wondering where this was going. "You want to make a deal with us?" I asked incredulously.

"I want to offer you another choice," her delicate fingers touched my cheek and Rayn's as she glanced back and forth between us. "I like the two of you, and I *see* what you truly are. The thought of your end, the end of your potential, it hurts my heart. Would you make another choice...instead of continuing as hunters, as destroyers of our kind? Could you choose another path?"

Another path?

"Become a vampire?!" I jumped to the first conclusion, reacting without considering what she really meant. It was my prejudice, my old habit surging forward again. Whether it was the stress or the fear, my ire was up, and I was finding the anger mighty difficult to control. "No! Never!"

A look of controlled patience crossed Ulgania's face. It seemed she realized that I had misunderstood. Her intense eyes locked onto mine with force, making me feel both insignificant and adored at the same time. The way a parent might look at a child when they are being lied to. "If the life of your dearest love depended on it, there is nothing you wouldn't do, correct?"

213

The tone of her voice held no threat, but for some reason, I still felt threatened. A surge of terror seeped in and colored my anger, and I was fully prepared to fall to my knees and beg for our lives, for Rayn's life. "Don't, please. I—"

But the woman only laughed, "It is no threat; it is simply fact. You would do anything, even that most hated of things, the thing that you would never do otherwise, to save your sweet Rayn. You see? That is how you have lied to us and to yourself."

She was right, of course. I sighed, and my shoulders dropped, "I would rather die…than become a vampire. But for Rayn, I'd do it in a heartbeat; I'd do…anything for her, to be with her."

Rayn hugged me hard, her face pressed to my chest, and I heard her whimper softly; she was crying.

"I know you would, as I would for Viar, *my* dearest love." Ulgania replied, "But I am not asking you to become a vampire. Nor am I threatening to allow Viarudian to kill you or your lady. What I am offering you is The Dark Gift."

"Ulgania!" Viar's soft yet powerful voice cut in, his huge eyes growing larger with shock, his hand on her arm, drawing her attention back to him again. "We cannot give The Dark Essence to hunters!"

I turned to Rayn as she tilted her sweet face up to me, her eyes still leaking tears, her body trembling against mine. We were both speechless, speaking only with our eyes, our hearts.

The male creature's voice grew louder, "You would gift this killer with what *we* have?" Despite his astonishment and resistance, in his voice and expression, there was a powerful respect and softness toward his woman.

I understood how he was feeling all too well.

"You can sense it in them, can't you, my love?" The woman urged, "Touch them again, put your flesh against theirs, and feel their souls, the deepest depths of their cores. I promise you will agree with me. They *are* worthy."

The look in his strange eyes and the intense emotions he displayed only further confused me. Oh, his anger remained, his distaste for what I was, what I'd done—it was all there. But there was also a melting of the proverbial ice between us, an understanding and compassion that made me think, oddly, of my father. That was not a comfortable association, so I rejected it immediately, even as I found myself wanting to actually like Viarudian and Ulgania.

In a swift, fluid motion, Viarudian was back. Rayn and I found ourselves standing beside each other again with his palms pressed to our cheeks, his eyes moving back and forth between us. I couldn't move a muscle, and I was sure it was the same for Rayn. One by one, Viar locked eyes with us, spending what felt like a considerable amount of time digging into our startled gazes as if seeking treasure there, which I suppose he was.

Then, he removed his hands and took a step back. "You," his voice was a breath of wind through deep caverns, his long, sharp finger pointed at me emphatically, "are not the same as you once were."

What?

What did he mean by that? Had he read my mind? Did he discover the details of my past and how much I'd changed after becoming a hunter? Was that what he was referring to?

"Of course, I'm not the same as I was. Is anyone after what I've gone through?" I replied with a shrug, "You wouldn't recognize me before my family was *destroyed* by vampires." It was impossible to keep the sneer out of my voice or the scathing look out of my expression.

He seemed unaffected by my ire, "That is not what I refer to, young one. You are no longer simply human."

Wait! What was he saying? I could not have heard him correctly.

"It has already begun," his smile was brief, but knowing, "So close to the vampires for so many years, it could not have been avoided."

"Close to the…" My heart raced, and sweat broke out on my skin. "What the hell are you getting at?"

"Exposure." He smiled broadly, and the effect on his not-quite-human face was unsettling, to say the least. "Exposure to The Dark Essence. It is tenacious, The Dark, always wanting, searching, needing…and it is *inside* you, even now. Has been for some time. It works on you so very slowly."

I gaped at him, skin hot, eyes wide as his declaration washed over me, but I struggled to accept what he said. I simply couldn't…. "Th-the…b-blood, you mean?"

He nodded.

No! *Shit!* No!

"But I've never been bitten, never drank vampire blood before. Haven't even gotten the stuff in my mouth, miraculously." That *was* a miracle, with all the vamp blood I'd shed, the gory messes I'd made, but I was sure I hadn't ever swallowed any.

The creature chuckled low and slow, "You need not swallow the stuff."

There was *no* way! I couldn't get my head around the idea that I was infected with vampire taint! How the hell!? And what about the other hunters, all of them exposed as much as I was, or perhaps even more so? Were they all cursed, too?

215

Or was this creature simply lying to me? Attempting to manipulate me in some way? Certainly, he was using his mental powers on me, on my mind, my body, after I'd expressly asked him not to.

"You do not believe me," he mused with a rueful chuckle, "but that matters not. You *are* forever changed and changing every second. You will evolve into a Darkling one way or another, but my guess is The Dark will follow the dictates of the thing that 'tainted' you, as Dark Essence typically does. Rarely, when vampires are the source, does The Dark manifest into something different, and yet, occasionally, it has."

He really wasn't making a lick of sense, "But, I'm warded against vampires and the vampire curse." Suddenly, it hit me: I hadn't always been warded! Was I tainted as far back as my early days before coming to the UK? But then, wouldn't Fedelma have sensed it in me before giving me those tattoos, or wouldn't the tattoos be a problem on a vampire's skin? God, the endless questions I had.

"Look," I took a deep breath, trying to calm my brain and settle my racing heart. "How can I have these wards and be a vampire?"

"Your wards are not foolproof, and they are one reason the Darkness inside you progresses so slowly. But doubt not, it *does* progress, and it will, given time, *alter* the very nature of you and even your...*wards*."

It was true. Oh god, I knew it was true!

"How long?"

"Not long," he replied.

"So, it happened after I was warded."

He nodded.

"What about the other hunters?"

"Of course, I cannot know that."

Viarudian lifted his right hand as if to show me something; then, using the long, sharp nail of his middle finger, he sliced into the porcelain flesh of his thumb. He then captured a dollop of the rich—not red—violet blood that flowed freely before the wound resealed itself. He then rubbed the viscous stuff between his fingers, murmuring strange sounds, perhaps words, most definitely a spell, until that unnaturally dark purple blood began to separate into two substances, finally leaving behind only a smear of jet-black stuff. Was that the infamous "Dark Essence?"

"Give me your hand, vampire slayer."

I hesitated, "Why? What are you going to do?"

"Nothing that has not already begun." His look was sharp, calculating as he withdrew the proffered hand and said, "Would you prefer the raging, ravenous hunter, the unyielding craving for blood like

216

those you hunt so mercilessly and so desperately despise? To become the thing your hunter friends must put down with shining blade and cleansing fire?"

I scowled at him, "So what, then? Are you going to cure my vampire taint, make me human again?"

"I do not like the connotations of the word...*taint,*" he returned my scowl. "Human again? Do you truly believe I have such power? And even if I did, why would I do such a thing? That is no gift! That is a cruelty! No, you and your...*taint* will continue. Let me enlighten you further. Infinitesimal amounts of The Dark have seeped into you through your pores. How? Why? Because it has *chosen* you, young one. The Dark Essence finds in you a kindred soul. It desired to merge with you, and it works within you, if only at a snail's pace."

Chose me? What the hell?

Feeling a prickling in my skin, the gooseflesh rising on my arms, the hairs at the back of my neck standing up, the oddest reality suddenly settled over me. As unfathomable as it might seem coming from a hunter of vampires, I knew the darkness inside and felt the keen and burning truth in the kinship he described.

"Dark Essence has its own will." The creature turned his large, gemstone eyes to the black stuff now coating his fingers. "It chooses its desired vessel and manifests in whatever form it dictates. The being you become depends on many factors. Vampires are unique, quite singular in their ability to spread their kind. They are one of the only Darkling creatures who may gift The Dark. It is fundamental to the creatures they are. So, because you received The Dark from a vampire, you will become one yourself."

"No," I growled, "I won't. I'm stronger than—"

The creature laughed, not cruelly, but as a parent might laugh at an ignorant child. "Resistance is futile."

So I was to be the Locutus of vampires...apparently.

"Give me your hand." He repeated, gently but insistently, holding his left hand out to me.

Uneasy and unsure, I glanced at his woman, that stunning, unearthly beauty who had pleaded our case and made this option available. She smiled so comfortingly back at me—like an angel, beckoning me to partake of this most surreal sacrament.

Holding my breath, I then turned to look down at Rayn, who, in my heart, was even more stunning than that radiant being. Her eyes were swimming as they met mine with a powerful kind of... *encouragement.*

She *wanted* me to accept their offer?!

217

"You…want this?" I gasped, mystified.

"This is right, Spencer. Trust me, it is right. I felt it before we arrived here, and I can feel it now even more powerfully. *This* is why Fedelma sent us here. You see, it is not only you…. I am also changed."

My heart plummeted. I knew then that Rayn was vampirized, too. Had I known it before now? Had there been signs? Well, nothing obvious, but had I sensed it and refused to accept it? Probably. My Rayn would be a vampire in time, just as, apparently, I would be.

"Fedelma knows about me, though I don't think she knows about you. We addressed it during my initiation to become her successor. It showed up during the first stage of my training, but she didn't tell me until much later. I was terrified, Spence. I thought she'd insist that I had to die and that all my dreams of working with her, of being with you, would be shattered. The idea of you finding out such a thing scared the hell out of me! I knew you would insist on being the one to kill me. Oh god, Spencer, what would that have done to you?"

I held her to my chest again, feeling sick, exhausted, helpless.

Rayn's voice drifted up to me tiredly, "Fedelma told me that something was coming for us. A new…well, she didn't know what it was, only that I must be prepared for it and to lead you into it when it presented itself. She told me, in the most emphatic terms, not to be afraid. And I know now *this* is that thing. Spencer, this is our destiny."

"Rayn…" I choked on the lump in my throat, mostly because I believed her and trusted her with my very soul. Resolved, I looked up at the creature who had remained frozen there with his left hand and those blackened fingers held out to me. My eyes locked on that jet substance as I lifted my right hand slowly, reluctantly, surrendering to this incomprehensible thing.

Gently, he grasped my arm and turned my hand palm up. Then he paused and gazed thoughtfully for a moment at the letters R A Y N before smearing that black substance across my wrist and right over Rayn's name.

Instinctively, I yanked my hand away, staring in wonder as the inky goop seeped right into my skin like so much quicksilver. Shocked, I rubbed at the flesh but felt no residue left behind.

As my startled eyes met the smiling woman's, then went to his strange, smiling face, the oddest, most intense physical sensation moved through my hand, then slowly seeped up my arm and crawled into my torso. It spread throughout my entire body in an instant, a wave of energy overtaking me that I can hardly describe.

An overwhelming shuddering sensation, similar to what you might describe as someone walking over your grave, utterly overtook me. It was so profound—a blissful sort of agony that required every ounce of self-control to prevent myself from writhing and wiggling like a madman. My skin, every inch that was inked by those runic tattoos, tingled, pulled, and burned far worse than the vampire ward ever had. And the marks themselves were changing, their shapes as well as their very nature and purpose. I could *feel* them, even though I couldn't see it happening.

Rayn had locked her arms around my middle, grasping onto me tightly as every muscle in my body went rigid. I grit my teeth, sucked in air through my clenched jaw, fisted and unfisted my hands, holding my tongue to avoid screaming like a madman until the heady anguish oh-so-slowly ebbed.

Once my addled nerve endings had quieted, I growled tightly, "What will happen to me now?" I was feeling scatterbrained and disoriented all over again and in a new way, finding it hard to think clearly, which made me incredibly frustrated.

With all patience and in his most benevolent savior's voice, Viarudian replied, "I have delivered you from the hunger. You will not suffer it now. Instead, you will be as I, and my beloved Ulgania. A Darkling."

I could not hold back the now completely natural trembling, simply from emotion and exhaustion, "Why would you do this for me...*to* me?" My voice was shaking, "You were ready to destroy me only moments ago. I was your enemy!"

"*Are* you still...truly, *my* enemy, Spencer?" It was the first time he'd spoken my name, and it sent shivers up and down my spine.

What was I to say to that? That I wasn't his enemy?

No, in fact, I was not. There was no desire in me, even after all he'd just put us through, to destroy him or either of those two beings. I doubted I could. They seemed impossible to kill—so ancient that, certainly, someone, or likely many someones, must have tried destroying at least him in the past and not succeeded. Didn't the woman say Viarudian had been locked away from her? Probably because he was *un*killable.

I needed to understand what he'd done by giving his Dark Essence. To me, it made absolutely no sense. He couldn't have only done it to make his woman happy, or maybe that was all it was.

"Please explain to me why you rewarded me with this...gift. You act as if you've blessed me...sanctified me. But you don't believe I deserve it. And what will happen to me? What curse have you doomed me with?"

"Curse," He laughed ruefully.

The woman's soft, cold hand cradled my cheek, and I turned to her, suddenly verklempt, eyes moist, burning, knowing…realizing that my very self, the core of who and what I was, had been irreversibly changed.

Ulgania's face shone like the brightness of a star to my troubled psyche, illuminating the darkness of my mind. Her smiling eyes brimmed with warmth and emotion that baffled yet helplessly endeared me to her and her strange lover…even to this new situation.

"You will be as we are," she said, "We do not hunger. We simply thrive."

I turned my leaking eyes to Rayn and cradled her sweet face in my hands.

"What about Rayn?" My voice caught on her name. She would be a vampire, and I was…something else.

"Love her," Ulgania whispered, her voice hot and sensual. "Love her, give of yourself to her, and you will pass your new Dark Essence into her. Viar has made it so."

"Am I…will I spread The Dark to others, then? How careful do I need to be?"

Viarudian shook his head, "No. Only once will you share, with your woman. Not all Darklings may spread the gift. It is only by The Dark Lord's will. Should he allow it, someday, you may be granted the ability."

"Then how am I sharing this with Rayn, exactly?"

"Because I have willed it so." Viar explained, "It is how I gifted The Dark to my Ulgania. Because of your devotion to each other, your coupling will pass it to her and create for you both a special bond. Unless you prefer that I—"

"No, no, I understand," I exclaimed.

My woman, *my* special bond!

Viarudian chuckled, "I thought not."

I wondered if, perhaps, I had tainted Rayn during sex, but it was a question not worth asking now because it didn't matter. I pressed my lips to hers as a soft acceptance of this new reality and to the easiest thing I had ever been asked to do: to love my woman.

When I pulled away, smiling down at her, Viarudian said, "Now, there is something you must see…"

XXII
FAMILY

Our host, my—benefactor?—led us deeper into the little house. The cottage was not as small as it appeared upon approach. Narrow in the front, it sprawled in the back, opening into a den, maybe half again the size of the smaller living room we had been standing in.

"You may ask how I could make this possible, this…thing that I shall reveal to you."

I did not care for the teasing tone of Viarudian's voice. My arm was around Rayn as we entered the den, then halted in the center of the room.

"Suffice it to say, the pieces fell into place."

Keeping to his senseless teases, Viarudian said no more. Then, after a subtle nod at Ulgania, he paused, closed his strange eyes, and grew utterly still, then he and his woman locked arms and left us standing there without another word.

Mystified, I looked down at Rayn just as the door across the room, opposite to the one we'd entered, opened.

I nearly collapsed.

There is no way to express my feelings at that moment!

Jaren?!

I had never stopped hunting for my brother. He literally seemed to have fallen off the face of the earth after killing our parents. I had come to the conclusion that, for some reason, Jaren didn't hunt in our town. Or if he did, I never discovered it. I routinely traveled out of town to hunt during those first ten years after Jaren's change but did not find any sign of him during all those hunts, either.

Year after year, I wondered, had it been a choice Jaren made not to hunt in our town, or had he destroyed himself the way he said he would in his confession/suicide note? I couldn't know for sure, but I seriously doubted he was dead by suicide. There was nothing in his demeanor on that fateful night to indicate he had any intention of killing *himself*. No remorse, no distress, or weakness of any kind. Only severe arrogance and vicious pride. Just like all vampires!

No, I knew that Jaren lived! He lived, and he killed…somewhere, and I was determined to find him and end him.

In all I'd read, nowhere did I find any way to rescue a vampire, to make them mortal again. I'd searched diligently through Clannon's library and throughout our travels all over Europe, studying any text or story I could lay my hands on and asking the wisest and most practiced hunters, gypsies, anyone, but to no avail.

It was a silly pursuit, and I always approached it dubiously. It wasn't that I didn't believe I'd find a way, but that I wondered if I *should* save him after what he'd done. I wondered if he could handle being saved, facing his monstrous acts with a human, un-vampire-tainted mind… those heartless and bloody murders laid bare before him. To gain that kind of awareness again would destroy him in a much more traumatic way than me simply killing him outright.

I didn't want my brother, as the Jaren I'd known before his fall, to feel that kind of pain.

Ultimately, part of me was relieved I discovered no cure. It made my work simpler: destroy the creature my brother was now and be done with it. It also, in some hopeful way, exonerated him in my heart. I believed that my brother was already dead before killing our folks. Dead of conscience, of his humanity. If some of those books I'd studied were accurate, then his vampire body had no soul, or it was essentially possessed. Whatever that thing was that had taken his body, it carried all the guilt, not him. That was my belief and my conviction.

Some accounts of vampires indicated that they were wholly the same people they were before the change—that the hunger in the early days drove them to a kind of disconnected insanity. The longer they lived, adjusting to their new state, the more they returned to a form of their previous human selves, at least mentally, if the change and their actions didn't drive them to insanity. Insanity seemed to be a given for most blood drinkers.

But I hated the idea that vampires could have a conscience, and I refused to believe it! To think that my brother, my poor brother, would have to live with himself, even as a vampire, after what he did! It sickened me simply to contemplate it.

It also brought my slaying into a whole new light, throwing so many questions into it, making it such a gray area that I could not accept it. So, I shoved those concepts completely out of my head. Otherwise, how was vampire slaying anything but cold-blooded murder?

Sure, the death penalty for killers can also be called "murder," and these creatures *were* killers, point blank! Still, I chose to see them as utter monsters with no censor, no remorse, just hungry, violent killing machines.

Monsters are monsters.

That perspective made the slaying so much more fulfilling!

But what's worse? Being moral of mind and doing monstrous things? Or being forever altered, losing all sense of right and wrong, and doing monstrous things? The human monster is far worse, in my opinion, and yet, I could not murder a man in cold blood. But I very well could be slaying monsters with a conscience.

How fucked up is that?

But, the truths, as I was about to discover, were far more convoluted than such a simple, black-and-white concept. I should have known it, and despite hints of it, like when Rayn encountered that young vamp with the tormented soul, still, I wasn't prepared for it.

You know how it is when you've searched for something for so long that it turns into a kind of obsession, always lurking in the back of your mind? Things happen, your focus shifts, and you...*almost* forget about your initial goal—then BAM! You finally find your original quarry out of the blue when you least expect it.

After all those years of searching, never giving up, my instinct had been correct!

There he stood in the doorway, big, strong, filling that opening with something, someone, that should not be there! My head reeled, and I heard Rayn gasp as she grasped my arm tightly.

He looked smaller than I remembered, or shorter, at least. I'd outstripped him by a couple of inches, which, at that moment, gave me a strange sense of superiority.

Coming back to the moment at hand, returning to that mission I'd set for myself, I reached inside my coat, grasped the handle of my scythe, and gently extracted myself from Rayn's hold; I stalked toward him as he strutted forward in that familiar, utterly confident, utterly fearless way of his.

Then I froze.

Jaren did the same.

All the air escaped my lungs, my heart locked, and I nearly collapsed to the floor.

How?!

How were *they* here?!

The scythe fell from my limp fingers. Rayn, who had rushed after me, snagged hold of my arm again, then she wrapped her arms around my middle.

"Oh, Spence!" I heard her cry, her voice breaking.

My parents, alive...?

Vampires!

Suddenly, I was a kid again—a broken, shattered, terrified little boy inside who had lost everything and suddenly regained some cruel, demented replacement.

It was as if my entire adult life was a rug now yanked out from under me. The foundation of my strength, everything I'd learned, gained, overcome in my endless struggles to prevail and succeed after my loss, crumbled to dust in the wake of this...this horrible—this wonderful—revelation!

I felt Rayn step back, and her warm, small hands grasped mine. Godsend!

Her presence was a rock, a crutch keeping me upright. Her soft, awe-filled voice drifted up to me, but I could scarcely make sense of what she said as my head swirled with a hurricane of scattered emotion, a disordered mass of memories, and fragmented knowledge. Thoughts cascaded and crashed into each other in a tumultuous attempt to understand what stood before me.

"Spencer," it was my mother's voice, my sweet, pretty little mother.

My sweet, pretty little *Monster.*

I turned my swimming gaze slowly from face to face: Jaren, Dad, then to her. She was stunning, lean, youthful, always fair-skinned, but more so now in that preternatural way. But her eyes, *their* eyes, all glowed with the furnace fire of the dark things they were. Red like the blood they drank to survive. Red like the blood frozen in my veins.

"Please, forgive your brother," she pleaded in her tender, oh-so-familiar motherly way.

I shook my head slowly, side to side, not so much defying her request as expressing my disbelief.

"How?" I rasped, my own voice small, quivering. "You...Mom..." I faltered but forced myself to continue, "Jaren k-killed you...so *cruelly!* I watched! I saw it, the hate in his eyes, how he did it! The viciousness!"

Slowly, my head cleared, memories coalescing, righting themselves like a spinning top coming to a standstill. I knew what I had witnessed, what I felt, that it was unmistakably real. My conviction, the very thing that had set me off on this journey of destruction, could not have been in error.

Yet here they were! Standing together right before my burning eyes.

"The hunger," Jaren's voice drew my attention to him reluctantly. I didn't want to look away from Mom.

The deeply seated feelings for and against my brother roiled inside me, mirrored in the way I glared at him, yet tempered by my confusion and the clear evidence before me.

"In the beginning, it's madness, Spence." He sighed, even laughed a little, "Feeding clears the madness; well, it did for me after you fled. I'd have followed you that night, you know—drained you dry, even after telling you I wouldn't do it. Perhaps my head had already begun to clear when I made that promise to you. You ran, then I saw what I'd done to Mom and Dad, so I gave them my blood, just as my sire had given hers to me."

My folks hadn't been dead? I'd escaped thinking they were gone and all was lost. And it was, just not in the way I'd thought.

"Your sire?" My curiosity overcame me. "Who did it to you?"

"It doesn't matter now, she's gone. *You* destroyed her." Jaren shrugged.

There was no anger in his voice, no accusation. It was simply a statement of fact.

A surreal kind of knowing swept over me. "Did she own a cat?" I asked, feeling weird speaking to Jaren like I used to, not like a hunter, like a brother. As if I'd completely forgotten what I was, what *he* was. As if I was somehow committing a sin against my calling by exchanging so casual a conversation.

"Big black cat," he smirked at me, holding his hand up to about the height of a wild panther.

The way he looked at me, spoke to me, made me feel half my size again.

My big brother...

It was clear no love was lost by the vampire woman's slaying.

Mom and Dad watched our exchange intently, silent and earnest.

"I wrote the note, for you, Spence, to protect you." He added.

I was nodding, understanding, finally, yet still profoundly confused.

"You left me unchanged, Jaren. Why didn't you just kill me along with the folks? You could have hunted me down later. Put me out of my...of my...misery. You knew I..." My voice cracked; I was falling apart again, just like a house of cards; I was about to completely lose it.

Rayn had been hugging my arm, rubbing it up and down, holding tightly to my hand to calm and support me. When I felt my body buckle, her arms flung around my middle again, keeping me up, pulling me back into myself. But she said nothing, just being there for me.

"You're magnificent, Spencer." Jaren grinned wide and warmly, making it particularly unnerving. All I could see was the cruel way he'd grinned at me before the killing…Before, I thought he'd killed our parents.

Those fangs of his were long, gleaming, not caked in blood like the last time I'd seen that terrible, gore-filled mouth with its wicked, wretched grimace!

"How could I steal away your growth?" He exclaimed, "You're incredible ascension? You're like a fucking phoenix, Spencer, rising from the ashes of your loss? Shoot, man, you went from sweet little brainiac to fucking badass, kickass Batman! Never in my wildest dreams would I have *ever* thought you'd turn into *this!*" He held his hands out to me, waving them up and down to indicate my size, my hunter getup, everything I now was.

All the things I'd gained and learned and accomplished crashed through my mind like a tide returning, or more like a tidal wave. And I felt a massive swelling of pride, of pain, of guilt knowing how proud my brother was of me.

Jaren laughed heartily, "And you got the fucking girl, man! *The* girl! *Your* girl!"

I was trembling in every limb at the conviction of his words, the love and respect in his voice. But I also felt the strength returning to my legs, my mind recovering again from this onslaught of unexpected revelations. And along with my shaking recovery came indecision.

What was I going to do now?

"A-are you…happy?" I asked, my voice a little stronger, eyes turning to my mother, then to my father.

"We're content, son." Dad smiled at me, mouth closed as if he were attempting to lessen the vampire effect by hiding his dangerous teeth.

Good luck with that! Those glowing crimson eyes could not be masked so easily!

Was this a nightmare or some insane delusion? My family was alive! Vampire creatures, but alive! God, I wanted to crash into them, to tumble into a big group hug and lose myself in kisses, relief, and unbridled joy!

226

It was my mother who broke away first and moved toward me with her precious arms extended. But I was still torn; couldn't help it, I was feeling both sick and oddly elated.

Visions flashed through my mind of creepy, mist-wreathed Ralphie Glick floating at the window in Salem's Lot, his fingernails scratching and scraping and screeching against the glass; *let me in…let me in…*

But I was moving toward my mother despite those fears, helpless to her pull, to the overwhelming desire to hold her in my arms again.

Rayn released me. Again, she trusted this most bizarre process, this incredible thing that seemed to go against everything I'd known and devoted myself to.

We, my dear family and I, wrapped ourselves into a cluster of tears, kisses, and embraces, like some fever dream I was sure I'd wake from any second.

Everything about that strange and incredible day felt unreal, surreal, impossible. I pulled Rayn in with us as tears streamed freely down my face, down hers, and even my vampire family's. It was a cleansing of my heart, a new awakening of my soul.

As our little love cluster calmed, I saw that Viarudian and Ulgania had returned; they stood together watching us, smiling like they were the parents and the rest of us the children—which, I suppose, they sort of were. It struck me then that none of us were mortal anymore. Not one of us in that room was a mundane, earthly mortal now. What that meant for me and my loved ones, I simply didn't know.

How would Clannon and the others handle this? Was Rayn now disqualified to be Nintach? Would Clannon disown me? My heart clenched at that thought! Would the hunters seek us out to destroy us? Could we even be destroyed?

"Spence, man, we need to talk." Jaren grasped my shoulder and shook it gently as I turned to him.

"Yeah, we really do," I replied. It was extremely strange looking down, just a little, into his eyes.

He cackled, "Shit, man, you're way too tall! Fucking bastard!"

"Jaren!" My mother exclaimed, making both of us laugh at the ridiculousness of my vampire mother scolding us for a few bad words.

Jaren led me into that back room, the one my vampire family had emerged from. It turned out to be a small apartment with two bedrooms and a bath. Rayn remained with my parents and those two mysterious ancient ones. I needed this one-on-one time with my brother. Whatever Rayn and I learned separately could be shared between us later.

I felt a powerful nostalgia as we sat across from each other in Jaren's windowless room, him on his bed and me in a small, plush chair. We used to sit just like this in his bedroom or mine all those years ago, and the discussions we had cascaded through my mind like waves crashing against everything that had happened since. I also felt a surge of excitement to finally, hopefully, begin to understand the questions that had plagued me over the years and many of the new ones burning my brain now.

"You want the whole story, I guess." Jaren rolled his eyes. He was toying with me. God, I'd missed that!

"I don't need a long-running series, just the cliff notes. Apparently, we have plenty of time for all the lurid details. First, tell me how the hell you ended up here in Scotland?"

"*That's* the first thing you want to know?" He laughed, "Alright, well, actually, it is a rather fantastic thing. Supernatural, super-science, you'll love it. Let me just give it all to you in order, okay? No sense jumping around."

I nodded.

"So, Clare, the vampire cat lady you killed, that bitch was a pain in my fucking ass! Oh, at first, I was smitten! God, yeah! Older woman, loaded, dead sexy—"

"Dead*ly* sexy!" I amended with a smirk.

"Ha, true enough. But, man, what a control freak *she* was! I won't go into all *those*…lurid details; not worth boring you with 'em. I will say that she was pretty pissed over me turning Mom and Dad! She screamed at me about how ridiculous it was that I'd want to vampirism my parents."

"She's right, Jaren, I don't get it either." I shrugged.

He gave me a long, dead-serious look, then sighed, "Spence, if anyone would understand why I did it, I'd have thought it would be you. I told you that hunger makes you mad and that feeding eases it. Early feeding is like that; the first feed is waaaay more than the rest, though. Puts you right out of your fucking mind. After you satisfy that mad craving, you return to your senses. Can you imagine what I felt when I saw…" Jaren closed his eyes, drew in a deep breath, the sudden blast of emotion evident in his handsome face.

228

"I understand. Look, Jaren, I've spent years with those images in my head, the way…" But I stopped myself. I wasn't there to chastise, to blame, and unload. Perhaps someday I would dump all my shit on Jaren. But now, I just wanted to hear his story. "I do get it, Jaren. I understand better now, so go on. Tell me what happened."

He nodded, smiled thankfully, and went on, "Clare wanted me to end them, and if I didn't, she'd do it herself or send one of her fucking goons to do it. Shitheads!"

I laughed, "Yeah, they weren't fun, but it was the cat that got me," I pulled my shirt up, displayed those big scars."

"Nice!" He exclaimed, then, needling me under his breath, said, "Show off."

I smirked at him as he continued his story.

"Needless to say, I took off immediately, left the bitch and we went into hiding. The folks and I skipped town, took up residence in a bed and breakfast, if you can believe that."

I frowned, "Did you kill the owner?"

"Yes." Jaren shrugged, but his expression remained serious. "Man, don't hate me for my vampire ways! The guy was old. A grumpy ol' sod. He was not long for this world anyway; I did him a favor. I really don't need you gettin' all fucking judgy on me right now." His tone was authoritative but not harsh.

"Fine, mister sensitive. I mean, I *have* been slaying your kind for a while now, and I know your ways. Nothing new to me. You drank the guy and took over his place. What next?"

Jaren grinned then and shook his head, "God, I *love* you like this— big, tough Spencer! Bein' all dominant with his big brother!"

"Just get on with it!" I smiled back, my face heating up.

"We weren't there long before Mom dragged Dad and me out to this remote area in the woods. Neither of us knew what she was doing, what any of her jabbering was about. She went on and on about some mysterious people, beings, that wanted to help vampires. I mean, helping vampires? What the hell? And beings? What? Aliens or some shit? Dad and I were baffled, but she was more animated and full of energy than I'd ever seen her, even in her mundane, mortal life. You know how subdued she's always been. You wouldn't have recognized her.

"But seeing her that way, it made us both so happy. Seriously! Since leaving you, Mom had been a total mess! Hand-wringing, nail-biting, tears and whining. God, the amount of times she begged me to go to you, to take *her* to you, to at least tell you we were okay! I can't even count!"

"Wait!" I suddenly realized there had been a completely normal funeral for my parents—nothing about their bodies going missing. Nothing strange at all happened once the "killings" were dealt with. "Jaren, how the hell was there a funeral? How could Mom and Dad have been vampires all this time, and I not know *something* was amiss?"

He shook his head, looked grim, "It wasn't easy, believe me. On the very night that I turned them, when I refused to take them to you or even to let you know that they were not dead and gone, neither Mom nor Dad would agree to simply disappearing *into the vampire world* with me. They insisted there needed to be a normal funeral so that you could move on and have closure. I had to figure something out.

"So, right there in their bedroom, after you left and after I had given them my blood and started the process of their change, I drained them both almost dry and left them there. Their bodies were in a real mess, and their vitals nonexistent, yet they did live a kind of half-life, undetectable by medicine. They would not die since the vampire change was happening. They were taken to be cremated, and I... well, I switched them out with two other bodies before the deed. Two of my...now don't go all righteous on me, man! Two of my victims that looked enough like them, same sizes, same general age, took their place."

"Shit, Jaren!" I dropped my face into my hands and tried to control the sick feeling welling up inside me. "Some other person's parents, someone's family, died to save—"

"Yes," he jumped on my words, "and it's all over now, so here's what happened next." My brother squirmed awkwardly in his seat before huffing, looking away from me, and continuing. I could feel his guilt, his profound discomfort. I said no more about it. "We went to this infamous clearing, to this infamous meeting mom was so eager for. Other vampires were there, strays, mostly. You know, vamps often form clusters, but some just don't join up with others. We call them strays."

"Yes, I know. I know pretty much everything there is to know about vampires, remember."

"Right, smart ass! Anyway, I'd say there were close to fifteen vampires there, including us three. That's when Viarudian and Ulgania showed up. And I mean, they literally just showed up! Out of thin air! POOF! And seeing them for the first time, I was, well, you've seen them now, so I don't need to express the effect they had on me, on all of us.

They walked out of literally nothing and right into the midst of our little group. That inexplicable act alone, of popping into existence like that, sent at least half of the vampires scurrying away in terror. Even preternatural creatures can get freaked out sometimes. They didn't come back.

The rest of us, perhaps seven in total, listened as Viar offered us the chance to go with him to…wherever it was he came from. He offered us safety and the chance at a new life. He offered freedom from the hunger, from the need to drink blood in order to thrive.

"Spence, none of the others took Viar and Ulga up on that offer. Only the three of us decided to go because we were a family, and we wanted out. We never asked for this curse—never wanted to be enslaved to the hunger. The other ones, the ones that refused, were mostly girls, and they *loved* what they had become, loved their power, their vampire nature. You'd be surprised how many vampires relish in what they are! It's a tough world out there—a world of danger, cruelty, and pain. So many people feel utterly powerless—*are* utterly powerless —to the forces around them. Brutality, assault, rape, trafficking, it's a constant threat to so many, and being a vampire gives these helpless people power. Power to feel safer, able to protect themselves."

"I get it," sighing, giving my brother a weak smile.

"So," he continued, "we followed these two…beings into that invisible door. Viarudian told us it was very old magic, utilized eons ago and taught to him by someone he once knew. We were fascinated, obviously, and frightened but also resolved. If this was some kind of trick, and we were following these creatures to our deaths, then so be it. Better for the world, eh? Better for you that we be dead and gone the way you thought we were anyway. But no, that was not the plan." He laughed, "Imagine our surprise when we emerged on the other side of that most incredible, magical doorway only to find ourselves right here in this mundane, humble little house!"

I shook my head, "You expected to step out onto some spacecraft or maybe a distant planet or dimension."

"Well, yeah! Of course, we did. Well, *I* did. I have no idea what Mom and Dad expected. But I will say, when we found ourselves in this cozy little place, Mom was elated! And, when Mom's elated, so is Dad…and so was I. Viar then offered us his Dark Gift, and we readily accepted. We trusted Viar, and his drop-dead-gorgeous lady. But still, if that black stuff he offered was going to kill us, we accepted that, too."

"I took it."

"Good!" Jaren grinned.

"Apparently," I shrugged, "I was already on the road to being a full-fledged vampire. Now, I won't have to drink blood."

"You won't! Not if you got The Dark Gift from Viar. The three of us haven't had to drink blood for years now!"

231

"But you get to keep the fangs, lucky bastard!" I joked.

"Give it time," Jaren winked, "Maybe you'll get them, too. The Dark Gift is…well, it changes you, and it likes the fanged look. Lots of Darklings have fangs, not only vampires. You'll get stronger, too. Not like you need it, freakin beast!"

"Shut up." I blushed.

XXIII
CHANGES

Rayn and I made our plans. At least our near-future plans. Even with all this bizarre, supernatural business going on, mundane world crap required our attention. First, I needed to return the rental car and pick up our things from Fedelma's place. Rayn and I would drive there, then get a taxi back to the cottage.

The little house was not home to Viar and Ulga. Apparently, the house belonged to Ulgania and was used as an in-between place for Darklings. There were many such places around the world, but the cottage was the primary place most dark creatures were brought.

The ancient and his lady made their home somewhere in a distant land—some secret place that they divulged to very few—being able to travel via that time/space door of his made distance no issue at all.

Once Rayn and I had returned to the Scottish cabin in the hills, we'd have Viar take us to my place in the States to sew things up there. The two of us had decided to move to Scotland for a time to be near my family. When we were ready, we'd call Jaren and plan to be picked up by Viar. This way, we'd avoid all the red tape, time, money, and effort of traveling by air.

We were creatures out of nature now, so vanishing seemed appropriate. I didn't have loved ones or friends in the US to worry about, but Rayn did have some close friends she'd need to placate. She'd tell them she met someone in Europe and was moving there permanently. Sweet and simple.

Initially, when Viar offered to take us wherever we needed to go, I had asked him to teach me how to travel that way myself so that we wouldn't need his help, but he said it would take far too long for me to master it, so we have a raincheck on that.

Shit! The idea of me, someday, mastering folding space/time into a doorway so I can go wherever the hell I want to go...

Bring it on!

The return to Fedelma's place felt surreal. Actually, every facet of life lately seemed to be more and more bizarre. Now, after all that had occurred, I understood why I'd been feeling like something extremely strange was coming. Shit, my family was alive! That still seemed utterly unreal to me! And, I was a changed man, a *truly* changed...creature? And Rayn, who was already altered permanently, would be changed yet again the next time we did the nasty. It was all too much for my squishy little brain to take, yet somehow, it all felt right, like destiny. Not that I really believed in destiny, did I? Maybe I did...

"What the hell is Fedelma going to think of all this?" I suddenly blurted out.

The ride had been silent, both of us lost in our own deep thoughts. Before we left, Rayn shared everything she, Viar, Ulga, and my parents had talked about. It was essentially the same story Jaren told me, but for a few added details imparted by our benevolent ancients. They told her about their mission to bring Darklings together for protection and learning. It was a calling given to Viarudian eons ago, granted to him by that oh-so-mysterious "Dark Lord." Darklings existed in many worlds, and due to their chaotic nature, each world had its own protectors assigned by the Lord of Darkness.

My feeble mind was blown again!

It seemed there were quite a few vampires and other dark creatures living around the area of Glasgow. They were everywhere, too, not only there. The European continents were particularly full of them. Viar and Ulga oversaw all of them, at least those that would allow themselves to be overseen. Some Darklings went rogue and did their own thing, refusing to become a part of any group or follow any kind of guidance, so all the ancient couple could do was keep watch over them from a distance.

This weird new reality sure was a lot to take in, but bloody hell, I loved it! Every freaky detail! Sure, I'd read loads of bizarre things in books, but soon, I'd be picking some ancient brains to learn more straight from the horse's mouth!

There was no time for that now; big changes were ahead, and a lot of adjusting to do.

Speaking of changes, the change within me was happening quickly. I could already feel big shifts in my senses, the way my body felt, even my mental acuity seemed sharper. But the biggest change was the boundless energy I was feeling! After a long night of incredible revelations, high emotion, and sheer insanity, I should have been exhausted both emotionally and physically, but I wasn't a bit tired. Shit, I could have gone a-slaying, run a damned marathon, and still had plenty of energy for fucking!

"What's funny?" Rayn asked when I chuckled to myself.

I smiled at her with a wink, "I'm already feeling my body, my very essence, shifting into whatever the hell I'm going to become. Feelin' pretty damned good, actually!" I did feel great, but I couldn't help but be nervous about such permanent and fundamental changes; who wouldn't be?

"Pull over."

I turned questioning eyes to her and slowed the car. "Why, you okay?"

Her hand slid between my legs, and the look on her face told me all I needed to know. I drove a bit further until I spotted a little car-sized cubby within a cluster of trees beside the road, just far enough into the foliage not to be seen by passing traffic.

It was chilly out, but I barely felt it as we moved to the backseat of the car, just like perfect dumb teenagers.

We were partially undressed, a little too eager to finish stripping, before I found myself on my back with Rayn straddling me. Her delicious heat enveloped "Little Spence," pulling him in hungrily and making me shudder with delight. We were off to the races—doin' the deed in that quiet place with the occasional car whizzing by. She sucked my seed into herself in more ways than one, and I was more than happy to give.

My stamina outlasted any of our previous sexual endeavors. I didn't even feel spent once we were done, but Rayn was feeling tired, so we chilled there for a while.

"I hope the change will happen quickly for me, too." She finally said as she lay in my arms.

The back seat was cramped, at least for me. Laying on my back with my legs sharply bent, I felt like a pretzel, a blissfully sated pretzel.

"So *that's* why you were so eager to *get it on*." I laughed, "You just wanted to take advantage of my Dark Gift!" I used a sinister voice for that last bit, making her laugh. I sighed, "I'm worried about how this will all be received by the old gal and the hunters."

"Hey," Rayn propped herself up on my chest and gave me a stern expression, "Fedelma told us to go, said we needed to go. She can't make a fuss. This is all *her* fault."

"True."

We kissed, dressed, then continued our trip.

Fedelma was not surprised one bit by any of it, which actually didn't surprise me. She had not known the true nature of the business, but she had been sure that we needed to experience it. Her burning interest in every detail kept us talking for hours. Sharing it all felt like admitting something deeply personal and uncomfortable to a parent, something one might keep from them for a long time, only to discover that they understood and fully supported you.

"What about Clan? How do you think he'll take this?" I asked her, knowing how well Fedelma knew him.

"You'll be off to London soon, yes?" She replied.

I nodded.

"I'll prepare him for ya." She said with an emphatic bob of her head.

"Really, you'll give him a quick call and lay it all out before we get there, will you?" I teased in mock sarcasm, then I shook my head, "I don't know… Honestly, I prefer to tell Clan myself, in person. This is a huge, life-altering…*destiny*-altering thing! It should come from me."

"Suit yourself, gorgeous," the old gal shrugged. "Yer scared to tell him, I know. Just thought I could help."

"I'm not scared." I wasn't, truly. I was just…uneasy. "That said, do you think he'll go all hunter on us? I mean, we're *not* vampires. We're Darklings, not blood drinkers."

She waved a dismissive hand, "You'll be fine. No, hunters don't destroy those who pose no danger to mankind. He may be shocked, especially to learn he might, himself, be tainted."

That was what I figured, but it was nice to get confirmation.

Late the following day, Rayn and I arrived in London, and, as usual, Clannon picked us up at the train station with my personal cabby, Kevin. Smart and savvy fella that he is, Clan felt something was off with us immediately. Exactly *what* he thought, I couldn't imagine.

"So, it appears a lot happened while you were in Glasgow," he said in a voice tinged with veiled concern.

I glanced at Rayn, then met Clan's too-dark gaze. He was looking quite intense, and I didn't know what to say to him. How do you open up such a "can of worms" conversation? Not exactly something to do with Kevin right there, able to hear everything we said. Poor Kev had no clue what we were really all about, and we weren't about to enlighten him. That's why Clan was being so careful about his tone.

"You want to talk about this now, or later, over a brandy?" I asked casually, giving Clan a knowing look.

"Oh, *that* interesting, eh?" His voice was playful, but his eyes were deadly serious as they bore into mine.

"You could say that," I replied.

Rayn turned to me as if to add her own comment, then started, eyes wide with warning and her hand going to her mouth. Clan was also giving me a powerfully pointed stare.

"What?" I asked, mystified, "Something on my face?"

She relayed all I needed to know by pointing to her own eyes with her fore and middle fingers. Apparently, the change was already beginning to show in my pupils! Red flames burned there! I was a bona fide Darkling, and somehow, I was going to have to hide that strangeness from Kevin. Immediately, I dropped my head and let my long hair create a curtain over my face, wishing I had dark sunglasses to hide behind.

Tilting my head carefully while still keeping it down, I turned to Clan, but we both remained silent as we stared—him at my forever-changed, glowing red eyes—and me at the big, triple scars running down his cheek—reminders of our battle with Erskine.

God, I thought desperately; *Clan must think I've been vampirized...* which I had been, but not knowing the rest of it, what must be going through his head?

"I can hardly wait to hear all about your *fun* and *interesting* trip," Clannon mumbled, turning his worried gaze out the window. The balance of the ride was silent.

Finally, we pulled up to Clan's place, and I feigned feeling sick to avoid interacting with Kevin too closely. Keeping my hair over my face, I shuffled to Clan's door and waited; then, I gave Kevin a friendly wave to thank him for the ride so I didn't seem too rude.

Stepping inside, that homey feeling swept over me again, just like it always did at Clan's place. And yet, I felt keenly out of place there now, out of place everywhere, actually. I was no longer the normal human hunter who first stepped over his threshold.

Quietly, we followed our host to that back room-cum-study where he kept his arcane library and where I'd previously slept. He left us there momentarily to retrieve a bottle of brandy and three glasses. When he appeared in the doorway, he paused and looked at the two of us with keen interest as we sat there looking like disobedient children about to be scolded.

He sighed heavily, then entered, poured our drinks at his desk, and gave us each a glass. Then, pulling his desk chair around closer to us, he seated himself. We watched as he took a generous sip of his brandy, and then he said, "You are not setting off my wards the way a vampire would, and yet..." He let the sentiment drop and waited for us to explain.

The fact we wouldn't set off his wards had slipped my mind, and a small wave of relief washed over me. I gave him a faint smile but kept my eyes serious, "Clannon, there is a lot, and I mean *a lot* to tell you."

"I figured as much, hence the brandy," he smirked.

And so, we told it all.

"Spencer, my god! Your family!" He exclaimed, his eyes glistening with moisture.

Telling Fedelma that my family was alive had not hit me the way it did when telling Clannon. I was blubbering, and Rayn as well. "Pretty incredible." I finally replied a bit raspily.

We all let it out, sharing in a long moment of raw and pure emotion that made me love those two dear people more than ever. Finally, we calmed down, tears drying, a little tipsy as we sat silently and digested it all.

"So, some, if not all of us hunters are doomed then, eh? Doomed to become vampires—how ironic or perhaps appropro. It's difficult to tell, really." Clan shook his head. "What a reward, yet not so unexpected."

"Really?" I cocked my eyebrows at him, "you expected this?"

He shook his head, "Yes, and no. I mean, if you play with fire, you're likely to get burned."

"True."

"At least there's another option." Rayn added, "I'm sure Viarudian would be willing to give the Dark Gift to any of you so that you won't hunger for blood."

But Clannon didn't look so confident. "Are you so sure, Romayne? Why would that ancient being do such a thing for all of us, and what will we do if we're infected and he refuses?"

I shrugged, "Why for me and not you?"

"Perhaps you're special," Clan returned my shrug, "I'm sure such a creature does not go around gifting Dark Essence to just anyone, and certainly not so freely. Not to mention, we've killed his kind. I can't imagine he'd be eager to give us any kind of gift, especially the Dark Gift he prizes so highly."

But Rayn wasn't having it, "Viar does not give The Dark freely, Clannon, and you hunters aren't just anyone. Sure, you've killed their kind, but you didn't do it maliciously or with cruel intent. I'm convinced Viar gave the gift to Spencer because he could see his good heart, and he'll see the same in you."

Clannon smiled warmly at her kind words, "I suppose you're right," then he turned to me, "But the creature did seem to despise you at first. He even threatened to kill you."

"He did, but I think he might have been testing me. Oh, I'm not saying he wasn't genuinely angry. I saw it in his eyes: intense anger, even pain. I'm sure I'd be dead now had his lady not stopped him."

Clannon was visibly uneasy, and I couldn't blame him.

"I do want to know if any of us are tainted, so paying this ancient Darkling a visit is paramount since I know no other way to test that. If Fedelma couldn't sense it, and our tattoos don't warn us, then we're left with just one option. What I'd like to do is bring the hunters to Viarudian, if we can do that. Something needs to be done to prevent them from becoming full-fledged vampires. I do not want the horrid job of having to slay my closest friends! What it will mean, accepting the Dark Gift, and the changes that come with it, well, it's already happening to you, one of our own, so we should trust that."

"For me and Rayn, so far, so good."

She took my hand into hers and addressed Clannon: "Viar said we would be like him. His words were, We would not hunger but thrive."

"That does sound awfully nice, doesn't it." Clan smiled, but his skepticism was clear. "And yet, it is called 'The Dark Gift,' which in and of itself does not seem to bode well. Perhaps I'm being too negative, too cautious, but after so many years studying all things dark, one cannot help but think gloomily. And it's all been so sudden," he sighed heavily, "and I know you felt it was a kind of destiny."

"Fedelma told us to go, that it was our destiny, remember," Rayn interjected.

"Ah, Fedelma! The old bat has ever been a mystery," he grinned, relaxed a little at the mention of his old friend. "I trust her, and the both of you, with my life, which I assume means that I should trust you all about this."

The three of us exchanged silent looks, agreeing about that special trust, helpless to whatever fate had in store for us. Honestly, I was feeling increasingly good about the whole ordeal. Maybe it was the surge in energy, the power filling my core, the sharpening of my senses, my mind, my perceptions. Or perhaps it really was destiny, and I felt so comfortable because we were actually on the right track. I certainly hoped we were for the sake of myself, my friends, and especially my cherished woman!

"Let's get some rest," Clan rose from his seat, "and I'll call Fedelma and talk to her about all this before reaching out to Byron and the others."

Still, after so many days, I wasn't a bit tired, but I nodded and didn't mention it.

Rayn and I were left to ourselves to shower and relax. The place was small enough that we thought it best not to get too carried away fooling around. A little touchy-feely here and there, then some perusing of Clan's incredible library, filled our night. Rayn slept some, but I just couldn't. I read and entertained myself by watching my lovely lady doze.

The next day, once Clannon had shared with us the basics of his conversation with Fedelma, we all decided to meet in Glasgow. I called the cabin and spoke with Jaren, relaying to him our plan and desire to meet with Viarudian. Although the ancient Darkling would make no promises about The Dark Gift, he did agree to meet all of us and assured us that he would not destroy the hunters, at least not during *this* meeting.

What a relief. I thought to myself worriedly after hanging up the phone.

Clannon, Rayn, and I arrived in Glasgow a few days later. We met Byron, Kenna, and Gerard at Fedelma's place before heading to the hills and our fateful meeting with the ancients. Fedelma came along with us, though she had no interest in asking for The Dark Gift herself. She just wanted to meet Viarudian and Ulgania, and she insisted she was ready for death whenever it came for her, more curious about what lay beyond the veil than continuing an endless life.

"We're endless already! Souls never die! And there's nothing to fear in shedding your body," she'd said as we loaded ourselves into another rental car. "It's better than this place! I want to see what all the afterlife has to offer and remember who I really am!"

Fedelma was one of a kind!

The drive was quite animated. We'd shared the summarized version with the other hunters of our experiences with the ancients and what little we knew about our new, altered state, so there were a million questions over the handful of hours it took us to get there.

Finally, pulling up to the humble little cottage, it all looked so mundane: the cozy little house, green, lush hillside, cobblestone walkway up to the front door. But as we drew nearer, our steps faltered. It was the effect that ancient energy was having on our wards, especially the mortal hunters.

I had moved ahead of them, with Rayn beside me, and when I noticed they had fallen behind, I turned and smirked over my shoulder, "See? We haven't been takin' the mick." I knew they didn't think we'd been pulling their leg, but I couldn't resist teasing them about it.

Once inside, my family greeted everyone with that familiar, loving warmth, which only further made the experience feel surreal for me. Mom had even cooked up a big dinner. The smells wafting in the air when we crossed the threshold sent my heart soaring and my stomach growling. God, I loved Mom's cooking, and Dad wasn't too shabby in the kitchen, either.

I realized then that hunger had also not plagued me since the change started. I couldn't remember the last time I ate or slept. Well, yeah, I could, actually. I had eaten my last meal the day I discovered my family was still alive. And now, seeing them all again and smelling that wonderful food, finally, I was feeling hungry again.

We Darkling creatures may not need to eat or drink (except for the vampires, that is), but we could if we desired it, and I was very much looking forward to digging into my mother's wonderful cooking!

After dinner, we gathered in the living room—the same room where we first met Viar and Ulga and where I laid unbelieving eyes on my family again.

There wasn't a lot of furniture in there. But there was a massive sectional sofa, two soft chairs, and a few little tables. Two midsize bookshelves flanked the kitchen door, and a fireplace perched catty-corner to the kitchen and just to the right of the door to the back bedrooms.

After-dinner chat was rather mundane compared to the talk we'd had on the way up. Everyone seemed relaxed and comfortable, enjoying themselves until, quite literally, out of nowhere, Viarudian and Ulgania appeared smack dab in the center of the room.

Kenna gasped, and Byron, seated beside her, stared at the newcomers with eyes like dinner plates. Everyone hastily stood up out of respect. It was the aura pouring off of those two incredible beings, the woman's beauty and the sheer strangeness, the weirdly handsome alienness of the male.

Viar smiled his unusual smile, which I was getting used to, yet I'm sure it unnerved the others. I realized suddenly that those special, invisible tattoos no longer glowed in the ancient's presence. I assumed it was due to the fact I was now a Darkling.

"The hunters," Viarudian announced in his hypnotic voice, and with a controlled kind of patience, a dark god entertaining mere mortals.

With her delicate hand on his arm, Ulgania also smiled, a much warmer, open expression compared to her companion. "Welcome, my friends."

Seeing how the men struggled not to ogle her, I couldn't suppress a smile. Both Rayn and I had warned them how gorgeous she was, but nothing could have prepared them.

Clannon took a step forward and extended his hand. It was a natural, automatic gesture, even in this odd situation.

Knowing the custom, Viar took his hand, moving in that slow, graceful way of his. They shook their greeting briefly, and then Clannon smiled. His voice trembled ever so slightly when he said, "It is an honor to make your acquaintance, Viarudian and Ulgania." Humbly and with great manners, he bowed his head.

"Your respect is appreciated," the ancient male replied. He then turned his attention to the rest, who approached and exchanged greetings in much the same way.

There was no standing on ceremony and no casual exchanges after this. Right away, Viar began his examination, starting with Clannon and working his way to the last.

We learned that Clan, Byron, and Kenna were all tainted. I could tell it affected them greatly. They sat now in their seats, lost in deep thought and consideration regarding their uncertain futures.

Gerard was the last. Viarudian placed his large hands on either side of the Frenchman's head, just as he'd done with the others, and locked eyes with him. Holding him in that unmoving state, he studied, felt, and searched Gerard's soul, his very core. The process went much faster than it had with the others.

"If the Dark Gift does not choose you, but is given to you now, you may die." Viarudian finally said.

Gerard blinked up at him, confused, "I am not tainted, am I? Is it that you are referring to?"

"It is." Viar let his gaze sweep the others, "You all have tiny vestiges of The Dark within you, but your friend here is clean. You all desire that I should gift you as I gifted Spencer. To alter the course of your Darkness. To tame the blood thirst that will eventually consume you. The Dark has chosen you, each of you, so that if I agree to do this for you, and if you agree to my stipulations in order to accommodate your wishes, you will all change in the way Spencer is changing.

"But to give The Dark to one who has crossed such intimate paths with Darklings, specifically vampires, and yet has *not* become tainted, there is no guarantee that The Dark will choose him." Turning to look down at Gerard, Viar cocked his head to the side, his voice low and eerily soothing, "Do you fear death, hunter?"

"Fear…death? No, I do not fear to die. And yet, I do not wish it. My life may be a troubled one, but I am not ready for it to end, mon amie."

Viar nodded, "Then The Dark Gift is not for you. If I were to give it, then perhaps, there is a chance it might choose you. But, there is also a chance that it may *not* choose you, and you would very likely die. There is no way to guess about such things, for The Dark is random, chaotic, willful, and powerful. It will enact itself upon you however it chooses. I have seen many outcomes, and I assure you, there are endless eventualities that I could not hope to fathom."

"It is alright," Gerard replied with a smile and a resolute nod of his head, "I choose to stay as I am. If I am not on l'itinéraire to vampirism, then I see no reason to tempt les Parques." He seated himself beside my mother, who patted his leg comfortingly as if he were another son.

The ancients watched all of this with keen interest, especially Viar, who seemed to be judging every look, every move, every single word that came out of the hunter's mouths.

"Many Darklings have died at your hands," the ancient creature mused, or was it blame?

All eyes were on Viar now. I could feel what they felt, simply out of empathy, having been there before, knowing the effect that creature had on me when I first encountered him. He still had the effect, even now, but I was more accustomed, or perhaps it was the fact that some of his darkness now worked within me. I felt calm, concerned…but calm.

Viar continued, "You seek a savior from your condition. I sense you, each of you, and as it was with Spencer, I feel no malice, from you. You have acted upon a series of deeply engrained human morals, which might be commendable. You may argue that there is no questioning your motives. That you saved the lives of your humankind by destroying those dangerous and deadly vampires. I cannot deny the nature of such Darklings. And you are right…you are right. But my mission to protect The Dark Lord's children stands. Spencer, and now Rayn, have joined our ranks, and they will find their redemption and play their own part in this mission.

"But what shall you do, you hunters? Clannon Colfeld, Byron and Kenna Craig? If I offer you The Dark Gift, you must meet my terms. You shall no longer hunt to slaughter. Instead, you will hunt to save, to minister, and to protect Darkling kind. If that promise cannot be made this day, to me, and thus to The Dark Lord, then I shall be left with the conundrum of releasing you out into the world to continue your bloody work, or of ending you right here and now."

XXIV
JUDGEMENT

Byron rose slowly and confidently to his feet, "With all due respect, Viarudian, vampires are dangerous. We did what had to be done. Is it not moral and right to rid the world of such threats? I understand you have a mission, a duty, to protect your Darklings. But you cannot blame us for protecting ourselves and our kind?"

Kenna joined Byron, sliding her hand into his as she stood beside him, "We have been doing the very same thing you're doing, protecting our own, only on opposite sides and apparently without a full understanding."

"Darkling numbers are few here in this world, not including the Nethers, whose numbers are quite large, yet they are not as participatory as others of our kind. We have worked ceaselessly to prevent and rein in the slaughter of mortals." Viar replied with emotion, "Vampirism is looked upon in a different light by other Darklings, although not looked down upon. The hunger is what makes them different from the rest of us. It can be debilitating and fierce—an incredible driving force unique to vampires. We do not condemn it, for it is the will of their Dark Essence to which all dark creatures are connected. We respect the will of The Dark as a thing unto itself, a gift of metamorphosis, of enrichment, of life elevated.

"Life…Death, for Darklings are far different concepts when compared to mortality. You humans fear death fiercely, and your lifespans are so very fleeting, a mere drop in the vast sea of eternity."

"Our lives may be fleeting, but they are important to us, valued! From our perspective, they feel long, very long indeed, and while they are often difficult, they are also cherished." Clannon added.

But Viar continued without responding to Clan's sentiments, "You mortals, destroy your own lives, and the lives of others in endless ways and so carelessly, and while many of your kind do not believe in any continuation after death. Oh, what a sad and empty thing that is. To believe in such a final end, while sending life after life into oblivion.

"And you, hunters, what of you? Do *you* believe that death is the ultimate end? Do you believe that when you send one of *ours* to their doom, that they cease forever to exist in any form or any realm?

"Vampires, and all Darklings, most certainly *do* have souls, but you have acted in such a way that, if you do believe that death means ceasing to exist in all forms...in any state, in any way at all, then your killings would be most cruel indeed! Oh, how vile it is to destroy a thing so utterly in your unfeeling, misguided eyes! Tell me now, I must know, do you believe death is final?"

"We all believe in life after death," Fedelma spoke up firmly for the hunters. "All of our hunters believe so because they're taught as much. Learnin' about and embracin' the afterlife's part of their trainin'. If they did not hold such beliefs prior to coming to me for their hunter education, then they *will* believe by the time I'm done with 'em, or they'll not become a hunter."

But the witch's most earnest assurance was not good enough for Viar. His large, strange eyes moved from one face to another, waiting for each person's response: "I understand what you were *taught* to believe, but do you *truly* believe?"

Each hunter nodded, and Clannon spoke for the group, "We believe in an afterlife, yes—"

The ancient cut in, "*An* afterlife, but there are many."

With a nod, Clannon conceded his point, then continued, "That said, we have also believed that vampires are either soulless or inhabited by some demonic power, because much of the literature we've studied postulates as much. It has been thought that when a human is turned into a vampire, their souls move on to the afterlife, while either an external entity, force, or power overtakes the body, or the body goes on without a soul, thirsting and incapable of empathy or compassion. Many writings have proposed that the missing soul causes a vampire's fierce hunger. Therefore, we believed that when we slayed a vampire, there would be no final ending of a human's existence, or, more properly, no destruction or damning of a noble soul, only the ending of a hollow, or debased monster upon our world."

"Such beliefs as you describe are in error, mere guesses, and yet, you have subscribed to them wholeheartedly, and acted on them as unassailable truths, with violence and finality." Viar began pacing the

248

room in clear agitation, his long, tapered fingers working in that manic way I'd seen when Rayn and I first met him. Clearly, he struggled greatly with the decision to bring the other hunters into the Darkling fold. Doing so for me was one thing, but perpetuating it to the others, despite numbering only three, seemed to disturb the ancient being greatly.

We all exchanged worried glances between us. I was feeling more uneasy as Viar's frenetic energy filled the room. Concern for the welfare of my friends was growing steadily. Maybe this whole meeting was a bad idea.

"Humankind excels at misguided beliefs," Viar's voice was low; it seemed like he was speaking more to himself than to us, thinking out loud because he wanted us to hear his mental deliberations. "The most erroneous of ideas become the most powerful 'truths' in the human heart and mind." His voice slowly rose in volume, along with his agitation, "Oh, and the misunderstandings, the misjudgments! Breeding atrocities, so great, so ghastly! Flabbergasting! You mortals! You paint some picture within your *limited* psyches based on *limited* information, manipulation, and grossly clouded judgments, then you adhere to it as if it were the very foundation of your being. A slippery slope, a cliff of loose rock and jagged shale, all waiting for you to step wrongly…to realize you are incorrect about everything you believed so vehemently: the ill-born hate, the fury against those you wrongly hate, the rending of your very soul when you realize you've been misled, sending you tumbling and crashing away when that foundation of what you thought made you who you are, turns out to be nothing but error upon error upon error! But to admit your error? No, no, you rage and tantrum and refuse to believe you could ever be wrong! Such pride! Empty pride!"

Viar was rambling now, lecturing us, flying off on a tangent that had us all riveted to our seats, sweating, hearts racing.

"And your arrogance! Your unworthy sense of entitlement! Like you are owed whatever you may desire without earning it! Clinging to your haughty delusions of superiority, to your lies with such stubborn tenacity! Refusing to learn, to grow, to let your bad ideas go. Refusing to accept that you could ever err in your thinking! Refusing humility, compassion, empathy. Oh, and how you follow so blindly those who would mislead and stomp you to dust for their own gain! The fool and the heathen leading fools and heathens! And how you attack others who do not see the world as you see it, do not believe the things you believe, or know what you *think* you know. But you do *not* know, for you know so little as to be all but nothing. To condemn others with such vile venom! Such, such—"

249

"My love," Ulgania had stepped into his pacing path and drawn herself into his arms, hugging his middle and calming his tirade with her soft voice and tender embrace.

The ancient male stilled immediately, his screwed up face relaxing into calm repose, only showing the faintest hint of lingering concern. The raging flames of his large, jewel eyes went from ruby red to his indigo blue again as they drank in Ulgania's unearthly beauty.

Her love for him radiated out from her very person, easing the heavy miasma he had created in the room.

Seeing Viar's response to Ulgania's touch and feeling the surge of their love tame his growing agitation made my heart surge as I reached for Rayn, to feel her soft skin, her warmth.

Viar curled into Ulgania's embrace, his eternal love, his most precious and trusted companion. The intense strength of their connection spoke to my heart because I knew what he was feeling all too well.

"You have observed much during your long life, my love," Ulga stroked his head, pressed her lips to his cheek, "even as you were locked away for so very long, you listened to the world, with your ability to hear and to feel, and to probe, even at far distances with the lonesome fingers of your searching, esoteric mind. Over the ages, you felt so much. Cut off from everything, and with such an incredible mind as yours, how could you not pay attention? Eons passed before you: the wars, violence, and hate… the lies, betrayals, manipulations. It is all true, those terrible things you say, and yet there *is* also love. Those powerful voices of division and derision may scream the loudest, but their power is by far not the strongest. Not *all* of humankind is hopelessly lost to debased minds.

"My Eternity, what of me? Am I, your most devoted, not different than all that? And yet, I once was mortal, before you found me and loved me and brought me to you, heart, body, and soul. And furthermore, are such terrible traits as you express even relevant here? These hunters, if they hated and were so lost as not to have the ability to turn the mirror upon themselves, to see their own faults, and to grow from them, would they have come here, into your awesome presence, so trusting and so willing? Would they have come in the *way* they have come to us, not with blades to cleave a head from a body, but with trust, curiosity, and need?"

"Need…" Viar sighed, "Oh yes, they need. They fear their vampirism and seek salvation from it for their own gain. Always, they are selfish for their many, many needs."

"No!" Clannon shot to his feet, and I, with him.

We exchanged a glance, and I went first, "I started hunting to save others, to protect, not to destroy for destruction's sake."

"It was the same for me." Clan added, "I did it out of a sense of duty."

"And revenge…" Viarudian added testily.

I could not deny that, nor could Clannon, but I replied, "Fine, there was an element of revenge for our losses and misery. But it was not the pure driving force for our work. We only wanted to prevent more deaths, and stop the pain we had suffered from happening to others."

"That's right," Kenna added. "We humans might not be able to completely avoid those dark emotions like revenge or hatred, but we choose to recognize and overcome them. We choose strength over weakness as our motivation."

My brave, sweet Rayn rose to her feet and went to Viar and Ulga, laying her hand on his hand that was rested on Ulga's shoulder. He looked down into my brave woman's upturned face, "Can you feel it, Viarudian?" Rayn smiled hopefully, her voice sweet but strong, "Do you sense the compassion in these hunters, these people, our *friends*, how good they are, how well-intentioned they are? There is not one soul present in this room with a black heart."

Looking at us all again, the ancient creature's eyes softened, and after a long, silent moment, he stood straighter, and the ends of his mouth curled into a gentle smile. "I can feel it, young one. And while my sentiments are not in error, I admit that I have been unfair to you and yours."

"Tell me," Clannon said as he moved closer to Viar, and the rest of us followed, "You say we are infected due to our battles with vampires. But what about those we have been intimate with? I have sons, two sons and their mothers. Could they also be infected?"

I was grateful Clan didn't mention *my* Lovarti tryst. I hadn't told Rayn about *that* yet.

"Potentially, although it is unlikely." Viar answered, "As I've stated, The Dark Essence has its own will. That said, not all Darklings can gift their essence to others. The Dark Lord restricts its spread, to varying degrees. He enjoys the worlds and realms, the endless variety of their flora and fauna as they naturally are, and he does not want The Dark, with its tenacious and constant desire to spread itself into all things, to completely overtake all of the realms."

I found it interesting that Viar's description of this enigmatic Dark Lord, which one might think would be a villain, was not much like the "dark lords" of fiction. Sauron, Palpatine, Voldemort, heck, even in religion, Lucifer constantly sought to spread his evil to overpower all goodness. But not so, apparently, for the mysterious lord of Darklings. The young vampires," Viar continued, "and Darklings in general, they need guidance, not death."

"But the irredeemable of them, the cruel and the sadistic ones?" I insisted, "You, yourself, said that death is not the terrible thing we mortals make it out to be. Let us, then, send those souls, those irreversibly damaged souls, on to the other side where, maybe they can, I don't know, learn from their mistakes, make progress in some way? Viarudian, let us do what we do best: hunt."

The creature stared hard at me, his large, intense eyes brimming with doubts and deep consideration. Then, he sighed, "I have tried, during my time, to avoid the destruction of our kind at all costs. The vampire is a tragic creature, you see. Its lusts rage through the human soul, changing it, as the body is changed. Some rise above, conquer its forces and are capable of existing in harmony with their cravings. While others allow the power and the hunger to drive and degrade them. With their heavy emotions and evil tendencies, some human souls truly do become monsters. I have destroyed a handful of such unfortunates in my time."

"*You* have killed vampires?" I gasped. After everything he'd just lectured us about, this surprised me.

"Reluctantly, I have, yes." The regret in Viar's voice was painful to hear and feel. His emotions wafting through the room like a sudden gust of wind.

"Those unwilling to accept your dark version of redemption," I offered.

He nodded slowly, "The hopelessly violent and ravenous ones— the ones who could not ever regain their compassion, if they had any to begin with. The ones filled only with loathing and destruction. Who revel in dominance over, and the wanton destruction of, others."

"We have monstrous humans, too, as you so eloquently stated during your rant," I smiled disarmingly at him since my statement was not meant to be critical, "and throughout history, we have found it prudent, even at times necessary, to put the worst of our criminals to death."

"So, then, let *us* hunt those Darklings that are lost and harming others." Clannon pleaded, "We can bring them to you, or lead you to them, if you prefer, so that you can hold a trial or simply make your judgment concerning how best to deal with them, whether sending them through to their afterlife, or giving them help here, to conquer what sinister or desperate motivations drive them; it can be your call.

Now that we understand a vampire's true nature, we hunters can serve in a different way."

With obvious discomfort yet a certain air of relenting, Viar replied, "Giving The Dark Gift is a decision I hesitate to make on my own."

"My love," Ulga said softly, "I am sure our lord would trust you to delegate your duties. Surely, he would expect as much."

"Delegate to Darklings, yes, but to mortal hunters?"

"Many Darklings were once mortals." She argued.

"Yes, but most were gifted with Dark Matter directly from The Dark Lord himself."

"Except for those of us changed by vampires," I interjected, and Viar nodded his head slowly. He was coming around.

Ulga added, "Must all the work and discipline fall upon our shoulders? These hunters, they are trained and prepared…and willing."

The ancient creature smiled at his woman, looking so human, so natural, despite his strange, otherworldly aspect, that I nearly forgot what he was…nearly.

Finally, Viar acquiesced. We hunters would serve The Dark Lord through him. We would be Darklings and protect our kind, as well as mortals.

In much the same way as Viar had done with me, he gifted that ebony essence to the other hunters, and each of them, Clannon, Byron, and Kenna, became a part of our new Dark Hunter fraternity.

Later, after the ancients had departed and we were all gathered in that quiet room to reflect upon all that had occurred, we agreed that, for us, making such an immense decision felt a lot like leaping off a cliff, as entering the unknown always did.

"But every day of life is an unknown until it happens," Rayn had said.

And I added, "We were all infected anyway; our futures were heading in one, not great direction; we'd be vampires if nothing were done. So we've at least traded a pretty disgusting, perilous unknown for one that promises to be better."

No one could argue that!

Near midnight, only a few hours after that big, future-changing meeting, Viarudian dropped Rayn and me off back in the States at our mountain cabin. "Dropped us off" sounds so simple, but it was even simpler than that! One step through an oval doorway, and bam! We were standing in front of my house thousands of miles from where we just were. Needless to say, my head was reeling, but I regained my equilibrium pretty quickly.

"You will get accustomed to it," Viar assured me.

I shrugged, "It's not like taking a single step forward made me dizzy; it's just the sheer strangeness of it, that's all."

He smiled in his unusual way before stepping back through that doorway and vanishing as if he'd never been there.

"Can't say I agree with him. I'll never get used to that!" I exclaimed.

"You will," Rayn cheerfully assured me, "We're going to live a long ol' time, aren't we? It'll be old hat before you know it!"

Laughing, I carried our bags inside with her bobbing along beside me.

Whenever I traveled like a normal human, I typically took a cab to the airport. Lucky, too, because we weren't without wheels. I checked the Mustang over, tested it out, and found it was running just fine despite being left undriven for so long.

Rayn asked if we could go to her house for the night, and I agreed. She had been increasingly concerned about her place after being away so long. I *still* wasn't tired. Hadn't yet felt the need to sleep or rest, and apparently, it was the same for her. So, we hopped in and headed out, arriving at her place a tad after 2:00 a.m.

"God, Spence, this is so surreal!" she said softly beside me.

Everything looked so average, so run of the mill normal to the eyes of two people who had just been through a plethora of wackiness —two people who were now changed both in body and in mind. Rayn and I turned to each other, preternatural eyes glowing red, and shared an unspoken emotion before exiting the car.

We'd barely stepped through her front door when a new sensation washed over us. It affected both our newly enhanced senses and wards —our *altered* wards, their sensations also altered. I glanced down at her before we both turned in unison to discover we weren't alone.

XXV
AN END & A BEGINNING

"Aurel?!" Rayn exclaimed.

What the actual fuck was *he* doing here?

I was moving before thinking—muscle memory kicking in, springing forward so quickly, so unnaturally fast, that I nearly lost control of myself. But I had become quite good at controlling my body in battle, so I was able to hold it together and keep from falling on my face.

Rayn hollered at me, at the both of us, but I wasn't hearing her words. I'd shifted into protection mode.

Aurel was ready for me, fangs bared, talons out. I carried no weapons, not prepared for a hunt since that wasn't our purpose—it was down to hand-to-hand combat.

And yes, being unarmed was mighty out of character for me, but my entire world had been utterly flipped on its head, and I was distracted by all those fundamental changes, as well as the shift in my hunter duties.

First thing I realized was, my tattoos weren't protecting me like they used to. They might have alerted me to Aurel's presence, but there was no sign he was in any way repelled by them.

We grappled fiercely, my Martial Arts and general fight training, plus increasing strength, helped some, but I was still not at vampire-level yet, so he was pretty quickly able to get me into a tight headlock, which royally pissed me off! Then, the unthinkable happened, and the fucking bastard sank his stinkin' teeth into my neck!

Now, *that* was a strange sensation! After battling vamps for years, feeling those four (top and bottom) sharp dagger teeth pierce my flesh…

He bit me under my jaw, one of his top fangs stabbed right into that tender spot where the pulse beats beneath the skin. Oddly, it didn't actually hurt like I thought it would. It felt like pressure, and there was a form of pain, I guess. It's difficult to put into words. It didn't hurt, and yet, it did.

Oh, and I was fighting him with all I had, although it was to no avail. I felt Rayn close to us, her hands beating like bird wings against Aurel, occasionally hitting me. It wasn't that her hits felt weak; it was more the fact that I was not entirely present. There was an exchange of information happening between the vampire and me. As he gulped my blood, it felt as if I was under some kind of hypnosis, sleepwalking, dreaming.

Suddenly, he released me with a gasp, and my legs gave right out from under me. I crumbled, Rayn's arms around me, but I quickly returned to myself. The brief faint was simply due to the sudden cut-off of our information exchange, not because of any weakness due to blood loss. Benefits of being a Darkling, I guessed.

"I've watched for a while." Aurel was saying as I returned to myself.

I could hear him where he stood a few feet behind me.

"When you told me to leave," he continued, "I stayed away at first. But after a time, I got curious. I…missed you, Rayn. I searched for you, but you never came home. You had simply vanished, but your things were still here. You were coming back; I knew it. So I kept an eye on your house, waiting until you returned. I was worried about you."

The guy really was smitten with my Rayn; I couldn't blame him. Still, I didn't like it. Didn't like him one bit.

"Thanks for keeping an eye on the place for me," she replied kindly, which, honestly, irked me.

I came to my feet, and, turning, I scowled at him. His lips were clean, no sign on his skin that he'd just stolen a chunk of my blood. "She's fine, as you can see." I growled, "So you can get the hell out of here, now."

"Spence," Rayn gently touched my chest, her other arm around my waist, asking me to ease up on her former boyfriend. I reluctantly complied, for the moment.

"A lot has changed, Aurel." Her voice was soft and caring…toward *him*. God, it was annoying!

"I can see that," his pale, glowing eyes narrowed—no contacts this time—yet they were strangely emotional, even—what?—hurt?... scared? "What's happened to you...to the both of you?"

I wondered what he was thinking, seeing us with the delicate beginnings of fangs and the red glow in our eyes, matching his own— we must have appeared to be vampires like him. Or could he sense there was a difference, that we were more than just vamps? He must have gleaned some details from feeding on me.

"Didn't you get it all out just now, when you fucking sucked my blood?" I sneered at him.

He narrowed his eyes at me and scowled back, "What I saw were snatches, like a dream. *Your* memories, didn't make any damned sense." He said it as if my head was faulty, and perhaps it is, though I knew it was just a cheap dig at me.

I remembered then why he probably couldn't get much out of me. It was the wards. Fedelma had described their ability to block a vampire from reading a hunter, how the information is blurry or muddled, and impossible to decipher. Seems those powers remained, even if the physical protections hadn't.

My mental experience as he drank from me? Well, it was a mild sensation of the act of drinking as if looking out from his perception, his senses; the satisfaction, taste, and feel of the blood, my blood, in his mouth, and sliding down his throat. It was calming, peaceful, even blissful, at the time. But thinking back on it afterward kind of makes me feel ill.

Aurel was studying Rayn again, his expression odd and hard to read, "You're a hunter now. Wow." His tone was scathing, yet I could swear there was a hint of admiration in it.

Rayn sighed, "I'll explain it all to you sometime, Aurel, but it's too much now." Turning to me, her eyes were full of purpose and pleading.

But I was confused. Couldn't imagine what she was wordlessly trying to ask me. I shrugged at her, and she turned back to the vampire, "You should come back with us."

"No way, Rayn! What?" The exclamation burst out before I had time to think about what I was saying. Then I remembered our new calling, and as much as I hated to admit it, Aurel *did* seem redeemable.

Bastard.

Rayn ignored my outburst and kept her eyes on the vampire.

Of course, he looked mighty confused, "Come where, Rayn?"

Maybe he wouldn't want to go. I hoped he wouldn't want to go.

"To Europe," Rayn replied.

"Why would I leave?" He spread his arms wide, shrugged, laughed a little, "I've got a great life here, Rayn: my clubs, my art, friends, connections. I have no desire to abandon all that. And why would you invite me anyway? You have...*him*, don't you? You've clearly...moved on." His burning eyes flicked to me in disgust—jealousy, plain and simple.

Well, that goes both ways, bub. I thought.

Maybe the creature had gotten the idea in his head that he could win Rayn back, seduce her with his 'irresistible' goth boy vampire-ness. But now that I was...well, special too, there was no longer anything to set him apart.

The three of us stood in awkward silence for a few minutes. I was poised, ready to stop Rayn if she began to divulge things to Aurel that I didn't think he should know. But why was I so opposed to being open about Viarudian and the Darklings? What was I protecting? Aurel was one of us. We were meant to find and vet vampires for their levels of cruelty, how dangerous they were, then judge whether they needed to be brought to Viar or destroyed.

God, I wanted to end him, but as much as it pained me, Aurel did not seem to deserve slaying.

"Hey, answer me this," I broke the silence, "How do you handle your kills, Aurel? How violent, sadistic, and cruel are you when you go out to dinner every night?"

Aurel huffed, scowled at me, and shook his head, "What the hell are you asking me that for? Like it's any business of yours!"

I wanted to strangle him, but I controlled myself. Barely.

Before I could respond, Rayn held a hand up and said, "As blunt and unnecessarily harsh as Spence asked that question, there *is* a reason we need to know, and I think I can answer for you. Correct me if I'm wrong, Aurel, but I don't think you go out and viciously slaughter people."

"No, I don't." The vamp replied flatly.

"You aren't a creature without any morals," she continued in her matter-of-fact way, "and you have, after many years as a vampire, come to find peace with the hunger. You have gained control over your craving, so it doesn't rule you anymore. Am I right?"

The look on the vampire's face as he stared at Rayn made me uneasy. It was filled with respect and warmth that had me cringing inwardly. The guy loved her, and what she'd said seemed to strike a chord with him. He was visibly moved, and I actually felt a twinge of compassion for the guy, although it could not outweigh my disdain.

"You've learned a lot, haven't you? Though it's not the kind of thing…" His thought trailed off, then he continued on another track, "I have lived a *very* long time, Rayn, and in all that time, more than two hundred years, I've worked to control the hunger and myself. Vampirism is not easy. Well, it's not easy for one who doesn't want to lose themselves to it. Some do, I didn't."

"I know," she replied, smiling at him.

"So," I grumbled, "you're not interested in coming with us—"

Rayn cut me off, "To learn about your origins and meet other Darklings that are *not* vampires?" It was like she was tempting him, trying to entice him. I wanted her to stop.

He smiled, fangs still stained a little pink from my blood: jerk!

"I know there are other dark creatures, although I've rarely encountered them. Our origin, as I understand it, comes from a single, mysterious being that began the Dark Curse in a time immemorial. But I know nothing more about it."

Rayn shrugged, "We don't have all the answers either. Not yet. But we've been promised that we will know everything."

"Then come back and tell me all about it sometime." He smiled knowingly at her, gave me a wary look, then turned his gaze back to Rayn, "I'm not ready to leave here just yet. Perhaps once I've had a full lifetime of fun, and when it's time to move on to the next, then I'll consider it. I'm still 'young' to the mortals in my circle. But that won't last forever. And I already spent most of my vampire life in Europe. Wore out my welcome over there," he shook his head, remembering, "and I'm quite enjoying my time here now, in the new world."

Relieved he wasn't joining us, I smiled broadly, joyously, and he rolled his eyes at me; then Rayn left my side, walked over to the stinkin' vamp, and embraced him. It seemed to shock him as much as it annoyed me. But I knew she was mine and felt no fear of him stealing her away.

After I told him to control his baby bats and to keep those deaths under control, Aurel agreed, as much as he hated me "ordering him around," and finally left. Thank god.

The two of us got to work. I helped Rayn pack up the things she wanted to keep. It wasn't much: family stuff like photos, keepsakes, and heirlooms that were small enough to carry in a few available boxes and bags. She stuffed several pieces of clothing, shoes, and a few accessories into a single case, but left most of her clothes behind; then, we headed back to my place with a carload.

It took several weeks, working day and night (we still hadn't slept), to get her house cleared out and on the market. Some of her belongings would remain behind in my cabin; the most important would come with us to the United Kingdom.

After all was said and done, we spent some quality time at the cabin before contacting Jaren to arrange our return. Notable here is the moment Rayn stumbled upon my old school notebook, you know, the one where I kept all my silly writing? Well, just as she had read over my shoulder way back when, I caught her from behind, curled up in my chair reading. She was fully absorbed in that same old horror story that I never let her finish in school.

"Shit," I mumbled under my breath, laughing at her when she jumped and squealed, jolted from her reading by my sudden appearance. "You finally got your stinkin' little mitts on that thing, did you?" I shoved my big ol' body into that chair beneath her, settling her comfortably on my lap.

She kissed my cheek, then gave me a stern look, "Spence, this is good stuff! Seriously, why were you so shy about sharing it?"

I shrugged, smirked, "Never thought it was worth sharing, just chicken scratch and my weird brain on paper."

"I'll type this up for you if you like." She grinned.

Fine, I'd let her do it; if she liked it that much, why deny her? I nodded, then shook my head at her as she settled into me as if I were simply an extension of that chair. I encircled her tiny waist with my arms, and she lost herself again in reading.

Then she started reading aloud, acting out each character, narrating like a pro, and it made the whole thing sound so much better than it really was!

My little actress.

I nuzzled into her with a little rumble in her ear.

She had to finish her reading later…

Ulgania retrieved us when we were ready to go, and let me tell you, there was no way I'd ever have the patience to travel normally after using that oval doorway to pass our selected belongings through from my cabin in the midwestern United States to the cottage on that Glasgow hillside! God, but what the world wouldn't do to have that ability!

Rayn and I were married at one of our favorite spots in the Scottish hills. It was more of a spiritual bonding than a traditional wedding. Fedelma performed the ceremony, and it was, quite literally, magical! My little, restored family and our hunter friends, as vital to me as my natural kin, were there, of course.

I was concerned that Rayn would be disappointed not to marry in the States, where her few family members and her friends could attend. She had not lived as a hermit, like me, and I knew there were people she cared deeply about that she'd left behind. But she assured me she was truly happy with me, making me promise not to concern myself with such things.

Her happiness was vitally important to me, and I would have done any damned thing for her, even let her go if that was what she wanted. It was not something I ever cared to entertain because my silly little heart couldn't stand the thought of losing her. But for her, I'd take a bullet, so...

Thankfully, it seemed I hadn't yet run her off. And I truly believed she *was* happy with me because of the way she smiled at me and the joy that I worked so ceaselessly to give her.

Oh, I could be a real dunce sometimes. We certainly weren't Mister and Missus Perfect. But we both understood each other and ourselves, and it made riding out those tougher times bearable, even occasionally, enjoyable. It's funny how being with Rayn made even the tough times feel like an adventure rather than torture.

After the wedding, we moved from place to place, hesitating to settle anywhere permanently. Most of our time was spent with my family before and after our nuptials. Quality time that brought me and my folks back together in a wholly new way. I even asked Dad all those questions I hadn't asked in my younger days—all the stuff you're too shy to ask as a kid, or you think of saying and asking after you lose a loved one. I was truly getting to know him for the first time, and I was shocked at how much he was like me.

Jaren and I simply picked up where we left off, well, after I massively unloaded on him. I spilled it all, every stinking thought, emotion, judgment, all the pain! He took it really well, actually, and by the time everything was out in the open, the two of us were in tears... not from anguish, but from uncontrollable laughter.

That's Jaren for ya. Turn trauma into a joke fest. I don't mean he didn't take my emotions seriously and respond accordingly. Still, he had a way of stripping away all the melodrama, simplifying things down to their base elements, then laughing at how ridiculous it all is.

My brother, one of a kind!

Rayn and I also grew considerably closer to Viar and Ulgania. It was our discussions with them that ultimately determined our next steps.

Our reluctance to settle down overseas proved to be instinctual. Clannon reminded me of my duty to be the head of hunters in the States. To take up the mantle of our new calling: to save, rather than slay vampires and other dangerous Darklings, and to find fellow hunters in the US, as he and the others would be recruiting in Europe.

That said, I would not be required to live in the States for this calling. Due to the changes in our nature, we Darklings could not so easily mingle with humankind. We would need to disappear from the ever-more-surveilled modern world and make our home in a safe place, a place ideal for us.

That place, according to Viarudian, was the forbidden dark wood, known as The Jangel Tarik. It was remotely located in the depths of The Persian Gulf, a part of the world I never imagined I'd live in.

I'd read about Earth's shunned forests, places mankind dared never venture. But this one in particular, far older and much more bizarre than the rest, stood out in stark contrast to the others. It was a forest recorded in the very oldest of manuscripts—a large patch of deeply, darkly shrouded land feared and shunned for eons upon eons.

Viar and his lady took us there, and the experience was, frankly, astounding. We stepped out of that oval, magical door into the very center of those mystical woods.

Looming massively before us, in a spot near where we were to set up house, was a highly unusual tree.

The behemoth's pale gray body and limbs were a series of jumbled knots; all twirled together in a tangled mass. Sprouting from its hearty trunk were a plethora of bark-covered tapering arms and fingers, all curling in and out and around themselves. Adorned with ebony, violet, and burgundy leaves, their shapes and sizes varied: pointy tips with tiny creepers that sprang from the leaf's edges, giving the appearance of curly hairs or wiry filaments.

Viar told us how that tree was special and that the portion we were looking at was part of an eternal shrub that grew in all realms!

Mind-blowing!

I had seen mention of a great, mysterious tree in *Kor Borholden's Dark Whispers*—a sadly brief description. It was possibly also included in the *Tome of Sohrakian Source*, but how that book was written so confused readers that no one was entirely sure what was being described. Otherwise, the other esoteric books had very few details about that special tree. I had considered it a myth until seeing it with my own eyes.

Countless Darkling creatures and a myriad of foliage thrived in that place, and all were benevolent to us since we were a part of their world now; even the plants were sentient. Yes, you really could commune with any and all Darkling plants! Incredible!

That camaraderie did not, of course, extend to humans who might dare venture there, which happened very rarely since the land was both warded to protect it and, due to its dangers and the lack of control mankind had over it, was protected and restricted by local governments.

Near that tree was where we built our new homes: a house for Rayn and me, my parents, and a place for Jaren. Living so remotely in the world would not be difficult for us, and relocating was far simpler than you might think. With Viar's assistance, we utilized the portal to transport the materials we needed for building and the things we required to live. Once I had learned how to utilize that magical oval door myself, then we were able to go literally anywhere we wanted! One single step and we could shop for necessities across the planet, find recreation at the drop of a hat, or I could go about my new hunter duties in the States or wherever in the world I was needed.

And guess who decided to join up and become a hunter? That's right, my brother. Of course, Jaren would want to be a part of it, and he was even more suited to it than I was; at least, that's how I felt. And *this* time, instead of him teaching me, I was his teacher, guiding him through the entire process as Clannon had done with me and I'd done with Rayn. Jaren also learned directly from Clan, Byron, and Gerard.

Let me tell you! Having my brother, my rock, at my side in this new hunter venture was, well, the most incredible feeling. I get verklempt just thinking about it.

As our Darkling natures ascended, Rayn and I began to shun the day, and night became our element. Those blacker-than-black entities, the Nethers, began to gather to us like moths to a flame, as they always do to the oldest of our kind—it was the ancient essence of Viar that did it, making us stand out far more dramatically than, say, the "baby bat" vampires. But those were not the only Darklings drawn to us. The creatures of the dark forest, those most dreamlike, often nightmarish beings, quickly became our friends and companions. The place felt like some twisted, spooky version of a classic Disney cartoon!

Heck, I was living within my very own horror-fantastic heaven! Wicked!

Clannon and the other hunters took their time making any kind of move out of the mortal world. They knew they would need to at some point, but they loved their homes and were loathe to leave them. Rayn and I often visited them, especially Clan, who invited us over quite regularly to stay with him.

At the moment I'm finishing up this very manuscript, I am seated at Clannon's desk. It was Clan who insisted I write my story way back when I first visited London. And when he said he wanted to bind it into a book to add to his collection, well, how could I refuse such an honor? Not that I believe my humble tale, written in my middling, often crass manner, deserves such treatment.

Initially, I declined to do it. I told him, "Look, Clan, what I write won't be worthy of your incredible artistry. But if I do this, it's going to be me, casual, raw, direct. I'm not going to flower it up or anything."

"I wouldn't expect you to, Spencer." Clan replied, "We hunters have many, quite old texts to study from, but we need new and modern takes, accounts happening now, and what you've seen and experienced will be invaluable to both current and future hunters. And now that it's all changed, your account will be the first to guide us into this new reality."

I was humbled, nervous, and hesitant to proceed, but I also agreed with Clan.

Still, I know he'll make it look like a masterpiece, if only on the outside, with one of his meticulously bound and beautifully unique leather covers!

And I must admit that writing this all down *has* been cathartic in a way I hadn't anticipated. Clan often mentioned how keeping journals helped to clear and unmuddle his head and that expressing it all in words made facing traumas and mental difficulties more bearable.

He was right, of course. I haven't felt so clear-headed and unburdened in quite a while. Of course, that might also be due to my newly enhanced state. Or having Rayn at my side, which has always uplifted me in more ways than one. Or, perhaps it was having my family back. So many factors played into my new and profound sense of calmness and enthusiasm, quite different from my old, lonely, singular hunting days. Days that now feel like another lifetime.

So, this is it.

This is my story.

And here I am—this new creature, surrounded by loved ones and facing countless unfathomable mysteries ahead. Where will I go from here? I don't know. It's a strange thing, this awkward feeling of not knowing my future after so long on a road of well-defined, well-determined direction. After becoming a hunter, I had no doubts about what I did. There were no diversions from my stalwart path, nothing but drive and purpose.

Now? I feel a bit like a fish out of water. A priest without a church. A car without wheels. Who am I and what do I do next?

Don't get me wrong. Those questions don't frighten me. On the contrary, I feel excitement unlike I've ever felt before about my future, our future—a very *long*, and hopefully good, future.

Only time will tell...

THE END

If you enjoyed this work, please leave a review; thank you.

ABOUT THE AUTHOR

KM Taylor is an artist and author of the Codex Sohrakia series. Her other works include *Codex Sohrakia II: The Athanasy Pact, Fearless Vampire Hunter,* and *The Devil's Conquest.* Both *Codex Sohrakia: The Gifted Dark* and *The Devil's Conquest* have received great reception and award recognition.

KM's interests and inspirations gravitate to dark fantasy, romance, and the supernatural. She also loves Science Fiction and plans to write in that genre eventually. KM has written in many genres over the years and in several formats, including science, health and nutrition, poetry, short stories, and fan fiction. Currently, she is working on several stand-alone future novels as well as the next installment in the Codex Sohrakia series.

To learn more, please visit CodexSohrakia.com.